THE SIGNET CLASSIC POETRY SERIES is under the general editorship of poet, lecturer, and teacher JOHN HOLLANDER.

Mr. Hollander's first volume of poetry, *A Crackling of Thorns,* won the Yale Series of Younger Poets Awards for 1958. He was a recipient of a National Institute of Arts and Letters grant (1963) and has been a member of the Wesleyan University Press Poetry Board and the Bollingen Poetry Translation Prize Board. Mr. Hollander is Professor of English at Hunter College.

Selected Poetry and Prose of Byron is edited by poet, critic, and author W. H. Auden. Mr. Auden was awarded the King George Gold Medal for poetry in 1937, a Pulitzer Prize in 1948, and the Feltrinelli Prize in 1957. He is the editor of *The Oxford Book of Light Verse.* His many volumes include *The Double Man, For the Time Being, The Age of Anxiety, Nones, The Shield of Achilles, On the Frontier,* and *Journey to a War.*

George Gordon, Lord Byron

SELECTED POETRY
AND PROSE

Edited by W. H. Auden

The Signet Classic Poetry Series
GENERAL EDITOR: JOHN HOLLANDER

PUBLISHED BY
THE NEW AMERICAN LIBRARY, NEW YORK AND TORONTO
THE NEW ENGLISH LIBRARY LIMITED, LONDON

First Printing, December, 1966

Library of Congress Catalog Card No. 66:28979

SIGNET TRADEMARK REG. U.S. PAT. OFF. AND FOREIGN COUNTRIES
REGISTERED TRADEMARK—MARCA REGISTRADA
HECHO EN CHICAGO, U.S.A.

SIGNET CLASSICS *are published* in the United States
by The New American Library, Inc.,
1301 Avenue of the Americas, New York, New York 10019,
in Canada *by The New American Library of Canada Limited,*
295 King Street East, Toronto 2, Ontario,
in the United Kingdom *by The New English Library Limited,*
Barnard's Inn, Holborn, London, E.C. 1, England

PRINTED IN THE UNITED STATES OF AMERICA

Contents

Introduction

Of the poets whom histories of English literature indiscriminately lump together as the Romantics, the three who enjoyed great and immediate success in their own lifetime were Scott, Byron, and, some way behind, Tom Moore. Between 1812 and 1817, for example, Byron's poems brought him in about two thousand pounds a year, a formidable sum for those days.

The extent to which taste has changed can be roughly gauged from looking at the courses devoted to this period by the average college English Department. Today, the poet most lectured upon is, I should guess, the one who was virtually unknown in his own time, William Blake—followed by Wordsworth, Coleridge, Keats, and Shelley, in that order. Scott the novelist is still widely read, Scott the poet by few. Moore, aside from a few songs in anthologies, is hardly read at all. And Byron? I wonder. I have no idea how many readers he still has, but, as one of them, I find the poems that made his reputation among his contemporaries, *Childe Harold* and the Tales, unreadable. Had he died in the first half of 1817, I should now be seconding his own verdict on his work up till that date, as stated when he wrote to Moore:

> If I live ten years longer, you will see, however, that all is not over with me—I don't mean in literature, for that is nothing; and it may seem odd enough to say, I do not think it is my vocation.

If I had to introduce Byron to a student who knew nothing of his work, I would tell him: "Before you attempt to read any of the poetry, read *all* of the prose, his letters and journals. Once you have read these, you will be able, when you come to the poems, to recognize immediately which are authentic and which are bogus. You will find, I think, that only three are of major importance: *Beppo, The Vision of Judgment,* and *Don Juan,* all of them written, incidentally, in the same meter."

It does not matter where one opens the prose; from the earliest years till the end, the tone of voice rings true and utterly unlike anybody else's.

This place is wretched enough—a villainous chaos of din and drunkenness, nothing but hazard and burgundy, hunting, mathematics, and Newmarket, riot and racing. Yet it is a paradise compared with the eternal dulness of Southwell. Oh! the misery of doing nothing but make *love, enemies,* and *verses.*

(1807)

Dined *versus* six o' the clock. Forgot that there was a plum-pudding (I have added, lately, *eating* to my "family of vices" and had dined before I knew it. Drank half a bottle of some sort of spirits—probably spirits of wine; for what they call brandy, rum, etc, etc, here is nothing but spirits of wine, colored accordingly. Did *not* eat two apples, which were placed by way of dessert. Fed the two cats, the hawk, and the tame (but *not tamed*) crow. Read Mitford's *History* of Greece—Xenophon's *Retreat of the Ten Thousand.* Up to this present moment writing, 6 minutes before 8 o' the clock—French hours, not Italian.

Hear the carriage—order pistols and great coat—necessary articles. Weather cold—carriage open, and inhabitants rather savage—rather treacherous and highly inflamed by politics. Fine fellows though—good materials for a nation. Out of chaos God made a world, and out of high passions come a people.

Clock strikes—going out to make love. Somewhat perilous but not disagreeable. Memorandum—a new screen put up today. It is rather antique but will do with a little repair.

(1821)

In the poems and plays, on the other hand—even the later ones—at any moment the voice may go off-key. It is instructive, and sad, to compare the journal of 1816, which he kept for Augusta while traveling through the Alps, with the alpine scenes in *Manfred,* written the following year—in which he also wrote his first major poem, *Beppo.* The scenes are based upon the Journal—sometimes whole phrases are repeated word for word—but while the Journal is vital and exciting, the play is dead and a big bore.

If a romantic poet is one who believes, and writes in accordance with the belief, that Imagination is a power of vision which enables man to perceive the sacred truth behind sensory phenomena and therefore the noblest of all the mental faculties, then Byron was, by profession and in practice, one of the least romantic poets who ever lived.

Long before he was able to make his poetry conform to them, he had arrived at very definite convictions about the nature of poetry, and was well aware that they were at odds with those prevalent among his contemporaries. Nearly all of the poetry being written in his time, including his own, was, he felt, on the wrong track. The only poets on the right track were those still writing in the Augustan tradition, Crabbe and Rogers, and they, compared with their masters, Dryden and Pope, were but epigones.

Byron's aesthetic theories, like those of any poet, were in part a set of working rules to help him write the kind of poetry it was in him to write, and in part an attempt to justify himself for not writing the kind of poetry for which he lacked the talent. The reason for his admiration for Dryden and Pope becomes clear when one considers the style he arrived at once he found himself as a poet. Like him, they were "realists" who, instead of creating imaginary characters and landscapes, described living people and existing things; and, also like him, they were "worldly"—that is to say their primary poetic concern was neither with nonhuman nature nor with their own personal emotions, but with man as a social-political animal, with how men and women behave to each other, with the motives behind and the rationalized excuses they give for their actions. For a time Byron's admiration for them led him astray because he imagined that their sort of poetry could only be written in the medium they employed—the heroic couplet. This, he was to discover, was not the case, but of that more later.

As for his limitations, no other English poet, probably, has been so utterly deficient in the power of invention, and therefore so incapable of appreciating it.

> I hate *things* all *fiction;* and therefore the *Merchant* and *Othello* have no great associations to me.

> I detest [painting] unless it reminds me of something I have seen, or think it possible to see, for which [reason] I spew upon and abhor all the Saints and subjects of one half of the impostures I see in the churches and palaces.
>
> (1817)

To be unable to invent is to be unable to dramatize, even to dramatize oneself. Byron's poetry only sounds authentic when he speaks directly in the first person as Byron. When, as in *Childe Harold* or *The Corsair* or *Manfred,* he attempts to create a hero who is a projection of himself, he fails, because, as in a bad portrait, the reader cannot help noticing both the resemblance and the failure to resemble.

With the exception of Don Juan, all the "byronic" heroes are melancholics. From his letters and journals, it is evident that Byron himself suffered deeply all his life from depressions. It would have been surprising if he had not. A strain of violence and erratic behavior in both the Byrons and the Gordons, a childhood of genteel poverty spent with a hysterical mother and no father, a deformed foot, and, evidently, some kind of glandular malfunction that made him prone to obesity—though short, at the age of eighteen he weighed 194 pounds—all must have been a burden difficult for any boy to bear. In addition he hints at extraordinary happenings, probably sexual, of which he dare not speak openly.

His letters and journals, however, also make it clear that from the beginning the riposte of his imagination, reason, and moral courage to his depressions was to make a joke of them. "A joke," said Nietzsche, "is an epitaph on an emotion," and it is probable that all great comedians suffer from melancholia: a poet who can successfully express tragic and sad emotions need not be sad himself; indeed, he may quite possibly be temperamentally cheerful.

Byron's genius was essentially a comic one, and his poetic history is a quest, finally successful, to discover the right verse vehicle for a comic poet in his time. His admiration of Dryden and Pope initially misled him into thinking that, like them, he was intended to be a satirist. Satire and Comedy overlap—satirists are often funny and comedians satirical—but their goals are essentially different. The goal of satire is reform; the goal of comedy, acceptance. Satire attempts to show that the behavior of an individual or a group within society violates the laws of ethics or common sense on the assumption that once the majority are aware of the facts, they will become morally indignant and either compel the violators to mend their ways or render them socially and politically impotent. Comedy, on the other hand, is concerned with the illusions, and self-deceptions, which all men indulge in, as to what they and the world they live in are really like, and cannot, so long as they remain human, help being. The object of the comic exposure is not a special individual or a special social group, but every man or human society as a whole. Satire is angry and optimistic—it believes that the evil it attacks can be abolished; Comedy is good-tempered and pessimistic—it believes that however much we may wish we could, we cannot change human nature and must make the best of a bad job.

Now and again, as in his attacks on Southey and the Duke of Wellington, Byron writes as a satirist.

> You are "the best of cut-throats":—do not start;
> The phrase is Shakespeare's, and not misapplied:
> War's a brain-spattering, windpipe-slitting art,
> Unless her cause by right be sanctified.
> If you have acted *once* a generous part,

The world, not the world's masters, will decide,
And I shall be delighted to learn who,
Save you and yours, have gained by Waterloo?
(*Don Juan*, Canto Nine, lines 25–32)

But his predominant and constant concern is, in his own words, "to giggle and make giggle."

Poor Julia's heart was in an awkward state;
She felt it going, and resolved to make
The noblest effort for herself and mate,
For honor's, pride's, religion's, virtue's sake;
Her resolutions were most truly great;
And almost might have made a Tarquin quake:
She prayed the Virgin Mary for her grace
As being the best judge of a lady's case.

She vowed she never would see Juan more,
And next day paid a visit to his mother,
And looked extremely at the opening door,
Which, by the Virgin's grace, let in another;
Grateful she was, and yet a little sore—
Again it opens—it can be no other,
'Tis surely Juan now—No! I'm afraid
That night the Virgin was no longer prayed.
(*Don Juan*, Canto One, lines 593–608)

Byron is not holding Julia up to ridicule as either a hypocrite or a slut. The conflict between her conscience and her desire, between the demands of the Virgin and those of Aphrodite, is perfectly genuine. Byron does not pass judgment on this; he simply states that human nature is like that, and that, in his experience, if Aphrodite has opportunity on her side, the Madonna is seldom victorious—so that, in sexual matters, we ought to be tolerant of human frailty.

In the work of no other poet, I think, is the success or failure of a poem so closely bound up with the choice of meter and stanza form. His first successful poems are occasional verses, many of them written in anapestic quatrains, a form introduced into English poetry by

"Monk" Lewis, who had learned it from German, and perfected by Scott and Moore. This is a good vehicle for "light" verse but only on a small scale: a long poem with a wide range of subject matter cannot be written in it. His poems in octosyllabic couplets, *To a Lady* and *Sam Rogers,* for example, are also always successful. A long comic poem can be written in this meter, as we know from *Hudibras,* and I believe that his two satires, *English Bards and Scotch Reviewers* and *Hints from Horace,* might have been triumphant instead of only moderate successes if he had chosen to write them in octosyllabics instead of heroic couplets. For any poet of his generation it would have been impossible to write a heroic couplet without at all times hearing the personal "tune" and the aphoristic stamp that Pope had given it—and, in consequence, producing a copy that could not hope to be as good as the original. Long before he discovered the mock-heroic ottava rima, Byron realized the comic possibilities of feminine rhymes, but, in his heroic couplets, the masculine ending of the typical Popean line is too much in his ear to allow him to use them freely. There are only three couplets with feminine rhymes in *English Bards and Scotch Reviewers* and only one in *Hints from Horace.* Lastly, though funny things can be said in it, the Popean couplet is not a comic form—i.e., it does not itself make what it says funny, and is therefore not the ideal medium for a poet like Byron, who is primarily not a satirist but a comedian.

When Byron writes anapests he is sure of himself, but in heroic couplets he becomes self-conscious and stiff. For example:

> Men are more easily made than machinery—
>   Stockings fetch better prices than lives—
> Gibbets on Sherwood will heighten the scenery,
>   Showing how Commerce on Liberty thrives.
>   (*An Ode to the Framers of the Frame Bill,*
>   lines 13–16)

> The *landed interest* (you may understand
> The phrase much better leaving out the *land*)—

The land self-interest groans from shore to shore,
For fear that plenty should attain the poor.
              (*The Age of Bronze,* lines 598–601)

The trouble with the Tales is that Byron is trying to
write a kind of poetry for which he was unsuited. Metri-
cally, they are always adequate, and in *The Siege of
Corinth* his handling of the "sprung" rhythm of *Christabel*
is sometimes very exciting.

> As the spring-tides, with heavy plash,
> From the cliff's invading dash
> Huge fragments, sapped by the ceaseless flow,
> Till white and thundering down they go,
> Like the avalanche's snow
> On the Alpine vales below;
> Thus at length, outbreathed and worn,
> Corinth's sons were downward borne
> By the long and oft renewed
> Charge of the Moslem multitude.
> In firmness they stood, and in masses they fell,
> Heaped by the host of the infidel,
> Hand to hand, and foot to foot.
> Nothing there, save death, was mute. . . .

In the case of *Childe Harold,* on the other hand, one
does not know which was the most disastrous, his choice
of hero or his choice of meter. At the time, he had only
read a short extract from *The Faerie Queene,* and one is
not surprised to learn that when, some years later, Leigh
Hunt tried to make him read the whole poem, he hated
it. The Spenserian stanza is essentially slow in tempo, and
Byron is only at his ease with rapid tempi. Consequently,
he failed completely to understand its mechanics. As
George Saintsbury says:

> Over and over again [in *The Faerie Queene*] you will
> find stanzas where no two consecutive lines have the
> same pause; and very often there is *no* pause very
> strongly marked, so that the verses are punctuated only
> by the rhyme. Further, there is constant enjambement

between the lines. In the final Alexandrines Spenser suc-
ceeds in varying largely, though he does not deliberately
avoid, that strict middle pause which the metre invites
in most modern languages, and especially in English. . . .

Byron is prodigal of strong and generally centripetal
breaks. The Byronic line is almost always neither more
nor less than a half-couplet of very fair, sometimes ex-
cellent quality, more or less middle-paused. *Childe
Harold* is couplets with their rhymes wrenched into
Spenserian order, and with a Drydenian, not a Spen-
serian, Alexandrine thrust in at regular (and therefore
hopelessly unDrydenian) intervals. As a general rule, he
does not know how to fit on the Alexandrine so as to
make it an organic part of the stanza.

    (*The History of English Prosody,* Vols. I and II)

A comparison of a stanza from *The Faerie Queene* and
a stanza from *Childe Harold,* picked at random, will show
the truth of Saintsbury's remarks.

> They to him hearken, as beseemeth meete,
> And pass on forward: so their way does ly,
> That one of those same islands, which doe fleet
> In the wide sea, they needes must passen by,
> Which seemd so sweet and pleasaunt to the eye,
> That it would tempt a man to touchen there:
> Upon the banck they sitting did espy
> A daintie damsell, dressing of her heare,
> By whom a little skippet floting did appeare.
>   (*F.Q.* Book II, Canto XII, stanza 14)

> Yet are thy skies as blue, thy crags as wild;
> Sweet are thy groves, and verdant are thy fields,
> Thine olive ripe as when Minerva smiled,
> And still his honeyed wealth Hymettus yields;
> There the blithe bee his fragrant fortress builds,
> The freeborn wanderer of thy mountain-air;
> Apollo still thy long, long summer gilds,
> Still in his beam Mendeli's marbles glare;
> Art, Glory, Freedom fail, but Nature still is fair.
>   (*C.H.* Canto II, stanza 87)

Childe Harold, that gloomy young man with independent means, that rebel without a cause, who wanders about the earth misanthroping among ruins and desolate places, has little heroic appeal to us, but with young persons in 1812, on the Continent as well as in England, he was a smashing hit; and, before considering the poetry of Byron's last and greatest period, we might pause to examine why this should have been so. No explanation can be more than partial and tentative, but it seems to me that one important factor must have been a feeling of political despair among liberal-minded people. In his youth Byron had been a passionate admirer of Napoleon, and in this he certainly was not alone. With our advantages of hindsight, it seems extraordinary that anyone should have thought of Napoleon as a liberator—to us he looks more like a prototype of Hitler—but we must remember what the social and political conditions were of which a liberal-minded Englishman in the period between 1790 and 1820 had firsthand knowledge. In the annals of English literature and English military history, this period is one of glory, but to a political or social historian it is very grim indeed. Political power was entirely in the hands of a tiny group of great landowners who were able to ignore all interests but their own, and whose only method of dealing with social distress was to imprison or hang those who complained. The criminal law was the most savage in Europe, conditions in the mines and factories were of a concentration-camp-like horror, freedom of speech and assembly were frequently suspended.

Nor, with the coming of peace in 1815, was there any improvement. On the contrary, Reaction seemed more securely in the saddle than ever. Childe Harold, one guesses, appealed to those who, like his creator, were sufficiently comfortably situated not to suffer personally from social injustice, and idealistic enough to desire a juster society, but unwilling or unable to engage in political action to secure one. Byron's maiden speech in the House of Lords was an attack on the Frame-Maker's Bill, a piece of savagely repressive legislation, and it is interesting to speculate as to what his political career might have been had the scandal caused by the breakup of his marriage not persuaded him to leave England. Would he have been able to overcome his natural inclination to act alone and learn to work with others? Would he have modified his view that liberty is a gift to be graciously bestowed on the masses by their betters? Could he ever have conquered his besetting sin, impatience, which is a grave defect in a poet, but quite fatal in a politician? "When a man hath no freedom to fight for at home," he wrote in 1820, but was this really so? To be sure, the Tories were still all-powerful, and the Whigs were not to form a government before 1830; but there were men in Parliament, including his friend Hobhouse, who did not despair but continued to fight for Reform, and their patient efforts did in time compel the Tories against their will to enact liberal measures. The Criminal Law was reformed and the Corn Laws modified in 1827, and in 1829 the Catholics were emancipated. Such questions, and the criticism they imply, would not arise had Byron been content, like Pope, to devote his life to perfecting his poetry, instead of desiring to win fame as an effective man of action as well. The two desires are incompatible; making and acting are both full-time occupations.

From this digression let us return to the poetry. Byron's three major poems are all written in an ottava rima that differs from the conventional form of that stanza in English by imitating more exactly its form in Italian. Byron knew Italian well and had read Casti and Pulci, but he does not seem to have realized the comic possibilities of such an imitation until he read Frere's *The Monks and the Giants*.

Italian is a polysyllabic language; most of its words end on an unaccented syllable, and rhymes are easy to find. Italian ottava rima, therefore, is usually hendecasyllabic with feminine rhymes. The stanza has great structural advantages. As a unit, eight lines give space enough to describe a single event or to elaborate upon a single idea without having to run on to the next stanza. If, on the other hand, a poet wishes to make several short statements, the arrangement of the rhymes allows him to pause at will without fragmentizing the stanza, for his statements will always be linked by a rhyme. In Italian, therefore, ottava rima became a maid-of-all-work stanza that would fit any subject, comic or tragic.

When English poets first took it over, they instinctively shortened the lines to decasyllabics with masculine rhymes.

> All suddenly dismaid, and hartless quite
> He fled abacke and catching hastie holde
> Of a young alder hard behinde him pight,
> It rent, and streight aboute him gan beholde
> What God or Fortune would asist his might.
> But whether God or Fortune made him bold
> It's hard to read; yet hardie will he had
> To oveercome, that made him less adrad.
>   (Spenser, *Vergil's Gnat*)

The almost insuperable obstacle to this stanza in English as a vehicle for serious poetry lies in the paucity of rhymes in our language. It is almost impossible to write a poem of any length in it without having to use banal rhymes, or to pad the line or distort the natural order of words in order to get a rhyme. Yeats, who wrote some of his finest poems in it, circumvented this problem by a liberal use of half-rhymes and by ending lines with words that are almost dactyls, so that the rhyming syllable is only slightly accented. In the opening stanza of *Nineteen Hundred and Nineteen,* for example, only two of the lines rhyme exactly.

> Many ingenious lovely things are gone
> That seemed sheer miracle to the multitude,
> Protected from the circle of the moon
> That pitches common things about. There stood
> Amid the ornamental bronze and stone
> An ancient image made of olive wood—
> And gone are Phidias' famous ivories
> And all the golden grasshoppers and bees.

But in Byron's day half-rhymes were still considered illegitimate. One of his few good "serious" poems, *Epistle to Augusta,* is written in the standard English form of the stanza, but the difficulties it presents prevent the poem from achieving perfection.

And for the remnant which may be to come
I am content; and for the past I feel
Not thankless—for within the crowded sum
Of struggles, happiness at times would steal;
And for the present, I would not benumb
My feelings further.—Nor shall I conceal
That with all this I still can look around,
And worship Nature with a thought profound.
                              (lines 113–120)

The words *sum* and *steal,* the phrase *Nor shall I conceal,*
and the inversion *thought profound* are more dictated by
the necessity to rhyme than by the thought.

The secret Frere discovered, and communicated to
Byron, was that the very qualities which make ottava
rima unsuited in English to serious poetry make it an
ideal comic vehicle, particularly if its difficulties are ap-
parently increased by following the Italian original more
closely in the use of double and triple rhymes, for in
English, unlike Italian, nearly all of these are comic. In
the process of composition, as every poet knows, the re-
lation between experience and language is always dia-
lectical, but in the finished product it must always appear
to the reader to be a one-way relationship. In serious
poetry thought, emotion, event, must always appear to
dictate the diction, meter, and rhyme in which they are
embodied; vice versa, in comic poetry it is the words,
meter, rhyme, which must appear to create the thoughts,
emotions, and events they require. Speaking of the reputed
cause of Keats's death, Byron writes:

'Tis strange the mind, that very fiery Particle,
Should let itself be snuffed out by an Article.

(Incidentally, his first draft of the couplet ran: " 'Tis
strange the mind should let such phrases quell its/Chief
impulse with a few frail paper pellets.") The reader can-
not help observing that if, instead of a fiery particle,
Keats's mind had been, let us say, "an organ made for
thinking," then the *Edinburgh Review* could never have

hurt his feelings, and he would have died, not of consumption but of over-drinking.

Again, while in serious poetry detectable padding of lines is fatal, the comic poet should appear openly and unashamedly to pad.

> An Arab horse, a stately stag, a barb
> New broke, a camelopard, a gazelle.
> No—none of these will do—and then their garb!
> Their veil and petticoat—Alas! to dwell
> Upon such things would very near absorb
> A canto—then their feet and ankles—well,
> Thank heaven I've got no metaphor quite ready,
> (And so, my sober Muse—come, let's be steady.)

In *Beppo* and *Don Juan,* the form itself obliges Byron to keep interrupting the narrative to comment upon it and affairs in general in his own person, and these digressions are the true heart of the poems. The real hero of both is Byron himself. Speaking of *Don Juan,* Mr. M. K. Joseph writes:

> The actual amount of digression varies surprisingly in different parts of the poem. . . . The average of the whole poem is about one-third; but in the earlier cantos (I–VIII—up to Ismail) he seems to have aimed at something like a quarter. Sometimes it goes well below this, in particularly active cantos, such as II (the shipwreck) and V (the seraglios); only once does it rise well above it, in Canto III (Juan and Haidée), where it amounts to almost forty percent. But when Juan reaches St. Petersburg, the percentage increases immediately, shooting up to nearly sixty percent; Canto XII, with its elaborate comments on women and the marriage market, carries over seventy percent on a slender thread of narrative—the highest in the whole poem. None of the later cantos go below forty percent, except for XIII (about thirty percent) and the last, XVI, which drops suddenly below twenty percent again; but in these two, much of the material centered on Juan is concerned to broaden the social picture—Norman Abbey, the house

party, meals, Lord Henry as magistrate—rather than to
advance the actual story.

(*Byron, the Poet*)

Don Juan himself, unlike previous byronic heroes, is
not, thank goodness, gloomy. Far from being a defiant
rebel against the laws of God and man, his most con-
spicuous traits are his good temper and his social adapta-
bility. Wherever chance takes him—to a pirate's lair, a
harem in Mohammedan Constantinople, a court in Greek
Orthodox Russia, a country house in Protestant England—
he immediately adapts himself and is accepted as an
agreeable fellow. Though by birth a Spaniard and a Catho-
lic, and therefore an outsider from an Englishman's point
of view, he is the perfect embodiment of that very British
notion that a gentleman should succeed at everything he
does without appearing to make an effort. In his sexual
life, especially when one remembers the mythical monster
of depravity after whom he is named, his most striking
quality is passivity. Not only is he not very promiscuous—
in the course of two years he sleeps with five women, a
poor showing by comparison with the 1,003 Spanish
ladies of Leporello's Catalogue Aria or even Byron's "200
odd Venetian pieces"—but he seduces none of them.
In three cases he is seduced—by Julia, Catherine, the
Duchess of Fitz-Fulk—and in the other two, circum-
stances outside his control bring him together with Haidée
and Dudu, and no persuasion on his part is needed. The
Don Juan of the myth is by definition incapable of love,
but Byron's hero, though he cannot quite play Tristan to
her Isolde and commit suicide when he is parted from
Haidée, has been genuinely in love with her.
When one compares him with what we know of his
creator, he seems to be a daydream of what Byron would
have liked to be but wasn't. Physically he is unblemished
and one cannot imagine him having to diet to keep his
figure; socially he is always at his ease and his behavior
in perfect taste. In the adventures ascribed to him, Byron
seems also to be offering a self-defense for his own life.
Aware that he was believed by many to be the heartless

seducer and atheist of the legend, Byron says, as it were, to his accusers: "The legendary Don Juan does not exist. I will show you what the life of a man who gets the reputation for being a Don Juan is really like."

Though not as great a bore as Childe Harold, Don Juan cannot be called a very interesting character; fortunately, though, Byron has discovered a genre of poetry in which the character of its official hero does not matter.

There is a passage in Walter Bagehot which would make an excellent epigraph for *Don Juan.*

There seems to be an unalterable contradiction between the human mind and its employments. How can a *soul* be a merchant? What relation to an immortal being have the price of linseed, the tare on tallow, or the brokerage on hemp? Can an undying creature debit *petty expenses* and charge for *carriage paid?* The soul ties its shoes; the mind washes its hands in a basin. All is incongruous.

As a biological organism, man is subject like all living creatures to the impersonal drives like hunger and sex; as a social-political individual much of his behavior, thinking, and morality is conditioned by the particular social group or groups in which the accident of birth or economic necessity have placed him; and as a unique person who can say *I* in response to the *thou's* of other persons, he transcends his time and his place, can choose to think and act for himself, accept personal responsibility for the consequences, and is capable alike of heroism or baseness, sanctity or corruption. These three aspects of human nature—the biological, the social, and the personal—are seldom in complete accord, which is why man is essentially a comic creature. While praying, his thoughts of God are suddenly distracted by a pretty face; while courting, his thoughts of the beloved are suddenly encroached upon by the desire for a beefsteak; half of the statements he makes in the first-person singular, his *I-know* or *I-believe,* though uttered with passionate conviction, are not really his but the unexamined presuppositions of the nation or class to which he happens to belong.

It is such contradictions that Byron, in *Don Juan,* is continually delighted to expose. He is not a cynic; he does not say, for instance, that all love is only lust, all goodness a sham—a mask assumed in order to cut a good figure in society—or all heroism only ambition. What he does attack is what he calls *cant,* the proneness of human beings, in order to think well of themselves, to pretend that their motives and feelings are always of the noblest and purest character, and that lust, greed, social climbing, desire for fame, etc., are vices that beset other people, not themselves.

To cite one minor example, his criticism of Wordsworth is less a criticism of Wordsworth, I think, than of those who were making a sacred cult of the Lake Poet. Byron certainly did not deny that the contemplation of Nature can arouse feelings of awe, joy, dread, and wonder—in several poems he describes similar experiences—but he knew that the cause of such feelings is not as self-evident as the contemplator imagines.

Young Juan wandered by the glassy brooks,
Thinking unutterable things; he threw
Himself at length within the leafy nooks
Where the wild branch of the cork forest grew:
There poets find materials for their books,
And every now and then we read them through,
So that their plan and prosody are eligible,
Unless, like Wordsworth, they prove unintelligible.

* * *

He thought about himself, and the whole earth,
Of man the wonderful, and of the stars,
And how the deuce they ever could have birth;
And then he thought of earthquakes, and of wars,
How many miles the moon might have in girth,
Of air-balloons, and of the many bars
To perfect knowledge of the boundless skies;—
And then he thought of Donna Julia's eyes.

In thoughts like these true wisdom may discern
Longings sublime, and aspirations high,
Which some are born with, but the most part learn

To plague themselves withal, they know not why:
'Twas strange that one so young should thus concern
His brain about the action of the sky;
If *you* think 'twas philosophy that this did,
I can't help thinking puberty assisted.
      (*Don Juan,* Canto One, lines 713–720, 729–744)

His other objection to the wordsworthian cult of Nature is his conviction that fascinating as the study of Nature may be, this should, at least in a poet, take second place; his first concern should be the study of man. The poet who ignores man will soon falsify even his descriptions of natural landscape by omitting the human elements that are almost always present. In his own description of a "sublime" landscape, Byron is careful to include the profanely human.

A green field is a sight which makes him pardon
The absence of that more sublime construction,
Which mixes up vines, olives, precipices,
Glaciers, volcanoes, oranges and ices.

In the history of English poetry before the so-called Romantic Age, comic poetry is comparatively rare: some of Chaucer, some of Dunbar, Skelton, Samuel (*Hudibras*) Butler. Dryden and Pope, though they often write funny lines, cannot be classified as comic poets. But from 1800 onward comic poetry has flourished. Byron, Moore (especially in his political poems), Praed, Hood, Barham, Lear, and Carroll (slightly to one side), W. S. Gilbert, J. K. Stephen, Calverley, and in this century the best of Chesterton and Belloc, not to mention the anonymous host of limerick writers, represent a tradition without which English poetry would be very much the poorer, and of them all, Byron is by far the greatest. Whatever its faults, *Don Juan* is the most original poem in English; nothing like it had ever been written before. Speaking for myself, I don't feel like reading it very often, but when I do, it is the only poem I want to read: no other will do.

W. H. AUDEN

Background Dates

GENERAL	YEAR	ENGLISH POETRY
Mozart, *Don Giovanni*	1787	
Kant, *Critique of Practical Reason*	1788	
United States Constitution ratified		
Bentham, *An Introduction to the Principles of Morals and Legislation*. (Utilitarianism)	1789	Blake, *Songs of Innocence, The Book of Thel*
Erasmus Darwin, *The Loves of the Plants*		
Fall of the Bastille		
White, *Natural History and Antiquities of Selborne*		
	1790	Blake, *The Marriage of Heaven and Hell*
Boswell, *The Life of Samuel Johnson*	1791	Burns, *Tam o' Shanter*
De Sade, *Justine*		
Wollstonecraft, *A Vindication of the Rights of Women*	1792	Ritson, *Ancient Songs from the Time of Henry III to the Revolution*
		Rogers, *The Pleasures of Memory*
Carnot's *levée en masse* (universal military conscription)	1793	Blake, *America: A Prophecy*
Decimal System adopted by the National Assembly		Wordsworth, *An Evening Walk*
Execution of Louis XVI		
Reign of Terror		
England and France at war		
Dalton, *Meteorological Observations and Essays* (beginnings of an atomic theory)		

GENERAL	YEAR	ENGLISH POETRY
Godwin, *Political Justice*		
Paley, *A View of the Evidences of Christianity*	1794	Blake, *Songs of Innocence and Experience*
Radcliffe, *Mysteries of Udolpho*		
Slavery abolished in French Colonies		
Lewis, *The Monk*	1796	
Goethe, *Hermann und Dorothea*	1797	
Malthus, *The Principle of Population as it affects the Future Improvement of Society*	1798	Wordsworth and Coleridge, *Lyrical Ballads*
Income Tax introduced in England		
Napoleon's *coup* of the 18th Brumaire	1799	
Corresponding Societies Bill (limiting freedom of assembly, speech and press)		
	1800	Moore, *Odes of Anacreon* Wordsworth and Coleridge, *Lyrical Ballads, Vol. II*
Gauss, *Disquisitiones Arithmeticae* (higher mathematics as an independent science)	1801	
Pestalozzi, *How Gertrude teaches her children* (theory of education by doing)		
Peace of Amiens	1802	Scott begins editing *Minstrelsy of the Scottish Border*
War with France resumed	1803	
Construction of the Caledonian Ship Canal begun by Telford (finished 1821)		
Code Napoléon	1804	Blake, *Milton*
	1805	Scott, *Lay of the Last Minstrel*
	1805–6	Wordsworth, *The Prelude* (first version, not published until 1926)
	1806	Scott, *Ballads and Lyrical Pieces*

GENERAL	YEAR	ENGLISH POETRY
Hegel, *Phenomenology of the Spirit*	1807	Moore, *A Selection of Irish Melodies*
Charles and Mary Lamb, *Tales from Shakespeare*		Wordsworth, *Poems in Two Volumes* (including *Ode on Intimations of Immortality*)
Goethe, *Faust, Part I*	1808	Scott, *Marmion*
Lamarck, *Zoological Philosophy*	1809	
Schlegel, *Lectures on Dramatic Art and Literature*	1809 11	
	1810	Crabbe, *The Borough*
Goya, *Desastres de la guerra*	1810–13	Scott, *The Lady of the Lake*
George III permanently insane	1811	
Prince of Wales appointed Prince Regent		
Austen, *Sense and Sensibility*		
Luddite Riots	1811–14	
Napoleon's Russian Campaign	1812	
Grimm, *Kinder und Hausmärchen*	1812–14	
First gas-lighting in London	1813	Shelley, *Queen Mab*
Austen, *Pride and Prejudice*		
Battle of Leipsig. Napoleon abdicates and retires to Elba	1814	Wordsworth, *The Excursion*
Stephenson's locomotive		
Scott, *Waverley*		
Congress of Vienna	1814–15	
Napoleon escapes. Battle of Waterloo. Income tax repealed (not reintroduced until 1842)	1815	Wordsworth, *The White Doe of Rylstone*
Corn Bill, forbidding import of cheap grain		
Austen, *Emma*	1816	Coleridge, *Christabel*
Scott, *Old Mortality*		Shelley, *Alastor*
Peacock, *Headlong Hall*		Hunt, *The Story of Rimini*
Habeas Corpus suspended	1817	Keats, *Poems*
Coleridge, *Biographia Literaria*		Moore, *Lallah Rookh*
Ricardo, *Principles of Political Economy and Taxation*		

Mary Shelley, *Frankenstein*	1818	Keats, *Endymion*
Bowdler, *The Family Shakespeare* (improper words expurgated)		
Scott, *The Heart of Midlothian*		
"Manchester Massacre." The Six Acts (repressive legislation)	1819	Keats, *Ode to a Nightingale*
Scott, *Ivanhoe*		Shelley, *The Cenci*
Schopenhauer, *The World as Will and Idea*		Wordsworth, *Peter Bell*
Death of George III, accession of George IV	1820	Keats, *La Belle Dame Sans Merci, Lamia, Hyperion,* etc.
		Shelley, *Prometheus Unbound*
		Wordsworth, *Sonnets to the River Duddon*
		Clare, *Poems, Descriptive of Rural Life and Scenery*
Lamb, *Essays of Elia*	1820–23	
Beginning of Greek War of Independence	1821	Shelley, *Adonais, Epipsychidion*
James Mill, *Elements of Political Economy*		Clare, *The Village Minstrel*
Saint-Simon, *The Industrial System*		
Scott, *Kenilworth*		
Hazlitt, *Table Talk*	1821–22	
De Quincey, *Confessions of an English Opium Eater*	1822	Beddoes, *The Bride's Tragedy*
Scott, *Peveril of the Peak*		Darley, *The Errors of Ecstasie*
		Rogers, *Italy, Part I*

A General Note on the Text

The overall textual policy for the Signet Classic Poetry series attempts to strike a balance between the convenience and dependability of total modernization, on the one hand, and the authenticity of an established text on the other. Starting with the Restoration and Augustan poets, the General Editor has set up the following guidelines for the individual editors:

Modern American spelling will be used, although punctuation may be adjusted by the editor of each volume when he finds it advisable. In any case, syllabic final "ed" will be rendered with grave accent to distinguish it from the silent one, which is written out without apostrophe (e.g., "to gild refinèd gold," but "askèd" rather than "ask'd"). Archaic words and forms are to be kept, naturally, whenever the meter or the sense may require it.

In the case of poets from earlier periods, the text is more clearly a matter of the individual editor's choice, and the type and degree of modernization has been left to his decision. But, in any event, archaic typographical conventions ("i," "j," "u," "v," etc.) have all been normalized in the modern way.

JOHN HOLLANDER

A Note on this Edition

The text of the poems used here is based on that of the edition published by John Murray Publishers, Ltd., London (*The Works of Lord Byron with his Letters and Journals & his Life,* edited by Thomas Moore, 17 vols., 1832–33), with the modernizations standard to this series. That of the letters is from *The Letters and Journals,* edited by R. E. Prothero, 6 vols., 1898–1901, also published by John Murray. For permission to use passages and a letter not printed in that edition, the editor is grateful to Sir John Murray and Charles Scribner's Sons, New York, as well as to the Yale University Library.

W. H. AUDEN

Chronology

1788   January 22. George Gordon Byron born in London.

1798   May 19. Becomes sixth Lord Byron and inherits Newstead Abbey, to which he moves.

1801   Enters Harrow.

1805   Enters Trinity College, Cambridge.

1806   *Fugitive Pieces* privately printed.

1807   *Hours of Idleness* published and later attacked in *Edinburgh Review.*

1809   Takes seat in House of Lords. *English Bards and Scotch Reviewers* published. Journeys with Hobhouse in Portugal, Spain, Malta, Albania.

1810   Continues travels in Greece and Turkey. Swims the Hellespont.

1811   Returns to England.

1812   *Childe Harold's Pilgrimage;* Cantos I and II bring immediate fame.

1813   *The Giaour; The Bride of Abydos.*

1814   *The Corsair; Lara.*

1815   January 2. Marries Annabella Milbanke. Augusta Ada born December 10. *Hebrew Melodies* published.

1816   January 15. Lady Byron leaves him. April 25. Departs from England, after being snubbed by society, never to return. Spends summer in Geneva with Shelley, Mary Godwin, and Claire Clairmont. Journeys to Venice with Hobhouse. *Childe Harold,* Canto III; *The Prisoner of Chillon; The Siege of Corinth,* all published.

1817   January 12. Birth of his daughter, Allegra, to Claire Clairmont. *Manfred* published.

1818   *Childe Harold,* Canto IV. *Beppo,* prefiguring *ottava rima* of *Don Juan.* Meets Teresa Guiccioli and moves to Ravenna with her.

1819   *Don Juan,* Cantos I and II; *Mazeppa.*

1820   Lives in Pisa.

1821   *Don Juan,* Cantos III–V; *Marino Faliero; Cain; Sardanapalus.*

1822   Allegra dies. Shelley drowns in July. Moves to Genoa. *The Vision of Judgment* published in Leigh Hunt's *The Liberal.*

1823   Sails for Greece. *Don Juan,* Cantos VI–XIV; *Heaven and Earth; The Age of Bronze; The Island.*

1824   April 19. Dies at Missolonghi. *The Deformed Transformed; Don Juan,* Cantos XV and XVI.

Selected Bibliography

Editions of the Works:

The Works of Byron. 13 volumes. London: John Murray, 1898–1904. *Poetry.* E. H. Coleridge (ed.). 7 volumes; *Letters and Journals.* R. H. Prothero (ed.). 6 volumes.

Don Juan. T. G. Steffan and W. W. Pratt (eds.). Variorum edition. Austin, Texas: University of Texas Press; London: Nelson, 1957.

His Very Self and Voice: Collected Conversations of Lord Byron. E. J. Lovell (ed.). New York: The Macmillan Co., 1954.

Biographies:

Marchand, Leslie A. *Byron, a Biography.* 3 volumes. New York: Alfred A. Knopf, Inc., 1957; London: John Murray, 1958.

Nicholson, Harold G. *Byron, the Last Journey.* Boston: Houghton Mifflin Company, 1924; London: Constable & Co., 1940 (new ed.).

Quennell, Peter. *Byron in Italy.* New York: The Viking Press, Inc.; London: William Collins Sons & Co., 1941.

———. *The Years of Fame.* New York: The Viking Press, Inc.; London: Faber & Faber, Ltd., 1935.

Background Information:

The Diaries of Tom Moore. J. B. Priestly (ed.). New York: The Macmillan Co., 1925.

The Life and Letters of Anne Isabella, Lady Noël Byron. E. C. Mayne (ed.). New York: Charles Scribner's Sons; London: Constable & Co., 1929.

Guiccioli, Teresa, Countess. *My Recollections of Lord Byron.* 1868.

Hobhouse, John Cam (Lord Broughton). *A Journal Through Albania.* London, 1813.

————. *Recollections of a Long Life.* 6 volumes. London: John Murray, 1909–11.

Trelawney, Edward John. *Recollections of the Last Days of Shelley and Byron.* New York: Philosophical Library; London: Folio Society Ltd., 1952.

Criticism:

Boyd, Elizabeth French. *Byron's Don Juan.* New York: Humanities Press; London: Routledge & Kegan Paul Ltd., 1958.

Joseph, M. K. *Byron the Poet.* London: Victor Gollancz Ltd., 1964.

Knight, George Wilson. *Lord Byron, Christian Virtues.* New York: Oxford University Press, 1953.

Lovell, Ernest J. *Byron: The Record of a Quest.* Austin, Texas: University of Texas Press, 1950.

Ridenour, George M. *The Style of Don Juan.* New Haven: Yale University Press; London: Oxford University Press, 1960.

Thorslev Jr., Peter L. *The Byronic Hero: Types and Prototypes.* Minneapolis: University of Minnesota Press, 1962.

PART ONE: Poems

TO A LADY

WHO PRESENTED TO THE AUTHOR A LOCK OF HAIR
BRAIDED WITH HIS OWN, AND APPOINTED A NIGHT IN
DECEMBER TO MEET HIM IN THE GARDEN

These locks, which fondly thus entwine,
In firmer chains our hearts confine
Than all th' unmeaning protestations
Which swell with nonsense love orations.
Our love is fixed, I think we've proved it,   5
Nor time, nor place, nor art have moved it;
Then wherefore should we sigh and whine,
With groundless jealousy repine,
With silly whims and fancies frantic,
Merely to make our love romantic?   10
Why should you weep like Lydia Languish,
And fret with self-created anguish?
Or doom the lover you have chosen,

On winter nights to sigh half frozen;
15 In leafless shades to sue for pardon,
Only because the scene's a garden?
For gardens seem, by one consent
(Since Shakespeare set the precedent,
Since Juliet first declared her passion),
20 To form the place of assignation.
Oh! would some modern muse inspire,
And seat her by a sea-coal fire;
Or had the bard at Christmas written,
And laid the scene of love in Britain,
25 He surely, in commiseration,
Had changed the place of declaration.
In Italy I've no objection,
Warm nights are proper for reflection;
But here our climate is so rigid,
30 That love itself is rather frigid:
Think on our chilly situation,
And curb this rage for imitation.
Then let us meet, as oft we've done,
Beneath the influence of the sun;
35 Or, if at midnight I must meet you,
Within your mansion let me greet you:
There we can love for hours together,
Much better, in such snowy weather,
Than placed in all th' Arcadian groves
40 That ever witnessed rural loves;
Then, if my passion fail to please,
Next night I'll be content to freeze;
No more I'll give a loose to laughter,
But curse my fate for ever after.

TO GEORGE, EARL DELAWARR°

Oh yes, I will own we were dear to each other;
    The friendships of childhood, though fleeting, are
        true;
The love which you felt was the love of a brother,
    Nor less the affection I cherished for you.

But Friendship can vary her gentle dominion,   5
    The attachment of years in a moment expires;
Like Love, too, she moves on a swift-waving pinion,
    But glows not, like Love, with unquenchable fires.

Full oft have we wandered through Ida together,
    And blessed were the scenes of our youth, I allow: 10
In the spring of our life, how serene is the weather!
    But winter's rude tempests are gathering now.

No more with affection shall memory blending,
    The wonted delights of our childhood retrace:
When pride steels the bosom, the heart is unbending,   15
    And what would be justice appears a disgrace.

However, dear George, for I still must esteem you—
    The few whom I love I can never upbraid—
The chance which has lost may in future redeem you,
    Repentance will cancel the vow you have made.   20

I will not complain, and though chilled is affection,
    With me no corroding resentment shall live:
My bosom is calmed by the simple reflection,
    That both may be wrong, and that both should
        forgive.

0 **To George, Earl Delawarr** schoolfriend of Byron's, later governor
of Bombay.

25 You knew that my soul, that my heart, my existence,
    If danger demanded, were wholly your own;
You knew me unaltered by years or by distance,
    Devoted to love and to friendship alone.

You knew—but away with the vain retrospection!
30   The bond of affection no longer endures;
Too late you may droop o'er the fond recollection,
    And sigh for the friend who was formerly yours.

For the present, we part—I will hope not forever;
    For time and regret will restore you at last:
35 To forget our dissension we both should endeavor,
    I ask no atonement but days like the past.

EGOTISM. A LETTER TO
J. T. BECHER°

If fate should seal my Death tomorrow
    (Though much *I* hope she will *postpone* it),
I've held a share of *Joy* and *Sorrow,*
    Enough for *Ten;* and *here* I *own* it.

5 I've lived, as many other men live,
    And yet, I think, with more enjoyment;
For could I through my days again live,
    I'd pass them in the *same* employment.

0 **Egotism . . . Becher** The Reverend John Thomas Betcher, Vicar of
Rumpton and Midsomer Norton, Notts., advised and encouraged the
young poet.

That *is* to say, with *some exception,*
   For though I will not make confession,   *10*
I've seen too much of man's deception
   Ever again to trust profession.

Some sage *Mammas* with gesture haughty,
   Pronounce me quite a youthful Sinner—
But *Daughters* say, "although he's naughty,   *15*
   You must not check a *Young Beginner!*"

I've loved, and many damsels know it—
   But whom I don't intend to mention,
As *certain stanzas* also show it,
   Some say *deserving Reprehension.*   *20*

Some ancient Dames, of virtue fiery
   (Unless Report does much belie them),
Have lately made a sharp Inquiry,
   And much it *grieves* me to *deny* them.

Two whom I loved had *eyes* of *Blue,*   *25*
   To which I hope you've no objection;
The *Rest* had eyes of *darker Hue*—
   Each Nymph, of course, was *all perfection.*

But here I'll close my *chaste* Description,
   Nor say the deeds of animosity;   *30*
For *silence* is the best prescription,
   To *physic* idle curiosity.

Of *Friends* I've known a *goodly Hundred*—
   For finding *one* in each acquaintance,
By *some deceived,* by others plundered,   *35*
   Friendship, to me, was not *Repentance.*

At *School* I thought like other *Children;*
   Instead of *Brains,* a fine Ingredient,
Romance, my *youthful Head bewildering,*
   To *Sense* had made me disobedient.   *40*

A victim, *nearly*, from affection,
　　To certain *very precious scheming*,
The still remaining recollection
　　Has *cured* my *boyish soul* of *Dreaming*.

45　By Heaven! I rather would forswear
　　The Earth, and all the joys reserved me,
Than dare again the *specious Snare*,
　　From which *my Fate* and *Heaven preserved* me.

Still I possess some Friends who love me—
50　In each a much esteemed and true one;
The Wealth of Worlds shall never move me
　　To quit their Friendship, for a new one.

But Becher! you're a *reverend pastor*,
　　Now take it in consideration,
55　Whether for penance I should fast, or
　　Pray for my *sins* in expiation.

I own myself the child of *Folly*,
　　But not so wicked as they make me—
I soon must die of melancholy,
60　If *Female* smiles should e'er forsake me.

Philosophers have *never doubted*,
　　That *Ladies' Lips* were made for *kisses!*
For *Love!* I could not live without it,
　　For such a *cursèd* place as *This is*.

65　Say, Becher, I shall be forgiven!
　　If *you* don't warrant my salvation,
I must resign all *Hopes* of *Heaven!*
　　For, *Faith*, I can't withstand Temptation.

QUERIES TO CASUISTS

The Moralists tell us that Loving is Sinning,
    And always are prating about and about it,
But as Love of Existence itself's the beginning,
    Say, what would Existence itself be without it?

They argue the point with much furious Invective,   5
    Though perhaps 'twere no difficult task to con-
      fute it;
But if Venus and Hymen should once prove defec-
      tive,
    Pray who would there be to defend or dispute it?

EPITAPH ON JOHN ADAMS, OF SOUTHWELL

A CARRIER, WHO DIED OF DRUNKENNESS

John Adams lies here, of the parish of Southwell,
A *Carrier* who *carried* his can to his mouth well;
He *carried* so much, and he *carried* so fast,
He could *carry* no more—so was *carried* at last;
For, the liquor he drank being too much for one,   5
He could not *carry* off—so he's now *carri-on*.
                       September, 1807

"WHEN WE TWO PARTED"

When we two parted
   In silence and tears,
Half broken-hearted
   To sever for years,
5 Pale grew thy cheek and cold,
   Colder thy kiss;
Truly that hour foretold
   Sorrow to this.

The dew of the morning
10   Sunk chill on my brow—
It felt like the warning
   Of what I feel now.
Thy vows are all broken,
   And light is thy fame;
15 I hear thy name spoken,
   And share in its shame.

They name thee before me,
   A knell to mine ear;
A shudder comes o'er me—
20   Why wert thou so dear?
They know not I knew thee,
   Who knew thee too well:—
Long, long shall I rue thee,
   Too deeply to tell.

25 In secret we met—
   In silence I grieve
That thy heart could forget,
   Thy spirit deceive.
If I should meet thee
30   After long years,
How should I greet thee?—
   With silence and tears.

1808

LINES TO MR. HODGSON°

WRITTEN ON BOARD THE LISBON PACKET

Huzza! Hodgson, we are going,
  Our embargo's off at last;
Favorable breezes blowing
  Bend the canvas o'er the mast.
From aloft the signal's streaming,   5
  Hark! the farewell gun is fired;
Women screeching, tars blaspheming,
  Tell us that our time's expired.
       Here's a rascal
       Come to task all,   10
  Prying from the custom-house;
       Trunks unpacking
       Cases cracking,
  Not a corner for a mouse
'Scapes unsearched amid the racket,   15
Ere we sail on board the Packet.

Now our boatmen quit their mooring,
  And all hands must ply the oar;
Baggage from the quay is lowering,
  We're impatient—push from shore.   20
"Have a care! that case holds liquor—
  Stop the boat—I'm sick—oh Lord!"
"Sick, ma'am, damme, you'll be sicker,
  Ere you've been an hour on board."
       Thus are screaming   25
       Men and women,
  Gemmen, ladies, servants, Jacks;
       Here entangling,
       All are wrangling,

0 **Mr. Hodgson** tutor at King's College, Cambridge, when Byron
went up to Trinity.

30   Stuck together close as wax.—
      Such the general noise and racket,
      Ere we reach the Lisbon Packet.

      Now we've reached her, lo! the captain,
          Gallant Kidd, commands the crew;
35   Passengers their berths are clapt in,
          Some to grumble, some to spew.
      "Hey day! call you that a cabin?
          Why 'tis hardly three feet square;
      Not enough to stow Queen Mab in—
40   Who the deuce can harbor there?"
                  "Who, sir? plenty—
                  Nobles twenty
          Did at once my vessel fill."—
                  "Did they? Jesus,
45   How you squeeze us!
          Would to God they did so still:
      Then I'd 'scape the heat and racket
      Of the good ship, Lisbon Packet."

      Fletcher! Murray! Bob! where are you?
50   Stretched along the deck like logs—
      Bear a hand, you jolly tar, you!
          Here's a rope's end for the dogs.
      Hobhouse muttering fearful curses,
          As the hatchway down he rolls,
55   Now his breakfast, now his verses,
          Vomits forth—and damns our souls.
                  "Here's a stanza
                  On Braganza—
          Help!"—"A couplet?"—"No, a cup
60   Of warm water—"
                  "What's the matter?"
          "Zounds! my liver's coming up;
      I shall not survive the racket
      Of this brutal Lisbon Packet."

65   Now at length we're off for Turkey,
          Lord knows when we shall come back!

Breezes foul and tempests murky
   May unship us in a crack.
But, since life at most a jest is,
   As philosophers allow,   *70*
Still to laugh by far the best is,
   Then laugh on—as I do now.
        Laugh at all things,
        Great and small things,
   Sick or well, at sea or shore;   *75*
        While we're quaffing,
        Let's have laughing—
Who the devil cares for more?—
Some good winc! and who would lack it,
Ev'n on board the Lisbon Packet?   *80*
               Falmouth Roads, June 30, 1809

WRITTEN AFTER SWIMMING
FROM SESTOS TO ABYDOS

If, in the month of dark December,
   Leander,[6] who was nightly wont
(What maid will not the tale remember?)
   To cross thy stream, broad Hellespont!

If, when the wintry tempest roared,   *5*
   He sped to Hero, nothing loth,

2 **Leander** legendary lover who swam the Hellespont each night to
Sestos and his lady Hero, returning at dawn. Byron and a friend
made the swim six days before this poem was written.

And thus of old thy current poured,
    Fair Venus! how I pity both!

For *me,* degenerate modern wretch,
10   Though in the genial month of May,
My dripping limbs I faintly stretch,
    And think I've done a feat today.

But since he crossed the rapid tide,
    According to the doubtful story,
15 To woo—and—Lord knows what beside,
    And swam for Love, as I for Glory;

'Twere hard to say who fared the best:
    Sad mortals! thus the Gods still plague you!
He lost his labor, I my jest;
20   For he was drowned, and I've the ague.
                    May 9, 1810

from ENGLISH BARDS and SCOTCH REVIEWERS (lines 103–142)

THE EPIGONES

    Time was, ere yet in these degenerate days
Ignoble themes obtained mistaken praise,
When sense and wit with poesy allied,
No fabled graces, flourished side by side;
5 From the same fount their inspiration drew,
And, reared by taste, bloomed fairer as they grew.

Then, in this happy isle, a Pope's pure strain
Sought the rapt soul to charm, nor sought in vain;
A polished nation's praise aspired to claim,
And raised the people's, as the poet's fame.   10
Like him great Dryden poured the tide of song,
In stream less smooth, indeed, yet doubly strong.
Then Congreve's scenes could cheer, or Otway's melt—
For nature then an English audience felt.
But why these names, or greater still, retrace,   15
When all to feebler bards resign their place?
Yet to such times our lingering looks are cast,
When taste and reason with those times are past.
Now look around, and turn each trifling page,
Survey the precious works that please the age;   20
This truth at least let satire's self allow,
No dearth of bards can be complained of now.
The loaded press beneath her labor groans,
And printers' devils shake their weary bones;
While Southey's epics cram the creaking shelves,   25
And Little's° lyrics shine in hot-pressed twelves.
Thus saith the preacher: "Nought beneath the sun
Is new"; yet still from change to change we run:
What varied wonders tempt us as they pass!
The cowpox, tractors, galvanism, and gas,   30
In turns appear, to make the vulgar stare,
Till the swollen bubble bursts—and all is air!
Nor less new schools of Poetry arise,
Where dull pretenders grapple for the prize:
O'er taste awhile these pseudo-bards prevail;   35
Each country book-club bows the knee to Baal,
And, hurling lawful genius from the throne,
Erects a shrine and idol of its own;
Some leaden calf—but whom it matters not,
From soaring Southey down to groveling Stott.°   40

26 **Little's** Thomas Moore's early pseudonym.   40 **Stott** Stott, better
known in the *Morning Post* by the name of Hafiz. This personage is
at present the most profound explorer of the bathos. [Byron's note.]

from HINTS FROM HORACE
(lines 221–262)

A LIFE

Observe his simple childhood's dawning days,
His pranks, his prate, his playmates, and his plays;
Till time at length the mannish tyro weans,
And prurient vice outstrips his tardy teens!

5   Behold him Freshman! forced no more to groan
O'er Virgil's devilish verses and—his own;
Prayers are too tedious, lectures too abstruse,
He flies from Tavell's frown° to "Fordham's Mews"
(Unlucky Tavell! doomed to daily cares
10 By pugilistic pupils, and by bears);
Fines, tutors, tasks, conventions threat in vain,
Before hounds, hunters, and Newmarket plain.
Rough with his elders, with his equals rash,
Civil to sharpers, prodigal of cash;
15 Constant to nought—save hazard and a whore,
Yet cursing both—for both have made him sore;
Unread (unless, since books beguile disease,
The pox becomes his passage to degrees);
Fooled, pillaged, dunned, he wastes his terms away,
20 And, unexpelled perhaps, retires M.A.;
Master of arts! as *hells* and *clubs* proclaim,
Where scarce a blackleg bears a brighter name!

Launched into life, extinct his early fire,
He apes the selfish prudence of his sire;
25 Marries for money, chooses friends for rank,
Buys land, and shrewdly trusts not to the Bank;

8 **Tavell's frown** The Rev. F. G. Tavell, tutor of Trinity College while Byron was at Cambridge, and presumably a disciplinarian.

Sits in the Senate; gets a son and heir;
Sends him to Harrow, for himself was there.
Mute, though he votes, unless when called to cheer,
His son's so sharp—he'll see the dog a peer!   30

Manhood declines—age palsies every limb;
He quits the scene—or else the scene quits him;
Scrapes wealth, o'er each departing penny grieves,
And avarice seizes all ambition leaves;
Counts cent per cent, and smiles, or vainly frets,   35
O'er hoards diminished by young Hopeful's debts;
Weighs well and wisely what to sell or buy,
Complete in all life's lessons—but to die.
Peevish and spiteful, doting, hard to please,
Commending every time, save times like these;   40
Crazed, querulous, forsaken, half forgot,
Expires unwept—is buried—let him rot!

from CHILDE HAROLD
(Canto II, Stanzas 73, 74, 85–90)

GREECE

Fair Greece, sad relic of departed worth!
Immortal, though no more; though fallen, great!
Who now shall lead thy scattered children forth,
And long accustomed bondage uncreate?
Not such thy sons who whilome did await,   5
The hopeless warriors of a willing doom,
In bleak Thermopylae's sepulchral strait—

Oh! who that gallant spirit shall resume,
Leap from Eurotas'° banks, and call thee from the
    tomb?

10   Spirit of freedom! when on Phyle's brow
    Thou sat'st with Thrasybulus° and his train,
    Couldst thou forbode the dismal hour which now
    Dims the green beauties of thine Attic plain?
    Not thirty tyrants now enforce the chain,
15   But every carle can lord it o'er thy land;
    Nor rise thy sons, but idly rail in vain,
    Trembling beneath the scourge of Turkish hand,
From birth till death enslaved; in word, in deed, un-
    manned.

*   *   *

And yet how lovely in thine age of woe,
20   Land of lost gods and godlike men, art thou!
    Thy vales of evergreen, thy hills of snow,
    Proclaim thee Nature's varied favorite now;
    Thy fanes, thy temples to thy surface bow,
    Commingling slowly with heroic earth,
25   Broke by the share of every rustic plough
    (So perish monuments of mortal birth,
So perish all in turn, save well-recorded Worth);

Save where some solitary column mourns
    Above its prostrate brethren of the cave;
30   Save where Tritonia's airy shrine adorns
    Colonna's° cliff, and gleams along the wave;
    Save o'er some warrior's half-forgotten grave,
    Where the gray stones and unmolested grass
    Ages, but not oblivion, feebly brave,
35   While strangers only not regardless pass,
Lingering like me, perchance, to gaze, and sigh
    "Alas!"

9 **Eurotas'** Laconia's principal river.   11 **Thrasybulus** Athenian
naval commander who siezed and held Phyle, above Athens, in the
late fifth century B.C.   31 **Colonna's** a reference to the Temple of
Athens, built on Sunium or Cape Colonna.

Yet are thy skies as blue, thy crags as wild;
Sweet are thy groves, and verdant are thy fields,
Thine olive ripe as when Minerva smiled,
And still his honeyed wealth Hymettus° yields;   40
There the blithe bee his fragrant fortress builds,
The freeborn wanderer of thy mountain air;
Apollo still thy long, long summer gilds,
Still in his beam Mendeli's marbles° glare;
Art, Glory, Freedom fail, but Nature still is fair.   45

Where'er we tread 'tis haunted, holy ground;
No earth of thine is lost in vulgar mold,
But one vast realm of wonder spreads around,
And all the Muse's tales seem truly told,
Till the sense aches with gazing to behold   50
The scenes our earliest dreams have dwelt upon:
Each hill and dale, each deepening glen and wold
Defies the power which crushed thy temples gone:
Age shakes Athena's tower but spares gray Marathon.

The sun, the soil, but not the slave, the same;   55
Unchanged in all except its foreign lord—
Preserves alike its bounds and boundless fame
The Battlefield, where Persia's victim horde
First bowed beneath the brunt of Hellas' sword,
As on the morn to distant Glory dear,   60
When Marathon became a magic word,
Which uttered, to the hearer's eye appear
The camp, the host, the fight, the conqueror's career,

The flying Mede, his shaftless broken bow;
The fiery Greek, his red pursuing spear;   65
Mountains above, Earth's, Ocean's plain below;
Death in the front, Destruction in the rear!
Such was the scene—what now remaineth here?
What sacred trophy marks the hallowed ground,
Recording Freedom's smile and Asia's tear?   70

---

40 **Hymettus** a mountain overlooking Athens, famous for its honey
and its marble.   44 **Mendeli's marbles** the famous Pendelic marble
used in Athenian architecture.

The rifled urn, the violated mound,
The dust thy courser's hoof, rude stranger, spurns
    around.

AN ODE TO THE FRAMERS OF
THE FRAME BILL°

[First published in the *Morning Chronicle,* March 2, 1812.]

Oh well done Lord Eldon! and better done Rider!
    Britannia must prosper with councils like yours;
Hawkesbury, Harrowby, help you to guide her,
    Whose remedy only must kill ere it cures:
5   Those villains, the Weavers, are all grown refractory,
    Asking some succor for Charity's sake—
So hang them in clusters round each Manufactory,
    That will at once put an end to *mistake.*

The rascals, perhaps, may betake them to robbing,
10   The dogs to be sure have got nothing to eat—
So if we can hang them for breaking a bobbin,
    'Twill save all the Government's money and meat:
Men are more easily made than machinery—
    Stockings fetch better prices than lives—
15 Gibbets on Sherwood will heighten the scenery,
    Showing how Commerce on Liberty thrives!

0 An Ode . . . Frame Bill On February 20, 1812, a repressive bill
providing the death penalty for protesting weavers who broke their
frames was passed by the House of Commons and sent to the House
of Lords, where Byron spoke vigorously against it in his maiden
speech.

Justice is now in pursuit of the wretches,
    Grenadiers, Volunteers, Bow-street Police,
Twenty-two Regiments, a score of Jack Ketches,
    Three of the Quorum and two of the Peace;   *20*
Some Lords, to be sure, would have summoned the
      Judges,
    To take their opinion, but that they ne'er shall,
For LIVERPOOL such a concession begrudges.
    So now they're condemned by *no Judges* at all.

Some folks for certain have thought it was shocking,   *25*
    When Famine appeals and when Poverty groans,
That life should be valued at less than a stocking,
    And breaking of frames lead to breaking of bones.
If it should prove so, I trust, by this token
    (And who will refuse to partake in the hope?),   *30*
That the frames of the fools may be first to be *broken,*
    Who, when asked for a *remedy,* sent them a *rope.*

THE DESTRUCTION OF
SENNACHERIB

The Assyrian came down like the wolf on the fold,
And his cohorts were gleaming in purple and gold;
And the sheen of their spears was like stars on the sea,
When the blue wave rolls nightly on deep Galilee.

Like the leaves of the forest when Summer is green,   *5*
That host with their banners at sunset were seen:
Like the leaves of the forest when Autumn hath blown,
That host on the morrow lay withered and strown.

For the Angel of Death spread his wings on the blast,
10 And breathed in the face of the foe as he passed;
And the eyes of the sleepers waxed deadly and chill,
And their hearts but once heaved, and forever grew
    still!

And there lay the steed with his nostril all wide,
But through it there rolled not the breath of his pride:
15 And the foam of his gasping lay white on the turf,
And cold as the spray of the rock-beating surf.

And there lay the rider distorted and pale,
With the dew on his brow and the rust on his mail;
And the tents were all silent, the banners alone,
20 The lances unlifted, the trumpet unblown.

And the widows of Ashur are loud in their wail,
And the idols are broke in the temple of Baal;
And the might of the Gentile, unsmote by the sword,
Hath melted like snow in the glance of the Lord!
                         Seaham, February 17, 1815

STANZAS FOR MUSIC

There's not a joy the world can give like that it takes
    away,
When the glow of early thought declines in feeling's
    dull decay;
'Tis not on youth's smooth cheek the blush alone,
    which fades so fast,
But the tender bloom of heart is gone, ere youth itself
    be past.

Then the few whose spirits float above the wreck of
 happiness   5
Are driven o'er the shoals of guilt, or ocean of excess:
The magnet of their course is gone, or only points in
 vain
The shore to which their shivered sail shall never
 stretch again.

Then the mortal coldness of the soul like death itself
 comes down;
It cannot feel for others' woes, it dare not dream its
 own;   10
That heavy chill has frozen o'er the fountain of our
 tears,
And though the eye may sparkle still, 'tis where the
 ice appears.

Though wit may flash from fluent lips, and mirth dis-
 tract the breast,
Through midnight hours that yield no more their
 former hope of rest;
'Tis but as ivy leaves around the ruined turret wreath,   15
All green and wildly fresh without, but worn and gray
 beneath.

Oh could I feel as I have felt—or be what I have been,
Or weep as I could once have wept, o'er many a
 vanished scene;
As springs in deserts found seem sweet, all brackish
 though they be,
So, midst the withered waste of life, those tears would
 flow to me.   20

March, 1815

STANZAS FOR MUSIC

There be none of Beauty's daughters
   With a magic like thee;
And like music on the waters
   Is thy sweet voice to me:
5 When, as if its sound were causing
   The charmèd ocean's pausing,
   The waves lie still and gleaming,
   And the lulled winds seem dreaming.

And the midnight moon is weaving
10   Her bright chain o'er the deep;
Whose breast is gently heaving,
   As an infant's asleep:
So the spirit bows before thee,
To listen and adore thee;
15 With a full but soft emotion,
Like the swell of Summer's ocean.

March 28 [1816]

DARKNESS

I had a dream, which was not all a dream.
The bright sun was extinguished, and the stars
Did wander darkling in the eternal space,
Rayless, and pathless, and the icy earth

Swung blind and blackening in the moonless air;   5
Morn came and went—and came, and brought no day,
And men forgot their passions in the dread
Of this their desolation; and all hearts
Were chilled into a selfish prayer for light.
And they did live by watchfires—and the thrones,   10
The palaces of crownèd kings—the huts,
The habitations of all things which dwell,
Were burnt for beacons; cities were consumed,
And men were gathered round their blazing homes
To look once more into each other's face.   15
Happy were those who dwelt within the eye
Of the volcanos, and their mountain torch:
A fearful hope was all the world contained;
Forests were set on fire—but hour by hour
They fell and faded—and the crackling trunks   20
Extinguished with a crash—and all was black.
The brows of men by the despairing light
Wore an unearthly aspect, as by fits
The flashes fell upon them; some lay down
And hid their eyes and wept; and some did rest   25
Their chins upon their clenchèd hands, and smiled;
And others hurried to and fro, and fed
Their funeral piles with fuel, and looked up
With mad disquietude on the dull sky,
The pall of a past world; and then again   30
With curses cast them down upon the dust,
And gnashed their teeth and howled. The wild birds
   shrieked,
And, terrified, did flutter on the ground,
And flap their useless wings; the wildest brutes
Came tame and tremulous; and vipers crawled   35
And twined themselves among the multitude,
Hissing, but stingless—they were slain for food.
And War, which for a moment was no more,
Did glut himself again;—a meal was bought
With blood, and each sate sullenly apart   40
Gorging himself in gloom. No love was left;
All earth was but one thought—and that was death,
Immediate and inglorious; and the pang

Of famine fed upon all entrails—men
45 Died, and their bones were tombless as their flesh;
The meager by the meager were devoured,
Even dogs assailed their masters, all save one,
And he was faithful to a corse, and kept
The birds and beasts and famished men at bay,
50 Till hunger clung them, or the dropping dead
Lured their lank jaws. Himself sought out no food,
But with a piteous and perpetual moan,
And a quick desolate cry, licking the hand
Which answered not with a caress—he died.
55 The crowd was famished by degrees; but two
Of an enormous city did survive,
And they were enemies. They met beside
The dying embers of an altar place,
Where had been heaped a mass of holy things
60 For an unholy usage; they raked up,
And shivering scraped with their cold skeleton hands
The feeble ashes, and their feeble breath
Blew for a little life, and made a flame
Which was a mockery. Then they lifted up
65 Their eyes as it grew lighter, and beheld
Each other's aspects—saw, and shrieked, and died—
Even of their mutual hideousness they died,
Unknowing who he was upon whose brow
Famine had written Fiend. The world was void,
70 The populous and the powerful was a lump,
Seasonless, herbless, treeless, manless, lifeless—
A lump of death—a chaos of hard clay.
The rivers, lakes, and ocean all stood still,
And nothing stirred within their silent depths;
75 Ships sailorless lay rotting on the sea,
And their masts fell down piecemeal; as they dropped
They slept on the abyss without a surge—
The waves were dead; the tides were in their grave,
The Moon, their mistress, had expired before;
80 The winds were withered in the stagnant air,
And the clouds perished; Darkness had no need
Of aid from them—She was the Universe.

Diodati, July, 1816

EPISTLE TO AUGUSTA

My sister! my sweet sister! if a name
Dearer and purer were, it should be thine.
Mountains and seas divide us, but I claim
No tears, but tenderness to answer mine:
Go where I will, to me thou art the same—   5
A loved regret which I would not resign.
There yet are two things in my destiny—
A world to roam through, and a home with thee.

The first were nothing—had I still the last,
It were the haven of my happiness;   10
But other claims and other ties thou hast,
And mine is not the wish to make them less.
A strange doom is thy father's son's, and past
Recalling, as it lies beyond redress;
Reversed for him our grandsire's° fate of yore—   15
He had no rest at sea, nor I on shore.

If my inheritance of storms hath been
In other elements, and on the rocks
Of perils, overlooked or unforeseen,
I have sustained my share of worldly shocks,   20
The fault was mine; nor do I seek to screen
My errors with defensive paradox;
I have been cunning in mine overthrow,
The careful pilot of my proper woe.

Mine were my faults, and mine be their reward.   25
My whole life was a contest, since the day
That gave me being, gave me that which marred
The gift—a fate, or will, that walked astray;
And I at times have found the struggle hard,
And thought of shaking off my bonds of clay.   30

15 **grandsire** Admiral John Byron was the poet's grandfather.

But now I fain would for a time survive,
If but to see what next can well arrive.

Kingdoms and empires in my little day
I have outlived, and yet I am not old;
35   And when I look on this, the petty spray
Of my own years of trouble, which have rolled
Like a wild bay of breakers, melts away;
Something—I know not what—does still uphold
A spirit of slight patience;—not in vain,
40 Even for its own sake, do we purchase pain.

Perhaps the workings of defiance stir
Within me—or perhaps a cold despair,
Brought on when ills habitually recur,
Perhaps a kinder clime, or purer air
45   (For even to this may change of soul refer,
And with light armor we may learn to bear),
Have taught me a strange quiet, which was not
The chief companion of a calmer lot.

I feel almost at times as I have felt
50   In happy childhood; trees, and flowers, and brooks,
Which do remember me of where I dwelt
Ere my young mind was sacrificed to books,
Come as of yore upon me, and can melt
My heart with recognition of their looks;
55   And even at moments I could think I see
Some living thing to love—but none like thee.

Here are the Alpine landscapes which create
A fund for contemplation;—to admire
Is a brief feeling of a trivial date;
60   But something worthier do such scenes inspire:
Here to be lonely is not desolate,
For much I view which I could most desire,
And, above all, a lake° I can behold
Lovelier, not dearer, than our own of old.

63 lake Lake Geneva (Leman).

Oh that thou wert but with me!—but I grow   65
The fool of my own wishes, and forget
The solitude, which I have vaunted so,
Has lost its praise in this but one regret;
There may be others which I less may show;—
I am not of the plaintive mood, and yet   70
I feel an ebb in my philosophy,
And the tide rising in my altered eye.

I did remind thee of our own dear Lake,
By the old Hall which may be mine no more.
Leman's is fair; but think not I forsake   75
The sweet remembrance of a dearer shore:
Sad havoc Time must with my memory make
Ere *that* or *thou* can fade these eyes before;
Though, like all things which I have loved, they are
Resigned forever, or divided far.   80

The world is all before me; I but ask
Of Nature that with which she will comply—
It is but in her summer's sun to bask,
To mingle with the quiet of her sky,
To see her gentle face without a mask,   85
And never gaze on it with apathy.
She was my early friend, and now shall be
My sister—till I look again on thee.

I can reduce all feelings but this one,
And that I would not;—for at length I see   90
Such scenes as those wherein my life begun,
The earliest—even the only paths for me:
Had I but sooner learnt the crowd to shun,
I had been better than I now can be;
The passions which have torn me would have slept;   95
I had not suffered, and *thou* hadst not wept.

With false Ambition what had I to do?
Little with Love, and least of all with Fame;
And yet they came unsought, and with me grew,
And made me all which they can make—a name.   100

Yet this was not the end I did pursue;
Surely I once beheld a nobler aim.
But all is over—I am one the more
To baffled millions which have gone before.

105　And for the future, this world's future may
From me demand but little of my care;
I have outlived myself by many a day;
Having survived so many things that were;
My years have been no slumber, but the prey
110　Of ceaseless vigils; for I had the share
Of life which might have filled a century,
Before its fourth in time had passed me by.

And for the remnant which may be to come,
I am content; and for the past I feel
115　Not thankless—for within the crowded sum
Of struggles, happiness at times would steal;
And for the present, I would not benumb
My feelings further.—Nor shall I conceal
That with all this I still can look around,
120　And worship Nature with a thought profound.

For thee, my own sweet sister, in thy heart
I know myself secure, as thou in mine;
We were and are—I am, even as thou art—
Beings who ne'er each other can resign;
125　It is the same, together or apart,
From life's commencement to its slow decline
We are entwined—let death come slow or fast,
The tie which bound the first endures the last!

Diodati, 1816

"SO WE'LL GO NO MORE A ROVING"

[To Thomas Moore, Venice, February 28, 1817.]

So we'll go no more a roving
  So late into the night,
Though the heart be still as loving,
  And the moon be still as bright.

For the sword outwears its sheath,   5
  And the soul wears out the breast,
And the heart must pause to breathe,
  And Love itself have rest.

Though the night was made for loving,
  And the day returns too soon,   10
Yet we'll go no more a roving
  By the light of the moon.

"MY BOAT IS ON THE SHORE"

[To Thomas Moore, July 10, 1817.]

My boat is on the shore,
  And my bark is on the sea;
But, before I go, Tom Moore,
  Here's a double health to thee!

5 Here's a sigh to those who love me,
  And a smile to those who hate;
 And, whatever sky's above me,
  Here's a heart for every fate.

 Though the ocean roar around me,
10 Yet it still shall bear me on;
 Though a desert should surround me,
  It hath springs that may be won.

 Were 't the last drop in the well,
  As I gasped upon the brink,
15 Ere my fainting spirit fell,
  'Tis to thee that I would drink.

 With that water, as this wine,
  The libation I would pour
 Should be—peace with thine and mine,
20 And a health to thee, Tom Moore.

"DEAR DOCTOR, I HAVE READ
YOUR PLAY"

[To John Murray, August 21, 1817. Murray had writ-
ten to Byron: "Polidori has sent me his tragedy! Do me
the kindness to send by return of post a *delicate* declen-
sion of it, which I engage faithfully to copy."]

Dear Doctor,° I have read your play,
Which is a good one in its way—

1 **Doctor** John William Polidori, Byron's personal physician.

Purges the eyes and moves the bowels,
And drenches handkerchiefs like towels
With tears, that, in a flux of grief,   5
Afford hysterical relief
To shattered nerves and quickened pulses,
Which your catastrophe convulses.
  I like your moral and machinery;
Your plot, too, has such scope for Scenery;   10
Your dialogue is apt and smart;
The play's concoction full of art;
Your hero raves, your heroine cries,
All stab, and everybody dies.
In short, your tragedy would be   15
The very thing to hear and see;
And for a piece of publication,
If I decline on this occasion,
It is not that I am not sensible
To merits in themselves ostensible,   20
But—and I grieve to speak it—plays
Are drugs—mere drugs, sir—nowadays.
I had a heavy loss by *Manuel*—
Too lucky if it prove not annual,—
And Sotheby, with his damned *Orestes*   25
(Which, by the way, the old Bore's best is),
Has lain so very long on hand
That I despair of all demand.
I've advertised, but see my books,
Or only watch my Shopman's looks;—   30
Still *Ivan, Ina,* and such lumber,
My back-shop glut, my shelves encumber.
  There's Byron, too, who once did better,
Has sent me, folded in a letter,
A sort of—it's no more a drama   35
Than *Darnley, Ivan,* or *Kehama;*
So altered since last year his pen is,
I think he's lost his wits at Venice,

. . . .

In short, sir, what with one and t'other,
I dare not venture on another.   40

I write in haste; excuse each blunder;
The Coaches through the street so thunder!
My Room's so full; we've Gifford here
Reading MSS., with Hookham Frere,
45 Pronouncing on the nouns and particles
Of some of our forthcoming Articles.
    The *Quarterly*—Ah, sir, if you
Had but the Genius to review!—
A smart Critique upon St. Helena,
50 Or if you only would but tell in a
Short compass what—but, to resume:
As I was saying, sir, the Room—
The Room's so full of wits and bards,
Crabbes, Campbells, Crokers, Freres, and Wards
55 And others, neither bards nor wits:—
My humble tenement admits
All persons in the dress of gent.,
From Mr. Hammond to Dog Dent.
    A party dines with me today,
60 All clever men, who make their way;
Crabbe, Malcolm, Hamilton, and Chantrey,
Are all partakers of my pantry.
They're at this moment in discussion
On poor De Staël's late dissolution.
65 Her book, they say, was in advance—
Pray Heaven! she tell the truth of France!
'Tis said she certainly was married
To Rocca, and had twice miscarried,
No—not miscarried, I opine—
70 But brought to bed at forty-nine.
Some say she died a Papist; Some
Are of opinion *that*'s a Hum;
I don't know that—the fellow, Schlegel,
Was very likely to inveigle
75 A dying person in compunction
To try the extremity of Unction.
But peace be with her! for a woman
Her talents surely were uncommon.
Her Publisher (and Public too)
80 The hour of her demise may rue—

For never more within his shop he—
Pray—was not she interred at Coppet?
Thus run our time and tongues away.—
But, to return, sir, to your play:
Sorry, sir, but I cannot deal,   85
Unless 'twere acted by O'Neill.
My hands are full, my head so busy,
I'm almost dead, and always dizzy;
And so, with endless truth and hurry,
Dear Doctor, I am yours,   90
                              JOHN MURRAY.

                                   August, 1817

ON SAM ROGERS°

Question and Answer

QUESTION

Nose and chin would shame a knocker;
Wrinkles that would puzzle Cocker;
Mouth which marks the envious scorner,
With a scorpion in each corner,
Turning its quick tail to sting you   5
In the place that most may wring you;
Eyes of leadlike hue, and gummy;
Carcass picked out from some mummy;
Bowels (but they were forgotten,
Save the liver, and that's rotten);   10

0 **Sam Rogers** justly forgotten poet, banker, and man-about-town,
famous for his breakfast-parties and his malice.

Skin all sallow, flesh all sodden—
Form the devil would frighten God in.
Is 't a corpse stuck up for show,
Galvanized at times to go?
15 With the Scripture in connection,
New proof of the resurrection?
Vampire, ghost, or ghoul, what is it?
I would walk ten miles to miss it.

ANSWER

Many passengers arrest one,
20 To demand the same free question.
Shorter's my reply, and franker—
That's the Bard, the Beau, the Banker.
Yet if you could bring about
Just to turn him inside out,
25 Satan's self would seem less sooty,
And his present aspect—Beauty.
Mark that (as he masks the bilious
Air, so softly supercilious)
Chastened bow, and mock humility,
30 Almost sicken to servility;
Hear his tone (which is to talking
That which creeping is to walking,
Now on all fours, now on tiptoe);
Hear the tales he lends his lip to;
35 Little hints of heavy scandals;
Every friend in turn he handles;
All which women or which men do,
Glides forth in an innuendo,
Clothed in odds and ends of humor—
40 Herald of each paltry rumor,
From divorces down to dresses,
Women's frailties, men's excesses,
All which life presents of evil
Make for him a constant revel.
45 You're his foe, for that he fears you,
And in absence blasts and sears you:
You're his friend—for that he hates you,

First caresses, and then baits you—
Darting on the opportunity
When to do it with impunity: 50
You are neither—then he'll flatter,
Till he finds some trait for satire;
Hunts your weak point out, then shows it
Where it injures to disclose it,
In the mode that's most invidious,   55
Adding every trait that's hideous—
From the bile, whose blackening river
Rushes through his Stygian liver.
Then he thinks himself a lover—
Why? I really can't discover,   60
In his mind, age, face, or figure;
Viper-broth might give him vigor,—
Let him keep the caldron steady,
He the venom has already.
For his faults—he has but *one*—   65
'Tis but envy, when all's done.
He but pays the pain he suffers,
Clipping, like a pair of snuffers,
Lights which ought to burn the brighter
For this temporary blighter.   70
He's the cancer of his species,
And will eat himself to pieces—
Plague personified, and famine—
Devil, whose sole delight is damning.

For his merits, would you know 'em?   75
Once he wrote a pretty Poem.

[*1818*]

BALLAD

(to the tune of "Sally in Our Alley")

Of all the twice ten thousand bards
    That ever penned a canto,
Whom Pudding or whom Praise rewards
    For lining a portmanteau;
5 Of all the poets ever known,
    From Grub Street to Fop's Alley,
The Muse may boast—the World must own
    There's none like pretty Gally!°

He writes as well as any Miss,
10   Has published many a poem;
The shame is yours, the gain is his,
    In case you should not know 'em:
He has ten thousand pounds a year—
    I do not mean to vally—
15 His songs at sixpence would be dear,
    So give them gratis, Gally!

And if this statement should seem queer,
    Or set down in a hurry,
Go, ask (if he will be sincere)
20   His bookseller—John Murray.
Come, say, how many have been sold,
    And don't stand shilly-shally,
Of bound and lettered, red and gold,
    Well printed works of Gally.

25 For Astley's circus Upton writes,
    And also for the Surry (*sic*);
Fitzgerald weekly still recites,
    Though grinning Critics worry:

8 Gally Galley Knight, a poetaster.

70

Miss Holford's Peg, and Sotheby's Saul,
   In fame exactly tally;   *30*
From Stationer's Hall to Grocer's Stall
   They go—and so does Gally.

He rode upon a Camel's hump
   Through Araby the sandy,
Which surely must have hurt the rump   *35*
   Of this poetic dandy.
His rhymes are of the costive kind,
   And barren as each valley
In deserts which he left behind
   Has been the Muse of Gally.   *40*

He has a Seat in Parliament,
   Is fat and passing wealthy;
And surely he should be content
   With these and being healthy:
But Great Ambition will misrule   *45*
   Men at all risks to sally—
Now makes a poet—now a fool,
   And *we* know *which*—of Gally.

Some in the playhouse like to row,
   Some with the Watch to battle.   *50*
Exchanging many a midnight blow
   To Music of the Rattle.
Some folks like rowing on the Thames
   Some rowing in an Alley,
But all the Row my fancy claims   *55*
   Is *rowing* of my *Gally*.

"WHEN A MAN HATH NO FREEDOM TO FIGHT FOR AT HOME"

[To Thomas Moore, November 5, 1820.]

When a man hath no freedom to fight for at home,
    Let him combat for that of his neighbors;
Let him think of the glories of Greece and of Rome,
    And get knocked on the head for his labors.
5 To do good to mankind is the chivalrous plan,
    And is always as nobly requited;
Then battle for freedom wherever you can,
    And, if not shot or hanged, you'll get knighted.

from CHILDE HAROLD
(Canto IV, Stanzas 1–4)

VENICE

I stood in Venice on the Bridge of Sighs,°
A palace and a prison on each hand:
I saw from out the wave her structures rise
As from the stroke of the enchanter's wand:
5 A thousand years their cloudy wings expand

1 **Bridge of Sighs** leads from the Doge's palace to the San Marco prison; it is a celebrated sentimental monument.

Around me, and a dying Glory smiles
O'er the far times, when many a subject land
Looked to the wingèd Lion's° marble piles,
Where Venice sate in state, throned on her hundred
    isles!

She looks a sea Cybele,° fresh from ocean,   *10*
Rising with her tiara of proud towers
At airy distance, with majestic motion,
A ruler of the waters and their powers:
And such she was;—her daughters had their dowers
From spoils of nations, and the exhaustless East   *15*
Poured in her lap all gems in sparkling showers:
In purple was she robed, and of her feast
Monarchs partook, and deemed their dignity
    increased.

In Venice Tasso's echoes° are no more,
And silent rows the songless gondolier;   *20*
Her palaces are crumbling to the shore,
And music meets not always now the ear:
Those days are gone—but Beauty still is here;
States fall, arts fade—but Nature doth not die,
Nor yet forget how Venice once was dear,   *25*
The pleasant place of all festivity,
The revel of the earth, the masque° of Italy!

But unto us she hath a spell beyond
Her name in story, and her long array
Of mighty shadows, whose dim forms despond   *30*
Above the dogeless city's vanished sway:
Ours is a trophy which will not decay
With the Rialto; Shylock and the Moor

----

8 **wingèd Lion** The Lion of St. Mark, patron saint of the city, sur-
mounts two columns in the piazzetta nearby.   10 **Cybele** The mother-
goddess was represented with a towery crown.   19 **Tasso's echoes**
Venetian gondoliers used to sing stanzas from *Jerusalem Delivered*.
(Consider the equivalent: London cabmen reciting Spenser!)
27 **masque** Masques and revels were Renaissance court dramas, with
music and elaborate stage effects—prototypical operas.

And Pierre can not be swept or worn away—
35   The keystones of the arch! though all were o'er,
For us repeopled were the solitary shore.

from CHILDE HAROLD
(Canto IV, Stanzas 177–184)

"OH THAT THE DESERT WERE MY DWELLING-PLACE"

Oh that the Desert were my dwelling-place,
With one fair Spirit for my minister,
That I might all forget the human race,
And, hating no one, love but only her!
5   Ye Elements, in whose ennobling stir
I feel myself exalted, can ye not
Accord me such a being? Do I err
In deeming such inhabit many a spot,
Though with them to converse can rarely be our lot?

10   There is a pleasure in the pathless woods
There is a rapture on the lonely shore,
There is society where none intrudes,
By the deep Sea, and music in its roar:
I love not Man the less, but Nature more,
15   From these our interviews, in which I steal
From all I may be or have been before,
To mingle with the Universe, and feel
What I can ne'er express, yet cannot all conceal.

Roll on, thou deep and dark blue Ocean, roll!
Ten thousand fleets sweep over thee in vain;   20
Man marks the earth with ruin, his control
Stops with the shore; upon the watery plain
The wrecks are all thy deed, nor doth remain
A shadow of man's ravage, save his own,
When, for a moment, like a drop of rain,   25
He sinks into thy depths with bubbling groan,
Without a grave, unknelled, uncoffined, and unknown.

His steps are not upon thy paths, thy fields
Are not a spoil for him—thou dost arise
And shake him from thee; the vile strength he
    wields   30
For earth's destruction thou dost all despise,
Spurning him from thy bosom to the skies,
And send'st him, shivering in thy playful spray
And howling, to his Gods, where haply lies
His petty hope in some near port or bay,   35
And dashest him again to earth:—there let him lay.

The armaments which thunderstrike the walls
Of rock-built cities, bidding nations quake
And monarchs tremble in their capitals,
The oak leviathans, whose huge ribs make   40
Their clay creator the vain title take
Of lord of thee and arbiter of war—
These are thy toys, and, as the snowy flake,
They melt into thy yeast of waves, which mar
Alike the Armada's pride or spoils of Trafalgar.°   45

Thy shores are empires, changed in all save thee—
Assyria, Greece, Rome, Carthage, what are they?
Thy waters washed them power while they were
    free,
And many a tyrant since; their shores obey
The stranger, slave, or savage; their decay   50
Has dried up realms to deserts:—not so thou,

45 **Alike . . . Trafalgar** Storms accounted for losses suffered by both
the Spanish Armada in 1588 and the French fleet in 1805.

Unchangeable save to thy wild waves' play;
Time writes no wrinkle on thine azure brow;
Such as creation's dawn beheld, thou rollest now.

55   Thou glorious mirror, where the Almighty's form
Glasses itself in tempests; in all time,
Calm or convulsed—in breeze, or gale, or storm,
Icing the pole, or in the torrid clime
Dark-heaving;—boundless, endless, and sublime—
60   The image of Eternity—the throne
Of the Invisible; even from out thy slime
The monsters of the deep are made; each zone
Obeys thee; thou goest forth, dread, fathomless, alone.

And I have loved thee, Ocean! and my joy
65   Of youthful sports was on thy breast to be
Borne, like thy bubbles, onward. From a boy
I wantoned with thy breakers—they to me
Were a delight; and if the freshening sea
Made them a terror—'twas a pleasing fear,
70   For I was as it were a child of thee,
And trusted to thy billows far and near,
And laid my hand upon thy mane—as I do here.

PART ONE: Prose

To The Hon. Augusta Byron°
Burgage Manor, August 18th, 1804

My dearest Augusta,

    I seize this interval of my *amiable* mother's absence this afternoon, again to inform you, or rather to desire to be informed by you, of what is going on. For my own part I can send nothing to amuse you, excepting a repetition of my complaints against my tormentor, whose *diabolical* disposition (pardon me for staining my paper with so harsh a word) seems to increase with age, and to acquire new force with Time. The more I see of her the more my dislike augments; nor can I so entirely conquer the appearance of it, as to prevent her from perceiving my opinion; this, so far from calming the Gale, blows it into a *hurricane,* which threatens to destroy everything, till exhausted by its own violence, it is lulled into a sullen

---

Hon. Augusta Byron Byron's half sister, later Mrs. Leigh. It is possible, though not proven, that Byron was the father of her daughter, Elizabeth Medora.

torpor, which, after a short period, is again roused into fresh and revived frenzy, to me most terrible, and to every other Spectator astonishing. She then declares that she plainly sees I hate her, that I am leagued with her bitter enemies, viz. Yourself, Ld Carlisle° and Mr. Hanson° and, as I never Dissemble or contradict her, we are all *honored* with a multiplicity of epithets, too *numerous,* and some of them too *gross,* to be repeated. In this society, and in this amusing and instructive manner, have I dragged out a weary fortnight, and am condemned to pass another or three weeks as happily as the former. No captive Negro, or Prisoner of war, ever looked forward to their emancipation, and return to Liberty with more Joy, and with more lingering expectation, than I do to my escape from this maternal bondage, and this accursed place, which is the region of dullness itself, and more stupid than the banks of Lethe, though it possesses contrary qualities to the river of oblivion, as the detested scenes I now witness, make me regret the happier ones already passed, and wish their restoration.

Such Augusta is the happy life I now lead, such my *amusements.* I wander about hating everything I behold, and if I remained here a few months longer, I should become, what with *envy, spleen and all uncharitableness,* a complete *misanthrope,* but notwithstanding this,

Believe me, Dearest Augusta, ever yours, etc., etc.,

Byron

Ld. Carlisle Byron's guardian.   **Mr. Hanson** family solicitor to the Byrons.

To Elizabeth Bridget Pigot°

Trinity College, Cambridge, October 26th, 1807

My dear Elizabeth,

Fatigued with sitting up till four in the morning for the last two days at hazard, I take up my pen to inquire how your highness and the rest of my female acquaintance at the seat of archiepiscopal grandeur go on. I know I deserve a scolding for my negligence in not writing more frequently; but racing up and down the country for these last three months, how was it possible to fulfill the duties of a correspondent? Fixed at last for six weeks, I write, as *thin* as ever (not having gained an ounce since my reduction), and rather in better humor;—but, after all, Southwell was a detestable residence. Thank St. Dominica, I have done with it: I have been twice within eight miles of it, but could not prevail on myself to *suffocate* in its heavy atmosphere. This place is wretched enough—a villainous chaos of din and drunkenness, nothing but hazard and burgundy, hunting, mathematics, and Newmarket, riot and racing. Yet it is a paradise compared with the eternal dullness of Southwell. Oh! the misery of doing nothing but make *love, enemies,* and *verses*.

Next January (but this is *entre nous only,* and pray let it be so, or my maternal persecutor will be throwing her tomahawk at any of my curious projects) I am going to sea, for four or five months, with my cousin Captain Bettesworth, who commands the *Tartar,* the finest frigate in the navy. I have seen most scenes, and wish to look at a naval life. We are going probably to the Mediterranean, or to the West Indies, or—to the devil; and if there is a possibility of taking me to the latter, Bettesworth will do it; for he has received four and twenty wounds in different places, and at this moment possesses a letter from the late Lord Nelson, stating Bettesworth as the only officer in the navy who had more wounds than himself.

I have got a new friend, the finest in the world, a *tame*

Elizabeth Bridget Pigot She and her brother John were children of a Southwell family, and friendly neighbors to the Byrons.

bear. When I brought him here, they asked me what I meant to do with him, and my reply was, "He should *sit for a fellowship.*" Sherard will explain the meaning of the sentence, if it is ambiguous. This answer delighted them not. We have several parties here, and this evening a large assortment of jockies, gamblers, boxers, authors, parsons, and poets sup with me—a precious mixture, but they go on well together; and for me, I am a *spice* of every thing, except a jockey; by the bye, I was dismounted again the other day.

Thank your brother in my name for his treatise. I have written 214 pages of a novel—one poem of 380 lines,° to be published (without my name) in a few weeks, with notes,—560 lines of Bosworth Field, and 250 lines of another poem in rhyme, besides half a dozen smaller pieces. The poem to be published is a Satire. *Apropos,* I have been praised to the skies in the *Critical Review,* and abused greatly in another publication. So much the better, they tell me, for the sale of the book; it keeps up controversy, and prevents it being forgotten. Besides, the first men of all ages have had their share, nor do the humblest escape;—so I bear it like a philosopher. It is odd two opposite critiques came out on the same day, and out of five pages of abuse my censor only quotes *two lines* from different poems, in support of his opinion. Now, the proper way to *cut up* is to quote long passages, and make them appear absurd, because simple allegation is no proof. On the other hand, there are seven pages of praise, and more than my modesty will allow said on the subject. Adieu.

poem of 380 lines the first draft of *English Bards and Scotch Reviewers.*

To R. C. Dallas°

Dorant's, January 21, 1808

Sir,

Whenever leisure and inclination permit me the pleasure of a visit, I shall feel truly gratified in a personal acquaintance with one whose mind has been long known to me in his writings.

You are so far correct in your conjecture, that I am a member of the University of Cambridge, where I shall take my degree of A.M. this term; but were reasoning, eloquence, or virtue, the objects of my search, Granta is not their metropolis, nor is the place of her situation an "El Dorado," far less an Utopia. The intellects of her children are as stagnant as her Cam, and their pursuits limited to the church—not of Christ, but of the nearest benefice.

As to my reading, I believe I may aver, without hyperbole, it has been tolerably extensive in the historical department; so that few nations exist, or have existed, with whose records I am not in some degree acquainted, from Herodotus down to Gibbon. Of the classics, I know about as much as most schoolboys after a discipline of thirteen years; of the law of the land as much as enables me to keep "within the statute"—to use the poacher's vocabulary. I did study the "Spirit of Laws"° and the Law of Nations; but when I saw the latter violated every month, I gave up my attempts at so useless an accomplishment: —of geography, I have seen more land on maps than I should wish to traverse on foot; —of mathematics, enough to give me the headache without clearing the part affected; —of philosophy, astronomy, and metaphysics, more than I can comprehend; and of common sense so little, that I mean to leave a Byronian prize at each of our "Almae Matres" for the first discovery—though I rather fear that of the longitude will precede it.

I once thought myself a philosopher, and talked non-

R. C. Dallas a distant relative of Byron's, thirty years his senior. He helped Byron to get *Childe Harold* published, later sponged on him. "Spirit of Laws" Montesquieu's treatise.

81

sense with great decorum: I defied pain, and preached up equanimity. For some time this did very well, for no one was in *pain* for me but my friends, and none lost their patience but my hearers. At last, a fall from my horse convinced me bodily suffering was an evil; and the worst of an argument overset my maxims and my temper at the same moment: so I quitted Zeno for Aristippus, and conceive that pleasure constitutes the τὸ καλόν.°

In morality, I prefer Confucius to the Ten Commandments, and Socrates to St. Paul (though the two latter agree in their opinion of marriage). In religion, I favor the Catholic emancipation, but do not acknowledge the Pope; and I have refused to take the sacrament, because I do not think eating bread or drinking wine from the hand of an earthly vicar will make me an inheritor of heaven. I hold virtue, in general, or the virtues severally, to be only in the disposition, each a *feeling,* not a principle. I believe truth the prime attribute of the Deity, and death an eternal sleep, at least of the body. You have here a brief compendium of the sentiments of the *wicked* George, Lord Byron,° and, till I get a new suit, you will perceive I am badly clothed.

> I remain yours, etc.,
> Byron

To his mother

Prevesa, November 12, 1809

My dear mother,

I have now been some time in Turkey: this place is on the coast, but I have traversed the interior of the province of Albania on a visit to the Pacha. I left Malta in the

τὸ καλόν the Beautiful. **Lord Byron** The fifth lord was known as the "wicked lord."

Spider, a brig of war, on the 21st of September, and arrived in eight days at Prevesa. I thence have been about 150 miles, as far as Tepaleen, his Highness's country palace, where I staid three days. The name of the Pacha is *Ali,* and he is considered a man of the first abilities: he governs the whole of Albania (the ancient Illyricum), Epirus, and part of Macedonia. His son, Vely Pacha, to whom he has given me letters, governs the Morea, and he has great influence in Egypt; in short, he is one of the most powerful men in the Ottoman empire. When I reached Yanina, the capital, after a journey of three days over the mountains, through a country of the most picturesque beauty, I found that Ali Pacha was with his army in Illyricum, besieging Ibrahim Pacha in the castle of Berat. He had heard that an Englishman of rank was in his dominions, and had left orders in Yanina with the commandant to provide a house, and supply me with every kind of necessary *gratis;* and, though I have been allowed to make presents to the slaves, etc., I have not been permitted to pay for a single article of household consumption.

I rode out on the vizier's horses, and saw the palaces of himself and grandsons: they are splendid, but too much ornamented with silk and gold. I then went over the mountains through Zitza, a village with a Greek monastery (where I slept on my return), in the most beautiful situation (always excepting Cintra, in Portugal) I ever beheld. In nine days I reached Tepaleen. Our journey was much prolonged by the torrents that had fallen from the mountains, and intersected the roads. I shall never forget the singular scene on entering Tepaleen at five in the afternoon, as the sun was going down. It brought to my mind (with some change of *dress,* however) Scott's description of Branksome Castle in his *Lay,* and the feudal system. The Albanians, in their dresses (the most magnificent in the world, consisting of a long *white kilt,* gold-worked cloak, crimson velvet gold-laced jacket and waistcoat, silver-mounted pistols and daggers), the Tartars with their high caps, the Turks in their vast pelisses and turbans, the soldiers and black slaves with the horses, the former in groups in an immense large open gallery in front of the palace, the latter placed in a kind of cloister below it, two hundred steeds ready caparisoned to move in a moment, couriers entering or passing out with dispatches, the kettle-drums beating, boys calling the hour from the minaret of the mosque, altogether, with the singular appearance of the building itself, formed a new and delightful spectacle to a stranger. I was conducted to a very handsome apartment, and my health inquired after by the vizier's secretary, *à-la-mode Turque*.

The next day I was introduced to Ali Pacha. I was dressed in a full suit of staff uniform, with a very magnificent saber, etc. The vizier received me in a large room paved with marble; a fountain was playing in the center; the apartment was surrounded by scarlet ottomans. He received me standing, a wonderful compliment from a Mussulman, and made me sit down on his right hand. I have a Greek interpreter for general use, but a physician of Ali's named Femlario, who understands Latin, acted for me on this occasion. His first question was, why, at so early an age, I left my country?—(the Turks have no idea of traveling for amusement). He then said, the English minister, Captain Leake, had told him I was of a great family, and desired his respects to my mother; which I now, in the name of Ali Pacha, present to you. He said he was certain I was a man of birth, because I had small ears, curling hair, and little white hands, and expressed himself pleased with my appearance and garb. He told me to consider him as a father whilst I was in Turkey, and said he looked on me as his son. Indeed, he treated me like a child, sending me almonds and sugared sherbet, fruit and sweetmeats, twenty times a day. He begged me to visit him often, and at night, when he was at leisure. I then, after coffee and pipes, retired for the first time. I saw him thrice afterward. It is singular that the Turks, who have no hereditary dignities, and few great families, except the Sultans, pay so much respect to birth; for I found my pedigree more regarded than my title.

Today I saw the remains of the town of Actium, near which Antony lost the world, in a small bay, where two frigates could hardly maneuver: a broken wall is the sole remnant. On another part of the gulf stand the ruins of Nicopolis, built by Augustus in honor of his victory. Last night I was at a Greek marriage; but this and a thousand things more I have neither time nor *space* to describe.

His Highness is sixty years old, very fat, and not tall, but with a fine face, light-blue eyes, and a white beard; his manner is very kind, and at the same time he possesses that dignity which I find universal among the Turks. He has the appearance of anything but his real character, for he is a remorseless tyrant, guilty of the most horrible cruelties, very brave, and so good a general that they call him the Mahometan Buonaparte. Napoleon has twice offered to make him King of Epirus, but he prefers the English interest, and abhors the French, as he himself told me. He is of so much consequence, that he is much courted by both, the Albanians being the most warlike subjects of the Sultan, though Ali is only nominally dependent on the Porte; he has been a mighty warrior, but is as barbarous as he is successful, roasting rebels, etc., etc. Buonaparte sent him a snuffbox with his picture. He said the snuffbox was very well, but the picture he could excuse, as he neither liked it nor the original. His ideas of judging of a man's birth from ears, hands, etc., were curious enough. To me he was, indeed, a father, giving me letters, guards, and every possible accommodation. Our next conversations were of war and traveling, politics and England. He called my Albanian soldier, who attends me, and told him to protect me at all hazard; his name is Viscillie, and, like all the Albanians, he is brave, rigidly honest, and faithful; but they are cruel, though not treacherous, and have several vices but no meannesses. They are, perhaps, the most beautiful race, in point of countenance, in the world; their women are sometimes handsome also, but they are treated like slaves, *beaten,* and, in short, complete beasts of burden; they plough, dig, and sow. I found them carrying wood, and actually repairing the highways. The men are all soldiers, and war and the chase their sole occupations. The women are the laborers, which after all is no great hardship in so delightful a climate.

Yesterday, the 11th of November, I bathed in the sea; today is so hot that I am writing in a shady room of the English consul's, with three doors wide open, no fire, or even *fireplace,* in the house, except for culinary purposes.

I am going tomorrow, with a guard of fifty men, to Patras in the Morea, and thence to Athens, where I shall winter. Two days ago I was nearly lost in a Turkish ship of war, owing to the ignorance of the captain and crew, though the storm was not so violent. Fletcher° yelled after his wife, the Greeks called on all the saints, the Mussulmans on Allah; the captain burst into tears and ran below deck, telling us to call on God; the sails were split, the main yard shivered, the wind blowing fresh, the night setting in, and all our chance was to make Corfu, which is in possession of the French, or (as Fletcher pathetically termed it) "a watery grave." I did what I could to console Fletcher, but finding him incorrigible, wrapped myself up in my Albanian capote (an immense cloak), and lay down on deck to wait the worst. I have learnt to philosophize in my travels; and if I had not, complaint was useless. Luckily the wind abated, and only drove us on the coast of Suli, on the mainland, where we landed, and proceeded, by the help of the natives, to Prevesa again; but I shall not trust Turkish sailors in future, though the Pacha had ordered one of his own galliots to take me to Patras. I am therefore going as far as Missolonghi by land, and there have only to cross a small gulf to get to Patras.

Fletcher's next epistle will be full of marvels. We were one night lost for nine hours in the mountains in a thunderstorm, and since nearly wrecked. In both cases Fletcher was sorely bewildered, from apprehensions of famine and banditti in the first, and drowning in the second instance. His eyes were a little hurt by the lightning, or crying (I don't know which), but are now recovered. When you write, address to me at Mt. Strane's, English consul, Patras, Morea.

I could tell you I know not how many incidents that I

Fletcher William Fletcher, Byron's valet, who remained with him till his death.

think would amuse you, but they crowd on my mind as much as they would swell my paper, and I can neither arrange them in the one, nor put them down on the other, except in the greatest confusion. I like the Albanians much; they are not all Turks; some tribes are Christians. But their religion makes little difference in their manner or conduct. They are esteemed the best troops in the Turkish service. I lived on my route, two days at once, and three days again, in a barrack at Salora, and never found soldiers so tolerable, though I have been in the garrisons of Gibraltar and Malta, and seen Spanish, French, Sicilian, and British troops in abundance. I have had nothing stolen, and was always welcome to their provision and milk. Not a week ago an Albanian chief (every village has its chief, who is called Primate), after helping us out of the Turkish galley in her distress, feeding us, and lodging my suite, consisting of Fletcher, a Greek, two Athenians, a Greek priest, and my companion, Mr. Hobhouse, refused any compensation but a written paper stating that I was well received; and when I pressed him to accept a few sequins, "No," he replied; "I wish you to love me, not to pay me." These are his words.

It is astonishing how far money goes in this country. While I was in the capital I had nothing to pay by the vizier's order; but since, though I have generally had sixteen horses, and generally six or seven men, the expense has not been *half* as much as staying only three weeks in Malta, though Sir A. Ball, the governor, gave me a house for nothing, and I had only *one servant*. By the by, I expect Hanson to remit regularly; for I am not about to stay in this province forever. Let him write to me at Mr. Strane's, English consul, Patras. The fact is, the fertility of the plains is wonderful, and specie is scarce, which makes this remarkable cheapness. I am going to Athens, to study modern Greek, which differs much from the ancient, though radically similar. I have no desire to return to England, nor shall I, unless compelled by absolute want, and Hanson's neglect; but I shall not enter into Asia for a year or two, as I have much to see in Greece, and I may perhaps cross into Africa, at

least the Egyptian part. Fletcher, like all Englishmen, is
very much dissatisfied, though a little reconciled to the
Turks by a present of eighty piasters from the vizier,
which, if you consider everything, and the value of specie
here, is nearly worth ten guineas English. He has suffered
nothing but from cold, heat, and vermin, which those who
lie in cottages and cross mountains in a cold country must
undergo, and of which I have equally partaken with him-
self; but he is not valiant, and is afraid of robbers and
tempests. I have no one to be remembered to in England,
and wish to hear nothing from it, but that you are well,
and a letter or two on business from Hanson, whom you
may tell to write. I will write when I can, and beg you to
believe me,

                                   Your affectionate son,
                                   Byron
P.S.—I have some very "magnifiques" Albanian dresses,
the only expensive articles in this country. They cost fifty
guineas each, and have so much gold, they would cost
in England two hundred.

I have been introduced to Hussein Bey, and Mahmout
Pacha, both little boys, grandchildren of Ali, at Yanina;
they are totally unlike our lads, have painted complexions
like rouged dowagers, large black eyes, and features per-
fectly regular. They are the prettiest little animals I ever
saw, and are broken into the court ceremonies already.
The Turkish salute is a slight inclination of the head, with
the hand on the heart; intimates always kiss. Mahmout is
ten years old, and hopes to see me again; we are friends
without understanding each other, like many other folks,
though from a different cause. He has given me a letter
to his father in the Morea, to whom I have also letters
from Ali Pacha.

To Murray° November 14, 1813

. . . I don't care one lump of sugar for my *poetry;* but
for my *costume,* and my *correctness* on those points (of
which I think the funeral was a proof), I will combat
lustily. . . .

To S. T. Coleridge

13 Terrace, Piccadilly, October 18th, 1815

Dear Sir,

Your letter I have just received. I will willingly do
whatever you direct about the volumes in question—the
sooner the better: it shall not be for want of endeavor on
my part, as a negotiator with the "Trade" (to talk techni-
cally) that you are not enabled to do yourself justice.
Last spring I saw Wr. Scott. He repeated to me a con-
siderable portion of an unpublished poem of yours°—the
wildest and finest I ever heard in that kind of composition.
The title he did not mention, but I think the heroine's
name was Geraldine. At all events, the "toothless mastiff
bitch" and the "witch Lady," the description of the hall,
the lamp suspended from the image, and more particu-
larly of the girl herself as she went forth in the evening—
all took a hold on my imagination which I never shall
wish to shake off. I mention this, not for the sake of
boring you with compliments, but as a prelude to the

Murray John Murray (1778–1863). Byron's publisher (also Scott's).
Part owner of *The Edinburgh Review.* After the publication of the Fifth
Canto of *Don Juan,* Byron left him and went to John Hunt's, but they
remained personal friends. **poem of yours** i.e., *Christabel.*

hope that this poem is or is to be in the volumes you are now about to publish. I do not know that even "Love" or the "Antient Mariner" are so impressive—and to me there are few things in our tongue beyond these two productions. . . .

To Samuel Taylor Coleridge

Oct. 27th, 1815

Dear Sir,

I have the *Christabelle* safe, and am glad to see it in such progress; surely a little effort would complete the poem. On your question with W. Scott, I know not how to speak; he is a friend of mine, and, though I cannot contradict your statement, I must look to the most favorable part of it. All I have ever seen of him has been frank, fair, and warm in regard toward you, and when he repeated this very production it was with such mention as it deserves, and *that* could not be faint praise.

But I am partly in the same scrape myself, as you will see by the enclosed extract from an unpublished poem,° which I assure you was written before (not seeing your *Christabelle,* for that you know I never did till this day), but before I heard Mr. S. repeat it, which he did in June last, and this thing was begun in January and more than half written before the Summer. The coincidence is only in this particular passage, and, if you will allow me, in publishing it (which I shall perhaps do *quietly* in Murray's collected Edition of my rhymes—though not *separately*), I will give the extract from you, and state that the original

unpublished poem Section XIX of *The Siege of Corinth.*

thought and expression have been many years in the
Christabelle. The stories, scenes, etc., are in general quite
different; mine is the siege of Corinth in 1715, when the
Turks retook the Morea from the Venetians. The Ground
is quite familiar to me, for I have passed the Isthmus *six,*
I think—*eight,* times in my way to and fro. The hero is
a renegade, and, the night before the storm of the City,
he is supposed to have an apparition, or wraith of his
mistress, to warn him of his destiny, as he sits among the
ruins of an old temple.

I write to you in the greatest hurry. I know not what
you may think of this. If you like, I will cut out the
passage, and do as well as I can without—or what you
please.

Ever yours,

Byron

To Leigh Hunt°

13, Terrace, Piccadilly, September-October 30, 1815
My dear Hunt,

Many thanks for your books, of which you already
know my opinion. Their external splendor should not dis-
turb you as inappropriate—they have still more within
than without. I take leave to differ with you on Words-
worth, as freely as I once agreed with you; at that time
I gave him credit for a promise, which is unfulfilled. I
still think his capacity warrants all you say of *it* only, but
that his performances since *Lyrical Ballads* are miserably
inadequate to the ability which lurks within him: there is
undoubtedly much natural talent spilt over the *Excursion;*
but it is rain upon rocks—where it stands and stagnates,
or rain upon sands—where it falls without fertilizing.

Leigh Hunt poet and essayist (1784–1859).

Who can understand him? Let those who do, make him
intelligible. Jacob Behmen, Swedenborg, and Joanna
Southcote, are mere types of this arch-apostle of mystery
and mysticism. But I have done—no, I have not done, for
I have two petty, and perhaps unworthy objections in
small matters to make to him, which, with his pretensions
to accurate observation, and fury against Pope's false
translation of "the Moonlight scene in Homer," I wonder
he should have fallen into;—these be they:—He says of
Greece in the body of his book°—that it is a land of

> Rivers, fertile plains, and sounding shores,
> Under a cope of variegated sky.

The rivers are dry half the year, the plains are barren, and
the shores still and tideless as the Mediterranean can make
them; the sky is anything but variegated, being for
months and months but "darkly, deeply, beautifully
blue."—The next is in his notes, where he talks of our
"Monuments crowded together in the busy, etc., of a large
town," as compared with the "still seclusion of a Turkish
cemetery in some remote place." This is pure stuff; for
one monument in our churchyards there are ten in the
Turkish, and so crowded, that you cannot walk between
them; that is, divided merely by a path or road; and as to
"remote places," men never take the trouble in a bar-
barous country, to carry their dead very far; they must
have lived near to where they were buried. There are no
cemeteries in "remote places," except such as have the
cypress and the tombstone still left, where the olive and
the habitation of the living have perished. . . .
    These things I was struck with, as coming peculiarly in
my own way; and in both of these he is wrong; yet I
should have noticed neither, but for his attack on Pope
for a like blunder, and a peevish affectation about him of
despising a popularity which he will never obtain. I write
in great haste, and, I doubt, not much to the purpose;
but you have it hot and hot, just as it comes, and so let
it go. By the way, both he and you go too far against

book The lines quoted are from The Excursion IV, 718–20.

Pope's "So when the moon," etc.; it is no translation, I know; but it is not such false description as asserted. I have read it on the spot; there is a burst, and a lightness, and a glow about the night in the Troad, which makes the "planets vivid," and the "pole glowing." The moon is—at least the sky is, clearness itself; and I know no more appropriate expression for the expansion of such a heaven—o'er the scene—the plain—the sky—Ida—the Hellespont—Simois—Scamander—and the Isles—than that of a "flood of glory." I am getting horribly lengthy, and must stop: to the whole of your letter "I say ditto to Mr. Burke," as the Bristol candidate cried by way of electioneering harangue. You need not speak of morbid feelings and vexations to me; I have plenty; but I must blame partly the times, and chiefly myself: but let us forget them. *I* shall be very apt to do so when I see you next. Will you come to the theater and see our new management? You shall cut it up to your heart's content, root and branch, afterward, if you like; but come and see it! If not, I must come and see you.

Ever yours, very truly and affectionately,

Byron

ALPINE JOURNEY (a journal)

Sept 20th, [1816]

Up at 6. Off at 8. The whole of this day's journey at an average of between two thousand seven hundred to three thousand feet above the level of the sea. This valley, the longest, narrowest, and considered one of the finest of the Alps, little traversed by travelers. Saw the bridge of La Roche. The bed of the river very low and deep, between immense rocks, and rapid as anger;—a man and mule said to have tumbled over without damage (the mule was lucky at any rate: unless I knew the *man,* I should be loath to pronounce *him* fortunate). The people looked free, and happy, and *rich* (which last implies neither of the former): the cows superb; a Bull nearly leapt into the Charaban—"agreable companion in a post chaise"; Goats and Sheep very thriving. A mountain with enormous Glaciers to the right—the Kletsgeberg; further on, the Hockthorn—nice names—so soft!—Hockthorn, I believe, very lofty and craggy, patched with snow only; no Glaciers on it, but some good epaulettes of clouds.

Passed the boundaries, out of Vaud and into Bern Canton; French exchanged for a bad German; the district famous for Cheese, liberty, property, and no taxes. H[obhouse]° went to fish—caught none. Strolled to river: saw boy and kid; kid followed him like a dog; kid could not get over a fence, and bleated piteously; tried myself to help kid, but nearly overset both self and kid into the river. Arrived here about six in the evening. Nine o'clock —going to bed. H. in next room knocked his head against the door, and exclaimed of course against doors; not tired today, but hope to sleep nevertheless. Women gabbling below; read a French translation of Schiller. Good Night, Dearest Augusta.

Sept 21st

Off early. The valley of Simmenthal as before. Entrance to the plain of Thoun very narrow; high rocks, wooded to the top; river; new mountains, with fine Glaciers. Lake of Thoun; extensive plain with a girdle of Alps. Walked down to the Chateau de Schadau; view along the lake: crossed the river in a boat rowed by women: *women* went right for the first time in my recollection. Thoun a very pretty town. The whole day's journey Alpine and proud.

Sept 22nd

Left Thoun in a boat, which carried us the length of the lake in three hours. The lake small; but the banks fine; rocks down to the water's edge. Landed at Neuhause; passed Interlachen; entered upon a range of scenes beyond all description or previous conception. Passed a

Hobhouse John Cam Hobhouse, later Baron Broughton (1786–1869). Whig politician and a lifelong friend.

rock; inscription—2 brothers—one murdered the other;
just the place for it. After a variety of windings came to
an enormous rock. Girl with fruit—very pretty; blue eyes,
good teeth, very fair: long but good features—reminded
me rather of Fanny. Bought some of her pears, and
patted her upon the cheek; the expression of her face
very mild, but good, and not at all coquettish. Arrived at
the foot of the Mountain (the *Yung frau,* i.e., the Maiden);
Glaciers; torrents; one of these torrents *nine hundred* feet
in height of visible descent. Lodge at the Curate's. Set out
to see the Valley; heard an Avalanche fall, like thunder;
saw Glacier—enormous. Storm came on, thunder, light-
ning, hail; all in perfection and beautiful. I was on horse-
back; Guide wanted to carry my cane; I was going to
give it him, when I recollected that it was a Swordstick,
and I thought the lightning might be attracted toward him;
kept it myself; a good deal encumbered with it, and my
cloak, as it was too heavy for a whip, and the horse was
stupid, and stood still with every other peal. Got in, not
very wet; the Cloak being staunch. H. wet through; H.
took refuge in cottage; sent man, umbrella, and cloak
(from the Curate's when I arrived) after him. Swiss
Curate's house very good indeed—much better than most
English Vicarages. It is immediately opposite the torrent
I spoke of. The torrent is in shape curving over the rock,
like the *tail* of a white horse streaming in the wind, such
as it might be conceived would be that of the "*pale* horse"
on which *Death* is mounted in the Apocalypse. It is
neither mist nor water, but a something between both;
its immense height (nine hundred feet) gives it a wave,
a curve, a spreading here, a condensation there, wonder-
ful and indescribable. I think, upon the whole, that this
day has been better than any of this present excursion.

Sept 23rd

Before ascending the mountain, went to the torrent
(7 in the morning) again; the Sun upon it forming a
rainbow of the lower part of all colors, but principally
purple and gold; the bow moving as you move; I never
saw anything like this; it is only in the Sunshine. Ascended
the Wengen Mountain; at noon reached a valley on the

summit; left the horses, took off my coat, and went to the summit, 7,000 feet (English feet) above the level of the *sea,* and about 5,000 above the valley we left in the morning. On one side, our view comprised the *Yung frau* with all her glaciers; then the *Dent d'Argent,* shining like truth; then the Little Giant (the Kleiner Eigher); and the Great Giant (the Grosser Eigher), and last, but not least, the Wetterhorn. The height of Jungfrau is 13,000 feet above the sea, 11,000 above the valley; she is the highest of this range. Heard the Avalanches falling every five minutes nearly—as if God was pelting the Devil down from Heaven with snowballs. From where we stood, on the Wengen Alp, we had all these in view on one side: on the other, the clouds rose from the opposite valley, curling up perpendicular precipices like the foam of the Ocean of Hell, during a Springtide—it was white, and sulphury, and immeasurably deep in appearance. The side we ascended was (of course) not of so precipitous a nature; but on arriving at the summit, we looked down the other side upon a boiling sea of cloud, dashing against the crags on which we stood (these crags on one side quite perpendicular). Stayed a quarter of an hour; began to descend; quite clear from cloud on that side of the mountain. In passing the masses of snow, I made a snowball and pelted H. with it.

Got down to our horses again, ate something; remounted; heard the Avalanches still; came to a morass; H. dismounted; H. got over well: I tried to pass my horse over; the horse sank up to the chin, and of course he and I were in the mud together; bemired all over, but not hurt; laughed and rode on. Arrived at the Grindenwald; dined, mounted again, and rode to the higher Glacier— twilight, but distinct—very fine Glacier, like *a frozen hurricane.* Starlight, beautiful, but the devil of a path! Never mind, got safe in; a little lightning; but the whole of the day as fine in point of weather as the day on which Paradise was made. Passed *whole woods of withered pines, all withered;* trunks stripped and barkless, branches lifeless; done by a single winter—their appearance reminded me of me and my family.

Sept 24th

Set out at seven; up at five. Passed the black Glacier, the Mountain Wetterhorn on the right; crossed the Scheideck mountain; came to the *Rose* Glacier, said to be the largest and finest in Switzerland. I think the Bossons Glacier at Chamouni as fine; H. does not. Came to the Reichenback waterfall, two hundred feet high; halted to rest the horses. Arrived in the valley of Oberhasli; rain came on; drenched a little; only 4 hours' rain, however, in 8 days. Came to Lake of Brientz, then to town of Brientz; changed. H. hurt his head against door. In the evening, four Swiss Peasant Girls of Oberhasli came and sang the airs of their country; two of the voices beautiful—the tunes also: they sang too that *Tyrolese air* and song which you love, Augusta, because I love it—and I love, because you love it; they are still singing. Dearest, you do not know how I should have liked this, were you with me. The airs are so wild and original, and at the same time of great sweetness. The singing is over: but below stairs I hear the notes of a Fiddle, which bode no good to my night's rest. The *Lard* help us—I shall go down and see the dancing.

To Moore°   January 28, 1817

. . . I tremble for the "magnificence" which you attribute to the new *Childe Harold.*° I am glad you like it; it is a fine indistinct piece of poetical desolation, and my favorite. I was half mad during the time of its composition, between metaphysics, lakes, love unextinguishable, thoughts unutterable, and the nightmare of my own de-

Moore Tom Moore (1779–1852), Anglo-Irish poet.   **new Childe Harold** the Fourth Canto.

linquencies. I should, many a good day, have blown my brains out, but for the recollection that it would have given pleasure to my mother-in-law. . . .

To Moore   February 28, 1817

. . . If I live ten years longer, you will see, however, that it is not over with me—I don't mean in literature, for that is nothing; and it may seem odd enough to say, I do not think it is my vocation. But you will see that I shall do something or other—the times and fortune permitting—that "like the cosmogony, or creation of the world, will puzzle the philosophers of all ages." But I doubt whether my constitution will hold out. I have, at intervals, exorcised it most devilishly. . . .

To Murray   April 2, 1817

. . . I hate things *all fiction;* and therefore the *Merchant* and *Othello* have no great associations to me. . . . There should always be some foundation of fact for the most airy fabric, and pure invention is but the talent of a liar. . . .

To Murray   April 14, 1817

. . . You must recollect, however, that I know nothing of painting; and that I detest it, unless it reminds me of something I have seen, or think it possible to see, for which [reason] I spit upon and abhor all the Saints and subjects of one half the impostures I see in the churches and palaces; and when in Flanders, I never was so disgusted in my life as with Rubens and his eternal wives and infernal glare of colors, as they appeared to me; and in Spain I did not think much of Murillo and Velasquez. Depend upon it, of all the arts, it is the most artificial and unnatural, and that by which the nonsense of mankind is the most imposed upon. I never yet saw the picture—or the statue—which came within a league of my conception or expectation; but I have seen many mountains, and Seas, and Rivers, and views, and two or three women, who went as far beyond it—besides some horses; and a lion (at Veli Pasha's) in the Morea; and a tiger at supper in Exeter Change. . . .

To Murray   September 15, 1817

. . . With regard to poetry in general, I am convinced, the more I think of it, that *all* of us—Scott, Southey, Wordsworth, Moore, Campbell, I—are all in the wrong, one as much as the other; that we are upon a wrong revolutionary poetical system, or systems, not worth a damn in itself, and from which none but Rogers and

Crabbe are free; and that the present and next genera-
tions will finally be of this opinion. I am the more con-
firmed in this by having lately gone over some of our
classics, particularly *Pope,* whom I tried in this way—I
took Moore's poems and my own and some others, and
went over them side by side with Pope's, and I was really
astonished (I ought not to have been so) and mortified
at the ineffable distance in point of sense, harmony, effect,
and even *Imagination,* passion, and *Invention,* between
the little Queen Anne's man, and us of the Lower Empire.
Depend upon it, it is all Horace then, and Claudian now,
among us; and if I had to begin again, I would model
myself accordingly. Crabbe's the man, but he has got a
coarse and impracticable subject, and Rogers, the Grand-
father of living poetry, is retired upon half-pay. . . .

To Moore   February 2, 1818

   . . . I called Crabbe and Sam the fathers of present
Poesy; and said, that I thought—except them—*all* of
"us youth" were on a wrong tack. But I never said that
we did not sail well. Our fame will be hurt by *admiration*
and *imitation.* When I say *our,* I mean *all* (Lakers in-
cluded), except the postscript of the Augustans. The
next generation (from the quantity and facility of imita-
tion) will tumble and break their necks off our Pegasus,
who runs away with us; but we keep the *saddle,* because
we broke the rascal and can ride. But though easy to
mount, he is the devil to guide; and the next fellows must
go back to the riding school and the manège, and learn
to ride the "great horse." . . .

To James Wedderburn Webster   September 8, 1818

. . . You ask about Venice; I tell you, as before, that I do not think *you* would like it, at least few English do, and still fewer remain there. Florence and Naples are the Lazarettoes where they carry the infection of their Society; indeed, if there were as many of them in Venice as residents as Lot begged might be permitted to be the salvation of Sodom, it would not be my abode a week longer; for the reverse of the proposition, I should be sure that they would be the damnation of all pleasant or sensible society. I never see any of them when I can avoid it, and when, *occasionally,* they arrive with letters of recommendation, I do what I can for them, if they are sick—and, if they are well, I return my card for theirs, but little more.

Venice is not an expensive residence (unless a man chooses it). It has theaters, society, and profligacy rather more than enough. I keep four horses on one of the islands, where there is a beach of some miles along the Adriatic, so that I have daily exercise. I have my gondola, and about fourteen servants, including the nurse for a little girl (a natural daughter of mine),° and I reside in one of the Mocenigo palaces on the Grand Canal; the rent of the whole house, which is very large and furnished with linen, etc., etc., inclusive, is two hundred a year (and I gave more than I need have done). In the two years I have been at Venice, I have spent about *five* thousand pounds, and I need not have spent a *third* of this, had it not been that I have a passion for women which is expensive in its variety everywhere, but less so in Venice than in other cities. You may suppose that in *two years,* with a large establishment, horses, house, box at the opera, gondola, journeys, women, and Charity (for I have not laid out all upon my pleasures, but have bought occasionally a shilling's worth of salvation), villas in the country, another carriage and horses purchased for the country, books bought, etc., etc.—in short everything I

_____
daughter of mine Allegra, daughter of Claire Clairmont.

wanted, and *more* than I ought to have wanted, that the sum of five thousand pounds sterling is no great deal, particularly when I tell you that more than half was laid out in the Sex;—to be sure I have had plenty for the money, that's certain.

If you are disposed to come this way, you might live very comfortably, and even splendidly, for less than a thousand a year, and find a palace for the rent of one hundred, that is to say, an Italian palace; you know that all houses with a particular front are called so—in short an enormous house. But, as I said, I do not think you would like it, or rather that Lady Frances would not; it is not so gay here as it has been, and there is a monotony to many people in its Canals and the comparative silence of its streets. To me who have been always passionate for Venice, and delight in the dialect and naïvete of the people, and the romance of its old history and institutions and appearance, all its disadvantages are more than compensated for by the sight of a single gondola. The view of the Rialto, of the Piazza, and the Chaunt of Tasso (though less frequent than of old), are to me worth all the cities on earth, save Rome and Athens.

PART TWO: Poems

BEPPO

A VENETIAN STORY

"*Rosalind.* Farewell, Monsieur Traveler: Look, you lisp, and wear strange suits: disable all the benefits of your own country; be out of love with your Nativity, and almost chide God for making you that countenance you are; or I will scarce think you have swam in a *Gondola.*"

As You Like It, Act IV, Scene 1

Annotation of the Commentators.
"That is, been at *Venice,* which was much visited by the young English gentlemen of those times, and was then what *Paris* is *now*—the seat of all dissoluteness."

S. A. [Samuel Ayscough]

'Tis known, at least it should be, that throughout
    All countries of the Catholic persuasion,
Some weeks before Shrove Tuesday comes about,
    The people take their fill of recreation,
And buy repentance, ere they grow devout,   *5*
    However high their rank or low their station,

With fiddling, feasting, dancing, drinking, masquing,
And other things which may be had for asking.

The moment night with dusky mantle covers
10   The skies (and the more duskily the better),
The time less liked by husbands than by lovers
      Begins, and prudery flings aside her fetter;
And gaiety on restless tiptoe hovers,
      Giggling with all the gallants who beset her;
15 And there are songs and quavers, roaring, humming,
Guitars, and every other sort of strumming.

And there are dresses splendid, but fantastical,
      Masks of all times and nations, Turks and Jews,
And harlequins and clowns, with feats gymnastical,
20   Greeks, Romans, Yankee-doodles, and Hindoos;
All kinds of dress, except the ecclesiastical,
      All people, as their fancies hit, may choose,
But no one in these parts may quiz the clergy—
Therefore take heed, ye Freethinkers! I charge ye.

25 You'd better walk about begirt with briars,
      Instead of coat and smallclothes, than put on
A single stitch reflecting upon friars,
      Although you swore it only was in fun;
They'd haul you o'er the coals, and stir the fires
30   Of Phlegethon° with every mother's son,
Nor say one mass to cool the caldron's bubble
That boiled your bones, unless you paid them double.

But saving this, you may put on whate'er
      You like by way of doublet, cape, or cloak,
35 Such as in Monmouth Street, or in Rag Fair,
      Would rig you out in seriousness or joke;
And even in Italy such places are,
      With prettier name in softer accents spoke,
For, bating Covent Garden, I can hit on
40 No place that's called "Piazza" in Great Britain.

30 **Phlegethon** burning river in Hades.

This feast is named the Carnival, which being
   Interpreted, implies "farewell to flesh":
So called, because, the name and thing agreeing,
   Through Lent they live on fish both salt and fresh.
But why they usher Lent with so much glee in,   *45*
   Is more than I can tell, although I guess
'Tis as we take a glass with friends at parting,
In the stagecoach or packet, just at starting.

And thus they bid farewell to carnal dishes,
   And solid meats, and highly spiced ragouts,   *50*
To live for forty days on ill-dressed fishes,
   Because they have no sauces to their stews,
A thing which causes many "poohs" and "pishes,"
   And several oaths (which would not suit the Muse),
From travelers accustomed from a boy   *55*
To eat their salmon, at the least, with soy.

And therefore humbly I would recommend
   "The curious in fish-sauce," before they cross
The sea, to bid their cook, or wife, or friend,
   Walk or ride to the Strand, and buy in gross   *60*
(Or if set out beforehand, these may send
   By any means least liable to loss),
Ketchup, Soy, Chili-vinegar, and Harvey,
Or, by the Lord! a Lent will well-nigh starve ye;

That is to say, if your religion's Roman,   *65*
   And you at Rome would do as Romans do,
According to the proverb—although no man,
   If foreign, is obliged to fast; and you,
If Protestant, or sickly, or a woman;
   Would rather dine in sin on a ragout—   *70*
Dine and be d—d! I don't mean to be coarse,
But that's the penalty, to say no worse.

Of all the places where the Carnival
   Was most facetious in the days of yore,
For dance, and song, and serenade, and ball,   *75*
   And masque, and mime, and mystery, and more

Than I have time to tell now, or at all,
   Venice the bell from every city bore—
And at the moment when I fix my story,
80 That sea-born city was in all her glory.

They've pretty faces yet, those same Venetians,
   Black eyes, arched brows, and sweet expressions
      still;
Such as of old were copied from the Grecians,
   In ancient arts by moderns mimicked ill;
85 And like so many Venuses of Titian's
   (The best's at Florence—see it, if ye will),
They look when leaning over the balcony,
Or stepped from out a picture° by Giorgione,

Whose tints are truth and beauty at their best;
90   And when you to Manfrini's palace go,
That picture (howsoever fine the rest)
   Is loveliest to my mind of all the show;
It may perhaps be also to *your* zest,
   And that's the cause I rhyme upon it so:
95 'Tis but a portrait of his son, and wife,
And self; but *such* a woman! love in life!

Love in full life and length, not love ideal,
   No, nor ideal beauty, that fine name,
But something better still, so very real,
100   That the sweet model must have been the same;
A thing that you would purchase, beg, or steal,
   Wer't not impossible, besides a shame.
The face recalls some face, as 'twere with pain,
You once have seen, but ne'er will see again:

105 One of those forms which flit by us, when we
   Are young and fix our eyes on every face;
And, oh! the loveliness at times we see
   In momentary gliding, the soft grace,
The youth, the bloom, the beauty which agree,

---

88 **picture** Giorgione's famous *Tempest,* which Byron saw in a col-
lection in the Manfrini palace.

    In many a nameless being we retrace,   110
Whose course and home we knew not, nor shall know,
Like the lost Pleiad seen no more below.

I said that like a picture by Giorgione
    Venetian women were, and so they *are,*
Particularly seen from a balcony   115
    (For beauty's sometimes best set off afar),
And there, just like a heroine of Goldoni,
    They peep from out the blind, or o'er the bar;
And, truth to say, they're mostly very pretty,
And rather like to show it, more's the pity!   120

For glances beget ogles, ogles sighs,
    Sighs wishes, wishes words, and words a letter,
Which flies on wings of light-heeled Mercuries
    Who do such things because they know no better;
And then, God knows what mischief may arise   125
    When love links two young people in one fetter,
Vile assignations, and adulterous beds,
Elopements, broken vows and hearts and heads.

Shakespeare described the sex in Desdemona
    As very fair, but yet suspect in fame,   130
And to this day from Venice to Verona
    Such matters may be probably the same,
Except that since those times was never known a
    Husband whom mere suspicion could inflame
To suffocate a wife no more than twenty,   135
Because she had a *cavalier servente.*°

Their jealousy (if they are ever jealous)
    Is of a fair complexion altogether,
Not like that sooty devil of Othello's
    Which smothers women in a bed of feather,   140
But worthier of these much more jolly fellows;
    When weary of the matrimonial tether
His head for such a wife no mortal bothers,
But takes at once another, or another's.

136 **cavalier servente** There being no divorce in Italy at this time, the
institution of the publicly avowed lover existed.

145 Didst ever see a Gondola? For fear
    You should not, I'll describe it you exactly:
'Tis a long covered boat that's common here,
    Carved at the prow, built lightly, but compactly;
Rowed by two rowers, each called "Gondolier,"
150   It glides along the water looking blackly,
Just like a coffin clapt in a canoe,
Where none can make out what you say or do.

And up and down the long canals they go,
    And under the Rialto shoot along,
155 By night and day, all paces, swift or slow;
    And round the theaters, a sable throng,
They wait in their dusk livery of woe—
    But not to them do woeful things belong,
For sometimes they contain a deal of fun,
160 Like mourning coaches when the funeral's done.

But to my story.—'Twas some years ago,
    It may be thirty, forty, more or less,
The Carnival was at its height, and so
    Were all kinds of buffoonery and dress;
165 A certain lady went to see the show,
    Her real name I know not, nor can guess,
And so we'll call her Laura, if you please,
Because it slips into my verse with ease.

She was not old, nor young, nor at the years
170   Which certain people call a *"certain age,"*
Which yet the most uncertain age appears,
    Because I never heard, nor could engage
A person yet by prayers, or bribes, or tears,
    To name, define by speech, or write on page,
175 The period meant precisely by that word—
Which surely is exceedingly absurd.

Laura was blooming still, had made the best
    Of time, and time returned the compliment
And treated her genteelly, so that, dressed,
180   She looked extremely well where'er she went;

A pretty woman is a welcome guest,
   And Laura's brow a frown had rarely bent;
Indeed she shone all smiles, and seemed to flatter
Mankind with her black eyes for looking at her.

She was a married woman; 'tis convenient,   *185*
   Because in Christian countries 'tis a rule
To view their little slips with eyes more lenient;
   Whereas if single ladies play the fool
(Unless within the period intervenient
   A well-timed wedding makes the scandal cool),   *190*
I don't know how they ever can get over it,
Except they manage never to discover it.

Her husband sailed upon the Adriatic,
   And made some voyages, too, in other seas,
And when he lay in quarantine for pratique°   *195*
   (A forty days' precaution 'gainst disease),
His wife would mount, at times, her highest attic,
   For thence she could discern the ship with ease:
He was a merchant trading to Aleppo,
His name Giuseppe, called more briefly, Beppo.   *200*

He was a man as dusky as a Spaniard,
   Sunburnt with travel, yet a portly figure;
Though colored, as it were, within a tanyard,
   He was a person both of sense and vigor—
A better seaman never yet did man yard: *205*
   And *she*, although her manners showed no rigor,
Was deemed a woman of the strictest principle,
So much as to be thought almost invincible.

But several years elapsed since they had met;
   Some people thought the ship was lost, and some   *210*
That he had somehow blundered into debt,
   And did not like the thought of steering home:
And there were several offered any bet,
   Or that he would, or that he would not come,

---

195 **pratique** a clean bill of health after quarantine.

215 For most men (till by losing rendered sager)
Will back their own opinions with a wager.

'Tis said that their last parting was pathetic,
    As partings often are, or ought to be,
And their presentiment was quite prophetic
220   That they should never more each other see
(A sort of morbid feeling, half poetic,
    Which I have known occur in two or three),
When kneeling on the shore upon her sad knee,
He left this Adriatic Ariadne.

225 And Laura waited long, and wept a little,
    And thought of wearing weeds, as well she might;
She almost lost all appetite for victual,
    And could not sleep with ease alone at night;
She deemed the window-frames and shutters brittle
230   Against a daring housebreaker or sprite,
And so she thought it prudent to connect her
With a vice-husband, *chiefly* to *protect her*.

She chose (and what is there they will not choose,
    If only you will but oppose their choice?),
235 Till Beppo should return from his long cruise
    And bid once more her faithful heart rejoice,
A man some women like, and yet abuse—
    A coxcomb was he by the public voice;
A Count of wealth, they said, as well as quality,
240 And in his pleasures of great liberality.

And then he was a Count, and then he knew
    Music, and dancing, fiddling, French and Tuscan;
The last not easy, be it known to you,
    For few Italians speak the right Etruscan.
245 He was a critic upon operas, too,
    And knew all niceties of the sock and buskin;
And no Venetian audience could endure a
Song, scene, or air, when he cried *"seccatura!"*°

248 **"seccatura"** "A bore!" (Literally, "dryness").

His "bravo" was decisive, for that sound
   Hushed "Academie" sighed in silent awe;   *250*
The fiddlers trembled as he looked around,
   For fear of some false note's detected flaw.
The "prima donna's" tuneful heart would bound,
   Dreading the deep damnation of his "bah!"
Soprano, basso, even the contra-alto,   *255*
Wished him five fathom under the Rialto.

He patronized the Improvisatori,°
   Nay, could himself extemporize some stanzas,
Wrote rhymes, sang songs, could also tell a story,
   Sold pictures, and was skillful in the dance as   *260*
Italians can be, though in this their glory
   Must surely yield the palm to that which France
     has;
In short, he was a perfect cavaliero,
And to his very valet seemed a hero.

Then he was faithful, too, as well as amorous,   *265*
   So that no sort of female could complain,
Although they're now and then a little clamorous;
   He never put the pretty souls in pain;
His heart was one of those which most enamor us,
   Wax to receive, and marble to retain.   *270*
He was a lover of the good old school,
Who still become more constant as they cool.

No wonder such accomplishments should turn
   A female head, however sage and steady,
With scarce a hope that Beppo could return—   *275*
   In law he was almost as good as dead, he
Nor sent, nor wrote, nor showed the least concern,
   And she had waited several years already;
And really if a man won't let us know
That he's alive, he's *dead,* or should be so.   *280*

Besides, within the Alps, to every woman
   (Although, God knows, it is a grievous sin),

257 **Improvisatori** poets or singers who extemporized.

'Tis, I may say, permitted to have *two* men;
 I can't tell who first brought the custom in,
285 But "cavalier serventes" are quite common,
 And no one notices, nor cares a pin;
And we may call this (not to say the worst)
A *second* marriage which corrupts the *first*.

The word was formerly a *Cicisbeo*,
290 But *that* is now grown vulgar and indecent;
The Spaniards call the person a *Cortejo*,
 For the same mode subsists in Spain, though recent;
In short it reaches from the Po to Teio,
 And may perhaps at last be o'er the sea sent.
295 But Heaven preserve Old England from such courses!
Or what becomes of damage and divorces?

However, I still think, with all due deference
 To the fair *single* part of the Creation,
That married ladies should preserve the preference
300 In *tête-à-tête* or general conversation—
And this I say without peculiar reference
 To England, France, or any other nation—
Because they know the world, and are at ease,
And being natural, naturally please.

305 'Tis true, your budding Miss is very charming,
 But shy and awkward at first coming out,
So much alarmed that she is quite alarming,
 All Giggle, Blush; half Pertness and half Pout;
And glancing at *Mamma,* for fear there's harm in
310 What you, she, it, or they, may be about,
The Nursery still lisps out in all they utter—
Besides, they always smell of bread and butter.

But "cavalier servente" is the phrase
 Used in politest circles to express
315 This supernumerary slave, who stays
 Close to the lady as a part of dress,
Her word the only law which he obeys.
 His is no sinecure, as you may guess;

Coach, servants, gondola, he goes to call,
And carries fan and tippet,° gloves and shawl.   *320*

With all its sinful doings, I must say,
    That Italy's a pleasant place to me,
Who love to see the Sun shine every day,
    And vines (not nailed to walls) from tree to tree
Festooned, much like the back scene of a play   *325*
    Or melodrame, which people flock to see,
When the first act is ended by a dance
In vineyards copied from the south of France.

I like on Autumn evenings to ride out,
    Without being forced to bid my groom be sure   *330*
My cloak is round his middle strapped about,
    Because the skies are not the most secure;
I know too that, if stopped upon my route
    Where the green alleys windingly allure,
Reeling with *grapes* red wagons choke the way—   *335*
In England 'twould be dung, dust, or a dray.

I also like to dine on *becaficas,*°
    To see the Sun set, sure he'll rise tomorrow,
Not through a misty morning twinkling weak as
    A drunken man's dead eye in maudlin sorrow,   *340*
But with all Heaven t'himself; that day will break as
    Beauteous as cloudless, nor be forced to borrow
That sort of farthing candlelight which glimmers
Where reeking London's smoky caldron simmers.

I love the language, that soft bastard Latin,   *345*
    Which melts like kisses from a female mouth,
And sounds as if it should be writ on satin,
    With syllables which breathe of the sweet South,
And gentle liquids gliding all so pat in
    That not a single accent seems uncouth,   *350*
Like our harsh northern whistling, grunting guttural,
Which we're obliged to hiss, and spit, and sputter all.

320 **tippet** short, capelike scarf.   337 **becaficas** songbirds.

I like the women too (forgive my folly),
   From the rich peasant cheek of ruddy bronze,
355 And large black eyes that flash on you a volley
   Of rays that say a thousand things at once,
To the high dama's brow, more melancholy,
   But clear, and with a wild and liquid glance,
Heart on her lips, and soul within her eyes,
360 Soft as her clime, and sunny as her skies.

Eve of the land which still is Paradise!
   Italian beauty! didst thou not inspire
Raphael, who died in thy embrace, and vies
   With all we know of Heaven, or can desire,
365 In what he hath bequeathed us?—in what guise,
   Though flashing from the fervor of the lyre,
Would *words* describe thy past and present glow,
While yet Canova can create below?

"England! with all thy faults I love thee still,"°
370   I said at Calais and have not forgot it;
I like to speak and lucubrate my fill;
   I like the government (but that is not it);
I like the freedom of the press and quill;
   I like the Habeas Corpus (when we've got it);
375 I like a parliamentary debate,
Particularly when 'tis not too late;

I like the taxes, when they're not too many;
   I like a seacoal fire, when not too dear;
I like a beefsteak, too, as well as any;
380   Have no objection to a pot of beer;
I like the weather, when it is not rainy,
   That is, I like two months of every year.
And so God save the Regent, Church, and King!
Which means that I like all and every thing.

385 Our standing army, and disbanded seamen,
   Poor's rate, Reform, my own, the nation's debt,

369 **"England . . . still"** quoted from Cowper's *The Task*.

Our little riots just to show we're free men,
   Our trifling, bankruptcies in the Gazette,
Our cloudy climate, and our chilly women,
   All these I can forgive, and those forget,   *390*
And greatly venerate our recent glories,
And wish they were not owing to the Tories.

But to my tale of Laura—for I find
   Digression is a sin, that by degrees
Becomes exceeding tedious to my mind,   *395*
   And, therefore, may the reader too displease—
The gentle reader, who may wax unkind,
   And caring little for the author's ease,
Insist on knowing what he means, a hard
And hapless situation for a bard.   *400*

Oh that I had the art of easy writing
   What should be easy reading! could I scale
Parnassus, where the Muses sit inditing
   Those pretty poems never known to fail,
How quickly would I print (the world delighting)   *405*
   A Grecian, Syrian, or Assyrian tale;
And sell you, mixed with western sentimentalism,
Some samples of the finest Orientalism.

But I am but a nameless sort of person
   (A broken Dandy lately on my travels),   *410*
And take for rhyme, to hook my rambling verse on,
   The first that Walker's Lexicon unravels,
And when I can't find that, I put a worse on,
   Not caring as I ought for critics' cavils;
I've half a mind to tumble down to prose,   *415*
But verse is more in fashion—so here goes.

The Count and Laura made their new arrangement,
   Which lasted, as arrangements sometimes do,
For half a dozen years without estrangement;
   They had their little differences, too;   *420*
Those jealous whiffs, which never any change meant:
   In such affairs there probably are few

Who have not had this pouting sort of squabble,
From sinners of high station to the rabble.

425 But, on the whole, they were a happy pair,
        As happy as unlawful love could make them;
The gentleman was fond, the lady fair,
        Their chains so slight, 'twas not worth while to
            break them:
The world beheld them with indulgent air;
430   The pious only wished "the devil take them!"
He took them not; he very often waits,
And leaves old sinners to be young ones' baits.

But they were young: Oh! what without our youth
        Would love be! What would youth be without love!
435 Youth lends it joy, and sweetness, vigor, truth,
        Heart, soul, and all that seems as from above;
But, languishing with years, it grows uncouth—
        One of few things experience don't improve,
Which is, perhaps, the reason why old fellows
440 Are always so preposterously jealous.

It was the Carnival, as I have said
        Some six and thirty stanzas back, and so
Laura the usual preparations made,
        Which you do when your mind's made up to go
445 Tonight to Mrs. Boehm's masquerade,
        Spectator or partaker in the show;
The only difference known between the cases
Is—*here,* we have six weeks of "varnished faces."

Laura, when dressed, was (as I sang before)
450   A pretty woman as was ever seen,
Fresh as the Angel o'er a new inn door,
        Or frontispiece of a new Magazine,
With all the fashions which the last month wore,
        Colored, and silver paper leaved between
455 That and the title-page, for fear the press
Should soil with parts of speech the parts of dress.

They went to the Ridotto;—'tis a hall
   Where people dance, and sup, and dance again;
Its proper name, perhaps, were a masqued ball,
   But that's of no importance to my strain;   460
'Tis (on a smaller scale) like our Vauxhall,
   Excepting that it can't be spoiled by rain:
The company is "mixed" (the phrase I quote is
As much as saying, they're below your notice);

For a "mixed company" implies that save   465
   Yourself and friends and half a hundred more
Whom you may bow to without looking grave,
   The rest are but a vulgar set, the bore
Of public places, where they basely brave
   The fashionable stare of twenty score   470
Of well-bred persons, called *"the World"*; but I,
Although I know them, really don't know why.

This is the case in England; at least was
   During the dynasty of Dandies, now
Perchance succeeded by some other class   475
   Of imitated imitators:—how
Irreparably soon decline, alas!
   The demagogues of fashion: all below
Is frail; how easily the world is lost
By love, or war, and now and then by frost!   480

Crushed was Napoleon by the northern Thor,
   Who knocked his army down with icy hammer,
Stopped by the *elements,* like a whaler, or
   A blundering novice in his new French grammar;
Good cause had he to doubt the chance of war,   485
   And as for Fortune—but I dare not d—n her,
Because, were I to ponder to infinity,
The more I should believe in her divinity.

She rules the present, past, and all to be yet,
   She gives us luck in lotteries, love, and marriage;   490
I cannot say that she's done much for me yet;

Not that I mean her bounties to disparage,
    We've not yet closed accounts, and we shall see yet
    How much she'll make amends for past miscarriage;
495 Meantime the goddess I'll no more importune,
Unless to thank her when she's made my fortune.

To turn—and to return;—the devil take it!
    This story slips forever through my fingers,
Because, just as the stanza likes to make it,
500   It needs must be—and so it rather lingers;
This form of verse began, I can't well break it,
    But must keep time and tune like public singers;
But if I once get through my present measure,
I'll take another when I'm next at leisure.

505 They went to the Ridotto ('tis a place
    To which I mean to go myself tomorrow,
Just to divert my thoughts a little space,
    Because I'm rather hippish, and may borrow
Some spirits, guessing at what kind of face
510   May lurk beneath each mask; and as my sorrow
Slackens its pace sometimes, I'll make, or find,
Something shall leave it half an hour behind).

Now Laura moves along the joyous crowd,
    Smiles in her eyes, and simpers on her lips;
515 To some she whispers, others speaks aloud;
    To some she curtsies, and to some she dips,
Complains of warmth, and, this complaint avowed,
    Her lover brings the lemonade, she sips;
She then surveys, condemns, but pities still
520 Her dearest friends for being dressed so ill.

One has false curls, another too much paint,
    A third—where did she buy that frightful turban?
A fourth's so pale she fears she's going to faint,
    A fifth's look's vulgar, dowdyish, and suburban,
525 A sixth's white silk has got a yellow taint,
    A seventh's thin muslin surely will be her bane,

And lo! an eighth appears,—"I'll see no more!"°
For fear, like Banquo's kings, they reach a score.

Meantime, while she was thus at others gazing,
　　Others were leveling their looks at her;   530
She heard the men's half-whispered mode of praising,
　　And, till 'twas done, determined not to stir;
The women only thought it quite amazing
　　That, at her time of life, so many were
Admirers still—but men are so debased,   535
Those brazen creatures always suit their taste.

For my part, now, I ne'er could understand
　　Why naughty women—but I won't discuss
A thing which is a scandal to the land,
　　I only don't see why it should be thus;   540
And if I were but in a gown and band,
　　Just to entitle me to make a fuss,
I'd preach on this till Wilberforce and Romilly°
Should quote in their next speeches from my homily.

While Laura thus was seen and seeing, smiling,   545
　　Talking, she knew not why and cared not what,
So that her female friends, with envy broiling,
　　Beheld her airs and triumph, and all that;
And well dressed males still kept before her filing,
　　And passing bowed and mingled with her chat;   550
More than the rest one person seemed to stare
With pertinacity that's rather rare.

He was a Turk, the color of mahogany;
　　And Laura saw him, and at first was glad,
Because the Turks so much admire philogyny,   555
　　Although their usage of their wives is sad;
'Tis said they use no better than a dog any
　　Poor woman whom they purchase like a pad:
They have a number, though they ne'er exhibit 'em,
Four wives by law, and concubines *ad libitum.*   560

527 **"I'll see . . . more"** see *Macbeth,* IV, i.   543 **William Wilberforce
and Sir Samuel Romilly** were both reformers.

They lock them up, and veil, and guard them daily,
　　They scarcely can behold their male relations,
So that their moments do not pass so gaily
　　As is supposed the case with northern nations;
565　Confinement, too, must make them look quite palely:
　　And as the Turks abhor long conversations,
Their days are either passed in doing nothing,
Or bathing, nursing, making love, and clothing.

They cannot read, and so don't lisp in criticism;
570　　Nor write, and so they don't affect the muse;
Were never caught in epigram or witticism,
　　Have no romances, sermons, plays, reviews—
In harems learning soon would make a pretty schism!
　　But luckily these beauties are no "Blues,"
575　No bustling Botherbys have they to show 'em
"That charming passage in the last new poem—"

No solemn, antique gentleman of rhyme,
　　Who having angled all his life for fame,
And getting but a nibble at a time,
580　　Still fussily keeps fishing on, the same
Small "Triton of the minnows," the sublime
　　Of mediocrity, the furious tame,
The echo's echo, usher of the school
Of female wits, boy bards—in short, a fool—

585　A stalking oracle of awful phrase,
　　The approving "Good!" (by no means GOOD in law),
Humming like flies around the newest blaze,
　　The bluest of bluebottles you e'er saw,
Teasing with blame, excruciating with praise,
590　　Gorging the little fame he gets all raw,
Translating tongues he knows not even by letter,
And sweating plays so middling, bad were better.

One hates an author that's *all author,* fellows
　　In foolscap uniforms turned up with ink,
595　So very anxious, clever, fine, and jealous,
　　One don't know what to say to them, or think,

Unless to puff them with a pair of bellows;
   Of coxcombry's worst coxcombs e'en the pink
Are preferable to these shreds of paper,
These unquenched snuffings of the midnight taper.   *600*

Of these same we see several, and of others,
   Men of the world, who know the world like men,
Scott, Rogers, Moore, and all the better brothers,
   Who think of something else besides the pen;
But for the children of the "mighty mother's,"   *605*
   The would-be wits and can't-be gentlemen,
I leave them to their daily "tea is ready,"
Smug coterie, and literary lady.

The poor dear Mussulwomen whom I mention
   Have none of these instructive pleasant people,   *610*
And *one* to them would seem a new invention,
   Unknown as bells within a Turkish steeple;
I think 'twould almost be worthwhile to pension
   (Though best-sown projects very often reap ill)
A missionary author, just to preach   *615*
Our Christian usage of the parts of speech.

No chemistry for them unfolds her gases,
   No metaphysics are let loose in lectures,
No circulating library amasses
   Religious novels, moral tales, and strictures   *620*
Upon the living manners, as they pass us;
   No exhibition glares with annual pictures;
They stare not on the stars from out their attics,
Nor deal (thank God for that!) in mathematics.

Why I thank God for that is no great matter,   *625*
   I have my reasons, you no doubt suppose,
And as, perhaps, they would not highly flatter,
   I'll keep them for my life (to come) in prose;
I fear I have a little turn for satire,
   And yet methinks the older that one grows   *630*
Inclines us more to laugh than scold, though laughter
Leaves us so doubly serious shortly after.

Oh, Mirth and Innocence! Oh, Milk and Water!
   Ye happy mixtures of more happy days!
635 In these sad centuries of sin and slaughter,
   Abominable Man no more allays
His thirst with such pure beverage. No matter,
   I love you both, and both shall have my praise:
Oh, for old Saturn's reign of sugar-candy!—
640 Meantime I drink to your return in brandy.

Our Laura's Turk still kept his eyes upon her,
   Less in the Mussulman than Christian way,
Which seems to say, "Madam, I do you honor,
   And while I please to stare, you'll please to stay":
645 Could staring win a woman, this had won her,
   But Laura could not thus be led astray;
She had stood fire too long and well, to boggle
Even at this stranger's most outlandish ogle.

The morning now was on the point of breaking,
650   A turn of time at which I would advise
Ladies who have been dancing, or partaking
   In any other kind of exercise,
To make their preparations for forsaking
   The ballroom ere the sun begins to rise,
655 Because when once the lamps and candles fail,
His blushes make them look a little pale.

I've seen some balls and revels in my time,
   And stayed them over for some silly reason,
And then I looked (I hope it was no crime)
660   To see what lady best stood out the season;
And though I've seen some thousands in their prime,
   Lovely and pleasing, and who still may please on,
I never saw but one (the stars withdrawn)
Whose bloom could after dancing dare the dawn.

665 The name of this Aurora I'll not mention,
   Although I might, for she was naught to me
More than that patent work of God's invention,
   A charming woman whom we like to see;

But writing names would merit reprehension,
　Yet if you like to find out this fair *she,*   670
At the next London or Parisian ball
You still may mark her cheek, out-blooming all.

Laura, who knew it would not do at all
　To meet the daylight after seven hours sitting
Among three thousand people at a ball,   675
　To make her curtsy thought it right and fitting;
The Count was at her elbow with her shawl,
　And they the room were on the point of quitting,
When lo! those cursèd gondoliers had got
Just in the very place where they *should not.*   680

In this they're like our coachmen, and the cause
　Is much the same—the crowd, and pulling, hauling,
With blasphemies enough to break their jaws,
　They make a never intermitting bawling.
At home, our Bow Street gemmen keep the laws,   685
　And here a sentry stands within your calling;
But for all that, there is a deal of swearing,
And nauseous words past mentioning or bearing.

The Count and Laura found their boat at last,
　And homeward floated o'er the silent tide,   690
Discussing all the dances gone and past;
　The dancers and their dresses, too, beside;
Some little scandals eke: but all aghast
　(As to their palace stairs the rowers glide)
Sate Laura by the side of her Adorer,   695
When lo! the Mussulman was there before her.

"Sir," said the Count, with brow exceeding grave,
　"Your unexpected presence here will make
It necessary for myself to crave
　Its import? But perhaps 'tis a mistake;   700
I hope it is so; and, at once to waive
　All compliment, I hope so for *your* sake;
You understand my meaning, or you *shall.*"
"Sir" (quoth the Turk), " 'tis no mistake at all.

705 "That lady is *my wife!*" Much wonder paints
    The lady's changing cheek, as well it might;
But where an Englishwoman sometimes faints,
    Italian females don't do so outright;
They only call a little on their saints,
710   And then come to themselves, almost or quite:
Which saves much hartshorn, salts, and sprinkling
    faces,
And cutting stays, as usual in such cases.

She said—what could she say? Why, not a word:
    But the Count courteously invited in
715 The stranger, much appeased by what he heard:
    "Such things, perhaps, we'd best discuss within,"
Said he; "don't let us make ourselves absurd
    In public by a scene, nor raise a din,
For then the chief and only satisfaction
720 Will be much quizzing on the whole transaction."

They entered and for coffee called—it came,
    A beverage for Turks and Christians both,
Although the way they make it's not the same.
    Now Laura, much recovered, or less loth
725 To speak, cries "Beppo! what's your pagan name?
    Bless me! your beard is of amazing growth!
And how came you to keep away so long?
Are you not sensible 'twas very wrong?

"And are you *really, truly,* now a Turk?
730   With any other women did you wive?
Is't true they use their fingers for a fork?
    Well, that's the prettiest shawl—as I'm alive!
You'll give it me? They say you eat no pork.
    And how so many years did you contrive
735 To—bless me! did I ever? No, I never
Saw a man grown so yellow! How's your liver?

"Beppo! that beard of yours becomes you not;
    It shall be shaved before you're a day older:
Why do you wear it? Oh, I had forgot—

Pray don't you think the weather here is colder?   *740*
How do I look? You shan't stir from this spot
  In that queer dress, for fear that some beholder
Should find you out, and make the story known.
How short your hair is! Lord, how gray it's grown!"

What answer Beppo made to these demands   *745*
  Is more than I know. He was cast away
About where Troy stood once, and nothing stands;
  Became a slave of course, and for his pay
Had bread and bastinadoes, till some bands
  Of pirates landing in a neighboring bay,   *750*
He joined the rogues and prospered, and became
A renegado of indifferent fame.

But he grew rich, and with his riches grew so
  Keen the desire to see his home again,
He thought himself in duty bound to do so,   *755*
  And not be always thieving on the main;
Lonely he felt, at times, as Robin Crusoe,
  And so he hired a vessel come from Spain,
Bound for Corfu: she was a fine polacca,
Manned with twelve hands, and laden with tobacco.   *760*

Himself, and much (heaven knows how gotten!) cash
  He then embarked with risk of life and limb,
And got clear off, although the attempt was rash;
  He said that *Providence* protected him—
For my part, I say nothing, lest we clash   *765*
  In our opinions:—well, the ship was trim,
Set sail, and kept her reckoning fairly on,
Except three days of calm when off Cape Bonn.°

They reached the island, he transferred his lading
  And self and livestock to another bottom,   *770*
And passed for a true Turkey-merchant, trading
  With goods of various names, but I forgot 'em.
However, he got off by this evading,

768 **Cape Bonn** in Tunisia.

Or else the people would perhaps have shot him;
775 And thus at Venice landed to reclaim
His wife, religion, house, and Christian name.

His wife received, the patriach re-baptized him
    (He made the church a present, by the way);
He then threw off the garments which disguised him,
780   And borrowed the Count's smallclothes° for a day:
His friends the more for his long absence prized him,
    Finding he'd wherewithal to make them gay,
With dinners, where he oft became the laugh of them,
For stories—but *I* don't believe the half of them.

785 Whate'er his youth had suffered, his old age
    With wealth and talking make him some amends;
Though Laura sometimes put him in a rage,
    I've heard the Count and he were always friends.
My pen is at the bottom of a page,
790   Which being finished, here the story ends;
'Tis to be wished it had been sooner done,
But stories somehow lengthen when begun.

from ODE TO VENICE (lines 1–31)

VENICE

Oh Venice! Venice! when thy marble walls
    Are level with the waters, there shall be
A cry of nations o'er thy sunken halls,
    A loud lament along the sweeping sea!
5 If I, a northern wanderer, weep for thee,

---

780 **smallclothes** underwear.

What should thy sons do?—anything but weep:
And yet they only murmur in their sleep.
In contrast with their fathers—as the slime,
The dull green ooze of the receding deep,
Is with the dashing of the springtide foam   *10*
That drives the sailor shipless to his home,
Are they to those that were; and thus they creep,
Crouching and crablike, through their sapping streets.
Oh! agony—that centuries should reap
No mellower harvest! Thirteen hundred years   *15*
Of wealth and glory turned to dust and tears;
And every monument the stranger meets,
Church, palace, pillar, as a mourner greets;
And even the Lion all subdued appears,
And the harsh sound of the barbarian drum,   *20*
With dull and daily dissonance repeats
The echo of thy Tyrant's voice along
The soft waves, once all musical to song,
That heaved beneath the moonlight with the throng
Of gondolas—and to the busy hum   *25*
Of cheerful creatures, whose most sinful deeds
Were but the overbeating of the heart,
And flow of too much happiness, which needs
The aid of age to turn its course apart
From the luxuriant and voluptuous flood   *30*
Of sweet sensations, battling with the blood.

from CAIN

ACT II

SCENE 1

The Abyss of Space

Cain. I tread on air, and sink not; yet I fear
  To sink.

Lucifer.   Have faith in me, and thou shalt be
  Borne on the air, of which I am the prince.

Cain. Can I do so without impiety?

Lucifer. Believe—and sink not! doubt—and perish!
5   thus
  Would run the edict of the other God,
  Who names me demon to his angels; they
  Echo the sound to miserable things,
  Which, knowing naught beyond their shallow senses,
10 Worship the word which strikes their ear, and deem
  Evil or good what is proclaimed to them
  In their abasement. I will have none such:
  Worship or worship not, thou shalt behold
  The worlds beyond thy little world, nor be
15 Amerced for doubts beyond thy little life,
  With torture of *my* dooming. There will come
  An hour, when, tossed upon some water-drops,
  A man shall say to a man, "Believe in me,
  And walk the waters"; and the man shall walk
20 The billows and be safe. *I* will not say,
  Believe in *me,* as a conditional creed
  To save thee; but fly with me o'er the gulf
  Of space an equal flight, and I will show
  What thou dar'st not deny—the history
25 Of past, and present, and of future worlds.

Cain. Oh, god, or demon, or whate'er thou art,
  Is yon our earth?

Lucifer.   Dost thou not recognize
  The dust which formed your father?

Cain.   Can it be?
  Yon small blue circle, swinging in far ether,
  With an inferior circlet near it still,   30
  Which looks like that which lit our earthly night?
  Is this our Paradise? Where are its walls,
  And they who guard them?

Lucifer.   Point me out the site
  Of Paradise.

Cain.   How should I? As we move
  Like sunbeams onward, it grows small and smaller,   35
  And as it waxes little, and then less,
  Gathers a halo round it, like the light
  Which shone the roundest of the stars, when I
  Beheld them from the skirts of Paradise.
  Methinks they both, as we recede from them,   40
  Appear to join the innumerable stars
  Which are around us; and, as we move on,
  Increase their myriads.

Lucifer.   And if there should be
  Worlds greater than thine own, inhabited
  By greater things, and they themselves far more   45
  In number than the dust of thy dull earth,
  Though multiplied to animated atoms,
  All living, and all doomed to death, and wretched,
  What wouldst thou think?

Cain.   I should be proud of thought
  Which knew such things.

Lucifer.   But if that high thought were   50
  Linked to a servile mass of matter, and,
  Knowing such things, aspiring to such things,
  And science still beyond them, were chained down
  To the most gross and petty paltry wants,
  All foul and fulsome, and the very best   55
  Of thine enjoyments a sweet degradation,
  A most enervating and filthy cheat

To lure thee on to the renewal of
Fresh souls and bodies, all foredoomed to be
As frail and few so happy—

60 *Cain.*   Spirit! I
Know naught of death, save as a dreadful thing
Of which I have heard my parents speak, as of
A hideous heritage I owe to them
No less than life; a heritage not happy,
65 If I may judge, till now. But, spirit! if
It be as thou hast said (and I within
Feel the prophetic torture of its truth),
Here let me die: for to give birth to those
Who can but suffer many years, and die,
70 Methinks is merely propagating death,
And multiplying murder.

Lucifer.   Thou canst not
All die—there is what must survive.

Cain.   The Other
Spake not of this unto my father, when
He shut him forth from Paradise, with death
75 Written upon his forehead. But at least
Let what is mortal of me perish, that
I may be in the rest as angels are.

Lucifer. I am angelic: wouldst thou be as I am?

Cain. I know not what thou art: I see thy power,
80 And see thou show'st me things beyond *my* power,
Beyond all power of my born faculties,
Although inferior still to my desires
And my conceptions.

Lucifer.   What are they which dwell
So humbly in their pride as to sojourn
With worms in clay?

85 *Cain.*   And what art thou who dwellest
So haughtily in spirit, and canst range
Nature and immortality—and yet
Seem'st sorrowful?

Lucifer.   I seem that which I am;
  And therefore do I ask of thee, if thou
  Wouldst be immortal?

Cain.   Thou hast said, I must be   90
  Immortal in despite of me. I knew not
  This until lately—but since it must be,
  Let me, or happy or unhappy, learn
  To anticipate my immortality.

Lucifer. Thou didst before I came upon thee.

Cain.   How?   95

Lucifer. By suffering.

Cain.   And must torture be immortal?

Lucifer. We and thy sons will try. But now, behold!
  Is it not glorious?

Cain.   Oh, thou beautiful
  And unimaginable ether! and
  Ye multiplying masses of increased   100
  And still increasing lights! what are ye? what
  Is this blue wilderness of interminable
  Air, where ye roll along, as I have seen
  The leaves along the limpid streams of Eden?
  Is your course measured for ye? Or do ye   105
  Sweep on in your unbounded revelry
  Through an aerial universe of endless
  Expansion—at which my soul aches to think—
  Intoxicated with eternity?
  Oh God! Oh Gods! or whatsoe'er ye are!   110
  How beautiful ye are! how beautiful
  Your works, or accidents, or whatsoe'er
  They may be! Let me die as atoms die
  (If that they die), or know ye in your might
  And knowledge! My thoughts are not in this hour   115
  Unworthy what I see, though my dust is;—
  Spirit! let me expire, or see them nearer.

Lucifer. Art thou not nearer? look back to thine
  earth!

Cain. Where is it? I see nothing save a mass
    Of most innumerable lights.

120 *Lucifer.*   Look there!

Cain. I cannot see it.

Lucifer.   Yet it sparkles still.

Cain. That!—yonder!

Lucifer.   Yea.

Cain.   And wilt thou tell me so?
    Why, I have seen the fire-flies and fire-worms
    Sprinkle the dusky groves and the green banks
125 In the dim twilight, brighter than yon world
    Which bears them.

Lucifer. Thou hast seen both worms and worlds,
    Each bright and sparkling—what dost think of
        them?

Cain. That they are beautiful in their own sphere,
    And that the night, which makes both beautiful,
130 The little shining fire-fly in its flight,
    And the immortal star in its great course,
    Must both be guided.

Lucifer.   But by whom or what?

Cain. Show me.

Lucifer.   Dar'st thou behold?

Cain.   How know I what
    I *dare* behold? As yet, thou hast shown naught
    I dare not gaze on further.

135 *Lucifer.*   On, then, with me.
    Wouldst thou behold things mortal or immortal?

Cain. Why, what are things?

Lucifer.   *Both* partly; but what doth
    Sit next thy heart?

Cain.   The things I see.

Lucifer.   But what
Sate nearest it?

Cain.   The things I have not seen,
Nor ever shall—the mysteries of death.   140

Lucifer. What, if I show to thee things which have
    died,
As I have shown thee much which cannot die?

Cain. Do so.

Lucifer.   Away, then, on our mighty wings!

Cain. Oh, how we cleave the blue! The stars fade
    from us!
The earth! where is my earth? Let me look on it,   145
For I was made of it.

Lucifer.   'Tis now beyond thee,
Less, in the universe, than thou in it;
Yet deem not that thou canst escape it; thou
Shalt soon return to earth and all its dust:
'Tis part of thy eternity, and mine.   150

Cain. Where dost thou lead me?

Lucifer.   To what was before thee!
The phantasm of the world; of which thy world
Is but the wreck.

Cain.   What! is it not then new?

Lucifer. No more than life is; and that was ere thou
Or *I* were, or the things which seem to us   155
Greater than either. Many things will have
No end; and some, which would pretend to have
Had no beginning, have had one as mean
As thou; and mightier things have been extinct
To make way for much meaner than we can   160
Surmise; for *moments* only and the *space*
Have been and must be all *unchangeable*.
But changes make not death, except to clay;
But thou art clay, and canst but comprehend
That which was clay, and such thou shalt behold.   165

Cain. Clay, spirit! what thou wilt, I can survey.

Lucifer. Away, then!

Cain.   But the lights fade from me fast,
    And some till now grew larger as we approached
    And wore the look of worlds.

Lucifer.   And such they are.

Cain. And Edens in them?

Lucifer.   It may be.

170   *Cain*.   And men?

Lucifer. Yea, or things higher.

Cain.   Ay, and serpents too?

Lucifer. Wouldst thou have men without them? must
    no reptiles
    Breathe save the erect ones?

Cain.   How the lights recede!
    Where fly we?

Lucifer.   To the world of phantoms, which
175   Are beings past, and shadows still to come.

Cain. But it grows dark and dark—the stars are gone!

Lucifer. And yet thou seest.

Cain.   'Tis a fearful light!
    No sun, no moon, no lights innumerable—
    The very blue of the empurpled night
180   Fades to a dreary twilight, yet I see
    Huge dusky masses: but unlike the worlds
    We were approaching, which, begirt with light,
    Seemed full of life even when their atmosphere
    Of light gave way, and showed them taking shapes
185   Unequal, of deep valleys and vast mountains;
    And some emitting sparks, and some displaying
    Enormous liquid plains, and some begirt
    With luminous belts, and floating moons, which
       took
    Like them the features of fair earth:—instead,
    All here seems dark and dreadful.

Lucifer.   But distinct.   *190*
  Thou seekest to behold death and dead things?

Cain. I seek it not; but as I know there are
  Such, and that my sire's sin makes him and me,
  And all that we inherit, liable
  To such, I would behold at once what I   *195*
  Must one day see perforce.

Lucifer.   Behold!

Cain.   'Tis darkness.

Lucifer. And so it shall be ever; but we will
  Unfold its gates!

Cain.   Enormous vapors roll
  Apart—what's this?

Lucifer.   Enter!

Cain.   Can I return?

Lucifer. Return! be sure: how else should death be
    peopled?   *200*
  Its present realm is thin to what it will be,
  Through thee and thine.

Cain.   The clouds still open wide
  And wider, and make widening circles round us.

Lucifer. Advance!

Cain.   And thou?

Lucifer.   Fear me—without me thou
  Couldst not have gone beyond thy world. On! on! *205*
                  [*They disappear through the clouds.*]

from THE DEFORMED TRANSFORMED

PART III

SCENE 1

A Castle in the Apennines, surrounded by a wild but smiling country. Chorus of Peasants singing before the Gates.

Chorus

1

> The wars are over,
>   The spring is come;
> The bride and her lover
>   Have sought their home:
> 5 They are happy, we rejoice;
> Let their hearts have an echo in every voice!

2

> The spring is come; the violet's gone,
> The firstborn child of the early sun:
> With us she is but a winter's flower,
> 10 The snow on the hills cannot blast her bower,
> And she lifts up her dewy eye of blue
> To the youngest sky of the selfsame hue.

3

> And when the spring comes with her host
> Of flowers, that flower beloved the most
> 15 Shrinks from the crowd that may confuse
> Her heavenly odor and virgin hues.

4

Pluck the others, but still remember
Their herald out of dim December—
The morning star of all the flowers,
The pledge of daylight's lengthened hours;   20
Nor, midst the roses, e'er forget
The virgin, virgin violet.

Enter Caesar

Caesar (*singing*). The wars are all over,
  Our swords are all idle,
  The steed bites the bridle,
The casque's on the wall.   25
There's rest for the rover;
  But his armor is rusty,
  And the veteran grows crusty,
As he yawns in the hall.   30
  He drinks—but what's drinking?
  A mere pause from thinking!
No bugle awakes him with life-and-death call.

Chorus

But the hound bayeth loudly,
  The boar's in the wood,   35
And the falcon longs proudly
  To spring from her hood:
On the wrist of the noble
  She sits like a crest,
And the air is in trouble   40
  With birds from their nest

Caesar. Oh! shadow of glory!
  Dim image of war!
But the chase hath no story,
  Her hero no star,   45
Since Nimrod, the founder
  Of empire and chase,
Who made the woods wonder
  And quake for their race.

50   When the lion was young,
          In the pride of his might,
      Then 'twas sport for the strong
          To embrace him in fight;
      To go forth, with a pine
55   For a spear, 'gainst the mammoth,
      Or strike through the ravine
          At the foaming behemoth;
      While man was in stature
          As towers in our time,
60   The firstborn of Nature,
          And, like her, sublime!

                    Chorus

      But the wars are over,
          The spring is come;
      The bride and her lover
65   Have sought their home:
      They are happy, and we rejoice;
      Let their hearts have an echo from every voice!
                    [*Exeunt the Peasantry, singing.*]

      from THE ISLAND (lines 448–459)

      SUBLIME TOBACCO

      Sublime tobacco! which from east to west
      Cheers the tar's labor or the Turkman's rest;
      Which on the Moslem's ottoman divides
      His hours, and rivals opium and his brides;
5   Magnificent in Stamboul, but less grand,
      Though not less loved, in Wapping or the Strand;
      Divine in hookahs,° glorious in a pipe,

      7 **hookahs** Oriental water pipes.

When tipped with amber, mellow, rich, and ripe;
Like other charmers, wooing the caress
More dazzlingly when daring in full dress;   10
Yet thy true lovers more admire by far
Thy naked beauties—Give me a cigar!

from THE AGE OF BRONZE (lines 568–609)

THE PRICE OF CORN

Alas, the country! how shall tongue or pen
Bewail her now *uncountry* gentlemen?
The last to bid the cry of warfare cease,
The first to make a malady of peace.
For what were all these country patriots born?   5
To hunt, and vote, and raise the price of corn?°
But corn, like every mortal thing, must fall,
Kings, conquerors, and markets most of all.
And must ye fall with every ear of grain?
Why would you trouble Buonaparte's reign?   10
He was your great Triptolemus;° his vices
Destroyed but realms, and still maintained your prices;
He amplified to every lord's content
The grand agrarian alchemy, high *rent*.
Why did the tyrant stumble on the Tartars,   15
And lower wheat to such desponding quarters?
Why did you chain him on yon isle so lone?
The man was worth much more upon his throne.
True, blood and treasure boundlessly were spilt,

6 **corn** The so-called Corn Laws imposed prohibitive duties on im-
ported grain, keeping the price too high for the poor.   11 **Triptole-**
mus legendary hero who received seed-corn from Demeter and
passed the art of grain cultivation on to mankind.

20 But what of that? the Gaul may bear the guilt;
But bread was high, the farmer paid his way,
And acres told upon the appointed day.
But where is now the goodly audit ale?
The purse-proud tenant, never known to fail?
25 The farm which never yet was left on hand?
The marsh reclaimed to most improving land?
The impatient hope of the expiring lease?
The doubling rental? What an evil's peace!
In vain the prize excites the ploughman's skill,
30 In vain the Commons pass their patriot bill;
The *landed interest* (you may understand
The phrase much better leaving out the *land*)—
The land self-interest groans from shore to shore,
For fear that plenty should attain the poor.
35 Up, up again, ye rents! exalt your notes,
Or else the ministry will lose their votes,
And patriotism, so delicately nice,
Her loaves will lower to the market price;
For ah! "the loaves and fishes," once so high,
40 Are gone—their oven closed, their ocean dry,
And naught remains of all the millions spent,
Excepting to grow moderate and content.

THE VISION OF JUDGMENT°

Saint Peter sat by the celestial gate:
    His keys were rusty and the lock was dull,
So little trouble had been given of late;
    Not that the place by any means was full,

0 **The Vision of Judgment** This poem is an answer to Robert
Southey's *Vision of Judgment*, an eulogy of George III by a poet who
Byron felt had betrayed his earlier political liberalism to follow
Henry Pye as poet laureate. He had denounced Bryon as a founder
of the "Satanic School."

But since the Gallic era "eighty-eight"°   5
   The devils had ta'en a longer, stronger pull,
And "a pull all together," as they say
At sea—which drew most souls another way.

The angels all were singing out of tune,
   And hoarse with having little else to do,   10
Excepting to wind up the sun and moon,
   Or curb a runaway young star or two,
Or wild colt of a comet, which too soon
   Broke out of bounds o'er the ethereal blue,
Splitting some planet with its playful tail,   15
As boats are sometimes by a wanton whale.

The guardian seraphs had retired on high,
   Finding their charges past all care below;
Terrestrial business filled naught in the sky
   Save the recording angel's black bureau;   20
Who found, indeed, the facts to multiply
   With such rapidity of vice and woe,
That he had stripped off both his wings in quills,
And yet was in arrear of human ills.

His business so augmented of late years,   25
   That he was forced, against his will no doubt
(Just like those cherubs, earthly ministers),
   For some resource to turn himself about,
And claim the help of his celestial peers,
   To aid him ere he should be quite worn out   30
By the increased demand for his remarks;
Six angels and twelve saints were named his clerks.

This was a handsome board—at least for heaven;
   And yet they had even then enough to do,
So many conquerors' cars were daily driven,   35
   So many kingdoms fitted up anew;
Each day too slew its thousands six or seven,
   Till at the crowning carnage, Waterloo,

5 **"Eighty-eight"** 1788, the year preceding the French Revolution.

They threw their pens down in divine disgust—
40   The page was so besmeared with blood and dust.

This by the way; 'tis not mine to record
    What angels shrink from: even the very devil
On this occasion his own work abhorred,
    So surfeited with the infernal revel:
45   Though he himself had sharpened every sword,
    It almost quenched his innate thirst of evil.
    (Here Satan's sole good work deserves insertion—
    'Tis, that he has both generals° in reversion.)

Let's skip a few short years of hollow peace,
50   Which peopled earth no better, hell as wont,
And heaven none—they form the tyrant's lease,
    With nothing but new names subscribed upon 't:
'Twill one day finish: meantime they increase,
    "With seven heads and ten horns," and all in front,
55   Like Saint John's foretold beast;° but ours are born
Less formidable in the head than horn.

In the first year of freedom's second dawn°
    Died George the Third; although no tyrant, one
Who shielded tyrants, till each sense withdrawn
60   Left him nor mental nor external sun:
A better farmer ne'er brushed dew from lawn,
    A worse king never left a realm undone!
He died—but left his subjects still behind,
One half as mad, and t' other no less blind.

65   He died!—his death made no great stir on earth;
    His burial made some pomp; there was profusion
Of velvet, gilding, brass, and no great dearth
    Of aught but tears—save those shed by collusion;
For these things may be bought at their true worth;

48 **generals** Wellington and Napoleon   55 **beast** the beast of the
Apocalypse, Revelation 13.   57 **freedom's second dawn** In 1820,
George III died and revolutionary activity broke out in Italy, as
well as all over southern Europe.

Of elegy there was the due infusion—   70
Bought also; and the torches, cloaks, and banners,
Heralds, and relics of old Gothic manners,

Formed a sepulchral melodrame. Of all
    The fools who flocked to swell or see the show,
Who cared about the corpse? The funeral   75
    Made the attraction, and the black the woe.
There throbbed not there a thought which pierced the
        pall;
    And when the gorgeous coffin was laid low,
It seemed the mockery of hell to fold
The rottenness of eighty years in gold.   80

So mix his body with the dust! It might
    Return to what it *must* far sooner, were
The natural compound left alone to fight
    Its way back into earth, and fire, and air;
But the unnatural balsams merely blight   85
    What nature made him at his birth, as bare
As the mere million's base unmummied clay—
Yet all his spices but prolong decay.

He's dead—and upper earth with him has done;
    He's buried; save the undertaker's bill   90
Or lapidary scrawl, the world is gone
    For him, unless he left a German will.
But where's the proctor who will ask his son?
    In whom his qualities are reigning still,
Except that household virtue, most uncommon,   95
Of constancy to a bad, ugly woman.

"God save the king!" It is a large economy
    In God to save the like; but if he will
Be saving, all the better; for not one am I
    Of those who think damnation better still: 100
I hardly know too if not quite alone am I
    In this small hope of bettering future ill
By circumscribing, with some slight restriction,
The eternity of hell's hot jurisdiction.

105 I know this is unpopular; I know
    'Tis blasphemous; I know one may be damned
For hoping no one else may e'er be so;
    I know my catechism; I know we are crammed
With the best doctrines till we quite o'er flow;
    I know that all save England's church have
110   shammed,
And that the other twice two hundred churches
And synagogues have made a *damned* bad purchase.

God help us all! God help me too! I am,
    God knows, as helpless as the devil can wish,
115 And not a whit more difficult to damn
    Than is to bring to land a late-hooked fish,
Or to the butcher to purvey the lamb;
    Not that I'm fit for such a noble dish,
As one day will be that immortal fry
120 Of almost every body born to die.

Saint Peter sat by the celestial gate,
    And nodded o'er his keys; when, lo! there came
A wondrous noise he had not heard of late—
    A rushing sound of wind, and stream, and flame;
125 In short, a roar of things extremely great,
    Which would have made aught save a saint exclaim;
But he, with first a start and then a wink,
Said, "There's another star gone out, I think!"

But ere he could return to his repose,
130   A cherub flapped his right wing o'er his eyes—
At which Saint Peter yawned, and rubbed his nose:
    "Saint porter," said the angel, "prithee rise!"
Waving a goodly wing, which glowed, as glows
    An earthly peacock's tail, with heavenly dyes:
135 To which the saint replied, "Well, what's the matter?
Is Lucifer come back with all this clatter?"

"No," quoth the cherub; "George the Third is dead."
    "And who *is* George the Third?" replied the
       apostle:

"*What George? what Third?*" "The king of England,"
   said
   The angel. "Well! he won't find kings to jostle   140
Him on his way; but does he wear his head?
   Because the last we saw here° had a tussle,
And ne'er would have got into heaven's good graces,
Had he not flung his head in all our faces.

"He was, if I remember, king of France;   145
   That head of his, which could not keep a crown
On earth, yet ventured in my face to advance
   A claim to those of martyrs—like my own:
If I had had my sword, as I had once
   When I cut ears off, I had cut him down;   150
But having but my *keys,* and not my brand,
I only knocked his head from out his hand.

"And then he set up such a headless howl,
   That all the saints came out and took him in;
And there he sits by St. Paul, cheek by jowl;   155
   That fellow Paul—the parvenu! The skin
Of Saint Bartholomew, which makes his cowl
   In heaven, and upon earth redeemed his sin
So as to make a martyr, never sped
Better than did this weak and wooden head.   160

"But had it come up here upon its shoulders,
   There would have been a different tale to tell:
The fellow-feeling in the saints beholders
   Seems to have acted on them like a spell;
And so this very foolish head heaven solders   165
   Back on its trunk: it may be very well,
And seems the custom here to overthrow
Whatever has been wisely done below."

The angel answered, "Peter! do not pout:
   The king who comes has head and all entire,   170
And never knew much what it was about;

142 **the last we saw here** Louis XVI, guillotined in 1793.

He did as doth the puppet—by its wire,
  And will be judged like all the rest, no doubt:
  My business and your own is not to inquire
175 Into such matters, but to mind our cue—
  Which is to act as we are bid to do."

While thus they spake, the angelic caravan,
  Arriving like a rush of mighty wind,
Cleaving the fields of space, as doth its swan
180   Some silver stream (say Ganges, Nile, or Inde,
  Or Thames, or Tweed), and 'midst them an old man
    With an old soul, and both extremely blind,
  Halted before the gate, and in his shroud
  Seated their fellow-traveler on a cloud.

185 But bringing up the rear of this bright host
    A Spirit of a different aspect waved
His wings, like thunderclouds above some coast
    Whose barren beach with frequent wrecks is paved;
His brow was like the deep when tempest-tossed;
190   Fierce and unfathomable thoughts engraved
  Eternal wrath on his immortal face,
  And *where* he gazed a gloom pervaded space.

As he drew near, he gazed upon the gate
    Ne'er to be entered more by him or sin,
195 With such a glance of supernatural hate,
    As made Saint Peter wish himself within;
He pattered with his keys at a great rate,
    And sweated through his apostolic skin:
  Of course his perspiration was but ichor,
200 Or some such other spiritual liquor.

The very cherubs huddled all together,
    Like birds when soars the falcon; and they felt
A tingling to the tip of every feather,
    And formed a circle like Orion's belt
Around their poor old charge; who scarce knew
205   whither
    His guards had led him, though they gently dealt

With royal manes (for by many stories,
   And true, we learn the angels are all Tories).

As things were in this posture, the gate flew
   Asunder, and the flashing of its hinges   210
Flung over space an universal hue
   Of many-colored flame, until its tinges
Reached even our speck of earth, and made a new
   Aurora borealis spread its fringes
O'er the North Pole; the same seen, when ice-bound,   215
By Captain Parry's crew, in "Melville's Sound."°

And from the gate thrown open issued beaming
   A beautiful and mighty Thing of Light,
Radiant with glory, like a banner streaming
   Victorious from some world-o'erthrowing fight: 220
My poor comparisons must needs be teeming
   With earthly likenesses, for here the night
Of clay obscures our best conceptions, saving
Johanna Southcote° or Bob Southey raving.

'Twas the archangel Michael: all men know   225
   The make of angels and archangels, since
There's scarce a scribbler has not one to show,
   From the fiends' leader to the angels' prince.
There also are some altar-pieces, though
   I really can't say that they much evince   230
One's inner notions of immortal spirits;
But let the connoisseurs explain *their* merits.

Michael flew forth in glory and in good;
   A goodly work of him from whom all glory
And good arise; the portal past—he stood;   235
   Before him the young cherubs and saints hoary—
(I say *young,* begging to be understood
   By looks, not years; and should be very sorry

216 **Captain Parry's crew . . . Sound** In 1819, Sir William Edward
Parry explored and described Melville Bay in Greenland.
224 **Johanna Southcote** Joanna Southcott prophesied that she would
bear a new messiah in 1814.

To state, they were not older than St. Peter,
240 But merely that they seemed a little sweeter).

The cherubs and the saints bowed down before
     That arch-angelic hierarch, the first
Of essences angelical, who wore
     The aspect of a god; but this ne'er nursed
245 Pride in his heavenly bosom, in whose core
     No thought, save for his Maker's service, durst
Intrude, however glorified and high;
He knew him but the viceroy of the sky.

He and the somber silent Spirit met—
250   They knew each other both for good and ill;
Such was their power, that neither could forget
     His former friend and future foe; but still
There was a high, immortal, proud regret
     In either's eye, as if 'twere less their will
255 Than destiny to make the eternal years
     Their date of war, and their *champ clos* the spheres.

But here they were in neutral space: we know
     From Job, that Satan hath the power to pay
A heavenly visit thrice a year or so;
260   And that "the sons of God," like those of clay,
Must keep him company; and we might show
     From the same book, in how polite a way
The dialogue is held between the Powers
Of Good and Evil—but 'twould take up hours.

265 And this is not a theologic tract,
     To prove with Hebrew and with Arabic
If Job be allegory or a fact,
     But a true narrative; and thus I pick
From out the whole but such and such an act
270   As sets aside the slightest thought of trick.
'Tis every tittle true, beyond suspicion,
And accurate as any other vision.

The spirits were in neutral space, before
   The gate of heaven; like eastern thresholds is
The place where Death's grand cause is argued o'er,   *275*
   And souls dispatched to that world or to this;
And therefore Michael and the other wore
   A civil aspect: though they did not kiss,
Yet still between his Darkness and his Brightness
There passed a mutual glance of great politeness.   *280*

The Archangel bowed, not like a modern beau,
   But with a graceful oriental bend,
Pressing one radiant arm just where below
   The heart in good men is supposed to tend.
He turned as to an equal not too low,   *285*
   But kindly; Satan met his ancient friend
With more hauteur, as might an old Castilian
Poor noble meet a mushroom rich civilian.

He merely bent his diabolic brow
   An instant; and then raising it, he stood   *290*
In act to assert his right or wrong, and show
   Cause why King George by no means could or
     should
Make out a case to be exempt from woe
   Eternal, more than other kings, endued
With better sense and hearts, whom history mentions,   *295*
Who long have "paved hell with their good inten-
   tions."

Michael began: "What wouldst thou with this man,
   Now dead, and brought before the Lord? What ill
Hath he wrought since his mortal race began,
   That thou canst claim him? Speak! and do thy will,   *300*
If it be just: if in his earthly span
   He hath been greatly failing to fulfill
His duties as a king and mortal, say,
And he is thine; if not, let him have way."

"Michael!" replied the Prince of Air, "even here,   *305*
   Before the Gate of him thou servest, must

I claim my subject: and will make appear
That as he was my worshiper in dust,
So shall he be in spirit, although dear
310   To thee and thine, because nor wine nor lust
Were of his weaknesses; yet on the throne
He reigned o'er millions to serve me alone.

"Look to *our* earth, or rather *mine; it* was,
Once, more thy master's: but I triumph not
315 In this poor planet's conquest; nor, alas!
Need he thou servest envy me my lot:
With all the myriads of bright worlds which pass
In worship round him, he may have forgot
Yon weak creation of such paltry things:
320 I think few worth damnation save their kings—

"And these but as a kind of quit-rent, to
Assert my right as lord; and even had
I such an inclination, 'twere (as you
Well know) superfluous; they are grown so bad,
325 That hell has nothing better left to do
Than leave them to themselves: so much more mad
And evil by their own internal curse,
Heaven cannot make them better, nor I worse.

"Look to the earth, I said, and say again:
When this old, blind, mad, helpless, weak, poor
330   worm
Began in youth's first bloom and flush to reign,
The world and he both wore a different form,
And much of earth and all the watery plain
Of ocean called him king: through many a storm
335 His isles had floated on the abyss of time;
For the rough virtues chose them for their clime.

"He came to his scepter young; he leaves it old:
Look to the state in which he found his realm,
And left it; and his annals too behold,

How to a minion° first he gave the helm;   340
How grew upon his heart a thirst for gold,
　The beggar's vice, which can but overwhelm
The meanest hearts; and for the rest, but glance
Thine eye along America and France.

" 'Tis true, he was a tool from first to last   345
　(I have the workmen safe); but as a tool
So let him be consumed. From out the past
　Of ages, since mankind have known the rule
Of monarchs—from the bloody rolls amassed
　Of sin and slaughter—from the Caesar's school,   350
Take the worst pupil; and produce a reign
More drenched with gore, more cumbered with the
　　　slain.

"He ever warred with freedom and the free:
　Nations as men, home subjects, foreign foes,
So that they uttered the word 'Liberty!'   355
　Found George the Third their first opponent. Whose
History was ever stained as his will be
　With national and individual woes?
I grant his household abstinence; I grant
His neutral virtues, which most monarchs want;   360

"I know he was a constant consort; own
　He was a decent sire, and middling lord.
All this is much, and most upon a throne;
　As temperance, if at Apicius'° board,
Is more than at an anchorite's supper shown.   365
　I grant him all the kindest can accord;
And this was well for him, but not for those
Millions who found him what oppression chose.

"The New World shook him off; the Old yet groans
　Beneath what he and his prepared, if not   370
Completed: he leaves heirs on many thrones
　To all his vices, without what begot

340 **minion** the Earl of Bute, with the Duke of Grafton (see l. 564),
minister of George III.   364 **Apicius** a Roman epicure of the age of
Augustus.

Compassion for him—his tame virtues; drones
   Who sleep, or despots who have now forgot
375 A lesson which shall be retaught them, wake
Upon the thrones of earth; but let them quake!

"Five millions of the primitive, who hold
   The faith which makes ye great on earth, implored
A *part* of that vast *all* they held of old—
380   Freedom to worship—not alone your Lord,
Michael, but you, and you, Saint Peter! Cold
   Must be your souls, if you have not abhorred
The foe to Catholic participation
In all the license of a Christian nation.°

385 "True! he allowed them to pray God: but as
   A consequence of prayer, refused the law
Which would have placed them upon the same base
   With those who did not hold the saints in awe."
But here Saint Peter started from his place,
390   And cried, "You may the prisoner withdraw:
Ere heaven shall ope her portals to this Guelph,
While I am guard, may I be damned myself!

"Sooner will I with Cerberus exchange
   My office (and *his* is no sinecure)
395 Than see this royal Bedlam bigot range
   The azure fields of heaven, of that be sure!"
"Saint!" replied Satan, "you do well to avenge
   The wrongs he made your satellites endure;
And if to this exchange you should be given,
400 I'll try to coax *our* Cerberus up to heaven."

Here Michael interposed: "Good saint! and devil!
   Pray, not so fast; you both outrun discretion.
Saint Peter, you were wont to be more civil:
   Satan, excuse this warmth of his expression,
405 And condescension to the vulgar's level:

377–84 **Five millions . . . nation** This stanza refers to the withholding
of political rights from Roman Catholics by George III.

Even saints sometimes forget themselves in session.
Have you got more to say?"—"No."—"If you please,
I'll trouble you to call your witnesses."

Then Satan turned and waved his swarthy hand,
   Which stirred with its electric qualities   410
Clouds farther off than we can understand,
   Although we find him sometimes in our skies;
Infernal thunder shook both sea and land
   In all the planets, and hell's batteries
Let off the artillery, which Milton mentions   415
As one of Satan's most sublime inventions.

This was a signal unto such damned souls
   As have the privilege of their damnation
Extended far beyond the mere controls
   Of worlds past, present, or to come; no station   420
Is theirs particularly in the rolls
   Of hell assigned; but where their inclination
Or business carries them in search of game,
They may range freely—being damned the same.

They are proud of this—as very well they may,   425
   It being a sort of knighthood, or gilt key°
Stuck in their loins; or like to an *entré*
   Up the back stairs, or such freemasonry.
I borrow my comparisons from clay,
   Being clay myself. Let not those spirits be   430
Offended with such base low likenesses;
We know their posts are nobler far than those.

When the great signal ran from heaven to hell,
   About ten million times the distance reckoned
From our sun to its earth—as we can tell   435
   How much time it takes up, even to a second,
For every ray that travels to dispel
   The fogs of London, through which, dimly beaconed,
The weathercocks are gilt some thrice a year,
If that the *summer* is not too severe:—   440

426 **gilt key** the Lord Chamberlain's insignia.

I say that I can tell—'twas half a minute:
   I know the solar beams take up more time
Ere, packed up for their journey, they begin it;
   But then their telegraph is less sublime,
445 And if they ran a race, they would not win it
   'Gainst Satan's couriers bound for their own clime.
The sun takes up some years for every ray
To reach its goal—the devil not half a day.

Upon the verge of space, about the size
450   Of half-a-crown, a little speck appeared
(I've seen a something like it in the skies
   In the Aegean, ere a squall); it neared,
And, growing bigger, took another guise;
   Like an aerial ship it tacked, and steered,
455 Or *was* steered (I am doubtful of the grammar
Of the late phrase, which makes the stanza stammer;—

But take your choice); and then it grew a cloud;
   And so it was—a cloud of witnesses.
But such a cloud! No land e'er saw a crowd
460   Of locusts numerous as the heavens saw these;
They shadowed with their myriads space; their loud
   And varied cries were like those of wild geese
(If nations may be likened to a goose),
And realized the phrase of "hell broke loose."

465 Here crashed a sturdy oath of stout John Bull,
   Who damned away his eyes as heretofore:
There Paddy brogued "By Jasus!"—"What's your
   wull?"
   The temperate Scot exclaimed: the French ghost
   swore
In certain terms I shan't translate in full,
470   As the first coachman will; and 'midst the war,
The voice of Jonathan was heard to express,
"*Our* president is going to war, I guess."

Besides there were the Spaniard, Dutch, and Dane;
   In short, an universal shoal of shades,

From Otaheite's isle to Salisbury Plain,   475
    Of all climes and professions, years and trades,
Ready to swear against the good king's reign,
    Bitter as clubs in cards are against spades:
All summoned by this grand "subpoena," to
Try if kings mayn't be damned like me or you.   480

When Michael saw this host, he first grew pale,
    As angels can; next, like Italian twilight,
He turned all colors—as a peacock's tail,
    Or sunset streaming through a Gothic skylight
In some old abbey, or a trout not stale,   485
    Or distant lightning on the horizon by night,
Or a fresh rainbow, or a grand review
Of thirty regiments in red, green, and blue.

Then he addressed himself to Satan: "Why—
    My good old friend, for such I deem you; though   490
Our different parties make us fight so shy,
    I ne'er mistake you for a *personal* foe;
Our difference is *political,* and I
    Trust that, whatever may occur below,
You know my great respect for you: and this   495
Makes me regret whate'er you do amiss—

"Why, my dear Lucifer, would you abuse
    My call for witnesses? I did not mean
That you should half of earth and hell produce;
    'Tis even superfluous, since two honest, clean,   500
True testimonies are enough: we lose
    Our time, nay, our eternity, between
The accusation and defense: if we
Hear both, 'twill stretch our immortality."

Satan replied, "To me the matter is   505
    Indifferent, in a personal point of view:
I can have fifty better souls than this
    With far less trouble than we have gone through
Already; and I merely argued his
    Late majesty of Britain's case with you   510

Upon a point of form: you may dispose
Of him; I've kings enough below, God knows!"

Thus spoke the Demon (late call'd "multifaced"
    By multo-scribbling Southey).—"Then we'll call
515 One or two persons of the myriads placed
    Around our congress, and dispense with all
The rest," quoth Michael: "Who may be so graced
    As to speak first? there's choice enough—who shall
It be?" Then Satan answered, "There are many;
520 But you may choose Jack Wilkes° as well as any."

A merry, cockeyed, curious-looking sprite
    Upon the instant started from the throng,
Dressed in a fashion now forgotten quite;
    For all the fashions of the flesh stick long
525 By people in the next world; where unite
    All the costumes since Adam's, right or wrong,
From Eve's fig leaf down to the petticoat,
Almost as scanty, of days less remote.

The spirit looked around upon the crowds
530   Assembled, and exclaimed, "My friends of all
The spheres, we shall catch cold amongst these clouds;
    So let's to business: why this general call?
If those are freeholders I see in shrouds,
    And 'tis for an election that they bawl,
535 Behold a candidate with unturned coat!
Saint Peter, may I count upon your vote?"

"Sir," replied Michael, "you mistake; these things
    Are of a former life, and what we do
Above is more august; to judge of kings
540   Is the tribunal met: so now you know."
"Then I presume those gentlemen with wings,"
    Said Wilkes, "are cherubs; and that soul below
Looks much like George the Third, but to my mind
A good deal older—Bless me! is he blind?"

520 **Wilkes** John Wilkes (1727–1797) was an eloquent Parliamentary
attacker of George III.

"He is what you behold him, and his doom   545
   Depends upon his deeds," the Angel said.
"If you have aught to arraign in him, the tomb
   Gives license to the humblest beggar's head
To lift itself against the loftiest."—"Some,"
   Said Wilkes, "don't wait to see them laid in lead,   550
For such a liberty—and I, for one,
Have told them what I thought beneath the sun."

"*Above* the sun repeat, then, what thou hast
   To urge against him," said the Archangel. "Why,"
Replied the spirit, "since old scores are past,   555
   Must I turn evidence? In faith, not I.
Besides, I beat him hollow at the last,
   With all his Lords and Commons: in the sky
I don't like ripping up old stories, since
His conduct was but natural in a prince: 560

"Foolish, no doubt, and wicked, to oppress
   A poor unlucky devil without a shilling;
But then I blame the man himself much less
   Than Bute and Grafton, and shall be unwilling
To see him punished here for their excess,   565
   Since they were both damned long ago, and still in
Their place below: for me, I have forgiven,
And vote his 'habeas corpus' into heaven."

"Wilkes," said the Devil, "I understand all this;
   You turned to half a courtier ere you died,   570
And seem to think it would not be amiss
   To grow a whole one on the other side
Of Charon's ferry, you forget that *his*
   Reign is concluded; whatsoe'er betide,
He won't be sovereign more: you've lost your labor,   575
For at the best he will but be your neighbor.

"However, I knew what to think of it,
   When I beheld you in your jesting way
Flitting and whispering round about the spit
   Where Belial, upon duty for the day,   580

With Fox's lard° was basting William Pitt,
  His pupil; I knew what to think, I say:
That fellow even in hell breeds farther ills;
I'll have him *gagged*—'twas one of his own bills.

585 "Call Junius!"° From the crowd a shadow stalked,
  And at the name there was a general squeeze,
So that the very ghosts no longer walked
  In comfort, at their own aerial ease,
But were all rammed and jammed (but to be balked,
590 As we shall see), and jostled hands and knees,
Like wind compressed and pent within a bladder,
Or like a human colic, which is sadder.

The shadow came—a tall, thin, gray-haired figure,
  That looked as it had been a shade on earth;
595 Quick in its motions, with an air of vigor,
  But naught to mark its breeding or its birth:
Now it waxed little, then again grew bigger,
  With now an air of gloom, or savage mirth;
But as you gazed upon its features, they
600 Changed every instant—to *what,* none could say.

The more intently the ghosts gazed, the less
  Could they distinguish whose the features were:
The Devil himself seemed puzzled even to guess;
  They varied like a dream—now here, now there;
605 And several people swore from out the press,
  They knew him perfectly; and one could swear
He was his father: upon which another
Was sure he was his mother's cousin's brother:

Another, that he was a duke, or knight,
610 An orator, a lawyer, or a priest,
A nabob, a man-midwife: but the wight
  Mysterious changed his countenance at least

---

581 **Fox's lard** refers to the fatness of Charles James Fox, Whig
Statesman.   585 **Junius** pseudonym of an author of a series of public
letters attacking the government of George III; his actual identity is
still unknown.

As oft as they their minds: though in full sight
  He stood, the puzzle only was increased;
The man was a phantasmagoria in
Himself—he was so volatile and thin.   615

The moment that you had pronounced him *one,*
  Presto! his face changed, and he was another;
And when that change was hardly well put on,
  It varied, till I don't think his own mother   620
(If that he had a mother) would her son
  Have known, he shifted so from one to t'other;
Till guessing from a pleasure grew a task,
At this epistolary "Iron Mask."

For sometimes he like Cerberus would seem—   625
  "Three gentlemen at once" (as sagely says
Good Mrs. Malaprop); then you might deem
  That he was not even *one;* now many rays
Were flashing round him; and now a thick steam
  Hid him from sight—like fogs on London days: 630
Now Burke, now Tooke, he grew to people's fancies,
And certes often like Sir Philip Francis.

I've an hypothesis—'tis quite my own;
  I never let it out till now, for fear
Of doing people harm about the throne,   635
  And injuring some minister or peer
On whom the stigma might perhaps be blown:
  It is—my gentle public, lend thine ear!
'Tis, that what Junius we are wont to call
Was *really, truly,* nobody at all.   640

I don't see wherefore letters should not be
  Written without hands, since we daily view
Them written without heads; and books, we see,
  Are filled as well without the latter too:
And really till we fix on somebody   645
  For certain sure to claim them as his due,
Their author, like the Niger's mouth, will bother
The world to say if *there* be mouth or author.

"And who and what art thou?" the Archangel said.—
650   "For *that* you may consult my title page,"
Replied this mighty shadow of a shade:
   "If I have kept my secret half an age,
I scarce shall tell it now."—"Canst thou upbraid,"
   Continued Michael, "George Rex, or allege
655 Aught further?" Junius answered, "You had better
   First ask him for *his* answer to my letter:

"My charges upon record will outlast
   The brass of both his epitaph and tomb."—
"Repent'st thou not," said Michael, "of some past
660   Exaggeration? something which may doom
Thyself if false, as him if true? Thou wast
   Too bitter—is it not so?—in thy gloom
Of passion?"—"Passion!" cried the phantom dim,
"I loved my country, and I hated him.

665 "What I have written, I have written: let
   The rest be on his head or mine!" So spoke
Old "Nominis Umbra;"° and while speaking yet,
   Away he melted in celestial smoke.
Then Satan said to Michael, "Don't forget
   To call George Washington, and John Horne
670   Tooke,°
And Franklin";—but at this time there was heard
   A cry for room, though not a phantom stirred.

At length with jostling, elbowing, and the aid
   Of cherubim appointed to that post,
675 The devil Asmodeus to the circle made
   His way, and looked as if his journey cost
Some trouble. When his burden down he laid,
   "What's this?" cried Michael; "why, 'tis not a
   ghost?"

667 **"Nominis Umbra"** The *Letters of Junius* bore on its title page
the motto *Stat Nominis Umbra*: "A shadow stands for the name."
670 **John Horne Tooke** (1736–1812), a radical leader and a supporter
of the independence of the American colonies.

"I know it," quoth the incubus; "but he
Shall be one, if you leave the affair to me.   680

"Confound the renegado! I have sprained
    My left wing, he's so heavy; one would think
Some of his works about his neck were chained.
    But to the point; while hovering o'er the brink
Of Skiddaw° (where as usual it still rained),   685
    I saw a taper, far below me, wink,
And stooping, caught this fellow at a libel—
No less on history than the Holy Bible.

"The former is the devil's scripture, and
    The latter yours, good Michael; so the affair   690
Belongs to all of us, you understand.
    I snatched him up just as you see him there,
And brought him off for sentence out of hand:
    I've scarcely been ten minutes in the air—
At least a quarter it can hardly be: 695
I dare say that his wife is still at tea."

Here Satan said, "I know this man of old,
    And have expected him for some time here;
A sillier fellow you will scarce behold,
    Or more conceited in his petty sphere: 700
But surely it was not worthwhile to fold
    Such trash below your wing, Asmodeus dear:
We had the poor wretch safe (without being bored
With carriage) coming of his own accord.

"But since he's here, let's see what he has done."—   705
    "Done!" cried Asmodeus, "he anticipates
The very business you are now upon,
    And scribbles as if head clerk to the Fates.
Who knows to what his ribaldry may run,
    When such an ass as this, like Balaam's, prates?"—   710
"Let's hear," quoth Michael, "what he has to say;
You know we're bound to that in every way."

685 **Skiddaw** a mountain in the Lake country near Robert Southey's home.

Now the bard, glad to get an audience, which
 By no means often was his case below,
715 Began to cough, and hawk, and hem, and pitch
 His voice into that awful note of woe
To all unhappy hearers within reach
 Of poets when the tide of rhyme's in flow;
But stuck fast with his first hexameter,
720 Not one of all whose gouty feet would stir.

But ere the spavined dactyls could be spurred
 Into recitative, in great dismay
Both cherubim and seraphim were heard
 To murmur loudly through their long array;
725 And Michael rose ere he could get a word
 Of all his foundered verses under way,
And cried, "For God's sake, stop, my friend! 'twere
  best—
Non Di, non homines—you know the rest!"°

A general bustle spread throughout the throng,
730 Which seemed to hold all verse in detestation;
The angels had of course enough of song
 When upon service; and the generation
Of ghosts had heard too much in life, not long
 Before, to profit by a new occasion;
735 The monarch, mute till then, exclaimed, "What! what!
Pye° come again? No more—no more of that!"

The tumult grew; an universal cough
 Convulsed the skies, as during a debate,
When Castlereagh has been up long enough
740 (Before he was first minister of state,
I mean—the *slaves hear now*); some cried "Off, off!"
 As at a farce; till, grown quite desperate,
The bard Saint Peter prayed to interpose
(Himself an author) only for his prose.

---

728 **Non Di . . . rest** from Horace, *Ars Poetica* p. 372f. "Neither gods nor men nor booksellers can put up with mediocre poetry." 736 **Pye** Henry Pye, poet laureate before Southey, a proverbially bad poet.

The varlet was not an ill-favored knave;   745
  A good deal like a vulture in the face,
With a hook nose and a hawk's eye, which gave
  A smart and sharper-looking sort of grace
To his whole aspect, which, though rather grave,
  Was by no means so ugly as his case;   750
But that indeed was hopeless as can be,
Quite a poetic felony *de se.*

Then Michael blew his trump, and stilled the noise
With one still greater, as is yet the mode
On earth besides; except some grumbling voice,   755
Which now and then will make a slight inroad
Upon decorous silence, few will twice
  Lift up their lungs when fairly overcrowed
And now the bard could plead his own bad cause,
With all the attitudes of self-applause.   760

He said (I only give the heads)—he said,
  He meant no harm in scribbling; 'twas his way
Upon all topics; 'twas, besides, his bread,
  Of which he buttered both sides; 'twould delay
Too long the assembly (he was pleased to dread),   765
  And take up rather more time than a day,
To name his works—he would but cite a few—
Wat Tyler—Rhymes on Blenheim—Waterloo.

He had written praises of a regicide;
  He had written praises of all kings whatever;   770
He had written for republics far and wide,
  And then against them bitterer than ever;
For pantisocracy° he once had cried
  Aloud, a scheme less moral than 'twas clever;
Then grew a hearty anti-jacobin—   775
Had turned his coat—and would have turned his skin.

---

773 **pantisocracy** In the last decade of the eighteenth century.
Southey and Coleridge planned to set up a utopian community along
the banks of the Susquehanna River.

He had sung against all battles, and again
   In their high praise and glory; he had called
Reviewing "the ungentle craft," and then
780   Become as base a critic as e'er crawled—
Fed, paid, and pampered by the very men
   By whom his muse and morals had been mauled:
He had written much blank verse, and blanker prose,
And more of both than anybody knows.

785 He had written Wesley's life:—here turning round
   To Satan, "Sir, I'm ready to write yours,
In two octavo volumes, nicely bound,
   With notes and preface, all that most allures
The pious purchaser; and there's no ground
790   For fear, for I can choose my own reviewers:
So let me have the proper documents,
That I may add you to my other saints."

Satan bowed, and was silent. "Well, if you,
   With amiable modesty, decline
795 My offer, what says Michael? There are few
   Whose memoirs could be rendered more divine.
Mine is a pen of all work; not so new
   As it was once, but I would make you shine
Like your own trumpet. By the way, my own
800 Has more of brass in it, and is as well blown.

"But talking about trumpets, here's my Vision!
   Now you shall judge, all people; yes, you shall
Judge with my judgment, and by my decision
   Be guided who shall enter heaven or fall.
805 I settle all these things by intuition,
   Times present, past, to come, heaven, hell, and all,
Like King Alfonso.° When I thus see double,
I save the Deity some worlds of trouble."

807 **Alfonso** a king of Castile (died 1284) who claimed that if he had
been consulted at the creation of the world, he would have spared
the Maker some absurdities.

He ceased, and drew forth an MS.; and no
   Persuasion on the part of devils, or saints,   810
Or angels, now could stop the torrent; so
   He read the first three lines of the contents;
But at the fourth, the whole spiritual show
   Had vanished, with variety of scents
Ambrosial and sulphureous, as they sprang,   815
Like lightning, off from his "melodious twang."

Those grand heroics acted as a spell;
   The angels stopped their ears and plied their
      pinions;
The devils ran howling, deafened, down to hell;
   The ghosts fled, gibbering, for their own dominions 820
(For 'tis not yet decided where they dwell,
   And I leave every man to his opinions);
Michael took refuge in his trump—but, lo!
His teeth were set on edge, he could not blow!

Saint Peter, who has hitherto been known   825
   For an impetuous saint, upraised his keys,
And at the fifth line knocked the poet down;
   Who fell like Phaeton, but more at ease,
Into his lake, for there he did not drown;
   A different web being by the Destinies   830
Woven for the Laureate's final wreath, whene'er
Reform shall happen either here or there.

He first sank to the bottom—like his works,
   But soon rose to the surface—like himself;
For all corrupted things are buoyed like corks,   835
   By their own rottenness, light as an elf,
Or wisp that flits o'er a morass: he lurks,
   It may be, still, like dull books on a shelf,
In his own den, to scrawl some "Life" or "Vision,"
As Welborn° says—"the devil turned precisian."   840

840 **Welborn** a character in Philip Massinger's *A New Way to Pay
Old Debts.*

As for the rest, to come to the conclusion
    Of this true dream, the telescope is gone
Which kept my optics free from all delusion,
    And showed me what I in my turn have shown;
845 All I saw farther, in the last confusion,
    Was, that King George slipped into heaven for one;
And when the tumult dwindled to a calm,
I left him practicing the hundredth psalm.

ON THIS DAY I COMPLETE MY THIRTY-SIXTH YEAR

'Tis time this heart should be unmoved,
    Since others it hath ceased to move:
Yet, though I cannot be beloved,
    Still let me love!

5 My days are in the yellow leaf;
    The flowers and fruits of love are gone;
The worm, the canker, and the grief
    Are mine alone!

The fire that on my bosom preys
10   Is lone as some volcanic isle;
No torch is kindled at its blaze—
    A funeral pile.

The hope, the fear, the jealous care,
    The exalted portion of the pain
15 And power of love, I cannot share,
    But wear the chain.

But 'tis not *thus*—and 'tis not *here*—
  Such thoughts should shake my soul, nor *now*,
Where glory decks the hero's bier,
    Or binds his brow.   20

The sword, the banner, and the field,
  Glory and Greece, around me see!
The Spartan, borne upon his shield,
    Was not more free.

Awake! (not Greece—she *is* awake!)   25
  Awake, my spirit! Think through *whom*
Thy life-blood tracks its parent lake,
    And then strike home!

Tread those reviving passions down,
  Unworthy manhood!—unto thee   30
Indifferent should the smile or frown
    Of beauty be.

If thou regret'st thy youth, *why live?*
  The land of honorable death
Is here:—up to the field, and give   35
    Away thy breath!

Seek out—less often sought than found—
  A soldier's grave, for thee the best;
Then look around, and choose thy ground,
    And take thy rest.   40
               Missolonghi, January 22, 1824

PART TWO: Prose

To Moore September 19, 1818

. . . I have finished the first canto (a long one, of about 180 octaves) of a poem in the style and manner of *Beppo,* encouraged by the good success of the same. It is called *Don Juan,* and is meant to be a little quietly facetious upon everything. But I doubt whether it is not—at least, as far as it has yet gone—too free for these very modest days. However, I shall try the experiment anonymously; and if it don't take, it will be discontinued. It is dedicated to Southey in good, simple, savage verse, upon the Laureat's politics, and the way he got them. . . .

To Murray, January 25, 1819

. . . You will do me the favor to print privately (for private distribution) fifty copies of *Don Juan.* The list of men to whom I wish it to be presented, I will send hereafter. The other two poems had best be added to the collective edition: I do not approve of *their* being published separately. *Print Don Juan entire,* omitting, of course, the lines on Castlereagh, as I am not on the spot to meet him. I have a second Canto ready, which will be sent by and bye. By this post, I have written to Mr. Hobhouse, addressed to your care.

Yours very truly,

B.

P.S.—I have acquiesced in the request and representation; and having done so, it is idle to detail my arguments in favor of my own Self-love and "Poeshie"; but I *protest*. If the poem has poetry, it would stand; if not, fall: the rest is "leather and prunella," and has never yet affected any human production "pro or con." Dullness is the only annihilator in such cases. As to the Cant of the day, I despise it, as I have ever done all its other finical fashions, which become you as paint became the Antient Britons. If you admit this prudery, you must omit half Ariosto, La Fontaine, Shakespeare, Beaumont, Fletcher, Massinger, Ford, all the Charles Second writers; in short, *something* of most who have written before Pope and are worth reading, and much of Pope himself. *Read him*—most of you *don't*—but *do*—and I will forgive you; though the inevitable consequence would be that you would burn all I have ever written, and all your other wretched Claudians of the day (except Scott and Crabbe) into the bargain. I wrong Claudian, who *was* a *poet*, by naming him with such fellows; but he was the *ultimus Romanorum*, the tail of the Comet, and these persons are the tail of an old Gown cut into a waistcoat for Jackey; but being both *tails*, I have compared one with the other, though very unlike, like all Similies. I write in a passion and a Sirocco, and I was up till six this morning at the Carnival; but I *protest*, as I did in my former letter.

To Murray August 12, 1819

. . . You are right, Gifford is right, Crabbe is right, Hobhouse is right—you are all right, and I am all wrong; but do, pray, let me have that pleasure. Cut me up root and branch; quarter me in the *Quarterly;* send round my *disjecti membra poetae,* like those of the Levite's Concubine; make me, if you will, a spectacle to men and angels; but don't ask me to alter, for I can't:—I am obstinate and lazy—and there's the truth.

But, nevertheless, I will answer your friend Cohen, who objects to the quick succession of fun and gravity, as if in that case the gravity did not (in intention, at least) heighten the fun. His metaphor is, that "we are never scorched and drenched at the same time." Blessings on his experience! Ask him these questions about "scorching and drenching." Did he never play at Cricket, or walk a mile in hot weather? Did he never spill a dish of tea over himself in handing the cup to his charmer, to the great shame of his nankeen breeches? Did he never swim in the sea at Noonday with the Sun in his eyes and on his head, which all the foam of the Ocean could not cool? Did he never draw his foot out of a tub of too hot water, damning his eyes and his valet's. . . . Was he ever in a Turkish bath, that marble paradise of sherbet and Sodomy? Was he ever in a cauldron of boiling oil, like St. John? or in the sulphureous waves of hell? (where he ought to be for his "scorching and drenching at the same time"). Did he never tumble into a river or lake, fishing, and sit in his wet clothes in the boat, or on the bank, afterwards "scorched and drenched," like a true sportsman? "Oh for breath to utter!"—but make him my compliments; he is a clever fellow for all that—a very clever fellow.

You ask me for the plan of Donny Johnny: I *have* no plan—I *had* no plan; but I had or have materials; though if, like Tony Lumpkin, I am "to be snubbed so when I am in spirits," the poem will be naught, and the poet turn serious again. If it don't take, I will leave it off where it is, with all due respect to the Public; but if continued, it must be in my own way. You might as well make Hamlet (or Diggory) "act mad" in a strait waistcoat as trammel my buffoonery, if I am to be a buffoon: their gestures and my thoughts would only be pitiably absurd and ludicrously constrained. Why, Man, the Soul of such writing is its license; at least the *liberty* of that *license,* if one likes—*not* that one should abuse it: it is like trial by Jury and Peerage and the Habeas Corpus—a very fine thing, but chiefly in the *reversion;* because no one wishes to be tried for the mere pleasure of proving his possession of the privilege.

But a truce with these reflections. You are too earnest and eager about a work never intended to be serious. Do you suppose that I could have any intention but to giggle and make giggle?—a playful satire, with as little poetry as could be helped, was what I meant: and as to the indecency, do, pray, read in Boswell what *Johnson,* the sullen moralist, says of *Prior* and Paulo Purgante. . . .

To Murray April 6, 1819

Dear sir,

The Second Canto of *Don Juan* was sent, on Saturday last, by post, in 4 packets, two of 4, and two of three sheets each, containing in all two hundred and seventeen stanzas, octave measure. But I will permit no curtailments, except those mentioned about Castlereagh and the two *Bobs* in the Introduction. You shan't make *Canticles* of my cantos. The poem will please, if it is lively; if it is stupid, it will fail; but I will have none of your damned cutting and slashing. If you please, you may publish *anonymously;* it will perhaps be better; but I will battle my way against them all, like a Porcupine.

So you and Mr. Foscolo,° etc., want me to undertake what you call a "great work"? an Epic poem, I suppose, or some such pyramid. I'll try no such thing; I hate tasks. And then "seven or eight years"! God send us all well this day three months, let alone years. If one's years can't be better employed than in sweating poesy, a man had better be a ditcher. And works, too! is *Childe Harold* nothing? You have so many *"divine"* poems, is it nothing to have written a *Human* one? without any of your worn-out machinery. Why, man, I could have spun the thoughts of the four cantos of that poem into twenty, had I wanted to book-make, and its passion into as many modern tragedies. Since you want *length,* you shall have enough of *Juan,* for I'll make 50 cantos.

Mr. Foscolo Ugo Foscolo (1778–1827), Italian poet.

And Foscolo, too! Why does *he* not do something more than the *Letters of Ortis,* and a tragedy, and pamphlets? He has good fifteen years more at his command than I have: what has he done all that time:—proved his Genius, doubtless, but not fixed its fame, nor done his utmost.

Besides, I mean to write my best work in *Italian,* and it will take me nine years more thoroughly to master the language; and then if my fancy exist, and I exist too, I will try what I *can* do *really.* As to the Estimation of the English which you talk of, let them calculate what it is worth, before they insult me with their insolent condescension.

I have not written for their pleasure. If they are pleased, it is that they chose to be so; I have never flattered their opinions, nor their pride; nor will I. Neither will I make "Ladies books" *al dilettar le femine e la plebe.*° I have written from the fullness of my mind, from passion, from impulse, from many motives, but not for their "sweet voices."

I know the precise worth of popular applause, for few Scribblers have had more of it; and if I chose to swerve into their paths, I could retain it, or resume it, or increase it. But I neither love ye, nor fear ye; and though I buy with ye and sell with ye, and talk with ye, I will neither eat with ye, drink with ye, nor pray with ye. They made me, without my search, a species of popular Idol; they, without reason or judgment, beyond the caprice of their good pleasure, threw down the Image from its pedestal; it was not broken with the fall, and they would, it seems, again replace it—but they shall not. . . .

To Hobhouse August 20, 1819

. . . I hear nothing of *Don Juan* but in two letters from Murray; the first very tremulous, the second in better spirits.

al . . . plebe "to please the women and the crowd."

Of the fate of the "pome" I am quite uncertain, and do not anticipate much brilliancy from your silence. But I do not care. I am as sure as the Archbishop of Grenada that I never wrote better, and I wish you all better taste, but will not send you any pistoles. . . .°

To Kinnaird° October 26, 1819

. . . As to *Don Juan*, confess, confess—you dog and be candid—that it is the sublime of *that there* sort of writing —it may be bawdy, but is it not good English? It may be profligate, but is it not *life,* is it not the *thing?* Could any man have written it who has not lived in the world? and fooled in a post chaise? in a hackney coach? in a gondola? against a wall? in a court carriage? in a vis-à-vis— on a table? and under it? I have written about a hundred stanzas of a third canto, but it is a damned modest—the outcry has frighted me. I have such projects for the Don but the Cant is so much stronger then the * , nowadays, that the benefit of experience in a man who had well weighed the worth of both monosyllables must be lost to despairing posterity. . . .

To Murray April 23, 1820

. . . You say that *one half* is very good: you are wrong; for, if it were, it would be the finest poem in existence. *Where* is the poetry of which *one half* is good? is it the *Aeneid?* is it *Milton's?* is it *Dryden's?* is it anyone's except *Pope's* and *Goldsmith's,* of which *all* is good? and yet these two last are the poets your pond poets would ex-

pistoles allusion to Lesage's *Gil Blas.*   **Kinnaird** Douglas James William Kinnaird. Banker who attended to Byron's financial affairs.

plode. But if *one half* of the two new cantos be good in your opinion, what the devil would you have more? No— no: no poetry is *generally* good—only by fits and starts— and you are lucky to get a sparkle here and there. You might as well want a Midnight *all stars* as rhyme all perfect. . . .

To Murray February 16, 1821

. . . The 5th [Canto] is so far from being the last of D.J., that it is hardly the beginning. I meant to take him the tour of Europe, with a proper mixture of siege, battle, and adventure, and to make him finish as *Anacharsis Cloots* in the French revolution. To how many cantos this may extend, I know not, nor whether (even if I live) I shall complete it; but this was my notion: I meant to have made him a *Cavalier Servente* in Italy, and a cause for a divorce in England, and a Sentimental "Werther-faced man" in Germany, so as to show the different ridicules of the society in each of those countries, and to have displayed him gradually *gaté* and blasé as he grew older, as is natural. But I had not quite fixed whether to make him end in Hell, or in an unhappy marriage, not knowing which would be the severest. The Spanish tradition says Hell: but it is probably only an Allegory of the other state. You are now in possession of my notions on the subject. . . .

To Murray July 6, 1821

. . . At the particular request of the Contessa G. I have promised *not* to continue *Don Juan*. You will therefore look upon these 3 cantos as the last of that poem. She had read the two first in the French translation, and never

ceased beseeching me to write no more of it. The reason
of this is not at first obvious to a superficial observer of
FOREIGN manners; but it arises from the wish of all
women to exalt the *sentiment* of the passions, and to keep
up the illusion which is their empire. Now *Don Juan*
strips off this illusion, and laughs at that and most other
things. I never knew a woman who did *not* protect Rous-
seau, nor one who did not dislike de Grammont, *Gil Blas,*
and all the *comedy* of the passions, when brought out
naturally. . . .

To Moore August 27, 1822

. . . I have nearly (*quite three*) four new cantos of *Don
Juan* ready. I obtained permission from the female Censor
Morum of *my* morals to continue it, provided it were im-
maculate; so I have been as decent as need be. . . .

To Murray August 23, 1821

. . . With regard to the charges about the Shipwreck—
I think that I told both you and Mr. Hobhouse, years ago,
that there was not a *single circumstance* of it *not* taken
from *fact;* not, indeed, from any *single* shipwreck, but all
from *actual* facts of different wrecks. Almost all *Don Juan*
is *real* life, either my own, or from people I knew. By the
way, much of the description of the *furniture,* in Canto
3rd, is taken from *Tully's Tripoli* (pray *note this*), and the
rest from my own observation. Remember, I never meant
to conceal this at all, and have only not stated it, because
Don Juan had no preface nor name to it. If you think it
worth while to make this statement, do so, in your own

way. *I* laugh at such charges, convinced that no writer ever borrowed less, or made his materials more his own.

To Murray August 31, 1821

. . . I have received the *Juans,* which are printed so *carelessly,* especially the 5th Canto, as to be disgraceful to me, and not creditable to you. It really must be *gone over again* with the *Manuscript,* the errors are so gross— words added—changed—so as to make cacophony and nonsense. You have been careless of this poem because some of your Synod don't approve of it; but I tell you, it will be long before you see anything half so good as poetry or writing. Upon what principle have you omitted the *note* on Bacon and Voltaire? and one of the concluding stanzas sent as an addition? because it ended, I suppose, with—

> And do not link two virtuous souls for life
> Into that *moral Centaur,* man and wife?

Now, I must say, once for all, that I will not permit any human being to take such liberties with my writings because I am absent. I desire the omissions to be replaced (except the stanza on Semiramis)—particularly the stanza upon the Turkish marriages; and I request that the whole be carefully *gone over* with the MSS.

I never saw such stuff as is printed:—Gulleyaz instead of Gulbeyaz, etc. Are you aware that Gulbeyaz is a real name, and the other nonsense? I copied the *Cantos* out carefully, so that there is *no* excuse, as the Printer reads or at least *prints,* the MSS. of the plays without error.

If you have no feeling for your own reputation, pray have some little for mine. I have read over the poem carefully, and I tell you, *it is poetry.* Your little envious knot of parson-poets may say what they please: time will show that I am not in this instance mistaken.

Desire my friend Hobhouse to correct the press, especially of the last canto, from the Manuscript as it is: it is enough to drive one out of one's senses, to see the infernal torture of words from the original. For instance the line—

And *pair* their rhymes as Venus yokes her doves—

is printed—

And *praise* their rhymes, etc.

Also *"precarious"* for *"precocious";* and this line, stanza 133.—

And this strong extreme effect to tire no longer.

Now do turn to the Manuscript and see if I ever wrote such a *line*: it is *not verse.*

No wonder the poem should fail (which, however, it *won't,* you will see) with such things allowed to creep about it. Replace what is omitted, and correct what is so shamefully misprinted, and let the poem have fair play; and I fear nothing.

. . . You forget that all the fools in London (the chief purchasers of your publications) will condemn in me the stupidity of your printer. For instance, in the Notes to Canto Fifth, "the *Adriatic* shore of the Bosphorus," instead of the *Asiatic!!!* All this may seem little to you with your ministerial connections; but it is serious to me, who am thousands of miles off, and have no opportunity of not proving myself the fool your printer makes me, except your pleasure and leisure, forsooth.

The Gods prosper you, and forgive you, for I won't.

To Murray September 24, 1821

. . . I have been thinking over our late correspondence, and wish to propose to you the following articles for our future:—

1. ˢᵗˡʸ That you shall write to me of yourself, of the health, wealth, and welfare of all friends; but of *me* (*quoad me*) little or nothing.

2 ᵈˡʸ That you shall send me Soda powders, tooth powder, tooth brushes, or any such anti-odontalgic or chemical articles, as heretofore, *ad libitum,* upon being reimbursed for the same.

3 ᵈˡʸ That you shall *not* send me any modern, or (as they are called) *new,* publications in *English whatsoever,* save and excepting any writing, prose or verse, of (or reasonably presumed to be of) Walter Scott, Crabbe, Moore, Campbell, Rogers, Gifford, Joanna Baillie, *Irving* (the American), Hogg, Wilson (*Isle of Palms* Man), or *any* especial *single* work of fancy which is thought to be of considerable merit; *Voyages* and *travels,* provided that they are *neither in Greece, Spain, Asia Minor, Albania, nor Italy,* will be welcome: having traveled the countries mentioned, I know that what is said of them can convey nothing further which I desire to know about them. No other English works whatsoever.

4 ᵗʰˡʸ That you send me *no periodical works* whatsoever —*no Edinburgh, Quarterly, Monthly,* nor any Review, Magazine, Newspaper, English or foreign, of any description.

5 ᵗʰˡʸ That you send me *no* opinions whatsoever, either *good, bad,* or *indifferent,* of yourself, or your friends, or others, concerning any work, or works, of mine, past, present, or to come.

6 ᵗʰˡʸ That all negotiations in matters of business between you and me pass through the medium of the Honorable Douglas Kinnaird, my friend and trustee, or Mr. Hobhouse, as *Alter Ego,* and tantamount to myself during my absence, or presence.

Some of these propositions may at first seem strange, but they are founded. The quantity of trash I have received as books is incalculable, and neither amused nor instructed. Reviews and Magazines are at the best but ephemeral and superficial reading: *who thinks* of the *grand article* of *last year* in any *given review?* in the next place, if they regard *myself,* they tend to increase *Egotism;* if favorable, I do not deny that the praise *elates,* and if unfavorable, that the abuse *irritates*—the latter may conduct me to inflict a species of Satire, which would neither do good to you nor to your friends: *they* may smile *now,* and so may *you;* but if I took you all in hand, it would not be difficult to cut you up like gourds. I did as much by as powerful people at nineteen years old, and I know little as yet, in three and thirty, which should prevent me from making all your ribs Gridirons for your hearts, if such were my propensity. But it is *not.* Therefore let me hear none of your provocations. If anything occurs so very *gross* as to require my notice, I shall hear of it from my personal friends. For the rest, I merely request to be left in ignorance.

The same applies to opinions, *good, bad,* or *indifferent,* of persons in conversation or correspondence: these do not *interrupt,* but they *soil* the *current* of my *Mind.* I am sensitive enough, but *not* till I am *touched;* and *here* I am beyond the touch of the short arms of literary England, except the few feelers of the Polypus that crawl over the Channel in the way of Extract.

All these precautions *in* England would be useless: the libeler or the flatterer would there reach me in spite of all; but in Italy we know little of literary England, and think less, except what reaches us through some garbled and brief extract in some miserable Gazette. For *two years* (excepting two or three articles cut out and sent to *you,* by the post) I never read a newspaper which was not forced upon me by some accident, and know, upon the whole, as little of England as you all do of Italy, and God knows *that* is little enough, with all your travels, etc., etc., etc. The English travelers *know Italy* as *you* know Guernsey: how much is *that?*

If anything occurs so violently gross or personal as to require notice, Mr. Dˢ Kinnaird will let me *know;* but of *praise* I desire to hear *nothing.*

You will say, "to what tends all this?" I will answer THAT;—to keep my mind *free and unbiased* by all paltry and personal irritabilities of praise or censure;—to let my Genius take its natural direction, while my feelings are like the dead, who know nothing and feel nothing of all or aught that is said or done in their regard.

If you can observe these conditions, you will spare yourself and others some pain: let me not be worked upon to rise up; for if I do, it will not be for a little: if you can *not* observe these conditions, we shall cease to be correspondents, but *not friends;* for I shall always be

Yours ever and truly,

Byron

P.S.—I have taken these resolutions not from any irritation against *you* or *yours,* but simply upon reflection that all reading, either praise or censure, of myself has done me harm. When I was in Switzerland and Greece, I was out of the way of hearing either, and *how I wrote there!* In Italy I am out of the way of it too; but latterly, partly through my fault, and partly through your kindness in wishing to send me the *newest* and most periodical publications, I have had a crowd of reviews, etc., thrust upon me, which have bored me with their jargon, of one kind or another, and taken off my attention from greater objects. You have also sent me a parcel of trash of poetry, for no reason that I can conceive, unless to provoke me to write a new *English Bards.* Now *this* I wish to avoid; for if ever I *do,* it will be a strong production; and I desire peace, as long as the fools will keep their nonsense out of my way.

To Moore   March 4, 1822

. . . With respect to "Religion," can I never convince you that *I* have no such opinions as the characters in that drama,° which seems to have frightened everybody? Yet *they* are nothing to the expressions in Goethe's *Faust* (which are ten times hardier), and not a whit more bold than those of Milton's Satan. My ideas of a character may

that drama Byron's *Cain.*

run away with me: like all imaginative men, I, of course, embody myself with the character while I *draw* it, but not a moment after the pen is from off the paper.

I am no enemy to religion, but the contrary. As a proof, I am educating my natural daughter a strict Catholic in a convent of Romagna; for I think people can never have *enough* of religion, if they are to have any. I incline, myself, very much to the Catholic doctrines; but if I am to write a drama, I must make my characters speak as I conceive them likely to argue.

As to poor Shelley, who is another bugbear to you and the world, he is, to my knowledge, the *least* selfish and the mildest of men—a man who has made more sacrifices of his fortune and feelings for others than any I ever heard of. With his speculative opinions I have nothing in common, nor desire to have.

The truth is, my dear Moore, you live near the *stove* of society, where you are unavoidably influenced by its heat and its vapors. I did so once—and too much—and enough to give a color to my whole future existence. As my success in society was *not* inconsiderable, I am surely not a prejudiced judge upon the subject, unless in its favor; but I think it, as now constituted, *fatal* to all great original undertakings of every kind. I never courted it *then,* when I was young and high in blood, and one of its "curled darlings"; and do you think I would do so *now,* when I am living in a clearer atmosphere? One thing *only* might lead me back to it, and that is, to try once more if I could do any good in *politics;* but *not* in the petty politics I see now preying upon our miserable country.

Do not let me be misunderstood, however. If you speak your *own* opinions, they ever had, and will have, the greatest weight with *me.* But if you merely *echo* the *monde* (and it is difficult not to do so, being in its favor and its ferment), I can only regret that you should ever repeat anything to which I cannot pay attention.

But I am prosing. The gods go with you, and as much immortality of all kinds as may suit your present and all other existence.

DIARY—1821

Tomorrow is my birthday—that is to say, at twelve o' the clock, midnight, *i.e.* in twelve minutes, I shall have completed thirty and three years of age!!!—and I go to my bed with a heaviness of heart at having lived so long, and to so little purpose.

It is three minutes past twelve.—" 'Tis the middle of the night by the castle clock," and I am now thirty-three!

> *Eheu, fugaces, Posthume, Posthume,*
> *Labuntur anni;*°—

but I don't regret them so much for what I have done, as for what I *might* have done.

> Through life's road, so dim and dirty,
> I have dragged to three-and-thirty.
> What have these years left to me?
> Nothing—except thirty-three.

DIARY—1821

What is the reason that I have been, all my lifetime, more or less *ennuyé?* and that, if anything, I am rather less so now than I was at twenty, as far as my recollection serves? I do not know how to answer this, but I presume that it is constitutional—as well as the waking in low spirits, which I have invariably done for many years. Temperance and exercise, which I have practiced at times, and for a long time together vigorously and violently, made little or no difference. Violent passions did;—when under their immediate influence—it is odd, but I was in agitated, but *not* in depressed, spirits.

A dose of salts has the effect of a temporary inebriation, like light champagne, upon me. But wine and spirits make me sullen and savage to ferocity—silent, however,

---

Eheu . . . anni "Ah, Posthumes, how the swift years glide by . . ." See the opening of Horace *Ode* II, 14.

and retiring, and not quarrelsome, if not spoken to. Swimming also raises my spirits—but in general they are low, and get daily lower. That is *hopeless;* for I do not think I am so much *ennuyé* as I was at nineteen. The proof of this is, that then I must game, or drink, or be in motion of some kind, or I was miserable. At present, I can mope in quietness; and like being alone better than any company—except the lady's whom I serve. But I feel a something, which makes me think that, if I ever reach near to old age, like Swift, I shall die at "top" first. Only I do not dread idiotism or madness so much as he did. On the contrary, I think some quieter stages of both must be preferable to much of what men think the possession of their senses.

DIARY—1821

I have been considering what can be the reason why I always wake, at a certain hour in the morning, and always in very bad spirits—I may say, in actual despair and despondency, in all respects—even of that which pleased me overnight. In about an hour or two, this goes off, and I compose either to sleep again, or, at least, to quiet. In England, five years ago, I had the same kind of hypochondria, but accompanied with so violent a thirst that I have drank as many as fifteen bottles of soda water in one night, after going to bed, and been still thirsty—calculating, however, some lost from the bursting out and effervescence and overflowing of the soda water, in drawing the corks, or striking off the necks of the bottles from mere thirsty impatience. At present, I have *not* the thirst; but the depression of spirits is no less violent. . . .

What is it?—liver? In England, Le Man (the apothecary) cured me of the thirst in three days, and it had lasted as many years. I suppose that it is all hypochondria.

DETACHED THOUGHTS—1821–1822

People have wondered at the Melancholy which runs through my writings. Others have wondered at my personal gaiety; but I recollect once, after an hour, in which I had been sincerely and particularly gay, and rather brilliant, in company, my wife replying to me when I said (upon her remarking my high spirits) "and yet, Bell, I have been called and mis-called Melancholy—you must have seen how falsely, frequently." "No, B (she answered), it is not so: at *heart* you are the most melancholy of mankind, and often when apparently gayest."

DETACHED THOUGHTS—1821–1822

If I could explain at length the *real* causes which have contributed to increase this perhaps *natural* temperament of mine, this Melancholy which hath made me a byword, nobody would wonder; but this is impossible without doing much mischief. I do not know what other men's lives have been, but I cannot conceive anything more strange than some of the earlier parts of mine. I have written my memoirs, but omitted *all* the really *consequential* and *important* parts, from deference to the dead, the living, and to those who must be both.

DETACHED THOUGHTS

My Mother, before I was twenty, would have it that I was like Rousseau, and Madame de Staël used to say so too in 1813, and the *Edinburgh Review* has something of the sort in its critique of the 4th Canto of *Childe Harold*. I can't see any point of resemblance: he wrote prose, I verse: he was of the people, I of the Aristocracy: he was a philosopher, I am none: he published his first work at forty, I mine at eighteen: his first essay brought him universal applause, mine the contrary: he married his house-keeper, I could not keep house with my wife: he thought all the world in a plot against *him*, my little world seems to think *me* in a plot against it, if I may judge by their abuse in print and coterie: he liked Botany, I like flowers, and herbs, and trees, but know nothing of their pedigrees: he wrote Music, I limit my knowledge of it to what I catch by *Ear*—I never could learn anything by study, not even a language, it was all by rote and ear and memory: he had a bad memory, I *had* at least an excellent one (ask Hodgson the poet, a good judge, for he has an astonishing one); he wrote with hesitation and care, I with rapidity and rarely with pains: *he* could never ride nor swim "nor was cunning of fence," *I* am an excellent swimmer, a decent though not at all a dashing rider (having staved in a rib at eighteen in the course of scampering), and was sufficient of fence—particularly of the Highland broadsword; not a bad boxer when I could keep my temper, which was difficult, but which I strove to do ever since I knocked down Mr. Purling and put his knee-pan out (with the gloves on) in Angelo's and Jackson's rooms in 1806 during the sparring; and I was besides a very fair cricketer—one of the Harrow Eleven when we played against Eton in 1805. Besides, Rousseau's way of life, his country, his manners, his whole character, were so very different, that I am at a loss to conceive how such a comparison could have arisen, as it has done three several times, and all in rather a remarkable manner. I forgot to say, that *he* was also short-sighted, and that hitherto my eyes have been the contrary to such a degree that, in the largest theater of Bologna, I distinguished and read some busts and inscriptions painted near the stage, from a box so distant, and so *darkly* lighted, that none of the company (composed of young and very bright-eyed people—some of them in the same box) could make out a letter, and thought that it was a trick, though I had never been in that theater before.

Altogether, I think myself justified in thinking the comparison not well founded. I don't say this out of pique, for Rousseau was a great man, and the thing if true were flattering enough; but I have no idea of being pleased with a chimera.

DETACHED THOUGHTS

I liked the Dandies; they were always very civil to *me,* though in general they disliked literary people, and persecuted and mystified Madame de Staël, Lewis, Horace Twiss, and the like, damnably. . . . The truth is, that, though I gave up the business early, I had a tinge of Dandyism in my minority, and probably retained enough of it, to conciliate the great ones; at four and twenty; I had gamed and drank, and taken my degree in most dissipations; and having no pedantry, and not being overbearing, we ran quietly together. I knew them all more or less, and they made me a Member of Watier's (a superb Club at that time), being, I take it, the only literary man (except *two others,* both men of the world [M. and S.], in it.

DETACHED THOUGHTS

In general, I do not draw well with literary men: not that I dislike them, but I never know what to say to them after I have praised their last publication. There are several exceptions, to be sure: but then they have either been men of the world, such as Scott, and Moore, etc., or visionaries out of it, such as Shelley, etc.

DETACHED THOUGHTS

I sometimes wish that I had studied languages with more attention: those which I know, even the classical (Greek and Latin, in the usual proportion of a sixth-form boy), and a smattering of modern Greek, the Armenian and Arabic Alphabets, a few Turkish and Albanian phrases, oaths, or requests, Italian tolerably, Spanish less than tolerably, French to read with ease but speak with difficulty—or rather not at all—all have been acquired by ear or eye, and never by anything like Study. Like

"Edie Ochiltree," "I never dowed to bide a hard turn o' wark in my life."

To be sure, I set in zealously for the Armenian and Arabic, but I fell in love with some absurd womankind both times, before I had overcome the Characters; and at Malta and Venice left the profitable Orientalists for— for (no matter what), notwithstanding that my master, the Padre Pasquale Aucher (for whom, by the way, I compiled the major part of two Armenian and English Grammars), assured me "that the terrestial Paradise had been certainly in *Armenia*." I went seeking it—God knows where—did I find it? Umph! Now and then, for a minute or two.

DETACHED THOUGHTS

I am always most religious upon a sunshiny day; as if there were some association between an internal approach to greater light and purity, and the kindler of this dark lanthorn of our eternal existence.

The Night is also a religious concern; and even more so, when I viewed the Moon and Stars through Herschel's telescope, and saw that they were worlds.

DETACHED THOUGHTS

As to *political* slavery—so general—its man's own fault; if they *will* be slaves, let them! Yet it is but "a word and a blow." See how England formerly, France, Spain, Portugal, America, Switzerland, freed themselves! There is no one instance of a *long* contest, in which *men* did not triumph over Systems. If Tyranny misses her *first* spring, she is cowardly as the tiger, and retires to be hunted.

To Murray   February 21, 1820

. . . By the king's death Mr. H[obhouse], I hear, will stand for Westminster: I shall be glad to hear of his standing anywhere except in the pillory,° which, from the company he must have lately kept (I alway except Burdett, and Douglas K., and the genteel part of the reformers), was perhaps to be apprehended. I was really glad to hear it was for libel instead of larceny; for, though impossible in his own person, he might have been taken up by mistake for another at a meeting. . . . I am out of all patience to see my friends sacrifice themselves for a pack of blackguards, who disgust one with their Cause, although I have always been a friend to and a Voter for reform. . . . If we must have a tyrant, let him at least be a gentleman who has been bred to the business, and let us fall by the ax and not by the butcher's cleaver.

No one can be more sick of, or indifferent to, politics than I am, if they let me alone; but if the time comes when a part must be taken one way or the other, I shall pause before I lend myself to the views of such ruffians, although I cannot but approve of a Constitutional amelioration of long abuses.

Lord George Gordon, and Wilkes, and Burdett, and Horne Tooke, were all men of education and courteous deportment: so is Hobhouse; but as for these others, I am convinced that Robespierre was a Child, and Marat a Quaker in comparison of what they would be, could they throttle their way to power.

pillory Hobhouse had just been released from jail, where he had been sent on a charge of breach of privilege, for a pamphlet, "A Trifling Mistake in Thomas, Lord Erskine's Preface." He was elected.

To Mr. Mayer

English Consul at Prevesa, 1824

Sir,

Coming to Greece, one of my principal objects was to alleviate as much as possible the miseries incident to a warfare so cruel as the present. When the dictates of humanity are in question, I know no difference between Turks and Greeks. It is enough that those who want assistance are men, in order to claim the pity and protection of the meanest pretender to humane feelings. I have found here twenty-four Turks, including women and children, who have long pined in distress, far from the means of support and the consolations of their home. The Government has consigned them to me; I transmit them to Prevesa, whither they desire to be sent. I hope you will not object to take care that they may be restored to a place of safety, and that the Governor of your town may accept of my present. The best recompense I can hope for would be to find that I had inspired the Ottoman commanders with the same sentiments towards those unhappy Greeks who may hereafter fall into their hands. I beg you to believe me, etc.

N. Byron

To Moore

Missolonghi, Western Greece, March 4, 1824

My dear Moore,

Your reproach is unfounded—I have received two letters from you, and answered both previous to leaving Cephalonia. I have not been "quiet" in an Ionian island, but much occupied with business, as the Greek deputies (if arrived) can tell you. Neither have I continued *Don Juan,* nor any other poem. You go, as usual, I presume, by some newspaper report or other.

When the proper moment to be of some use arrived I came here; and am told that my arrival (with some other circumstances) *has* been of, at least, temporary advantage to the cause. I had a narrow escape from the Turks, and another from shipwreck, on my passage. On the 15th (or 16th) of February I had an attack of apoplexy, or epilepsy—the physicians have not exactly decided which, but the alternative is agreeable. My constitution, therefore, remains between the two opinions, like Mahomet's sarcophagus between the magnets. All that I can say is, that they nearly bled me to death, by placing the leeches too near the temporal artery, so that the blood could with difficulty be stopped, even with caustic. I am supposed to be getting better, slowly, however. But my homilies will, I presume, for the future, be like the Archbishop of Grenada's—in this case, "I order you a hundred ducats from my treasurer, and wish you a little more taste."

For public matters I refer you to Colonel Stanhope's and Capt. Parry's reports and to all other reports whatsoever. There is plenty to do—war without, and tumult within—they "kill a man a week," like Bob Acres in the country. Parry's artificers have gone away in alarm, on account of a dispute in which some of the natives and foreigners were engaged, and a Swede was killed, and a Suliote wounded. In the middle of their fright there was a strong shock of an earthquake; so, between that and the sword, they boomed off in a hurry, in despite of all dissuasions to the contrary. A Turkish brig run ashore, etc., etc., etc.

You, I presume, are either publishing or meditating that same. Let me hear from and of you, and believe me, in all events,

Ever and affectionately yours,

N. B.

PART THREE
Don Juan

DON JUAN
Dedication

1

Bob Southey! You're a poet—Poet laureate,
    And representative of all the race,
Although 'tis true that you turned out a Tory at
    Last—yours has lately been a common case;
And now, my Epic Renegade! what are ye at?   *5*
    With all the Lakers, in and out of place?
A nest of tuneful persons, to my eye
Like "four and twenty Blackbirds in a pye;"°

8 pye See note to *The Vision of Judgment.* l. 736.

II

"Which pye being opened they began to sing"
    (This old song and new simile holds good),
"A dainty dish to set before the King,"
        Or Regent, who admires such kind of food;—
And Coleridge, too, has lately taken wing,
        But like a hawk encumbered with his hood—
Explaining metaphysics to the nation—
I wish he would explain his Explanation.

III

You, Bob! are rather insolent, you know,
    At being disappointed in your wish
To supersede all warblers here below,
        And be the only Blackbird in the dish;
And then you overstrain yourself, or so,
        And tumble downward like the flying fish
Gasping on deck, because you soar too high, Bob,
And fall, for lack of moisture, quite a-dry, Bob!

IV

And Wordsworth, in a rather long *Excursion*
    (I think the quarto holds five hundred pages),
Has given a sample from the vasty version
        Of his new system to perplex the sages;
'Tis poetry—at least by his assertion,
        And may appear so when the Dog Star rages—
And he who understands it would be able
To add a story to the Tower of Babel.

V

You—Gentlemen! by dint of long seclusion
    From better company, have kept your own
At Keswick, and, through still continued fusion
        Of one another's minds, at last have grown
To deem as a most logical conclusion,
        That Poesy has wreaths for you alone:
There is a narrowness in such a notion,
Which makes me wish you'd change your lakes for
        ocean.

VI

I would not imitate the petty thought,
    Nor coin my self-love to so base a vice,
For all the glory your conversion brought,
    Since gold alone should not have been its price.
You have your salary; was 't for that you wrought?   *45*
    And Wordsworth has his place in the Excise.°
You're shabby fellows—true—but poets still,
And duly seated on the immortal hill.

VII

Your bays may hide the baldness of your brows—
    Perhaps some virtuous blushes;—let them go—   *50*
To you I envy neither fruit nor boughs—
    And for the fame you would engross below,
The field is universal, and allows
    Scope to all such as feel the inherent glow:
Scott, Rogers, Campbell, Moore, and Crabbe will try   *55*
'Gainst you the question with posterity.

VIII

For me, who, wandering with pedestrian Muses,
    Contend not with you on the wingèd steed,
I wish your fate may yield ye, when she chooses,
    The fame you envy and the skill you need;   *60*
And recollect a poet nothing loses
    In giving to his brethren their full meed
Of merit, and complaint of present days
Is not the certain path to future praise.

IX

He that reserves his laurels for posterity   *65*
    (Who does not often claim the bright reversion)
Has generally no great crop to spare it, he
    Being only injured by his own assertion;
And although here and there some glorious rarity
    Arise like Titan from the sea's immersion,   *70*

46 **Excise** Wordsworth accepted the post of Distributor of Stamps
for Westmorland County in 1813.

The major part of such appellants go
To—God knows where—for no one else can know.

X

If, fallen in evil days on evil tongues,
    Milton appealed to the Avenger, Time,
75 If Time, the Avenger, execrates his wrongs,
    And makes the word "Miltonic" mean *"sublime,"*
He deigned not to belie his soul in songs,
    Nor turn his very talent to a crime;
He did not loathe the Sire to laud the Son,
80 But closed the tyrant-hater he begun.

XI

Think'st thou, could he—the blind Old Man—arise
    Like Samuel from the grave, to freeze once more
The blood of monarchs with his prophecies,
    Or be alive again—again all hoar
85 With time and trials, and those helpless eyes,
        And heartless daughters—worn—and pale—and
            poor;
Would *he* adore a sultan? *he* obey
The intellectual eunuch Castlereagh?°

XII

Cold-blooded, smooth-faced, placid miscreant!
90   Dabbling its sleek young hands in Erin's gore,
And thus for wider carnage taught to pant,
    Transferred to gorge upon a sister shore,
The vulgarest tool that Tyranny could want,
    With just enough of talent, and no more,
95 To lengthen fetters by another fixed,
And offer poison long already mixed.

XIII

An orator of such set trash of phrase
    Ineffably—legitimately vile,

---

88 **Castlereagh** chief Tory statesman from 1812 to 1822, and op-
ponent of popular causes at home and abroad.

That even its grossest flatterers dare not praise,
    Nor foes—all nations—condescend to smile—   *100*
Not even a sprightly blunder's spark can blaze
    From that Ixion grindstone's ceaseless toil,
That turns and turns to give the world a notion
Of endless torments and perpetual motion.

XIV
A bungler even in its disgusting trade,   *105*
    And botching, patching, leaving still behind
Something of which its masters are afraid,
    States to be curbed and thoughts to be confined,
Conspiracy or Congress to be made—
    Cobbling at manacles for all mankind—   *110*
A tinkering slave-maker, who mends old chains,
With God and man's abhorrence for its gains.

XV
If we may judge of matter by the mind,
    Emasculated to the marrow *It*
Hath but two objects, how to serve and bind,   *115*
    Deeming the chain it wears even men may fit,
Eutropius° of its many masters—blind
    To worth as freedom, wisdom as to wit,
Fearless—because *no* feeling dwells in ice,
Its very courage stagnates to a vice.   *120*

XVI
Where shall I turn me not to *view* its bonds,
    For I will never *feel* them?—Italy!
Thy late reviving Roman soul desponds
    Beneath the lie this State-thing breathed o'er thee—
Thy clanking chain, and Erin's yet green wounds,   *125*
    Have voices, tongues to cry aloud for me.
Europe has slaves, allies, kings, armies still,
And Southey lives to sing them very ill.

---

117 **Eutropius** a eunuch and minister of the Roman emperor
Arcadius.

XVII

Meantime, Sir Laureate, I proceed to dedicate,
130   In honest simple verse, this song to you.
And, if in flattering strains I do not predicate,
    'Tis that I still retain my "buff and blue";°
My politics as yet are all to educate:
    Apostasy's so fashionable, too,
135 To keep *one* creed's a task grown quite Herculean;
Is it not so, my Tory, ultra-Julian?°

Venice, September 16, 1818

CANTO ONE

Julia

I

I want a hero: an uncommon want,
    When every year and month sends forth a new one,
Till, after cloying the gazettes with cant,
    The age discovers he is not the true one;
5 Of such as these I should not care to vaunt,
    I'll therefore take our ancient friend Don Juan—
We all have seen him, in the pantomime,
Sent to the devil somewhat ere his time.

II

Vernon, the butcher Cumberland, Wolfe, Hawke,
    Prince Ferdinand, Granby, Burgoyne, Keppel,
10   Howe,°

132 **"buff and blue"** colors of the Whigs.   136 **Julian** Julian the
Apostate.   9–10 **Vernon . . . Howe** renowned military and naval
leaders

Evil and good, have had their tithe of talk,
    And filled their sign posts then, like Wellesley°
      now;
Each in their turn like Banquo's monarchs stalk,
    Followers of fame, "nine farrow" of that sow:
France, too, had Buonaparté and Dumourier   *15*
Recorded in the *Moniteur* and *Courier*.

III

Barnave, Brissot, Condorcet, Mirabeau,
    Petion, Clootz, Danton, Marat, La Fayette,
Were French, and famous people, as we know:
    And there were others, scarce forgotten yet,   *20*
Joubert, Hoche, Marceau, Lannes, Desaix, Moreau,
    With many of the military set,
Exceedingly remarkable at times,
But not at all adapted to my rhymes.

IV

Nelson was once Britannia's god of war,   *25*
    And still should be so, but the tide is turned;
There's no more to be said of Trafalgar,
    'Tis with our hero quietly inurned;
Because the army's grown more popular,
    At which the naval people are concerned;   *30*
Besides, the prince is all for the land-service,
Forgetting Duncan, Nelson, Howe, and Jervis.

V

Brave men were living before Agamemnon
    And since, exceeding valorous and sage,
A good deal like him too, though quite the same none;   *35*
    But then they shone not on the poet's page,
And so have been forgotten:—I condemn none,
    But can't find any in the present age
Fit for my poem (that is, for my new one);
So, as I said, I'll take my friend Don Juan.   *40*

12 **Wellesley** the Duke of Wellington.

VI

Most epic poets plunge *in medias res*
   (Horace makes this the heroic turnpike road),
And then your hero tells, whene'er you please,
   What went before—by way of episode,
45 While seated after dinner at his ease,
   Beside his mistress in some soft abode,
Palace, or garden, paradise, or cavern,
Which serves the happy couple for a tavern.

VII

That is the usual method, but not mine—
50   My way is to begin with the beginning;
The regularity of my design
   Forbids all wandering as the worst of sinning,
And therefore I shall open with a line
   (Although it cost me half an hour in spinning)
55 Narrating somewhat of Don Juan's father,
And also of his mother, if you'd rather.

VIII

In Seville was he born, a pleasant city,
   Famous for oranges and women—he
Who has not seen it will be much to pity,
60   So says the proverb—and I quite agree;
Of all the Spanish towns is none more pretty,
   Cadiz perhaps—but that you soon may see;
Don Juan's parents lived beside the river,
A noble stream, and called the Guadalquivir.

IX

65 His father's name was José—*Don,* of course.—
   A true Hidalgo, free from every stain
Of Moor or Hebrew blood, he traced his source
   Through the most Gothic gentlemen of Spain;
A better cavalier ne'er mounted horse,
70   Or, being mounted, e'er got down again,
Than José, who begot our hero, who
Begot—but that's to come— Well, to renew:

X

His mother was a learnèd lady, famed
   For every branch of every science known
In every Christian language ever named,   75
   With virtues equaled by her wit alone,
She made the cleverest people quite ashamed,
   And even the good with inward envy groan,
Finding themselves so very much exceeded
In their own way by all the things that she did.   80

XI

Her memory was a mine: she knew by heart
   All Calderon and greater part of Lopé,
So that if any actor missed his part
   She could have served him for the prompter's copy;
For her Feinagle's° were an useless art,   85
   And he himself obliged to shut up shop—he
Could never make a memory so fine as
That which adorned the brain of Donna Inez.

XII

Her favorite science was the mathematical,
   Her noblest virtue was her magnanimity,   90
Her wit (she sometimes tried at wit) was Attic all,
   Her serious sayings darkened to sublimity;
In short, in all things she was fairly what I call
   A prodigy—her morning dress was dimity,
Her evening silk, or, in the summer, muslin,   95
And other stuffs, with which I won't stay puzzling.

XIII

She knew the Latin—that is, "the Lord's prayer,"
   And Greek—the alphabet—I'm nearly sure;
She read some French romances here and there,
   Although her mode of speaking was not pure;   100
For native Spanish she had no great care,
   At least her conversation was obscure;
Her thoughts were theorems, her words a problem,
As if she deemed that mystery would ennoble 'em.

85 **Feinagle's** a system for memory training.

XIV

105 She liked the English and the Hebrew tongue,
    And said there was analogy between 'em;
She proved it somehow out of sacred song,
    But I must leave the proofs to those who've seen
        'em;
But this I heard her say, and can't be wrong,
    And all may think which way their judgments lean
110   'em,
    " 'Tis strange—the Hebrew noun which means "I
        am,"
The English always use to govern d—n."

XV

Some women use their tongues—she *looked* a lecture,
    Each eye a sermon, and her brow a homily,
115 An all-in-all sufficient self-director,
    Like the lamented late Sir Samuel Romilly,°
The Law's expounder, and the State's corrector,
    Whose suicide was almost an anomaly—
One sad example more, that "All is vanity"
120 (The jury brought their verdict in "Insanity").

XVI

In short, she was a walking calculation,
    Miss Edgeworth's novels stepping from their covers,
Or Mrs. Trimmer's books° on education,
    Or *Coelebs' Wife*° set out in quest of lovers,
125 Morality's prim personification,
    In which not Envy's self a flaw discovers;
To others' share let "female errors fall,"
For she had not even one—the worst of all.

XVII

Oh! she was perfect past all parallel—
130   Of any modern female saint's comparison;
So far above the cunning powers of hell,
    Her guardian angel had given up his garrison;

116 **Romilly** Sir Samuel Romilly, Lady Byron's lawyer.   123 **Trimmer's books** moralistic children's tales.   124 **Coeleb's Wife** Hannah More's novel.

Even her minutest motions went as well
    As those of the best time-piece made by Harrison:
In virtues nothing earthly could surpass her,   135
Save thine "incomparable oil," Macassar!°

XVIII

Perfect she was, but as perfection is
    Insipid in this naughty world of ours,
Where our first parents never learned to kiss
    Till they were exiled from their earlier bowers,   140
Where all was peace, and innocence, and bliss
    (I wonder how they got through the twelve hours);
Don José, like a lineal son of Eve,
Went plucking various fruit without her leave.

XIX

He was a mortal of the careless kind,   145
    With no great love for learning, or the learnèd,
Who chose to go where'er he had a mind,
    And never dreamed his lady was concernèd;
The world, as usual, wickedly inclined
    To see a kingdom or a house o'erturnèd,   150
Whispered he had a mistress, some said *two*—
But for domestic quarrels *one* will do.

XX

Now Donna Inez had, with all her merit,
    A great opinion of her own good qualities;
Neglect, indeed, requires a saint to bear it,   155
    And such, indeed, she was in her moralities;
But then she had a devil of a spirit,
    And sometimes mixed up fancies with realities,
And let few opportunities escape
Of getting her liege lord into a scrape.   160

XXI

This was an easy matter with a man
    Oft in the wrong, and never on his guard;
And even the wisest, do the best they can,

136 **Macassar** a hair oil.

Have moments, hours, and days, so unprepared,
165 That you might "brain them with their lady's fan";
    And sometimes ladies hit exceeding hard,
    And fans turn into falchions in fair hands,
    And why and wherefore no one understands.

XXII

'Tis pity learnèd virgins ever wed
170   With persons of no sort of education,
    Or gentlemen, who, though well born and bred,
        Grow tired of scientific conversation:
    I don't choose to say much upon this head,
        I'm a plain man, and in a single station,
175 But—Oh! ye lords of ladies intellectual,
    Inform us truly, have they not hen-pecked you all?

XXIII

Don José and his lady quarreled—*why,*
    Not any of the many could divine,
Though several thousand people chose to try,
180   'Twas surely no concern of theirs nor mine;
    I loathe that low vice—curiosity;
        But if there's anything in which I shine,
    'Tis in arranging all my friends' affairs,
    Not having of my own domestic cares.

XXIV

185 And so I interfered, and with the best
        Intentions, but their treatment was not kind;
    I think the foolish people were possessed,
        For neither of them could I ever find,
    Although their porter afterwards confessed—
190   But that's no matter, and the worst's behind,
    For little Juan o'er me threw, down stairs,
    A pail of housemaid's water unawares.

XXV

A little curly-headed, good-for-nothing,
    And mischief-making monkey from his birth;
195 His parents ne'er agreed except in doting

Upon the most unquiet imp on earth;
Instead of quarreling, had they been but both in
  Their senses, they'd have sent young master forth
To school, or had him soundly whipped at home,
To teach him manners for the time to come.   *200*

XXVI

Don José and the Donna Inez led
  For some time an unhappy sort of life,
Wishing each other, not divorced, but dead;
  They lived respectably as man and wife,
Their conduct was exceedingly well-bred,   *205*
  And gave no outward signs of inward strife,
Until at length the smothered fire broke out,
And put the business past all kind of doubt.

XXVII

For Inez called some druggists and physicians,
  And tried to prove her loving lord was *mad;*   *210*
But as he had some lucid intermissions,
  She next decided he was only *bad;*
Yet when they asked her for her depositions,
  No sort of explanation could be had,
Save that her duty both to man and God   *215*
Required this conduct—which seemed very odd.

XXVIII

She kept a journal, where his faults were noted,
  And opened certain trunks of books and letters,
All which might, if occasion served, be quoted;
  And then she had all Seville for abettors,   *220*
Besides her good old grandmother (who doted),
  The hearers of her case became repeaters,
Then advocates, inquisitors, and judges,
Some for amusement, others for old grudges.

XXIX

And then this best and weakest woman bore   *225*
  With such serenity her husband's woes,
Just as the Spartan ladies did of yore,
Who saw their spouses killed, and nobly chose

Never to say a word about them more—
230   Calmly she heard each calumny that rose,
And saw *his* agonies with such sublimity,
That all the world exclaimed, "What magnanimity!"

XXX

No doubt this patience, when the world is damning us,
    Is philosophic in our former friends;
235   'Tis also pleasant to be deemed magnanimous,
    The more so in obtaining our own ends;
And what the lawyers call a *"malus animus"*°
    Conduct like this by no means comprehends;
Revenge in person 's certainly no virtue,
240   But then 'tis not *my* fault, if *others* hurt you.

XXXI

And if your quarrels should rip up old stories,
    And help them with a lie or two additional,
I'm not to blame, as you well know—no more is
    Anyone else—they were become traditional;
245   Besides, their resurrection aids our glories
    By contrast, which is what we just were wishing all:
And science profits by this resurrection—
Dead scandals form good subjects for dissection.

XXXII

Their friends had tried at reconciliation,
250   Then their relations, who made matters worse.
('Twere hard to tell upon a like occasion
    To whom it may be best to have recourse—
I can't say much for friend or yet relation):
    The lawyers did their utmost for divorce,
255   But scarce a fee was paid on either side
Before, unluckily, Don José died.

XXXIII

He died: and most unluckily, because,
    According to all hints I could collect

237 **Malus animus** malice aforethought.

From counsel learnèd in those kinds of laws
   (Although their talk's obscure and circumspect),   *260*
His death contrived to spoil a charming cause;
   A thousand pities also with respect
To public feeling, which on this occasion
Was manifested in a great sensation.

XXXIV

But, ah! he died; and buried with him lay   *265*
   The public feeling and the lawyers' fees:
His house was sold, his servants sent away,
   A Jew took one of his two mistresses,
A priest the other—at least so they say:
   I asked the doctors after his disease—   *270*
He died of the slow fever called the tertian,
And left his widow to her own aversion.

XXXV

Yet José was an honorable man,
   That I must say who knew him very well;
Therefore his frailties I'll no further scan   *275*
   Indeed there were not many more to tell;
And if his passions now and then outran
   Discretion, and were not so peaceable
As Numa's° (who was also named Pompilius),
He had been ill brought up, and was born bilious.   *280*

XXXVI

Whate'er might be his worthlessness or worth,
   Poor fellow! he had many things to wound him
Let's own—since it can do no good on earth—
   It was a trying moment that which found him
Standing alone beside his desolate hearth,   *285*
   Where all his household gods lay shivered round
     him:
No choice was left his feelings or his pride,
Save death or Doctors' Commons°—so he died.

279 **Numa** second legendary king of Rome, and a beneficient ruler.
288 **Doctors' Commons** divorce court.

XXXVII

Dying intestate, Juan was sole heir
290   To a chancery suit, and messuages,° and lands,
Which, with a long minority and care,
    Promised to turn out well in proper hands:
Inez became sole guardian, which was fair,
    And answered but to nature's just demands;
295 An only son left with an only mother
Is brought up much more wisely than another.

XXXVIII

Sagest of women, even of widows, she
    Resolved that Juan should be quite a paragon,
And worthy of the noblest pedigree
300   (His sire was of Castile, his dam from Aragon):
Then for accomplishments of chivalry,
    In case our lord the king should go to war again,
He learned the arts of riding, fencing, gunnery,
And how to scale a fortress—or a nunnery.

XXXIX

305 But that which Donna Inez most desired,
    And saw into herself each day before all
The learnèd tutors whom for him she hired,
    Was, that his breeding should be strictly moral:
Much into all his studies she inquired,
310   And so they were submitted first to her, all,
Arts, sciences, no branch was made a mystery
To Juan's eyes, excepting natural history.

XL

The languages, especially the dead,
    The sciences, and most of all the abstruse,
315 The arts, at least all such as could be said
    To be the most remote from common use,
In all these he was much and deeply read;
    But not a page of any thing that's loose,
Or hints continuation of the species,
320 Was ever suffered, lest he should grow vicious.

290 **messuages** estates.

XLI

His classic studies made a little puzzle,
   Because of filthy loves of gods and goddesses,
Who in the earlier ages raised a bustle,
   But never put on pantaloons or bodices;
His reverend tutors had at times a tussle,   *325*
   And for their Aeneids, Iliads, and Odysseys,
Were forced to make an odd sort of apology,
For Donna Inez dreaded the Mythology.

XLII

Ovid's a rake, as half his verses show him,
   Anacreon's morals are a still worse sample,   *330*
Catullus scarcely has a decent poem,
   I don't thing Sappho's Ode a good example,
Although Longinus tells us there is no hymn
   Where the sublime soars forth on wings more
     ample:
But Virgil's songs are pure, except that horrid one°   *335*
Beginning with "Formosum Pastor Corydon."

XLIII

Lucretius' irreligion is too strong,
   For early stomachs, to prove wholesome food;
I can't help thinking Juvenal was wrong,
   Although no doubt his real intent was good,   *340*
For speaking out so plainly in his song,
   So much indeed as to be downright rude;
And then what proper person can be partial
To all those nauseous epigrams of Martial?

XLIV

Juan was taught from out the best edition,   *345*
   Expurgated by learnèd men, who place,
Judiciously, from out the schoolboy's vision,
   The grosser parts; but, fearful to deface
Too much their modest bard by this omission,
   And pitying sore his mutilated case,   *350*
They only add them all in an appendix,
Which saves, in fact, the trouble of an index;

335 **horrid one** Virgil's second *Eclogue*

XLV

For there we have them all "at one fell swoop,"
    Instead of being scattered through the pages;
355 They stand forth marshaled in a handsome troop,
    To meet the ingenuous youth of future ages,
Till some less rigid editor shall stoop
    To call them back into their separate cages,
Instead of standing staring all together,
360 Like garden gods—and not so decent either.

XLVI

The Missal too (it was the family Missal)
    Was ornamented in a sort of way
Which ancient mass-books often are, and this all
    Kinds of grotesques illumined; and how they,
365 Who saw those figures on the margin kiss all,
    Could turn their optics to the text and pray,
Is more than I know—But Don Juan's mother
Kept this herself, and gave her son another.

XLVII

Sermons he read, and lectures he endured,
370   And homilies, and lives of all the saints;
To Jerome and to Chrysostom° inured,
    He did not take such studies for restraints;
But how faith is acquired, and then ensured,
    So well not one of the aforesaid paints
375 As Saint Augustine in his fine *Confessions,*
Which make the reader envy his transgressions.

XLVIII

This, too, was a sealed book to little Juan—
    I can't but say that his mamma was right,
If such an education was the true one.
380   She scarcely trusted him from out her sight;
Her maids were old, and if she took a new one,
    You might be sure she was a perfect fright;
She did this during even her husband's life—
I recommend as much to every wife.

371 **Jerome . . . Chrysostom** Church Fathers.

XLIX

Young Juan waxed in goodliness and grace;   385
   At six a charming child, and at eleven
With all the promise of as fine a face
   As e'er to man's maturer growth was given:
He studied steadily, and grew apace,
   And seemed, at least, in the right road to heaven,   390
For half his days were passed at church, the other
Between his tutors, confessor, and mother.

L

At six, I said, he was a charming child,
   At twelve he was a fine, but quiet boy;
Although in infancy a little wild,   395
   They tamed him down amongst them: to destroy
His natural spirit not in vain they toiled,
   At least it seemed so; and his mother's joy
Was to declare how sage, and still, and steady,
Her young philosopher was grown already.   400

LI

I had my doubts, perhaps I have them still,
   But what I say is neither here nor there:
I knew his father well, and have some skill
   In character— but it would not be fair
From sire to son to augur good or ill: 405
   He and his wife were an ill-sorted pair—
But scandal's my aversion—I protest
Against all evil speaking, even in jest.

LII

For my part I say nothing—nothing—but
   This I will say—my reasons are my own—   410
That if I had an only son to put
   To school (as God be praised that I have none),
'Tis not with Donna Inez I would shut
   Him up to learn his catechism alone,
No—no—I'd send him out betimes to college.   415
For there it was I picked up my own knowledge.

LIII

For there one learns—'tis not for me to boast,
    Though I acquired—but I pass over *that,*
As well as all the Greek I since have lost:
420   I say that there's the place—but *Verbum sat,*°
I think I picked up too, as well as most,
    Knowledge of matters—but no matter *what*—
I never married—but, I think, I know
That sons should not be educated so.

LIV

425   Young Juan now was sixteen years of age,
    Tall, handsome, slender, but well knit: he seemed
Active, though not so sprightly, as a page;
    And everybody but his mother deemed
Him almost man; but she flew in a rage
430   And bit her lips (for else she might have screamed)
If any said so, for to be precocious
Was in her eyes a thing the most atrocious.

LV

Amongst her numerous acquaintance, all
    Selected for discretion and devotion,
435   There was the Donna Julia, whom to call
    Pretty were but to give a feeble notion
Of many charms in her as natural
    As sweetness to the flower, or salt to ocean,
Her zone to Venus, or his bow to Cupid
440   (But this last simile is trite and stupid).

LVI

The darkness of her Oriental eye
    Accorded with her Moorish origin
(Her blood was not all Spanish, by the by;
    In Spain, you know, this is a sort of sin);
445   When proud Granada fell, and, forced to fly,
    Boabdil wept, of Donna Julia's kin
Some went to Africa, some stayed in Spain,
Her great-great-grandmamma chose to remain.

420 **Verbum sat** A word to the wise is sufficient.

LVII

She married (I forget the pedigree)
   With an Hidalgo, who transmitted down   *450*
His blood less noble than such blood should be;
   At such alliances his sires would frown,
In that point so precise in each degree
   That they bred *in and in,* as might be shown,
Marrying their cousins—nay, their aunts, and nieces,   *455*
Which always spoils the breed, if it increases.

LVIII

This heathenish cross restored the breed again,
   Ruined its blood, but much improved its flesh;
For from a root the ugliest in Old Spain
   Sprung up a branch as beautiful as fresh;   *460*
The sons no more were short, the daughters plain:
   But there's a rumor which I fain would hush,
'Tis said that Donna Julia's grandmamma
Produced her Don more heirs at love than law.

LIX

However this might be, the race went on   *465*
   Improving still through every generation,
Until it centered in an only son,
   Who left an only daughter; my narration
May have suggested that this single one
   Could be but Julia (whom on this occasion   *470*
I shall have much to speak about), and she
Was married, charming, chaste, and twenty-three.

LX

Her eye (I'm very fond of handsome eyes)
   Was large and dark, suppressing half its fire
Until she spoke, then through its soft disguise   *475*
   Flashed an expression more of pride than ire,
And love than either; and there would arise
   A something in them which was not desire,
But would have been, perhaps, but for the soul
Which struggled through and chastened down the
     whole.   *480*

LXI

Her glossy hair was clustered o'er a brow
   Bright with intelligence, and fair, and smooth;
Her eyebrow's shape was like th' aerial bow,
   Her cheek all purple with the beam of youth,
485 Mounting at times to a transparent glow,
   As if her veins ran lightning; she, in sooth,
Possessed an air and grace by no means common:
Her stature tall—I hate a dumpy woman.

LXII

Wedded she was some years, and to a man
490   Of fifty, and such husbands are in plenty;
And yet, I think, instead of such a ONE
   'Twere better to have TWO of five-and-twenty,
Especially in countries near the sun:
   And now I think on 't, *mi vien in mente,*°
495 Ladies even of the most uneasy virtue
Prefer a spouse who age is short of thirty.

LXIII

'Tis a sad thing, I cannot choose but say,
   And all the fault of that indecent sun,
Who cannot leave alone our helpless clay,
500   But will keep baking, broiling, burning on,
That howsoever people fast and pray,
   The flesh is frail, and so the soul undone:
What men call gallantry, and gods adultery,
Is much more common where the climate's sultry.

LXIV

505 Happy the nations of the moral North!
   Where all is virtue, and the winter season
Sends sin, without a rag on, shivering forth
   ('Twas snow that brought St. Anthony to reason);
Where juries cast up what a wife is worth,
510   By laying whate'er sum in mulct they please on
The lover, who must pay a handsome price,
Because it is a marketable vice.

494 **"mi vien in mente"** it occurs to me.

LXV

Alfonso was the name of Julia's lord,
  A man well looking for his years, and who
Was neither much beloved nor yet abhorred: *515*
  They lived together, as most people do,
Suffering each other's foibles by accord,
  And not exactly either *one* or *two;*
Yet he was jealous, though he did not show it,
For jealousy dislikes the world to know it.   *520*

LXVI

Julia was—yet I never could see why—
  With Donna Inez quite a favorite friend;
Between their tastes there was small sympathy,
  For not a line had Julia ever penned:
Some people whisper (but no doubt they lie,   *525*
  For malice still imputes some private end)
That Inez had, ere Don Alfonso's marriage,
Forgot with him her very prudent carriage;

LXVII

And that still keeping up the old connection,
  Which time had lately rendered much more chaste,   *530*
She took his lady also in affection,
  And certainly this course was much the best:
She flattered Julia with her sage protection,
  And complimented Don Alfonso's taste;
And if she could not (who can?) silence scandal,   *535*
At least she left it a more slender handle.

LXVIII

I can't tell whether Julia saw the affair
  With other people's eyes, or if her own
Discoveries made, but none could be aware
  Of this, at least no symptom e'er was shown;   *540*
Perhaps she did not know, or did not care,
  Indifferent from the first or callous grown:
I'm really puzzled what to think or say,
She kept her counsel in so close a way.

LXIX

545 Juan she saw, and, as a pretty child,
    Caressed him often—such a thing might be
Quite innocently done, and harmless styled,
    When she had twenty years, and thirteen he;
But I am not so sure I should have smiled
550   When he was sixteen, Julia twenty-three;
These few short years make wondrous alterations,
Particularly amongst sun-burnt nations.

LXX

Whate'er the cause might be, they had become
    Changed; for the dame grew distant, the youth shy,
555 Their looks cast down, their greetings almost dumb,
    And much embarrassment in either eye;
There surely will be little doubt with some
    That Donna Julia knew the reason why,
But as for Juan, he had no more notion
560 Than he who never saw the sea of ocean.

LXXI

Yet Julia's very coldness still was kind,
    And tremulously gentle her small hand
Withdrew itself from his, but left behind
    A little pressure, thrilling, and so bland
565 And slight, so very slight, that to the mind
    'Twas but a doubt; but ne'er magician's wand
Wrought change with all Armida's fairy art°
Like what this light touch left on Juan's heart.

LXXII

And if she met him, though she smiled no more,
570   She looked a sadness sweeter than her smile,
As if her heart had deeper thoughts in store
    She must not own, but cherished more the while
For that compression in its burning core;
    Even innocence itself has many a wile,
575 And will not dare to trust itself with truth,
And love is taught hypocrisy from youth.

567 **Armida's . . . art** the skill of the sorceress in Tasso's *Jerusalem Delivered.*

LXXIII

But passion most dissembles, yet betrays
    Even by its darkness; as the blackest sky
Foretells the heaviest tempest, it displays
    Its workings through the vainly guarded eye,   *580*
And in whatever aspect it arrays
    Itself, 'tis still the same hypocrisy;
Coldness or anger, even disdain or hate,
Are masks it often wears, and still too late.

LXXIV

Then there were sighs, the deeper for suppression,   *585*
    And stolen glances, sweeter for the theft,
And burning blushes, though for no transgression,
    Tremblings when met, and restlessness when left;
All these are little preludes to possession,
    Of which young passion cannot be bereft,   *590*
And merely tend to show how greatly love is
Embarrassed at first starting with a novice.

LXXV

Poor Julia's heart was in an awkward state;
    She felt it going, and resolved to make
The noblest efforts for herself and mate,   *595*
    For honor's, pride's, religion's, virtue's sake;
Her resolutions were most truly great,
    And almost might have made a Tarquin quake:
She prayed the Virgin Mary for her grace,
As being the best judge of a lady's case.   *600*

LXXVI

She vowed she never would see Juan more,
    And next day paid a visit to his mother,
And looked extremely at the opening door,
    Which, by the Virgin's grace, let in another;
Grateful she was, and yet a little sore—   *605*
    Again it opens, it can be no other,
'Tis surely Juan now—No! I'm afraid
That night the Virgin was no further prayed.

LXXVII

She now determined that a virtuous woman
610   Should rather face and overcome temptation,
That flight was base and dastardly, and no man
         Should ever give her heart the least sensation;
That is to say, a thought beyond the common
         Preference, that we must feel upon occasion
615 For people who are pleasanter than others,
But then they only seem so many brothers.

LXXVIII

And even if by chance—and who can tell?
         The devil's so very sly—she should discover
That all within was not so very well,
620   And, if still free, that such or such a lover
Might please perhaps, a virtuous wife can quell
         Such thoughts, and be the better when they're over;
And if the man should ask, 'tis but denial:
I recommend young ladies to make trial.

LXXIX

625 And then there are such things as love divine,
         Bright and immaculate, unmixed and pure,
Such as the angels think so very fine,
         And matrons who would be no less secure,
Platonic, perfect, "just such love as mine";
630   Thus Julia said—and thought so, to be sure;
And so I'd have her think, were I the man
On whom her reveries celestial ran.

LXXX

Such love is innocent, and may exist
         Between young persons without any danger.
635 A hand may first, and then a lip be kist;
         For my part, to such doings I'm a stranger,
But *hear* these freedoms form the utmost list
         Of all o'er which such love may be a ranger:
If people go beyond, 'tis quite a crime,
640 But not my fault—I tell them all in time.

LXXXI

Love, then, but love within its proper limits,
    Was Julia's innocent determination
In young Don Juan's favor, and to him its
    Exertion might be useful on occasion;
And, lighted at too pure a shrine to dim its   *645*
    Ethereal luster, with what sweet persuasion
He might be taught, by love and her together—
I really don't know what, nor Julia either.

LXXXII

Fraught with this fine intention, and well fenced
    In mail of proof—her purity of soul—   *650*
She, for the future of her strength convinced,
    And that her honor was a rock, or mole,
Exceeding sagely from that hour dispensed
    With any kind of troublesome control;
But whether Julia to the task was equal   *655*
Is that which must be mentioned in the sequel.

LXXXIII

Her plan she deemed both innocent and feasible,
    And, surely, with a stripling of sixteen
Not scandal's fangs could fix on much that's seizable,
    Or if they did so, satisfied to mean   *660*
Nothing but what was good, her breast was
    peaceable—
    A quiet conscience makes one so serene!
Christians have burnt each other, quite persuaded
That all the Apostles would have done as they did.

LXXXIV

And if in the meantime her husband died,   *665*
    But Heaven forbid that such a thought should cross
Her brain, though in a dream! (and then she sighed)
    Never could she survive that common loss;
But just suppose that moment should betide,
    I only say suppose it—*inter nos*.   *670*
(This should be *entre nous,* for Julia thought
In French, but then the rhyme would go for naught.)

LXXXV

I only say suppose this supposition:
    Juan being then grown up to man's estate
675 Would fully suit a widow of condition,
    Even seven years hence it would not be too late;
And in the interim (to pursue this vision)
    The mischief, after all, could not be great,
For he would learn the rudiments of love,
680 I mean the seraph way of those above.

LXXXVI

So much for Julia. Now we'll turn to Juan.
    Poor little fellow! he had no idea
Of his own case, and never hit the true one;
    In feelings quick as Ovid's Miss Medea,
685 He puzzled over what he found a new one,
    But not as yet imagined it could be a
Thing quite in course, and not at all alarming,
Which, with a little patience, might grow charming.

LXXXVII

Silent and pensive, idle, restless, slow,
690   His home deserted for the lonely wood,
Tormented with a wound he could not know,
    His, like all deep grief, plunged in solitude:
I'm fond myself of solitude or so,
    But then, I beg it may be understood,
695 By solitude I mean a sultan's, not
A hermit's, with a harem for a grot.

LXXXVIII

"Oh Love! in such a wilderness as this,
    Where transport and security entwine,
Here is the empire of thy perfect bliss,
700   And here thou art a god indeed divine."°
The bard I quote from does not sing amiss,
    With the exception of the second line,
For that same twining "transport and security"
Are twisted to a phrase of some obscurity.

697–700 **"Oh Love . . . divine"** quoted ("from memory" says Byron)
from Thomas Campbell's *Gertrude of Wyoming*.

LXXXIX

The poet meant, no doubt, and thus appeals   705
    To the good sense and senses of mankind,
The very thing which everybody feels,
    As all have found on trial, or may find,
That no one likes to be disturbed at meals
    Or love.—I won't say more about "entwined"   710
Or "transport," as we knew all that before,
But beg "Security" will bolt the door.

XC

Young Juan wandered by the glassy brooks,
    Thinking unutterable things; he threw
Himself at length within the leafy nooks   715
    Where the wild branch of the cork forest grew:
There poets find materials for their books,
    And every now and then we read them through,
So that their plan and prosody are eligible,
Unless, like Wordsworth, they prove unintelligible.   720

XCI

He, Juan (and not Wordsworth), so pursued
    His self-communion with his own high soul,
Until his mighty heart, in its great mood,
    Had mitigated part, though not the whole
Of its disease; he did the best he could   725
    With things not very subject to control,
And turned, without perceiving his condition,
Like Coleridge, into a metaphysician.

XCII

He thought about himself, and the whole earth,
    Of man the wonderful, and of the stars,   730
And how the deuce they ever could have birth;
    And then he thought of earthquakes, and of wars,
How many miles the moon might have in girth,
    Of air-balloons, and of the many bars
To perfect knowledge of the boundless skies;—   735
And then he thought of Donna Julia's eyes.

XCIII

In thoughts like these true wisdom may discern
    Longings sublime, and aspirations high,
Which some are born with, but the most part learn
740   To plague themselves withal, they know not why:
'Twas strange that one so young should thus concern
    His brain about the action of the sky;
If *you* think 'twas philosophy that this did,
I can't help thinking puberty assisted.

XCIV

745 He pored upon the leaves, and on the flowers,
    And heard a voice in all the winds; and then
He thought of wood-nymphs and immortal bowers,
    And how the goddesses came down to men:
He missed the pathway, he forgot the hours,
750   And when he looked upon his watch again,
He found how much old Time had been a winner—
He also found that he had lost his dinner.

XCV

Sometimes he turned to gaze upon his book,
    Boscan, or Garcilasso;°—by the wind
755 Even as the page is rustled while we look,
    So by the poesy of his own mind
Over the mystic leaf his soul was shook,
    As if 'twere one whereon magicians bind
Their spells, and give them to the passing gale,
760 According to some good old woman's tale.

XCVI

Thus would he while his lonely hours away
    Dissatisfied, nor knowing what he wanted;
Nor glowing reverie, nor poet's lay,
    Could yield his spirit that for which it panted,
765 A bosom whereon he his head might lay,
    And hear the heart beat with the love it granted,
With—several other things, which I forget,
Or which, at least, I need not mention yet.

754 Boscan . . . Garcilasso Spanish poets of the sixteenth century.

XCVII

Those lonely walks, and lengthening reveries,
   Could not escape the gentle Julia's eyes;   *770*
She saw that Juan was not at his ease;
   But that which chiefly may, and must surprise,
Is, that the Donna Inez did not tease
   Her only son with question or surmise:
Whether it was she did not see, or would not,   *775*
Or, like all very clever people, could not.

XCVIII

This may seem strange, but yet 'tis very common:
   For instance—gentlemen, whose ladies take
Leave to o'erstep the written rights of woman,
   And break the—Which commandment is 't they
      break?   *780*
(I have forgot the number, and think no man
   Should rashly quote, for fear of a mistake.)
I say, when these same gentlemen are jealous,
They make some blunder, which their ladies tell us.

XCIX

A real husband always is suspicious,   *785*
   But still no less suspects in the wrong place,
Jealous of someone who had no such wishes,
   Or pandering blindly to his own disgrace,
By harboring some dear friend extremely vicious;
   The last indeed's infallibly the case: *790*
And when the spouse and friend are gone off wholly,
He wonders at their vice, and not his folly.

C

Thus parents also are at times short-sighted;
   Though watchful as the lynx, they ne'er discover,
The while the wicked world beholds delighted,   *795*
   Young Hopeful's mistress, or Miss Fanny's lover,
Till some confounded escapade has blighted
   The plan of twenty years, and all is over;
And then the mother cries, the father swears,
And wonders why the devil he got heirs.   *800*

CI

But Inez was so anxious, and so clear
    Of sight, that I must think, on this occasion,
She had some other motive much more near
    For leaving Juan to this new temptation;
805 But what that motive was, I shan't say here;
    Perhaps to finish Juan's education,
Perhaps to open Don Alfonso's eyes,
In case he thought his wife too great a prize.

CII

It was upon a day, a summer's day;—
810   Summer's indeed a very dangerous season,
And so is spring about the end of May;
    The sun, no doubt, is the prevailing reason;
But whatsoe'er the cause is, one may say,
    And stand convicted of more truth than treason,
That there are months which nature grows more
815   merry in—
March has its hares, and May must have its heroine.

CIII

'Twas on a summer's day—the sixth of June:—
    I like to be particular in dates,
Not only of the age, and year, but moon;
820   They are a sort of post-house, where the Fates
Change horses, making history change its tune,
    Then spur away o'er empires and o'er states,
Leaving at last not much besides chronology,
Excepting the post-obits of theology.

CIV

825 'Twas on the sixth of June, about the hour
    Of half-past six—perhaps still nearer seven—
When Julia sate within as pretty a bower
    As e'er held houri in that heathenish heaven
Described by Mahomet, and Anacreon Moore,°
830   To whom the lyre and laurels have been given,

829 **Anacreon Moore** Thomas Moore, Byron's friend, translated the
Greek Anacreontic poems.

With all the trophies of triumphant song—
He won them well, and may he wear them long!

CV

She sate, but not alone; I know not well
   How this same interview had taken place,
And even if I knew, I should not tell—
   People should hold their tongues in any case;
No matter how or why the thing befell,
   But there were she and Juan, face to face—
When two such faces are so, 'twould be wise,
But very difficult, to shut their eyes.

CVI

How beautiful she looked! her conscious heart
   Glowed in her cheek, and yet she felt no wrong.
Oh Love! how perfect is thy mystic art,
   Strengthening the weak, and trampling on the
      strong,
How self-deceitful is the sagest part
   Of mortals whom thy lure hath led along—
The precipice she stood on was immense,
So was her creed in her own innocence.

CVII

She thought of her own strength, and Juan's youth,
   And of the folly of all prudish fears,
Victorious virtue, and domestic truth,
   And then of Don Alfonso's fifty years:
I wish these last had not occurred, in sooth,
   Because that number rarely much endears,
And through all climes, the snowy and the sunny,
Sounds ill in love, whate'er it may in money.

CVIII

When people say, "I've told you *fifty* times,"
   They mean to scold, and very often do;
When poets say, "I've written *fifty* rhymes,"
   They make you dread that they'll recite them too;
In gangs of *fifty*, thieves commit their crimes;

At *fifty* love for love is rare, 'tis true,
But then, no doubt, it equally as true is,
A good deal may be bought for *fifty* Louis.

CIX

865 Julia had honor, virtue, truth, and love,
    For Don Alfonso; and she inly swore,
By all the vows below to powers above,
    She never would disgrace the ring she wore,
Nor leave a wish which wisdom might reprove;
870   And while she pondered this, besides much more,
One hand on Juan's carelessly was thrown,
Quite by mistake—she thought it was her own;

CX

Unconsciously she leaned upon the other,
    Which played within the tangles of her hair:
875 And to contend with thoughts she could not smother
    She seemed by the distraction of her air.
'Twas surely very wrong in Juan's mother
    To leave together this imprudent pair,
She who for many years had watched her son so—
880 I'm very certain *mine* would not have done so.

CXI

The hand which still held Juan's, by degrees
    Gently, but palpably confirmed its grasp,
As if it said, "Detain me, if you please";
    Yet there's no doubt she only meant to clasp
885 His fingers with a pure Platonic squeeze:
    She would have shrunk as from a toad, or asp,
Had she imagined such a thing could rouse
A feeling dangerous to a prudent spouse.

CXII

I cannot know what Juan thought of this,
890   But what he did, is much what you would do;
His young lip thanked it with a grateful kiss,
    And then, abashed at its own joy, withdrew
In deep despair, lest he had done amiss—

Love is so very timid when 'tis new:
She blushed, and frowned not, but she strove to speak,   895
And held her tongue, her voice was grown so weak.

CXIII
The sun set, and up rose the yellow moon:
    The devil's in the moon for mischief; they
Who called her CHASTE, methinks, began too soon
    Their nomenclature; there is not a day,   900
The longest, not the twenty-first of June,
    Sees half the business in a wicked way
On which three single hours of moonshine smile—
And then she looks so modest all the while

CXIV
There is a dangerous silence in that hour,   905
    A stillness, which leaves room for the full soul
To open all itself, without the power
    Of calling wholly back its self-control;
The silver light which, hallowing tree and tower,
    Sheds beauty and deep softness o'er the whole,   910
Breathes also to the heart, and o'er it throws
A loving languor, which is not repose.

CXV
And Julia sate with Juan, half embraced
    And half retiring from the glowing arm,
Which trembled like the bosom where 'twas placed;   915
    Yet still she must have thought there was no harm,
Or else 'twere easy to withdraw her waist;
    But then the situation had its charm,
And then—God knows what next—I can't go on;
I'm almost sorry that I e'er begun.   920

CXVI
Oh Plato! Plato! you have paved the way,
    With your confounded fantasies, to more
Immoral conduct by the fancied sway
    Your system feigns o'er the controlless core
Of human hearts, than all the long array   925

Of poets and romancers:—You're a bore,
A charlatan, a coxcomb—and have been,
At best, no better than a go-between.

CXVII

And Julia's voice was lost, except in sighs,
930   Until too late for useful conversation;
The tears were gushing from her gentle eyes,
    I wish indeed they had not had occasion,
But who, alas! can love, and then be wise?
    Not that remorse did not oppose temptation;
935 A little still she strove, and much repented,
And whispering "I will ne'er consent"—consented.

CXVIII

'Tis said that Xerxes offered a reward
    To those who could invent him a new pleasure:
Methinks the requisition's rather hard,
940   And must have cost his majesty a treasure:
For my part, I'm a moderate-minded bard,
    Fond of a little love (which I call leisure);
I care not for new pleasures, as the old
Are quite enough for me, so they but hold.

CXIX

945 Oh Pleasure! you are indeed a pleasant thing,
    Although one must be damned for you, no doubt:
I make a resolution every spring
    Of reformation, ere the year run out,
But somehow, this my vestal vow takes wing,
950   Yet still, I trust it may be kept throughout:
I'm very sorry, very much ashamed,
And mean, next winter, to be quite reclaimed.

CXX

Here my chaste Muse a liberty must take—
    Start not! still chaster reader—she'll be nice hence-
955 Forward, and there is no great cause to quake;
    This liberty is a poetic license,
Which some irregularity may make
    In the design, and as I have a high sense

Of Aristotle and the Rules, 'tis fit
To beg his pardon when I err a bit.   960

CXXI

This license is to hope the reader will
   Suppose from June the sixth (the fatal day,
Without whose epoch my poetic skill
   For want of facts would all be thrown away),
But keeping Julia and Don Juan still   965
   In sight, that several months have passed; we'll say
'Twas in November, but I'm not so sure
About the day—the era's more obscure.

CXXII

We'll talk of that anon.—'Tis sweet to hear
   At midnight on the blue and moonlit deep   970
The song and oar of Adria's° gondolier,
   By distance mellowed, o'er the waters sweep;
'Tis sweet to see the evening star appear;
   'Tis sweet to listen as the night-winds creep
From leaf to leaf; 'tis sweet to view on high   975
The rainbow, based on ocean, span the sky.

CXXIII

'Tis sweet to hear the watchdog's honest bark
   Bay deep-mouthed welcome as we draw near home;
'Tis sweet to know there is an eye will mark
   Our coming, and look brighter when we come;   980
'Tis sweet to be awakened by the lark,
   Or lulled by falling waters; sweet the hum
Of bees, the voice of girls, the songs of birds,
The lisp of children, and their earliest words.

CXXIV

Sweet is the vintage, when the showering grapes   985
   In Bacchanal profusion reel to earth,
Purple and gushing: sweet are our escapes
   From civic revelry to rural mirth;
Sweet to the miser are his glittering heaps,

971 **Adria's** the Adriatic, thus Venice.

990   Sweet to the father is his first-born's birth,
Sweet is revenge—especially to women,
Pillage to soldiers, prize-money to seamen.

CXXV

Sweet is a legacy, and passing sweet
    The unexpected death of some old lady
995 Or gentleman of seventy years complete,
        Who've made "us youth" wait too—too long already
For an estate, or cash, or country seat,
    Still breaking, but with stamina so steady
That all the Israelites are fit to mob its
1000 Next owner for their double-damned post-obits.

CXXVI

'Tis sweet to win, no matter how, one's laurels,
    By blood or ink; 'tis sweet to put an end
To strife; 'tis sometimes sweet to have our quarrels,
    Particularly with a tiresome friend:
1005 Sweet is old wine in bottles, ale in barrels;
    Dear is the helpless creature we defend
Against the world; and dear the schoolboy spot
We ne'er forget, though there we are forgot.

CXXVII

But sweeter still than this, than these, than all,
1010   Is first and passionate love—it stands alone,
Like Adam's recollection of his fall;
        The tree of knowledge has been plucked—all's known—
And life yields nothing further to recall
    Worthy of this ambrosial sin, so shown,
1015 No doubt in fable, as the unforgiven
Fire which Prometheus filched for us from heaven.

CXXVIII

Man's a strange animal, and makes strange use
    Of his own nature, and the various arts,
And likes particularly to produce

Some new experiment to show his parts;   *1020*
This is the age of oddities let loose,
    Where different talents find their different marts;
You'd best begin with truth, and when you've lost
    your
Labor, there's a sure market for imposture.

CXXIX

What opposite discoveries we have seen!   *1025*
    (Signs of true genius, and of empty pockets.)
One makes new noses, one a guillotine,
    One breaks your bones, one sets them in their
        sockets;
But vaccination certainly has been
    A kind antithesis to Congreve's rockets,°   *1030*
With which the Doctor paid off an old pox,
By borrowing a new one from an ox.

CXXX

Bread has been made (indifferent) from potatoes;
    And galvanism has set some corpses grinning,
But has not answered like the apparatus   *1035*
    Of the Humane Society's beginning
By which men are unsuffocated gratis:
    What wondrous new machines have late been
        spinning!
I said the smallpox has gone out of late;
Perhaps it may be followed by the great.   *1040*

CXXXI

'Tis said the great came from America;
    Perhaps it may set out on its return—
The population there so spreads, they say
    'Tis grown high time to thin it in its turn,
With war, or plague, or famine, any way,   *1045*
    So that civilization they may learn;
And which in ravage the more loathsome evil is—
Their real lues, or our pseudo-syphilis?

1030 **Congreve's rockets** a new kind of explosive artillery shell.

CXXXII

This is the patent-age of new inventions
1050   For killing bodies, and for saving souls,
All propagated with the best intentions;
    Sir Humphry Davy's lantern,° by which coals
Are safely mined for in the mode he mentions,
    Tombuctoo travels, voyages to the Poles,
1055 Are ways to benefit mankind, as true,
Perhaps, as shooting them at Waterloo.

CXXXIII

Man's a phenomenon, one knows not what,
    And wonderful beyond all wondrous measure;
'Tis pity though, in this sublime world, that
1060   Pleasure's a sin, and sometimes sin's a pleasure;
Few mortals know what end they would be at,
    But whether glory, power, or love, or treasure,
The path is through perplexing ways, and when
The goal is gained, we die, you know—and then—

CXXXIV

1065 What then?—I do not know, no more do you—
    And so good night.—Return we to our story:
'Twas in November, when fine days are few,
    And the far mountains wax a little hoary,
And clap a white cape on their mantles blue;
1070   And the sea dashes round the promontory,
And the loud breaker boils against the rock,
And sober suns must set at five o'clock.

CXXXV

'Twas, as the watchmen say, a cloudy night;
    No moon, no stars, the wind was low or loud
1075 By gusts, and many a sparkling hearth was bright
    With the piled wood, round which the family crowd;
There's something cheerful in that sort of light,
    Even as a summer sky 's without a cloud:
I'm fond of fire, and crickets, and all that,
1080 A lobster salad, and champagne, and chat.

1052 **Davy's lantern** the coal miner's safety lamp invented in 1815.

CXXXVI
'Twas midnight—Donna Julia was in bed,
    Sleeping, most probably—when at her door
Arose a clatter might awake the dead,
    If they had never been awoke before,
And that they have been so we all have read,   1085
    And are to be so, at the least, once more;—
The door was fastened, but with voice and fist
First knocks were heard, then "Madam Madam—
    hist!

CXXXVII
"For God's sake, Madam—Madam—here's my master,
    With more than half the city at his back—   1090
Was ever heard of such a curst disaster!
    'Tis not my fault—I kept good watch—Alack!
Do pray undo the bolt a little faster
    They're on the stair just now, and in a crack
Will all be here; perhaps he yet may fly—   1095
Surely the window's not so *very* high!"

CXXXVIII
By this time Don Alfonso was arrived,
    With torches, friends, and servants in great number;
The major part of them had long been wived,
    And therefore paused not to disturb the slumber   1100
Of any wicked woman, who contrived
    By stealth her husband's temples to encumber:
Examples of this kind are so contagious,
Were *one* not punished, *all* would be outrageous.

CXXXIX
I can't tell how, or why, or what suspicion   1105
    Could enter into Don Alfronso's head;
But for a cavalier of his condition
    It surely was exceedingly ill-bred,
Without a word of previous admonition,
    To hold a levee round his lady's bed,   1110
And summon lackeys, armed with fire and sword,
To prove himself the thing he most abhorred.

CXL

Poor Donna Julia, starting as from sleep
　　(Mind—that I do not say—she had not slept),
1115 Began at once to scream, and yawn, and weep;
　　Her maid Antonia, who was an adept,
Contrived to fling the bedclothes in a heap,
　　As if she had just now from out them crept:
I can't tell why she should take all this trouble
1120 To prove her mistress had been sleeping double.

CXLI

But Julia mistress, and Antonia maid,
　　Appeared like two poor harmless women, who
Of goblins, but still more of men afraid,
　　Had thought one man might be deterred by two,
1125 And therefore side by side were gently laid,
　　Until the hours of absence should run through,
And truant husband should return, and say,
"My dear, I was the first who came away."

CXLII

Now Julia found at length a voice, and cried,
1130 　　"In heaven's name, Don Alfonso, what d'ye mean?
Has madness seized you? would that I had died
　　Ere such a monster's victim I had been!
What may this midnight violence betide,
　　A sudden fit of drunkenness or spleen?
1135 Dare you suspect me, whom the thought would kill?
Search, then, the room!"—Alfonso said, "I will."

CXLIII

He searched, *they* searched, and rummaged every-
　　　　where,
　　Closet and clothes' press, chest and window seat,
And found much linen, lace, and several pair
1140 　　Of stockings, slippers, brushes, combs, complete,
With other articles of ladies fair,
　　To keep them beautiful, or leave them neat:
Arras they pricked and curtains with their swords,
And wounded several shutters, and some boards.

CXLIV

Under the bed they searched, and there they found— 1145
   No matter what—it was not that they sought;
They opened windows, gazing if the ground
   Had signs or footmarks, but the earth said naught;
And then they stared each other's faces round:
   'Tis odd, not one of all these seekers thought,   1150
And seems to me almost a sort of blunder,
Of looking *in* the bed as well as under.

CXLV

During this inquisition, Julia's tongue
   Was not asleep—"Yes, search and search," she
      cried,
"Insult on insult heap, and wrong on wrong!   1155
   It was for this that I became a bride!
For this in silence I have suffered long
   A husband like Alfonso at my side;
But now I'll bear no more, nor here remain,
If there be law or lawyers in all Spain.   1160

CXLVI

"Yes, Don Alfonso! husband now no more,
   If ever you indeed deserved the name,
Is 't worthy of your years?—you have threescore—
   Fifty, or sixty, it is all the same—
Is 't wise or fitting, causeless to explore   1165
   For facts against a virtuous woman's fame?
Ungrateful, perjured, barbarous Don Alfonso,
How dare you think your lady would go on so?

CXLVII

"Is it for this I have disdained to hold
   The common privileges of my sex?   1170
That I have chosen a confessor so old
   And deaf, that any other it would vex,
And never once he has had cause to scold,
   But found my very innocence perplex
So much, he always doubted I was married—   1175
How sorry you will be when I've miscarried!

CXLVIII
"Was it for this that no Cortejo° e'er
    I yet have chosen from out the youth of Seville?
Is it for this I scarce went anywhere,
1180   Except to bullfights, mass, play, rout, and revel?
Is it for this, whate'er my suitors were,
    I favored none—nay, was almost uncivil?
Is it for this that General Count O'Reilly,°
Who took Algiers, declares I used him vilely?

CXLIX
1185 "Did not the Italian Musico Cazzani
    Sing at my heart six months at least in vain?
Did not his countryman, Count Corniani,
    Call me the only virtuous wife in Spain?
Were there not also Russians, English, many?
1190   The Count Strongstroganoff I put in pain,
And Lord Mount Coffeehouse, the Irish peer,
Who killed himself for love (with wine) last year.

CL
"Have I not had two bishops at my feet,
    The Duke of Ichar, and Don Fernan Nunez?
1195 And is it thus a faithful wife you treat?
    I wonder in what quarter now the moon is:
I praise your vast forbearance not to beat
    Me also, since the time so opportune is—
Oh, valiant man! with sword drawn and cocked trigger,
1200 Now, tell me, don't you cut a pretty figure?

CLI
"Was it for this you took your sudden journey,
    Under pretense of business indispensable,
With that sublime of rascals your attorney,
    Whom I see standing there, and looking sensible
1205 Of having played the fool? though both I spurn, he

1177 **Cortejo** publicly acknowledged lover. 1183 **O'Reilly** A
Spanish general of Irish descent, he was actually defeated in this
attempt.

Deserves the worst, his conduct's less defensible,
Because, no doubt, 'twas for his dirty fee,
And not from any love to you nor me.

CLII

"If he comes here to take a deposition,
    By all means let the gentleman proceed;   1210
You've made the apartment in a fit condition:
    There's pen and ink for you, sir, when you need—
Let every thing be noted with precision,
    I would not you for nothing should be fee'd—
But, as my maid's undressed, pray turn your spies out." 1215
"Oh!" sobbed Antonia, "I could tear their eyes out."

CLIII

"There is the closet, there the toilet, there
    The antechamber—search them under, over;
There is the sofa, there the great armchair,
    The chimney—which would really hold a lover.   1220
I wish to sleep, and beg you will take care
    And make no further noise, till you discover
The secret cavern of this lurking treasure—
And when 'tis found, let me, too, have that pleasure.

CLIV

"And now, Hidalgo! now that you have thrown   1225
    Doubt upon me, confusion over all,
Pray have the courtesy to make it known
    Who is the man you search for? how d'ye call
Him? what's his lineage? let him but be shown—
    I hope he's young and handsome—is he tall?   1230
Tell me—and be assured, that since you stain
My honor thus, it shall not be in vain.

CLV

"At least, perhaps, he has not sixty years,
    At that age he would be too old for slaughter,
Or for so young a husband's jealous fears   1235
    (Antonia! let me have a glass of water).
I am ashamed of having shed these tears,

They are unworthy of my father's daughter;
My mother dreamed not in my natal hour
1240 That I should fall into a monster's power.

CLVI

"Perhaps 'tis of Antonia you are jealous,
    You saw that she was sleeping by my side
When you broke in upon us with your fellows:
    Look where you please—we've nothing, sir, to hide;
1245 Only another time, I trust, you'll tell us,
    Or for the sake of decency abide
A moment at the door, that we may be
Dressed to receive so much good company.

CLVII

"And now, sir, I have done, and say no more;
1250   The little I have said may serve to show
The guileless heart in silence may grieve o'er
    The wrongs to whose exposure it is slow:
I leave you to your conscience as before,
    'Twill one day ask you *why* you used me so?
1255 God grant you feel not then the bitterest grief!—
Antonia! where's my pocket-handkerchief?"

CLVIII

She ceased, and turned upon her pillow; pale
    She lay, her dark eyes flashing through their tears,
Like skies that rain and lighten; as a veil,
1260   Waved and o'ershading her wan cheek, appears
Her streaming hair; the black curls strive, but fail,
    To hide the glossy shoulder, which uprears
Its snow through all;—her soft lips lie apart,
And louder than her breathing beats her heart.

CLIX

1265 The Senhor Don Alfonso stood confused;
    Antonia bustled round the ransacked room,
And, turning up her nose, with looks abused
    Her master and his myrmidons, of whom
Not one, except the attorney, was amused;

He, like Achates,° faithful to the tomb,   *1270*
So there were quarrels, cared not for the cause,
Knowing they must be settled by the laws.

CLX

With prying snub-nose, and small eyes, he stood,
   Following Antonia's motions here and there,
With much suspicion in his attitude;   *1275*
   For reputations he had little care;
So that a suit or action were made good,
   Small pity had he for the young and fair,
And ne'er believed in negatives, till these
Were proved by competent false witnesses.   *1280*

CLXI

But Don Alfonso stood with downcast looks,
   And, truth to say, he made a foolish figure;
When, after searching in five hundred nooks,
   And treating a young wife with so much rigor,
He gained no point, except some self-rebukes,   *1285*
   Added to those his lady with such vigor
Had poured upon him for the last half hour,
Quick, thick, and heavy—as a thundershower.

CLXII

At first he tried to hammer an excuse,
   To which the sole reply was tears and sobs,   *1290*
And indications of hysterics, whose
   Prologue is always certain throes, and throbs,
Gasps, and whatever else the owners choose:
   Alfonso saw his wife, and thought of Job's;
He saw too, in perspective, her relations,   *1295*
And then he tried to muster all his patience.

CLXIII

He stood in act to speak, or rather stammer,
   But sage Antonia cut him short before
The anvil of his speech received the hammer,
   With "Pray, sir, leave the room, and say no more,   *1300*

1270 **Achates** Aeneas's comrade.

Or madam dies."—Alfonso muttered, "D—n her,"
　　But nothing else, the time of words was o'er;
He cast a rueful look or two, and did,
He knew not wherefore, that which he was bid.

CLXIV

1305 With him retired his *posse comitatus,*
　　The attorney last, who lingered near the door
Reluctantly, still tarrying there as late as
　　Antonia let him—not a little sore
At this most strange and unexplained *hiatus*
1310 　In Don Alfonso's facts, which just now wore
An awkward look; as he revolved the case,
The door was fastened in his legal face.

CLXV

No sooner was it bolted, than—Oh shame!
　　Oh sin! Oh sorrow! and oh womankind!
1315 How can you do such things and keep your fame,
　　Unless this world, and t'other too, be blind?
Nothing so dear as an unfilched good name!
　　But to proceed—for there is more behind:
With much heartfelt reluctance be it said,
1320 Young Juan slipped half-smothered, from the bed.

CLXVI

He had been hid—I don't pretend to say
　　How, nor can I indeed describe the where—
Young, slender, and packed easily, he lay,
　　No doubt, in little compass, round or square;
1325 But pity him I neither must nor may
　　His suffocation by that pretty pair;
'Twere better, sure, to die so, than be shut
With maudlin Clarence° in his Malmsey butt.

CLXVII

And, secondly, I pity not, because
1330 　He had no business to commit a sin,
Forbid by heavenly, fined by human laws,

1328 **Clarence** See *Richard III,* I, IV.

At least 'twas rather early to begin;
But at sixteen the conscience rarely gnaws
  So much as when we call our old debts in
At sixty years, and draw the accounts of evil,   *1335*
And find a deucèd balance with the devil.

CLXVIII
Of his position I can give no notion:
  'Tis written in the Hebrew Chronicle,
How the physicians, leaving pill and potion,
  Prescribed, by way of blister, a young belle,   *1340*
When old King David's blood grew dull in motion,
  And that the medicine answered very well;
Perhaps 'twas in a different way applied,
For David lived, but Juan nearly died.

CLXIX
What's to be done? Alfonso will be back   *1345*
  The moment he has sent his fools away.
Antonia's skill was put upon the rack,
  But no device could be brought into play—
And how to parry the renewed attack?
  Besides, it wanted but few hours of day: *1350*
Antonia puzzled; Julia did not speak,
But pressed her bloodless lip to Juan's cheek.

CLXX
He turned his lip to hers, and with his hand
  Called back the tangles of her wandering hair;
Even then their love they could not all command,   *1355*
  And half forgot their danger and despair:
Antonia's patience now was at a stand—
  "Come, come, 'tis no time now for fooling there,"
She whispered, in great wrath—"I must deposit
This pretty gentleman within the closet: *1360*

CLXXI
"Pray, keep your nonsense for some luckier night—
  Who can have put my master in this mood?
What will become on't—I'm in such a fright,
  The devil's in the urchin, and no good—

1365 Is this a time for giggling? this a plight?
        Why, don't you know that it may end in blood?
    You'll lose your life, and I shall lose my place,
    My mistress all, for that half-girlish face.

CLXXII

    "Had it but been for a stout cavalier
1370   Of twenty-five or thirty (come, make haste)—
    But for a child, what piece of work is here!
        I really, madam, wonder at your taste
    (Come, sir, get in)—my master must be near:
        There, for the present, at the least, he's fast,
1375 And if we can but till the morning keep
    Our counsel—(Juan, mind, you must not sleep)."

CLXXIII

    Now, Don Alfonso entering, but alone,
        Closed the oration of the trusty maid:
    She loitered, and he told her to be gone,
1380   An order somewhat sullenly obeyed;
    However, present remedy was none,
        And no great good seemed answered if she staid:
    Regarding both with slow and sidelong view,
    She snuffed the candle, curtsied, and withdrew.

CLXXIV

1385 Alfonso paused a minute—then begun
        Some strange excuses for his late proceeding;
    He would not justify what he had done,
        To say the best, it was extreme ill-breeding;
    But there were ample reasons for it, none
1390   Of which he specified in this his pleading:
    His speech was a fine sample, on the whole,
    Of rhetoric, which the learned call "rigmarole."

CLXXV

    Julia said naught; though all the while there rose
        A ready answer, which at once enables
1395 A matron, who her husband's foible knows,
        By a few timely words to turn the tables,
    Which, if it does not silence, still must pose—

Even if it should comprise a pack of fables;
'Tis to retort with firmness, and when he
Suspects with *one,* do you reproach with *three.*   1400

CLXXVI

Julia, in fact, had tolerable grounds—
    Alfonso's loves with Inez were well known,
But whether 'twas that one's own guilt confounds—
    But that can't be, as has been often shown,
A lady with apologies abounds;—   1405
    It might be that her silence sprang alone
From delicacy to Don Juan's ear,
To whom she knew his mother's fame was dear.

CLXXVII

There might be one more motive, which makes two;
    Alfonso ne'er to Juan had alluded—   1410
Mentioned his jealousy, but never who
    Had been the happy lover, he concluded,
Concealed amongst his premises; 'tis true,
    His mind the more o'er this its mystery brooded;
To speak of Inez now were, one may say,   1415
Like throwing Juan in Alfonso's way.

CLXXVIII

A hint, in tender cases, is enough;
    Silence is best, besides there is a *tact*
(That modern phrase appears to me sad stuff,
    But it will serve to keep my verse compact)—   1420
Which keeps, when pushed by questions rather rough,
    A lady always distant from the fact.
The charming creatures lie with such a grace,
There's nothing so becoming to the face.

CLXXIX

They blush, and we believe them; at least I   1425
    Have always done so; 'tis of no great use,
In any case, attempting a reply,
    For then their eloquence grows quite profuse;
And when at length they're out of breath, they sigh,

1430   And cast their languid eyes down, and let loose
      A tear or two, and then we make it up;
      And then—and then—and then—sit down and sup.

CLXXX

Alfonso closed his speech, and begged her pardon,
      Which Julia half withheld, and then half granted,
1435 And laid conditions he thought very hard on,
      Denying several little things he wanted:
He stood like Adam lingering near his garden,
      With useless penitence perplexed and haunted,
Beseeching she no further would refuse,
1440 When, lo! he stumbled o'er a pair of shoes.

CLXXXI

A pair of shoes!—what then? not much, if they
      Are such as fit with ladies' feet, but these
(No one can tell how much I grieve to say)
      Were masculine; to see them, and to seize,
1445 Was but a moment's act.—Ah! well-a-day!
      My teeth begin to chatter, my veins freeze—
Alfonso first examined well their fashion,
And then flew out into another passion.

CLXXXII

He left the room for his relinquished sword,
1450   And Julia instant to the closet flew.
"Fly, Juan, fly! for heaven's sake—not a word—
      The door is open—you may yet slip through
The passage you so often have explored—
      Here is the garden key—Fly—fly—Adieu!
1455 Haste—haste! I hear Alfonso's hurrying feet—
Day has not broke—there's no one in the street."

CLXXXIII

None can say that this was not good advice,
      The only mischief was, it came too late;
Of all experience 'tis the usual price,
1460   A sort of income tax laid on by fate:
Juan had reached the room-door in a trice,

And might have done so by the garden gate,
But met Alfonso in his dressing gown,
Who threatened death—so Juan knocked him down.

CLXXXIV

Dire was the scuffle, and out went the light;   1465
   Antonia cried out "Rape!" and Julia "Fire!"
But not a servant stirred to aid the fight.
   Alfonso, pommeled to his heart's desire,
Swore lustily he'd be revenged this night;
   And Juan, too, blasphemed an octave higher;   1470
His blood was up: though young, he was a Tartar,
And not at all disposed to prove a martyr.

CLXXXV

Alfonso's sword had dropped ere he could draw it,
   And they continued battling hand to hand,
For Juan very luckily ne'er saw it;   1475
   His temper not being under great command,
If at that moment he had chanced to claw it,
   Alfonso's days had not been in the land
Much longer.—Think of husbands', lovers' lives!
And how ye may be doubly widows—wives!   1480

CLXXXVI

Alfonso grappled to detain the foe,
   And Juan throttled him to get away,
And blood ('twas from the nose) began to flow;
   At last, as they more faintly wrestling lay,
Juan contrived to give an awkward blow,   1485
   And then his only garment quite gave way;
He fled, like Joseph, leaving it; but there,
I doubt, all likeness ends between the pair.

CLXXXVII

Lights came at length, and men, and maids, who
    found
   An awkward spectacle their eyes before;   1490
Antonia in hysterics, Julia swooned,
   Alfonso leaning, breathless, by the door;

Some half-torn drapery scattered on the ground,
    Some blood, and several footsteps, but no more:
1495 Juan the gate gained, turned the key about,
And liking not the inside, locked the out.

CLXXXVIII
Here ends this canto.—Need I sing, or say,
    How Juan naked, favored by the night,
Who favors what she should not, found his way,
1500   And reached his home in an unseemly plight?
The pleasant scandal which arose next day,
    The nine days' wonder which was brought to light,
And how Alfonso sued for a divorce,
Were in the English newspapers, of course.

CLXXXIX
1505 If you would like to see the whole proceedings,
    The depositions, and the cause at full,
The names of all the witnesses, the pleadings
    Of counsel to nonsuit, or to annul,
There's more than one edition, and the readings
1510   Are various, but they none of them are dull;
The best is that in shorthand ta'en by Gurney,°
Who to Madrid on purpose made a journey.

CXC
But Donna Inez, to divert the train
    Of one of the most circulating scandals
1515 That had for centuries been known in Spain,
    At least since the retirement of the Vandals,
First vowed (and never had she vowed in vain)
    To Virgin Mary several pounds of candles;
And then, by the advice of some old ladies,
1520 She sent her son to be shipped off from Cadiz.

CXCI
She had resolved that he should travel through
    All European climes, by land or sea,
To mend his former morals, and get new,

1511 **Gurney** William Brodie Gurney was a famous shorthand reporter who recorded many eminent English trials.

Especially in France and Italy
(At least this is the thing most people do).   *1525*
   Julia was sent into a convent: she
Grieved, but, perhaps, her feelings may be better
Shown in the following copy of her Letter:—

CXCII
"They tell me 'tis decided; you depart:
   'Tis wise—'tis well, but not the less a pain;   *1530*
I have no further claim on your young heart.
   Mine is the victim, and would be again;
To love too much has been the only art
   I used;—I write in haste, and if a stain
Be on this sheet, 'tis not what it appears;   *1535*
My eyeballs burn and throb, but have no tears.

CXCIII
"I loved, I love you, for this love have lost
   State, station, heaven, mankind's, my own esteem,
And yet cannot regret what it hath cost,
   So dear is still the memory of that dream;   *1540*
Yet, if I name my guilt, 'tis not to boast,
   None can deem harshlier of me than I deem:
I trace this scrawl because I cannot rest—
I've nothing to reproach, or to request.

CXCIV
"Man's love is of man's life a thing apart,   *1545*
   'Tis woman's whole existence; man may range
The court, camp, church, the vessel, and the mart;
   Sword, gown, gain, glory, offer in exchange
Pride, fame, ambition, to fill up his heart,
   And few there are whom these cannot estrange;   *1550*
Men have all these resources, we but one,
To love again, and be again undone.

CXCV
"You will proceed in pleasure, and in pride,
   Beloved and loving many; all is o'er
For me on earth, except some years to hide   *1555*

My shame and sorrow deep in my heart's core;
These I could bear, but cannot cast aside
   The passion which still rages as before—
And so farewell—forgive me, love me—No,
1560 That word is idle now—but let it go.

CXCVI

"My breast has been all weakness, is so yet;
   But still I think I can collect my mind;
My blood still rushes where my spirit's set,
   As roll the waves before the settled wind;
1565 My heart is feminine, nor can forget—
   To all, except one image, madly blind;
So shakes the needle, and so stands the pole,
As vibrates my fond heart to my fixed soul.

CXCVII

"I have no more to say, but linger still,
1570   And dare not set my seal upon this sheet,
And yet I may as well the task fulfill,
   My misery can scarce be more complete:
I had not lived till now, could sorrow kill;
   Death shuns the wretch who fain the blow would
      meet,
1575 And I must even survive this last adieu,
And bear with life, to love and pray for you!"

CXCVIII

This note was written upon gilt-edged paper
   With a neat little crow-quill, slight and new:
Her small white hand could hardly reach the taper,
1580   It trembled as magnetic needles do,
And yet she did not let one tear escape her;
   The seal a sunflower; *"Elle vous suit partout,"*
The motto cut upon a white cornelian;
The wax was superfine, its hue vermilion.

CXCIX

1585 This was Don Juan's earliest scrape; but whether
   I shall proceed with his adventures is

Dependent on the public altogether;
  We'll see, however, what they say to this:
Their favor in an author's cap's a feather,
  And no great mischief's done by their caprice;   *1590*
And if their approbation we experience,
Perhaps they'll have some more about a year hence.

CC

My poem's epic, and is meant to be
  Divided in twelve books; each book containing,
With love, and war, a heavy gale at sea,   *1595*
  A list of ships, and captains, and kings reigning,
New characters; the episodes are three:
  A panoramic view of hell's in training,
After the style of Virgil and of Homer,
So that my name of Epic's no misnomer.   *1600*

CCI

All these things will be specified in time,
  With strict regard to Aristotle's rules,
The *Vade Mecum* of the true sublime,
  Which makes so many poets, and some fools:
Prose poets like blank verse, I'm fond of rhyme,   *1605*
  Good workmen never quarrel with their tools;
I've got new mythological machinery,
And very handsome supernatural scenery.

CCII

There's only one slight difference between
  Me and my epic brethren gone before,   *1610*
And here the advantage is my own, I ween
  (Not that I have not several merits more,
But this will more peculiarly be seen);
  They so embellish, that 'tis quite a bore
Their labyrinth of fables to thread through,   *1615*
Whereas this story's actually true.

CCIII

If any person doubt it, I appeal
  To history, tradition, and to facts,

To newspapers, whose truth all know and feel,
1620   To plays in five, and operas in three acts;
All these confirm my statement a good deal,
        But that which more completely faith exacts
Is that myself, and several now in Seville,
        Saw Juan's last elopement with the devil.

CCIV

1625 If ever I should condescend to prose,
        I'll write poetical commandments, which
Shall supersede beyond all doubt all those
        That went before; in these I shall enrich
My text with many things that no one knows,
1630   And carry precept to the highest pitch:
I'll call the work "Longinus o'er a Bottle,
Or, Every Poet his *own* Aristotle."

CCV

Thou shalt believe in Milton, Dryden, Pope;
        Thou shalt not set up Wordsworth, Coleridge,
            Southey;
1635 Because the first is crazed beyond all hope,
        The second drunk, the third so quaint and mouthy:
With Crabbe it may be difficult to cope,
        And Campbell's Hippocrene is somewhat drouthy:
Thou shalt not steal from Samuel Rogers, nor
1640 Commit—flirtation with the muse of Moore.

CCVI

Thou shalt not covet Mr. Sotheby's Muse,
        His Pegasus, nor anything that's his;°
Thou shalt not bear false witness like "the Blues"°
        (There's one, at least, is very fond of this);
1645 Thou shalt not write, in short, but what I choose:
        This is true criticism, and you may kiss—
Exactly as you please, or not—the rod;
But if you don't, I'll lay it on, by G—d!

1642 **his** William Sotheby, a minor poet and patron.   1643 **Blues**
bluestockings—female intellectuals like Lady Byron.

CCVII

If any person should presume to assert
   This story is not moral, first, I pray,   *1650*
That they will not cry out before they're hurt,
   Then that they'll read it o'er again, and say
(But, doubtless, nobody will be so pert)
   That this is not a moral tale, though gay;
Besides, in Canto Twelfth, I mean to show   *1655*
The very place where wicked people go.

CCVIII

If, after all, there should be some so blind
   To their own good this warning to despise,
Led by some tortuosity of mind,
   Not to believe my verse and their own eyes,   *1660*
And cry that they "the moral cannot find,"
   I tell him, if a clergyman, he lies;
Should captains the remark, or critics, make
They also lie too—under a mistake.

CCIX

The public approbation I expect,   *1665*
   And beg they'll take my word about the moral,
Which I with their amusement will connect
   (So children cutting teeth receive a coral);
Meantime, they'll doubtless please to recollect
   My epical pretensions to the laurel: *1670*
For fear some prudish readers should grow skittish,
I've bribed my grandmother's review—the British.

CCX

I sent it in a letter to the Editor,
   Who thanked me duly by return of post—
I'm for a handsome article his creditor;   *1675*
   Yet, if my gentle Muse he please to roast,
And break a promise after having made it her,
   Denying the receipt of what it cost,
And smear his page with gall instead of honey,
All I can say is—that he had the money.   *1680*

CCXI

I think that with this holy new alliance
    I may ensure the public, and defy
All other magazines of art or science,
    Daily, or monthly, or three-monthly; I
1685 Have not essayed to multiply their clients,
    Because they tell me 'twere in vain to try,
And that the *Edinburgh Review* and *Quarterly*
Treat a dissenting author very martyrly.

CCXII

"*Non ego hoc ferrem calidâ juventâ*
1690   *Consule Planco*," Horace° said, and so
Say I; by which quotation there is meant a
    Hint that some six or seven good years ago
(Long ere I dreamt of dating from the Brenta)
    I was most ready to return a blow,
1695 And would not brook at all this sort of thing
In my hot youth—when George the Third was King.

CCXIII

But now at thirty years my hair is gray
    (I wonder what it will be like at forty?
I thought of a peruke the other day)—
1700   My heart is not much greener; and, in short, I
Have squandered my whole summer while 'twas May,
    And feel no more the spirit to retort; I
Have spent my life, both interest and principal,
And deem not, what I deemed, my soul invincible.

CCXIV

1705 No more—no more—Oh! never more on me
    The freshness of the heart can fall like dew,
Which out of all the lovely things we see
    Extracts emotions beautiful and new,
Hived in our bosoms like the bag o' the bee:
1710   Think'st thou the honey with those objects grew?
Alas! 'twas not in them, but in thy power
To double even the sweetness of a flower.

1690 **Horace** In *Odes* III, xiv. "I should not have put up with this in the heat of my youth under Plancus's consulate."

CCXV

No more—no more—Oh! never more, my heart,
  Canst thou be my sole world, my universe!
Once all in all, but now a thing apart,   *1715*
  Thou canst not be my blessing or my curse:
The illusion's gone forever, and thou art
  Insensible, I trust, but none the worse,
And in thy stead I've got a deal of judgment,
Though heaven knows how it ever found a lodgment.   *1720*

CCXVI

My days of love are over; me no more
  The charms of maid, wife, and still less of widow,
Can make the fool of which they made before—
  In short, I must not lead the life I did do;
The credulous hope of mutual minds is o'er,   *1725*
  The copious use of claret is forbid too,
So for a good old-gentlemanly vice,
I think I must take up with avarice.

CCXVII

Ambition was my idol, which was broken
  Before the shrines of Sorrow, and of Pleasure;   *1730*
And the two last have left me many a token
  O'er which reflection may be made at leisure:
Now, like Friar Bacon's brazen head,° I've spoken,
  "Time is, Time was, Time's past":—a chymic°
    treasure
Is glittering youth, which I have spent betimes—   *1735*
My heart in passion, and my head on rhymes.

CCXVIII

What is the end of Fame? 'tis but to fill
  A certain portion of uncertain paper:
Some liken it to climbing up a hill,
  Whose summit, like all hills, is lost in vapor;   *1740*
For this men write, speak, preach, and heroes kill,

1733 **head** See Robert Greene's play *Friar Bacon and Friar Burgay.*
1734 **chymic** counterfeit.

And bards burn what they call their "midnight
taper,"
To have, when the original is dust,
A name, a wretched picture, and worse bust.

CCXIX

1745 What are the hopes of man? Old Egypt's King
Cheops erected the first pyramid
And largest, thinking it was just the thing
To keep his memory whole, and mummy hid;
But somebody or other rummaging,
1750   Burglariously broke his coffin's lid:
Let not a monument give you or me hopes,
Since not a pinch of dust remains of Cheops.

CCXX

But I, being fond of true philosophy,
Say very often to myself, "Alas!
1755 All things that have been born were born to die,
And flesh (which Death mows down to hay) is
grass;
You've passed your youth not so unpleasantly,
And if you had it o'er again—'twould pass—
So thank your stars that matters are no worse,
1760 And read your Bible, sir, and mind your purse."

CCXXI

But for the present, gentle reader! and
Still gentler purchaser! the bard—that's I—
Must, with permission, shake you by the hand,
And so "Your humble servant, and good-b'ye!"
1765 We meet again, if we should understand
Each other; and if not, I shall not try
Your patience further than by this short sample—
'Twere well if others followed my example.

CCXXII

"Go, little book, from this my solitude!
1770   I cast thee on the waters—go thy ways!
And if, as I believe, thy vein be good,

The world will find thee after many days."
When Southey's read, and Wordsworth understood,
    I can't help putting in my claim to praise—
The four first rhymes are Southey's, every line: *1775*
For God's sake, reader! take them not for mine.

Haidée

(from Canto Two, stanzas 104 216)

CIV

The shore looked wild, without a trace of man,
    And girt by formidable waves; but they
Were mad for land, and thus their course they ran,
    Though right ahead the roaring breakers lay:
A reef between them also now began   *5*
    To show its boiling surf and bounding spray,
But finding no place for their landing better,
They ran the boat for shore—and overset her.

CV

But in his native stream, the Guadalquivir,
    Juan to lave his youthful limbs was wont;   *10*
And having learnt to swim in that sweet river,
    Had often turned the art to some account:
A better swimmer you could scarce see ever,
    He could, perhaps, have passed the Hellespont,
As once (a feat on which ourselves we prided)   *15*
Leander, Mr. Ekenhead, and I did.°

16 **Leander . . . I did** It was with Lieutenant Ekenhead that Byron
swam the Hellespont in 1810. See note to *Written After Swim-
ming from Sestos to Abydos*, p. 45.

CVI

So, here, though faint, emaciated, and stark,
   He buoyed his boyish limbs, and strove to ply
With the quick wave, and gain, ere it was dark,
20   The beach which lay before him, high and dry:
The greatest danger here was from a shark,
   That carried off his neighbor by the thigh;
As for the other two, they could not swim,
So nobody arrived on shore but him.

CVII

25 Nor yet had he arrived but for the oar,
   Which, providentially for him, was washed
Just as his feeble arms could strike no more,
      And the hard wave o'erwhelmed him as 'twas
         dashed
Within his grasp; he clung to it, and sore
30   The waters beat while he thereto was lashed;
At last, with swimming, wading, scrambling, he
Rolled on the beach, half senseless, from the sea:

CVIII

There, breathless, with his digging nails he clung
   Fast to the sand, lest the returning wave,
35 From whose reluctant roar his life he wrung,
   Should suck him back to her insatiate grave:
And there he lay, full length, where he flung,
   Before the entrance of a cliff-worn cave,
With just enough of life to feel its pain,
40 And deem that it was saved, perhaps, in vain.

CIX

With slow and staggering effort he arose,
   But sunk again upon his bleeding knee
And quivering hand; and then he looked for those
   Who long had been his mates upon the sea;
45 But none of them appeared to share his woes,
   Save one, a corpse, from out the famished three,
Who died two days before, and now had found
An unknown barren beach for burial ground.

CX

And as he gazed, his dizzy brain spun fast,
 And down he sunk; and as he sunk, the sand *50*
Swam round and round, and all his senses passed:
 He fell upon his side, and his stretched hand
Drooped dripping on the oar (their jurymast),
 And, like a withered lily, on the land
His slender frame and pallid aspect lay, *55*
As fair a thing as e'er was formed of clay.

CXI

How long in his damp trance young Juan lay
 He knew not, for the earth was gone for him,
And time had nothing more of night nor day
 For his congealing blood, and senses dim; *60*
And how this heavy faintness passed away
 He knew not, till each painful pulse and limb,
And tingling vein, seemed throbbing back to life,
For Death, though vanquished, still retired with strife.

CXII

His eyes he opened, shut, again unclosed, *65*
 For all was doubt and dizziness; he thought
He still was in the boat, and had but dozed,
 And felt again with his despair o'erwrought,
And wished it death in which he had reposed,
 And then once more his feelings back were brought, *70*
And slowly by his swimming eyes was seen
A lovely female face of seventeen.

CXIII

'Twas bending close o'er his, and the small mouth
 Seemed almost prying into his for breath;
And chafing him, the soft warm hand of youth *75*
 Recalled his answering spirits back from death;
And, bathing his chill temples, tried to soothe
 Each pulse to animation, till beneath
Its gentle touch and trembling care, a sigh
To these kind efforts made a low reply. *80*

CXIV

Then was the cordial poured, and mantle flung
    Around his scarce-clad limbs; and the fair arm
Raised higher the faint head which o'er it hung;
    And her transparent cheek, all pure and warm,
85 Pillowed his deathlike forehead; then she wrung
    His dewy curls, long drenched by every storm;
And watched with eagerness each throb that drew
A sigh from his heaved bosom—and hers, too.

CXV

And lifting him with care into the cave,
90   The gentle girl, and her attendant—one
Young, yet her elder, and of brow less grave,
    And more robust of figure—then begun
To kindle fire, and as the new flames gave
    Light to the rocks that roofed them, which the sun
95 Had never seen, the maid, or whatsoe'er
She was, appeared distinct, and tall, and fair.

CXVI

Her brow was overhung with coins of gold,
    That sparkled o'er the auburn of her hair,
Her clustering hair, whose longer locks were rolled
100   In braids behind; and though her stature were
Even of the highest for a female mold,
    They nearly reached her heel; and in her air
There was a something which bespoke command,
As one who was a lady in the land.

CXVII

105 Her hair, I said, was auburn; but her eyes
    Were black as death, their lashes the same hue,
Of downcast length, in whose silk shadow lies
    Deepest attraction; for when to the view
Forth from its raven fringe the full glance flies,
110   Ne'er with such force the swiftest arrow flew;
'Tis as the snake late coiled, who pours his length,
And hurls at once his venom and his strength.

CXVIII

Her brow was white and low, her cheek's pure dye
    Like twilight rosy still with the set sun;
Short upper lip—sweep lips! that make us sigh   *115*
    Ever to have seen such; for she was one
Fit for the model of a statuary
    (A race of mere impostors, when all's done—
I've seen much finer women, ripe and real,
Than all the nonsense of their stone ideal).   *120*

CXIX

I'll tell you why I say so, for 'tis just
    One should not rail without a decent cause:
There was an Irish lady, to whose bust
    I ne'er saw justice done, and yet she was
A frequent model; and if e'er she must   *125*
    Yield to stern Time and Nature's wrinkling laws,
They will destroy a face which mortal thought
Ne'er compassed, nor less mortal chisel wrought.

CXX

And such was she, the lady of the cave:
    Her dress was very different from the Spanish,   *130*
Simpler, and yet of colors not so grave;
    For, as you know, the Spanish women banish
Bright hues when out of doors, and yet, while wave
    Around them (what I hope will never vanish)
The basquina and the mantilla, they   *135*
Seem at the same time mystical and gay.

CXXI

But with our damsel this was not the case:
    Her dress was many-colored, finely spun;
Her locks curled negligently round her face,
    But through them gold and gems profusely shone,   *140*
Her girdle sparkled, and the richest lace
    Flowed in her veil, and many a precious stone
Flashed on her little hand; but, what was shocking,
Her small snow feet had slippers, but no stocking.

CXXII

145 The other female's dress was not unlike,
      But of inferior materials: she
Had not so many ornaments to strike,
      Her hair had silver only, bound to be
Her dowry; and her veil, in form alike,
150   Was coarser; and her air, though firm, less free;
Her hair was thicker, but less long; her eyes
As black, but quicker, and of smaller size.

CXXIII

And these two tended him, and cheered him both
      With food and raiment, and those soft attentions,
155 Which are—(as I must own)—of female growth,
      And have ten thousand delicate inventions:
They made a most superior mess of broth,
      A thing which poesy but seldom mentions,
But the best dish that e'er was cooked since Homer's
160 Achilles ordered dinner° for new comers.

CXXIV

I'll tell you who they were, this female pair,
      Lest they should seem princesses in disguise;
Besides, I hate all mystery, and that air
      Of claptrap, which your recent poets prize;
165 And so, in short, the girls they really were
      They shall appear before your curious eyes,
Mistress and maid; the first was only daughter
Of an old man, who lived upon the water.

CXXV

A fisherman he had been in his youth,
170   And still a sort of fisherman was he;
But other speculations were, in sooth,
      Added to his connection with the sea,
Perhaps not so respectable, in truth:
      A little smuggling, and some piracy,

160 **Achilles . . . dinner** In Book IX of the *Iliad*, Achilles feasted
Ajax, Ulysses, and Phoenix.

Left him, at last, the sole of many masters   *175*
Of an ill-gotten million of piasters.°

CXXVI

A fisher, therefore, was he—though of men,
  Like Peter the Apostle—and he fished
For wandering merchant vessels, now and then,
  And sometimes caught as many as he wished;   *180*
The cargoes he confiscated, and gain
  He sought in the slave-market too, and dished
Full many a morsel for that Turkish trade,
By which, no doubt, a good deal may be made.

CXXVII

He was a Greek, and on his isle had built   *185*
  (One of the wild and smaller Cyclades)°
A very handsome house from out his guilt,
  And there he lived exceedingly at ease;
Heaven knows what cash he got or blood he spilt,
  A sad old fellow was he, if you please;   *190*
But this I know, it was a spacious building,
Full of barbaric carving, paint, and gilding.

CXXVIII

He had an only daughter, called Haidée,
  The greatest heiress of the Eastern Isles;
Besides, so very beautiful was she,   *195*
  Her dowry was as nothing to her smiles:
Still in her teens, and like a lovely tree
  She grew to womanhood, and between whiles
Rejected several suitors, just to learn
How to accept a better in his turn.   *200*

CXXIX

And walking out upon the beach, below
  The cliff, towards sunset, on that day she found,
Insensible—not dead, but nearly so—
  Don Juan, almost famished, and half drowned;
But being naked, she was shocked, you know,   *205*

---

175 **piasters** small coins.   186 **Cyclades** Aegean islands.

Yet deemed herself in common pity bound,
As far as in her lay, "to take him in,
A stranger" dying, with so white a skin.

CXXX

But taking him into her father's house
210   Was not exactly the best way to save,
But like conveying to the cat the mouse,
　　Or people in a trance into their grave;
Because the good old man had so much νοῦς,°
　　Unlike the honest Arab thieves so brave,
215　He would have hospitably cured the stranger
And sold him instantly when out of danger.

CXXXI

And therefore, with her maid, she thought it best
　　(A virgin always on her maid relies)
To place him in the cave for present rest:
220　And when, at last, he opened his black eyes,
Their charity increased about their guest;
　　And their compassion grew to such a size,
It opened half the turnpike gates to heaven—
(St. Paul says,° 'tis the toll which must be given).

CXXXII

225　They made a fire—but such a fire as they
　　Upon the moment could contrive with such
Materials as were cast up round the bay—
　　Some broken planks, and oars, that to the touch
Were nearly tinder, since so long they lay
230　A mast was almost crumbled to a crutch;
But, by God's grace, here wrecks were in such plenty,
That there was fuel to have furnished twenty.

CXXXIII

He had a bed of furs, and a pelisse,°
　　For Haidée stripped her sables off to make
235　His couch; and, that he might be more at ease,

213 νοῦς "mind."   224 **St. Paul says** In I Corinthians 13.
233 **pelisse** a capacious cloak.

And warm, in case by chance he should awake,
They also gave a petticoat apiece,
    She and her maid—and promised by daybreak
To pay him a fresh visit, with a dish
For breakfast, of eggs, coffee, bread, and fish.   *240*

CXXXIV

And thus they left him to his lone repose:
    Juan slept like a top, or like the dead,
Who sleep at last, perhaps (God only knows),
    Just for the present; and in his lulled head
Not even a vision of his former woes   *245*
    Throbbed in accursèd dreams, which sometimes
      spread
Unwelcome visions of our former years,
Till the eye, cheated, opens thick with tears.

CXXXV

Young Juan slept all dreamless:—but the maid,
    Who smoothed his pillow, as she left the den   *250*
Looked back upon him, and a moment staid,
    And turned, believing that he called again.
He slumbered; yet she thought, at least she said
    (The heart will slip, even as the tongue and pen),
He had pronounced her name—but she forgot   *255*
That at this moment Juan knew it not.

CXXXVI

And pensive to her father's house she went,
    Enjoining silence strict to Zoe, who
Better than her knew what, in fact, she meant,
    She being wiser by a year or two: *260*
A year or two's an age when rightly spent,
    And Zoe spent hers, as most women do,
In gaining all that useful sort of knowledge
Which is acquired in Nature's good old college.

CXXXVII

The morn broke, and found Juan slumbering still   *265*
    Fast in his cave, and nothing clashed upon

His rest; the rushing of the neighboring rill,
  And the young beams of the excluded sun,
Troubled him not, and he might sleep his fill;
270   And need he had of slumber yet, for none
Had suffered more—his hardships were comparative
To those related in my grand-dad's° "Narrative."

CXXXVIII

Not so Haidée: she sadly tossed and tumbled,
  And started from her sleep, and, turning o'er
Dreamed of a thousand wrecks, o'er which she
275   stumbled,
  And handsome corpses strewed upon the shore;
And woke her maid so early that she grumbled,
  And called her father's old slaves up, who swore
In several oaths—Armenian, Turk, and Greek—
280 They knew not what to think of such a freak.

CXXXIX

But up she got, and up she made them get,
  With some pretense about the sun, that makes
Sweet skies just when he rises, or is set;
  And 'tis, no doubt, a sight to see when breaks
285 Bright Phoebus, while the mountains still are wet
  With mist, and every bird with him awakes,
And night is flung off like a mourning suit
Worn for a husband—or some other brute.

CXL

I say, the sun is a most glorious sight:
290   I've seen him rise full oft, indeed of late
I have sat up on purpose all the night,
  Which hastens, as physicians say, one's fate;
And so all ye, who would be in the right
  In health and purse, begin your day to date
295 From daybreak, and when coffined at fourscore,
Engrave upon the plate, you rose at four.

272 **grand-dad** Commodore John Byron's account of a round-the-world expedition and its adversities, published 1768.

CXLI

And Haidée met the morning face to face;
   Her own was freshest, though a feverish flush
Had dyed it with the headlong blood, whose race
   From heart to cheek is curbed into a blush,   *300*
Like to a torrent which a mountain's base,
   That overpowers some Alpine river's rush,
Checks to a lake, whose waves in circles spread;
Or the Red Sea—but the sea is not red.

CXLII

And down the cliff the island virgin came,   *305*
   And near the cave her quick light footsteps drew,
While the sun smiled on her with his first flame,
   And young Aurora° kissed her lips with dew,
Taking her for a sister; just the same
   Mistake you would have made on seeing the two,   *310*
Although the mortal, quite as fresh and fair,
Had all the advantage, too, of not being air.

CXLIII

And when into the cavern Haidée stepped
   All timidly, yet rapidly, she saw
That like an infant Juan sweetly slept;   *315*
   And then she stopped, and stood as if in awe
(For sleep is awful), and on tiptoe crept
   And wrapped him closer, lest the air, too raw,
Should reach his blood, then o'er him still as death
Bent, with hushed lips, that drank his scarce-drawn
    breath.   *320*

CXLIV

And thus like to an angel o'er the dying
   Who die in righteousness, she leaned; and there
All tranquilly the shipwrecked boy was lying,
   As o'er him lay the calm and stirless air:
But Zoe the meantime some eggs was frying,   *325*
   Since, after all, no doubt the youthful pair

308 **Aurora** dawn.

Must breakfast, and betimes—lest they should ask it,
She drew out her provision from the basket.

CXLV

She knew that the best feelings must have victual,
330 And that a shipwrecked youth would hungry be;
Besides, being less in love, she yawned a little,
    And felt her veins chilled by the neighboring sea;
And so, she cooked their breakfast to a tittle;
    I can't say that she gave them any tea,
335 But there were eggs, fruit, coffee, bread, fish, honey,
With Scio wine—and all for love, not money.

CXLVI

And Zoe, when the eggs were ready, and
    The coffee made, would fain have wakened Juan;
But Haidée stopped her with her quick small hand,
340 And without word, a sign her finger drew on
Her lip, which Zoe needs must understand;
    And, the first breakfast spoiled, prepared a new one,
Because her mistress would not let her break
That sleep which seemed as it would ne'er awake.

CXLVII

345 For still he lay, and on his thin worn cheek
    A purple hectic played like dying day
On the snow-tops of distant hills; the streak
    Of sufferance yet upon his forehead lay,
Where the blue veins looked shadowy, shrunk, and
        weak;
350 And his black curls were dewy with the spray,
Which weighed upon them yet, all damp and salt,
Mixed with the stony vapors of the vault.

CXLVIII

And she bent o'er him, and he lay beneath,
    Hushed as the babe upon its mother's breast,
355 Drooped as the willow when no winds can breathe,
    Lulled like the depth of ocean when at rest,
Fair as the crowning rose of the whole wreath,

Soft as the callow cygnet in its nest;
In short, he was a very pretty fellow,
Although his woes had turned him rather yellow.   *360*

CXLIX

He woke and gazed, and would have slept again,
    But the fair face which met his eyes forbade
Those eyes to close, though weariness and pain
    Had further sleep a further pleasure made;
For woman's face was never formed in vain   *365*
    For Juan, so that even when he prayed
He turned from grisly saints, and martyrs hairy,
To the sweet portraits of the Virgin Mary.

CL

And thus upon his elbow he arose,
    And looked upon the lady, in whose cheek   *370*
The pale contended with the purple rose,
    As with an effort she began to speak;
Her eyes were eloquent, her words would pose,
    Although she told him, in good modern Greek,
With an Ionian accent, low and sweet,   *375*
That he was faint, and must not talk, but eat.

CLI

Now Juan could not understand a word,
    Being no Grecian; but he had an ear,
And her voice was the warble of a bird,
    So soft, so sweet, so delicately clear,   *380*
That finer, simpler music ne'er was heard;
    The sort of sound we echo with a tear,
Without knowing why—an overpowering tone,
Whence melody descends as from a throne.

CLII

And Juan gazed as one who is awoke   *385*
    By a distant organ, doubting if he be
Not yet a dreamer, till the spell is broke
    By the watchman, or some such reality,
Or by one's early valet's cursed knock;

390   At least it is a heavy sound to me,
Who like a morning slumber—for the night
Shows stars and women in a better light.

CLIII

And Juan, too, was helped out from his dream,
    Or sleep, or whatsoe'er it was, by feeling
395 A most prodigious appetite: the steam
    Of Zoe's cookery no doubt was stealing
Upon his senses, and the kindling beam
    Of the new fire, which Zoe kept up, kneeling,
To stir her viands, made him quite awake
400 And long for food, but chiefly a beefsteak.

CLIV

But beef is rare within these oxless isles;
    Goat's flesh there is, no doubt, and kid, and mutton,
And, when a holiday upon them smiles,
    A joint upon their barbarous spits they put on:
405 But this occurs but seldom, between whiles,
    For some of these are rocks with scarce a hut on;
Others are fair and fertile, among which
This, though not large, was one of the most rich.

CLV

I say that beef is rare, and can't help thinking
410   That the old fable of the Minotaur—
From which our modern morals, rightly shrinking,
    Condemn the royal lady's taste who wore
A cow's shape for a mask—was only (sinking
    The allegory) a mere type, no more,
415 That Pasiphae° promoted breeding cattle,
To make the Cretans bloodier in battle.

CLVI

For we all know that English people are
    Fed upon beef—I won't say much of beer,
Because 'tis liquor only, and being far

415 **Pasiphae** wife of King Minos of Crete, upon whom Zeus
fathered the Minotaur, half-bull, half-human.

From this my subject, has no business here;   420
We know, too, they are very fond of war,
    A pleasure—like all pleasures—rather dear;
So were the Cretans—from which I infer
That beef and battles both were owing to her.

CLVII

But to resume. The languid Juan raised   425
    His head upon his elbow, and he saw
A sight on which he had not lately gazed,
    As all his latter meals had been quite raw,
Three or four things, for which the Lord he praised,
    And, feeling still the famished vulture gnaw,   430
He fell upon whate'er was offered, like
A priest, a shark, an alderman, or pike.

CLVIII

He ate, and he was well supplied: and she,
    Who watched him like a mother, would have fed
Him past all bounds, because she smiled to see   435
    Such appetite in one she had deemed dead:
But Zoe, being older than Haidée,
    Knew (by tradition, for she ne'er had read)
That famished people must be slowly nursed,
And fed by spoonfuls, else they always burst.   440

CLIX

And so she took the liberty to state,
    Rather by deeds than words, because the case
Was urgent, that the gentleman, whose fate
    Had made her mistress quit her bed to trace
The seashore at this hour, must leave his plate,   445
    Unless he wished to die upon the place—
She snatched it, and refused another morsel,
Saying, he had gorged enough to make a horse ill.

CLX

Next they—he being naked, save a tattered
    Pair of scarce decent trousers—went to work,   450
And in the fire his recent rags they scattered,

And dressed him, for the present, like a Turk,
Or Greek—that is, although it not much mattered,
    Omitting turban, slippers, pistols, dirk—
455 They furnished him, entire, except some stitches,
With a clean shirt, and very spacious breeches.

CLXI

And then fair Haidée tried her tongue at speaking,
    But not a word could Juan comprehend,
Although he listened so that the young Greek in
460   Her earnestness would ne'er have made an end;
And, as he interrupted not, went eking
    Her speech out to her protégé and friend,
Till pausing at the last her breath to take,
She saw he did not understand Romaic.°

CLXII

465 And then she had recourse to nods, and signs,
    And smiles, and sparkles of the speaking eye,
And read (the only book she could) the lines
    Of his fair face, and found, by sympathy,
The answer eloquent, where the soul shines
470   And darts in one quick glance a long reply;
And thus in every look she saw expressed
A world of words, and things at which she guessed.

CLXIII

And now, by dint of fingers and of eyes,
    And words repeated after her, he took
475 A lesson in her tongue; but by surmise,
    No doubt, less of her language than her look:
As he who studies fervently the skies
    Turns oftener to the stars than to his book,
Thus Juan learned his alpha beta better
480 From Haidée's glance than any graven letter.

CLXIV

'Tis pleasing to be schooled in a strange tongue
    By female lips and eyes—that is, I mean,

464 **Romaic** demotic, or modern Greek.

When both the teacher and the taught are young,
    As was the case, at least, where I have been;
They smile so when one's right, and when one's
      wrong   485
    They smile still more, and then there intervene
Pressure of hands, perhaps even a chaste kiss;—
I learned the little that I know by this:

CLXV

That is, some words of Spanish, Turk, and Greek,
    Italian not at all, having no teachers;   490
Much English I cannot pretend to speak,
    Learning that language chiefly from its preachers,
Barrow, South, Tillotson, whom every week
    I study, also Blair,° the highest reachers
Of eloquence in piety and prose—   495
I hate your poets, so read none of those.

CLXVI

As for the ladies, I have naught to say,
    A wanderer from the British world of fashion,
Where I, like other "dogs, have had my day,"
    Like other men, too, may have had my passion—   500
But that, like other things, has passed away,
    And all her fools whom I *could* lay the lash on:
Foes, friends, men, women, now are naught to me
But dreams of what has been, no more to be.

CLXVII

Return we to Don Juan. He begun   505
    To hear new words, and to repeat them; but
Some feelings, universal as the sun,
    Were such as could not in his breast be shut
More than within the bosom of a nun:
    He was in love—as you would be, no doubt,   510
With a young benefactress—so was she,
Just in the way we very often see.

493-4 **Barrow . . . Blair** These were all seventeenth-century theologians, save for Hugh Blair, who wrote on rhetoric.

CLXVIII

And every day by daybreak—rather early
    For Juan, who was somewhat fond of rest—
515 She came into the cave, but it was merely
    To see her bird reposing in his nest;
And she would softly stir his locks so curly,
    Without disturbing her yet slumbering guest,
Breathing all gently o'er his cheek and mouth,
520 As o'er a bed of roses the sweet south.

CLXIX

And every morn his color freshlier came,
    And every day helped on his convalescence;
'Twas well, because health in the human frame
    Is pleasant, besides being true love's essence,
525 For health and idleness to passion's flame
    Are oil and gunpowder; and some good lessons
Are also learnt from Ceres and from Bacchus,
Without whom Venus will not long attack us.

CLXX

While Venus fills the heart (without heart really
530   Love, though good always, is not quite so good),
Ceres° presents a plate of vermicelli—
    For love must be sustained like flesh and blood
While Bacchus pours out wine, or hands a jelly:
    Eggs, oysters, too, are amatory food;
535 But who is their purveyor from above
Heaven knows—it may be Neptune, Pan, or Jove.

CLXXI

When Juan woke he found some good things ready,
    A bath, a breakfast, and the finest eyes
That ever made a youthful heart less steady,
540   Besides her maid's, as pretty for their size;
But I have spoken of all this already—
    And repetition's tiresome and unwise—
Well—Juan, after bathing in the sea,
Came always back to coffee and Haidée.

531 **Ceres** as goddess of grain.

CLXXII

Both were so young, and one so innocent,   545
   That bathing passed for nothing; Juan seemed
To her, as 'twere, the kind of being sent,
   Of whom these two years she had nightly dreamed,
A something to be loved, a creature meant
   To be her happiness, and whom she deemed   550
To render happy; all who joy would win
Must share it—Happiness was born a twin.

CLXXIII

It was such pleasure to behold him, such
   Enlargement of existence to partake
Nature with him, to thrill beneath his touch,   555
   To watch him slumbering, and to see him wake:
To live with him forever were too much;
   But then the thought of parting made her quake:
He was her own, her ocean-treasure, cast
Like a rich wreck—her first love, and her last.   560

CLXXIV

And thus a moon rolled on, and fair Haidée
   Paid daily visits to her boy, and took
Such plentiful precautions, that still he
   Remained unknown within his craggy nook;
At last her father's prows put out to sea,   565
   For certain merchantmen upon the look,
Not as of yore to carry off an Io,°
But three Ragusan vessels bound for Scio.°

CLXXV

Then came her freedom, for she had no mother,
   So that, her father being at sea, she was   570
Free as a married woman, or such other
   Female, as where she likes may freely pass,
Without even the encumbrance of a brother,
   The freest she that ever gazed on glass:

567 **Io** loved by Zeus, hated by Hera, carried off by Phoenician
merchants.   568 **Ragusan . . . Scio** Ragusa is Dubrovnik; Scio is the
Italian name for the island of Chios.

575 I speak of Christian lands in this comparison,
   Where wives, at least, are seldom kept in garrison.

CLXXVI
Now she prolonged her visits and her talk
   (For they must talk), and he had learnt to say
So much as to propose to take a walk—
580   For little had he wandered since the day
On which, like a young flower snapped from the stalk,
   Drooping and dewy on the beach he lay—
And thus they walked out in the afternoon,
And saw the sun set opposite the moon.

CLXXVII
585 It was a wild and breaker-beaten coast,
   With cliffs above, and a broad sandy shore,
Guarded by shoals and rocks as by an host,
   With here and there a creek, whose aspect wore
A better welcome to the tempest-tost;
590   And rarely ceased the haughty billow's roar,
Save on the dead long summer days, which make
The outstretched ocean glitter like a lake.

CLXXVIII
And the small ripple spilt upon the beach
   Scarcely o'erpassed the cream of your champagne,
595 When o'er the brim the sparkling bumpers reach,
   That spring-dew of the spirit! the heart's rain!
Few things surpass old wine; and they may preach
   Who please—the more because they preach in
      vain—
Let us have wine and woman, mirth and laughter,
600 Sermons and soda-water the day after.

CLXXIX
Man, being reasonable, must get drunk;
   The best of life is but intoxication:
Glory, the grape, love, gold, in these are sunk
   The hopes of all men, and of every nation;
605 Without their sap, how branchless were the trunk

Of life's strange tree, so fruitful on occasion:
But to return—Get very drunk; and when
You wake with headache, you shall see what then.

CLXXX

Ring for your valet—bid him quickly bring
    Some hock and soda water, then you'll know   *610*
A pleasure worthy Xerxes the great king;
    For not the blest sherbèt, sublimed with snow,
Nor the first sparkle of the desert spring,
    Nor Burgundy in all its sunset glow,
After long travel, ennui, love, or slaughter,   *615*
Vie with that draught of hock and soda water.

CLXXXI

The coast—I think it was the coast that I
    Was just describing Yes, it *was* the coast—
Lay at this period quiet as the sky,
    The sands untumbled, the blue waves untossed   *620*
And all was stillness, save the sea-bird's cry,
    And dolphin's leap, and little billow crossed
By some low rock or shelve, that made it fret
Against the boundary it scarcely wet.

CLXXXII

And forth they wandered, her sire being gone,   *625*
    As I have said, upon an expedition;
And mother, brother, guardian, she had none,
    Save Zoe, who, although with due precision
She waited on her lady with the sun,
    Thought daily service was her only mission,   *630*
Bringing warm water, wreathing her long tresses,
And asking now and then for cast-off dresses.

CLXXXIII

It was the cooling hour, just when the rounded
    Red sun sinks down behind the azure hill,
Which then seems as if the whole earth it bounded,   *635*
    Circling all nature, hushed, and dim, and still,
With the far mountain-crescent half surrounded

On one side, and the deep sea calm and chill
Upon the other, and the rosy sky,
640 With one star sparkling through it like an eye.

CLXXXIV

And thus they wandered forth, and hand in hand,
  Over the shining pebbles and the shells,
Glided along the smooth and hardened sand,
  And in the worn and wild receptacles
645 Worked by the storms, yet worked as it were planned,
  In hollow halls, with sparry roofs and cells,
They turned to rest; and, each clasped by an arm,
Yielded to the deep twilight's purple charm.

CLXXXV

They looked up to the sky, whose floating glow
650   Spread like a rosy ocean, vast and bright;
They gazed upon the glittering sea below,
  Whence the broad moon rose circling into sight;
They heard the waves splash, and the wind so low,
  And saw each other's dark eyes darting light
655 Into each other—and, beholding this,
Their lips drew near, and clung into a kiss;

CLXXXVI

A long, long kiss, a kiss of youth, and love,
  And beauty, all concentrating like rays
Into one focus, kindled from above;
660   Such kisses as belong to early days,
Where heart, and soul, and sense, in concert move,
  And the blood's lava, and the pulse a blaze,
Each kiss a heart-quake—for a kiss's strength,
I think, it must be reckoned by its length.

CLXXXVII

665 By length I mean duration; theirs endured
    Heaven knows how long—no doubt they never
      reckoned;
  And if they had, they could not have secured
    The sum of their sensations to a second:

They had not spoken; but they felt allured,
    As if their souls and lips each other beckoned,   *670*
Which, being joined, like swarming bees they clung—
Their hearts the flowers from whence the honey
      sprung.

CLXXXVIII

They were alone, but not alone as they
    Who shut in chambers think it loneliness;
The silent ocean, and the starlight bay,   *675*
    The twilight glow, which momently grew less,
The voiceless sands, and dropping caves, that lay
    Around them, made them to each other press,
As if there were no life beneath the sky
Save theirs, and that their life could never die.   *680*

CLXXXIX

They feared no eyes nor ears on that lone beach,
    They felt no terrors from the night, they were
All in all to each other: though their speech
    Was broken words, they *thought* a language there—
And all the burning tongues the passions teach   *685*
    Found in one sign the best interpreter
Of nature's oracle—first love—that all
Which Eve has left her daughters since her fall.

CXC

Haidée spoke not of scruples, asked no vows,
    Nor offered any; she had never heard   *690*
Of plight and promises to be a spouse,
    Or perils by a loving maid incurred;
She was all which pure ignorance allows,
    And flew to her young mate like a young bird;
And never having dreamt of falsehood, she   *695*
Had not one word to say of constancy.

CXCI

She loved, and was belovèd—she adored,
    And she was worshiped; after nature's fashion,
Their intense soul, into each other poured,

700   If souls could die, had perished in that passion—
     But by degrees their senses were restored,
         Again to be o'ercome, again to dash on;
     And, beating 'gainst *his* bosom, Haidée's heart
     Felt as if never more to beat apart.

     CXCII

705 Alas! they were so young, so beautiful,
         So lonely, loving, helpless, and the hour
     Was that in which the heart is always full,
         And, having o'er itself no further power,
     Prompts deeds eternity cannot annul,
710   But pays off moments in an endless shower
     Of hell-fire—all prepared for people giving
     Pleasure or pain to one another living.

     CXCIII

     Alas! for Juan and Haidée! they were
         So loving and so lovely—till then never,
715 Excepting our first parents, such a pair
         Had run the risk of being damned forever;
     And Haidée, being devout as well as fair,
         Had, doubtless, heard about the Stygian river,
     And hell and purgatory—but forgot
720 Just in the very crisis she should not.

     CXCIV

     They look upon each other, and their eyes
         Gleam in the moonlight; and her white arm clasps
     Round Juan's head, and his around her lies
         Half buried in the tresses which it grasps;
725 She sits upon his knee, and drinks his sighs,
         He hers, until they end in broken gasps;
     And thus they form a group that's quite antique,
     Half naked, loving, natural, and Greek.

     CXCV

     And when those deep and burning moments passed,
730   And Juan sunk to sleep within her arms,
     She slept not, but all tenderly, though fast,

Sustained his head upon her bosom's charms;
    And now and then her eye to heaven is cast,
    And then on the pale cheek her breast now warms,
Pillowed on her o'erflowing heart, which pants   *735*
With all it granted, and with all it grants.

CXCVI

An infant when it gazes on a light,
    A child the moment when it drains the breast,
A devotee when soars the Host in sight,
    An Arab with a stranger for a guest,   *740*
A sailor when the prize has struck in fight,
    A miser filling his most hoarded chest,
Feel rapture; but not such true joy are reaping
As they who watch o'er what they love while sleeping.

CXCVII

For there it lies so tranquil, so beloved,   *745*
    All that it hath of life with us is living;
So gentle, stirless, helpless, and unmoved,
    And all unconscious of the joy 'tis giving;
All it hath felt, inflicted, passed, and proved,
    Hushed into depths beyond the watcher's diving;   *750*
There lies the thing we love with all its errors
And all its charms, like death without its terrors.

CXCVIII

The lady watched her lover—and that hour
    Of Love's, and Night's, and Ocean's solitude,
O'erflowed her soul with their united power;   *755*
    Amidst the barren sand and rocks so rude
She and her wave-worn love had made their bower,
    Where naught upon their passion could intrude,
And all the stars that crowded the blue space
Saw nothing happier than her glowing face.   *760*

CXCIX

Alas! the love of women! it is known
    To be a lovely and a fearful thing;
For all of theirs upon that die is thrown,

And if 'tis lost, life hath no more to bring
765 To them but mockeries of the past alone,
And their revenge is as the tiger's spring,
Deadly, and quick, and crushing; yet, as real
Torture is theirs, what they inflict they feel.

CC

They are right; for man, to man so oft unjust,
770 Is always so to women; one sole bond
Awaits them, treachery is all their trust;
Taught to conceal, their bursting hearts despond
Over their idol, till some wealthier lust
Buys them in marriage—and what rests beyond?
775 A thankless husband, next a faithless lover,
Then dressing, nursing, praying, and all's over.

CCI

Some take a lover, some take drams or prayers,
Some mind their household, others dissipation,
Some run away, and but exchange their cares,
780 Losing the advantage of a virtuous station;
Few changes e'er can better their affairs,
Theirs being an unnatural situation,
From the dull palace to the dirty hovel:
Some play the devil, and then write a novel.°

CCII

785 Haidée was Nature's bride, and knew not this;
Haidée was Passion's child, born where the sun
Showers triple light, and scorches even the kiss
Of his gazelle-eyed daughters; she was one
Made but to love, to feel that she was his
790 Who was her chosen: what was said or done
Elsewhere was nothing. She had naught to fear,
Hope, care, nor love beyond, her heart beat *here*.

CCIII

And oh! that quickening of the heart, that beat!
How much it costs us! yet each rising throb

784 **novel** Lady Caroline Lamb's *Glenarron* (published 1816) con-
tained a treatment of her famous affair with Byron.

Is in its cause as its effect so sweet,   795
   That Wisdom, ever on the watch to rob
Joy of its alchemy, and to repeat
   Fine truths; even Conscience, too, has a tough job
To make us understand each good old maxim,
So good—I wonder Castlereagh° don't tax 'em.   800

CCIV

And now 'twas done—on the lone shore were plighted
   Their hearts; the stars, their nuptial torches, shed
Beauty upon the beautiful they lighted:
   Ocean their witness, and the cave their bed,
By their own feelings hallowed and united,   805
   Their priest was Solitude, and they were wed:
And they were happy, for to their young eyes
Each was an angel, and earth paradise.

CCV

Oh, Love! of whom great Caesar was the suitor,
   Titus the master, Antony the slave,   810
Horace, Catullus, scholars, Ovid tutor,
   Sappho the sage bluestocking, in whose grave
All those may leap who rather would be neuter—
   (Leucadia's rock still overlooks the wave)
Oh, Love! thou art the very god of evil,   815
For, after all, we cannot call thee devil.

CCVI

Thou makest the chaste connubial state precarious,
   And jestest with the brows of mightiest men:
Caesar and Pompey, Mahomet, Belisarius,
   Have much employed the muse of history's pen;   820
Their lives and fortunes were extremely various,
   Such worthies Time will never see again;
Yet to these four in three things the same luck holds,
They all were heroes, conquerors, and cuckolds.

800 **Castlereagh** the conservative British Foreign Secretary from
1812 to 1822.

CCVII

825 Thou makest philosophers; there's Epicurus
    And Aristippus,° a material crew!
Who to immoral courses would allure us
    By theories quite practicable too;
If only from the devil they would insure us,
830   How pleasant were the maxim (not quite new),
"Eat, drink, and love; what can the rest avail us?"
So said the royal sage Sardanapalus.°

CCVIII

But Juan! had he quite forgotten Julia?
    And should he have forgotten her so soon?
835 I can't but say it seems to me most truly a
    Perplexing question; but, no doubt, the moon
Does these things for us, and whenever newly a
    Strong palpitation rises, 'tis her boon,
Else how the devil is it that fresh features
840 Have such a charm for us poor human creatures?

CCIX

I hate inconstancy—I loathe, detest,
    Abhor, condemn, abjure the mortal made
Of such quicksilver clay that in his breast
    No permanent foundation can be laid;
845 Love, constant love, has been my constant guest,
    And yet last night, being at a masquerade,
I saw the prettiest creature, fresh from Milan,
Which gave me some sensations like a villain.

CCX

But soon Philosophy came to my aid,
850   And whispered, "Think of every sacred tie!"
"I will, my dear Philosophy!" I said,
    "But then her teeth, and then, oh, Heaven! her eye!
I'll just inquire if she be wife or maid,
    Or neither—out of curiosity."

---

826 **Aristippus** Greek Epicurean philosopher of the fourth century
B.C.   832 **Sardanapalus** last Assyrian king, about whose excesses of
pleasure Byron wrote a play in 1821.

"Stop!" cried Philosophy, with air so Grecian   855
(Though she was masqued then as a fair Venetian);

CCXI

"Stop!" so I stopped.—But to return: that which
   Men call inconstancy is nothing more
Then admiration due where nature's rich
   Profusion with young beauty covers o'er   860
Some favored object; and as in the niche
   A lovely statue we almost adore,
This sort of adoration of the real
Is but a heightening of the "beau ideal."

CCXII

'Tis the perception of the beautiful,   865
   A fine extension of the faculties,
Platonic, universal, wonderful,
   Drawn from the stars, and filtered through the skies,
Without which life would be extremely dull;
   In short, it is the use of our own eyes,   870
With one or two small senses added, just
To hint that flesh is formed of fiery dust.

CCXIII

Yet 'tis a painful feeling, and unwilling,
   For surely if we always could perceive
In the same object graces quite as killing   875
   As when she rose upon us like an Eve,
'Twould save us many a heartache, many a shilling
   (For we must get them anyhow, or grieve),
Whereas, if one sole lady pleased forever,
How pleasant for the heart, as well as liver!   880

CCXIV

The heart is like the sky, a part of heaven,
   But changes night and day, too, like the sky;
Now o'er it clouds and thunder must be driven,
   And darkness and destruction as on high:
But when it hath been scorched, and pierced, and
      riven,   885
   Its storms expire in water-drops; the eye

Pours forth at last the heart's blood turned to tears,
Which make the English climate of our years.

CCXV
The liver is the lazaret of bile,
890   But very rarely executes its function,
For the first passion stays there such a while,
    That all the rest creep in and form a junction,
Like knots of vipers on a dunghill's soil,
    Rage, fear, hate, jealousy, revenge, compunction,
895 So that all mischiefs spring up from this entrail,
Like earthquakes from the hidden fire called "central."

CCXVI
In the meantime, without proceeding more
    In this anatomy, I've finished now
Two hundred and odd stanzas as before,
900   That being about the number I'll allow
Each canto of the twelve, or twenty-four;
    And, laying down my pen, I make my bow,
Leaving Don Juan and Haidée to plead
For them and theirs with all who deign to read.

Their Poet
(from Canto Three, Stanzas 82–89)

LXXXII

Their poet, a sad trimmer, but no less
  In company a very pleasant fellow,
Had been the favorite of full many a mess
  Of men, and made them speeches when half
    mellow;
And though his meaning they could rarely guess,   *5*
  Yet still they deigned to hiccup or to bellow
The glorious meed of popular applause,
Of which the first ne'er knows the second cause.

LXXXIII

But now being lifted into high society,
  And having picked up several odds and ends   *10*
Of free thoughts in his travels for variety,
  He deemed, being in a lone isle, among friends,
That, without any danger of a riot, he
  Might for long lying make himself amends;
And, singing as he sung in his warm youth,   *15*
Agree to a short armistice with truth.

LXXXIV

He had traveled 'mongst the Arabs, Turks, and
    Franks,
  And knew the self-loves of the different nations:
And having lived with people of all ranks,
  Had something ready upon most occasions—   *20*
Which got him a few presents and some thanks.
  He varied with some skill his adulations;
To "do at Rome as Romans do," a piece
Of conduct was which he observed in Greece.

LXXXV

25 Thus, usually, when he was asked to sing,
        He gave the different nations something national;
    'Twas all the same to him—"God save the king,"
        Or *"Ça ira,"*° according to the fashion all:
    His muse made increment of any thing,
30   From the high lyric down to the low rational:
    If Pindar sang horse races, what should hinder
    Himself from being as pliable as Pindar?

LXXXVI

    In France, for instance, he would write a chanson;
        In England a six-canto quarto tale;
35 In Spain, he'd make a ballad or romance on
        The last war—much the same in Portugal;
    In Germany, the Pegasus he'd prance on
        Would be old Goethe's (see what says De Staël);°
    In Italy he'd ape the "Trecentisti";°
40 In Greece, he'd sing some sort of hymn like this t' ye:

1

        The isles of Greecs, the isles of Greece!
            Where burning Sappho loved and sung,
        Where grew the arts of war and peace,
            Where Delos rose, and Phoebus sprung!
45   Eternal summer gilds them yet,
        But all, except their sun, is set.

2

        The Scian and the Teian muse,°
            The hero's harp, the lover's lute,
        Have found the fame your shores refuse;
50   Their place of birth alone is mute
        To sounds which echo further west
        Than your sires' "Islands of the Blest."

28 **"Ça ira"** "It'll work"—a French revolutionary song. 38 **De Staël** Madame De Staël had stated that Goethe represented German literature in its entirety. 39 **Trecentisti"** fourteenth-century poets. 47 **Scian . . . Teian muse** Homer and Anacreon.

3

The mountains look on Marathon
 And Marathon looks on the sea
And musing there an hour alone,   55
 I dreamed that Greece might still be free;
For standing on the Persians' grave,
I could not deem myself a slave.

4

A king° sate on the rocky brow
 Which looks o'er sea-born Salamis;   60
And ships, by thousands, lay below,
 And men in nations;—all were his!
He counted them at break of day—
And when the sun set where were they?

5

And where are they? and where art thou, 65
 My country? On thy voiceless shore
The heroic lay is tuneless now—
 The heroic bosom beats no more!
And must thy lyre, so long divine,
Degenerate into hands like mine?   70

6

'Tis something, in the dearth of fame,
 Though linked among a fettered race,
To feel at least a patriot's shame,
 Even as I sing, suffuse my face;
For what is left the poet here?   75
For Greeks a blush—for Greece a tear.

7

Must *we* but weep o'er days more blest?
 Must *we* but blush?—Our fathers bled.
Earth! render back from out thy breast
 A remnant of our Spartan dead!   80
Of the three hundred grant but three,
To make a new Thermopylae!

59 **A king** Xerxes, who watched the defeat of his navy at Salamis.

8

What, silent still? and silent all?
    Ah! no;—the voices of the dead
85 Sound like a distant torrent's fall,
    And answer, "Let one living head,
But one arise—we come, we come!"
'Tis but the living who are dumb.

9

In vain—in vain: strike other chords;
90 Fill high the cup with Samian wine!
Leave battles to the Turkish hordes,
    And shed the blood of Scio's vine!
Hark! rising to the ignoble call—
How answers each bold Bacchanal!

10

95 You have the Pyrrhic dance as yet,
    Where is the Pyrrhic phalanx gone?
Of two such lessons, why forget
    The nobler and the manlier one?
You have the letters Cadmus gave—
100 Think ye he meant them for a slave?

11

Fill high the bowl with Samian wine!
    We will not think of themes like these!
It made Anacreon's song divine:
    He served—but served Polycrates—
105 A tyrant; but our masters then
Were still, at least, our countrymen.

12

The tyrant of the Chersonese
    Was freedom's best and bravest friend;
That tyrant was Miltiades!
110 Oh! that the present hour would lend
Another despot of the kind!
Such chains as his were sure to bind.

13
Fill high the bowl with Samian wine!
  On Suli's rock, and Parga's shore,
Exists the remnant of a line   *115*
  Such as the Doric mothers bore;
And there, perhaps, some seed is sown,
The Heracleidan blood might own.

14
Trust not for freedom to the Franks—
  They have a king who buys and sells: *120*
In native swords, and native ranks,
  The only hope of courage dwells;
But Turkish force, and Latin fraud,
Would break your shield, however broad.

15
Fill high the bowl with Samian wine!   *125*
  Our virgins dance beneath the shade—
I see their glorious black eyes shine;
  But gazing on each glowing maid,
My own the burning tear-drop laves,
To think such breasts must suckle slaves.   *130*

16
Place me on Sunium's marbled steep,
  Where nothing, save the waves and I,
May hear our mutual murmurs sweep;
  There, swanlike, let me sing and die:
A land of slaves shall ne'er be mine—   *135*
Dash down yon cup of Samian wine!

LXXXVII
Thus sung, or would, or could, or should have sung,
  The modern Greek, in tolerable verse;
If not like Orpheus quite, when Greece was young,
  Yet in these times he might have done much worse: *140*
His strain displayed some feeling—right or wrong;
  And feeling, in a poet, is the source
Of others' feeling; but they are such liars,
And take all colors—like the hands of dyers.

LXXXVIII

145 But words are things, and a small drop of ink,
      Falling like dew upon a thought, produces
   That which makes thousands, perhaps millions, think;
      'Tis strange, the shortest letter which man uses
   Instead of speech, may form a lasting link
150   Of ages; to what straits old Time reduces
   Frail man, when paper—even a rag like this,
   Survives himself, his tomb, and all that's his.

LXXXIX

   And when his bones are dust, his grave a blank,
      His station, generation, even his nation,
155 Become a thing, or nothing, save to rank
      In chronological commemoration,
   Some dull MS. oblivion long has sank,
      Or graven stone found in a barrack's station
   In digging the foundation of a closet,
160 May turn his name up, as a rare deposit.

Gulbeyaz

(from Canto Five, Stanzas 107–139)

CVII

   The lady eyed him o'er and o'er, and bade
      Baba retire, which he obeyed in style,
   As if well used to the retreating trade;
      And taking hints in good part all the while,
5 He whispered Juan not to be afraid,
      And looking on him with a sort of smile,

Took leave, with such a face of satisfaction
As good men wear who have done a virtuous action.

CVIII

When he was gone, there was a sudden change:
    I know not what might be the lady's thought,   *10*
But o'er her bright brow flashed a tumult strange,
    And into her clear cheek the blood was brought,
Blood-red as sunset summer clouds which range
    The verge of Heaven; and in her large eyes wrought,
A mixture of sensations might be scanned,   *15*
Of half voluptuousness and half command.

CIX

Her form had all the softness of her sex,
    Her features all the sweetness of the devil,
When he put on the cherub to perplex
    Eve, and paved (God knows how) the road to evil;   *20*
The sun himself was scarce more free from specks
    Than she from aught at which the eye could cavil;
Yet, somehow, there was something somewhere want-
    ing,
As if she rather *ordered* than was *granting*.

CX

Something imperial, or imperious, threw   *25*
    A chain o'er all she did; that is, a chain
Was thrown as 'twere about the neck of you—
    And rapture's self will seem almost a pain
With aught which looks like despotism in view:
    Our souls at least are free, and 'tis in vain   *30*
We would against them make the flesh obey—
The spirit in the end will have its way.

CXI

Her very smile was haughty, though so sweet;
    Her very nod was not an inclination;
There was a self-will even in her small feet,   *35*
    As though they were quite conscious of her sta-
    tion—

They trod as upon necks; and to complete
    Her state (it is the custom of her nation),
A poniard decked her girdle, as the sign
40 She was a sultan's bride (thank Heaven, not mine!).

CXII

"To hear and to obey" had been from birth
    The law of all around her; to fulfill
All fantasies which yielded joy or mirth.
    Had been her slaves' chief pleasure, as her will;
45 Her blood was high, her beauty scarce of earth:
    Judge, then, if her caprices e'er stood still;
Had she but been a Christian, I've a notion
We should have found out the "perpetual motion."

CXIII

Whate'er she saw and coveted was brought;
50   Whate'er she did *not* see, if she supposed
It might be seen, with diligence was sought,
    And when 'twas found straightway the bargain
      closed;
There was no end unto the things she bought,
    Nor to the trouble which her fancies caused;
55 Yet even her tyranny had such a grace,
The women pardoned all except her face.

CXIV

Juan, the latest of her whims, had caught
    Her eye in passing on his way to sale;
She ordered him directly to be bought,
60   And Baba, who had ne'er been known to fail
In any kind of mischief to be wrought,
    At all such auctions knew how to prevail:
She had no prudence, but he had; and this
Explains the garb which Juan took amiss.

CXV

65 His youth and features favored the disguise,
    And, should you ask how she, a sultan's bride,
Could risk or compass such strange fantasies,
    This I must leave sultanas to decide:

Emperors are only husbands in wives' eyes,
   And kings and consorts oft are mystified,   70
As we may ascertain with due precision,
Some by experience, others by tradition.

CXVI

But to the main point, where we have been tending:—
   She now conceived all difficulties past,
And deemed herself extremely condescending   75
   When, being made her property at last,
Without more preface, in her blue eyes blending
   Passion and power, a glance on him she cast,
And merely saying, "Christian, canst thou love?"
Conceived that phrase was quite enough to move.   80

CXVII

And so it was, in proper time and place;
   But Juan, who had still his mind o'erflowing
With Haidée's isle and soft Ionian face,
   Felt the warm blood, which in his face was glowing,
Rush back upon his heart, which filled apace,   85
   And left his cheeks as pale as snowdrops blowing;
These words went through his soul like Arab-spears,
So that he spoke not, but burst into tears.

CXVIII

She was a good deal shocked; not shocked at tears,
   For women shed and use them at their liking;   90
But there is something when man's eye appears
   Wet, still more disagreeable and striking,
A woman's teardrop melts, a man's half scars,
   Like molten lead, as if you thrust a pike in
His heart to force it out, for (to be shorter)   95
To them 'tis a relief, to us a torture.

CXIX

And she would have consoled, but knew not how:
   Having no equals, nothing which had e'er
Infected her with sympathy till now,
   And never having dreamt what 'twas to bear   100
Aught of a serious, sorrowing kind, although

There might arise some pouting petty care
To cross her brow, she wondered how so near
Her eyes another's eye could shed a tear.

CXX

105 But nature teaches more than power can spoil,
And, when a *strong* although a strange sensation
Moves—female hearts are such a genial soil
For kinder feelings, whatsoe'er their nation,
They naturally pour the "wine and oil,"
110   Samaritans in every situation;
And thus Gulbeyaz, though she knew not why,
Felt an odd glistening moisture in her eye.

CXXI

But tears must stop like all things else; and soon
Juan, who for an instant had been moved
115 To such a sorrow by the intrusive tone
Of one who dared to ask if "he *had* loved,"
Called back the stoic to his eyes, which shone
Bright with the very weakness he reproved;
And although sensitive to beauty, he
120 Felt most indignant still at not being free.

CXXII

Gulbeyaz, for the first time in her days,
Was much embarrassed, never having met
In all her life with aught save prayers and praise;
And as she also risked her life to get
125 Him whom she meant to tutor in love's ways
Into a comfortable tête-à-tête,
To lose the hour would make her quite a martyr,
And they had wasted now almost a quarter.

CXXIII

I also would suggest the fitting time
130 To gentlemen in any such like case,
That is to say in a meridian clime—
With us there is more law given to the chase,
But here a small delay forms a great crime:

So recollect that the extremest grace
Is just two minutes for your declaration—   *135*
A moment more would hurt your reputation.

CXXIV

Juan's was good; and might have been still better,
    But he had got Haidée into his head:
However strange, he could not yet forget her,
    Which made him seem exceedingly ill-bred.   *140*
Gulbeyaz, who looked on him as her debtor
    For having had him to her palace led,
Began to blush up to the eyes, and then
Grow deadly pale, and then blush back again.

CXXV

At length, in an imperial way, she laid   *145*
    Her hand on his, and bending on him eyes
Which needed not an empire to persuade,
    Looked into his for love, where none replies:
Her brow grew black, but she would not upbraid,
    That being the last thing a proud woman tries;   *150*
She rose, and pausing one chaste moment, threw
Herself upon his breast, and there she grew.

CXXVI

This was an awkward test, as Juan found,
    But he was steeled by sorrow, wrath, and pride:
With gentle force her white arms he unwound,   *155*
    And seated her all drooping by his side,
Then rising haughtily he glanced around,
    And looking coldly in her face, he cried,
"The prisoned eagle will not pair, nor I
Serve a Sultana's sensual fantasy.   *160*

CXXVII

"Thou ask'st if I can love? be this the proof
    How much I *have* loved—that I love not *thee!*
In this vile garb, the distaff, web, and woof
    Were fitter for me: Love is for the free!
I am not dazzled by this splendid roof,   *165*
    Whate'er thy power, and great it seems to be;

Heads bow, knees bend, eyes watch around a throne,
And hands obey—our hearts are still our own."

CXXVIII

This was a truth to us extremely trite;
170   Not so to her, who ne'er had heard such things:
She deemed her least command must yield delight,
    Earth being only made for queens and kings.
If hearts lay on the left side or the right
    She hardly knew, to such perfection brings
175 Legitimacy its born votaries, when
Aware of their due royal rights o'er men.

CXXIX

Besides, as has been said, she was so fair
    As even in a much humbler lot had made
A kingdom or confusion anywhere,
180   And also, as may be presumed, she laid
Some stress on charms, which seldom are, if e'er,
    By their possessors thrown into the shade:
She thought hers gave a double "right divine";
And half of that opinion's also mine.

CXXX

185 Remember, or (if you cannot) imagine,
    Ye, who have kept your chastity when young,
While some more desperate dowager has been waging
    Love with you, and been in the dogdays stung
By your refusal, recollect her raging!
190   Or recollect all that was said or sung
On such a subject; then suppose the face
Of a young downright beauty in this case.

CXXXI

Suppose—but you already have supposed,
    The spouse of Potiphar, the Lady Booby,
195 Phaedra, and all which story has disclosed
    Of good examples; pity that so few by
Poets and private tutors are exposed,
    To educate—ye youth of Europe—you by!

But when you have supposed the few we know,
You can't suppose Gulbeyaz' angry brow.   200

CXXXII

A tigress robbed of young, a lioness,
    Or any interesting beast of prey,
Are similes at hand for the distress
    Of ladies who cannot have their own way;
But though my turn will not be served with less,   205
    These don't express one half what I should say:
For what is stealing young ones, few or many,
To cutting short their hopes of having any?

CXXXIII

The love of offspring's nature's general law,
    From tigresses and cubs to ducks and ducklings;   210
There's nothing whets the beak, or arms the claw
    Like an invasion of their babes and sucklings;
And all who have seen a human nursery, saw
    How mothers love their children's squalls and
        chucklings;
This strong extreme effect (to tire no longer   215
Your patience) shows the cause must still be stronger.

CXXXIV

If I said fire flashed from Gulbeyaz' eyes,
    'Twere nothing—for her eyes flashed always fire;
Or said her cheeks assumed the deepest dyes,
    I should but bring disgrace upon the dyer,   220
So supernatural was her passion's rise;
    For ne'er till now she knew a checked desire:
Even ye who know what a checked woman is
(Enough, God knows!) would much fall short of this.

CXXXV

Her rage was but a minute's, and 'twas well—   225
    A moment's more had slain her; but the while
It lasted 'twas like a short glimpse of hell:
    Naught's more sublime than energetic bile,
Though horrible to see yet grand to tell,
    Like ocean warring 'gainst a rocky isle;   230

And the deep passions flashing through her form
Made her a beautiful embodied storm.

CXXXVI

A vulgar tempest 'twere to a typhoon
　　To match a common fury with her rage,
235 And yet she did not want to reach the moon,
　　Like moderate Hotspur on the immortal page;
Her anger pitched into a lower tune,
　　Perhaps the fault of her soft sex and age—
Her wish was but to "kill, kill, kill," like Lear's,
240 And then her thirst of blood was quenched in tears.

CXXXVII

A storm it raged, and like the storm it passed,
　　Passed without words—in fact she could not speak;
And then her sex's shame broke in at last,
　　A sentiment till then in her but weak,
245 But now it flowed in natural and fast,
　　As water through an unexpected leak;
For she felt humbled—and humiliation
Is sometimes good for people in her station.

CXXXVIII

It teaches them that they are flesh and blood,
250 　　It also gently hints to them that others,
Although of clay, are yet not quite of mud;
　　That urns and pipkins are but fragile brothers,
And works of the same pottery, bad or good,
　　Though not all born of the same sires and mothers:
255 It teaches—Heaven knows only what it teaches,
But sometimes it may mend, and often reaches.

CXXXIX

Her first thought was to cut off Juan's head;
　　Her second, to cut only his—acquaintance;
Her third, to ask him where he had been bred;
260 　　Her fourth, to rally him into repentance;
Her fifth, to call her maids and go to bed;
　　Her sixth, to stab herself; her seventh, to sentence

The lash to Baba:—but her grand resource
Was to sit down again, and cry of course.

Oh, Wellington

(from Canto Nine, Stanzas 1–9)

I

Oh, Wellington! (or "Villainton"—for Fame
   Sounds the heroic syllables both ways;
France could not even conquer your great name,
   But punned it down to this facetious phrase—
Beating or beaten she will laugh the same),
   You have obtained great pensions and much praise: 5
Glory like yours should any dare gainsay,
Humanity would rise, and thunder "Nay!"°

II

I don't think that you used Kinnaird quite well
   In Marinet's affair°—in fact, 'twas shabby,   10
And like some other things won't do to tell
   Upon your tomb in Westminster's old abbey.
Upon the rest 'tis not worthwhile to dwell,
   Such tales being for the tea-hours of some tabby;
But though your years as *man* tend fast to zero,   15
In fact your grace is still but a *young hero*.

---

8 **Nay!** Byron himself indicated, in a note, the pun on the name of
Marshall Ney. 10 **Marinet's affair** an alleged plot to assassinate
Wellington, revealed by one Marinet to Lord Kinnaird, with whom
the Duke fell out.

III

Though Britain owes (and pays you too) so much,
　　Yet Europe doubtless owes you greatly more:
You have repaired Legitimacy's crutch,
20　　A prop not quite so certain as before:
The Spanish, and the French, as well as Dutch,
　　Have seen, and felt, how strongly you *restore;*
And Waterloo has made the world your debtor
(I wish your bards would sing it rather better).

IV

25　You are "the best of cut-throats":—do not start;
　　The phrase is Shakespeare's,° and not misapplied:
War's a brain-spattering, windpipe-slitting art,
　　Unless her cause by right be sanctified.
If you have acted *once* a generous part,
30　　The world, not the world's masters, will decide,
And I shall be delighted to learn who,
Save you and yours, have gained by Waterloo?

V

I am no flatterer—you've supped full of flattery:
　　They say you like it too—'tis no great wonder.
35　He whose whole life has been assault and battery,
　　At last may get a little tired of thunder;
And swallowing eulogy much more than satire, he
　　May like being praised for every lucky blunder,
Called "Saviour of the Nations"—not yet saved,
40　And "Europe's Liberator"—still enslaved.

VI

I've done. Now go and dine from off the plate
　　Presented by the Prince of the Brazils,
And send the sentinel before your gate
　　A slice or two from your luxurious meals:
45　He fought, but has not fed so well of late.
　　Some hunger, too, they say the people feels:—
There is no doubt that you deserve your ration,
But pray give back a little to the nation.

26 **Shakespeare's** in *Macbeth,* III, IV.

VII

I don't mean to reflect—a man so great as
  You, my lord duke! is far above reflection: *50*
The high Roman fashion, too, of Cincinnatus,
  With modern history has but small connection:
Though as an Irishman you love potatoes,
  You need not take them under your direction;
And half a million for your Sabine farm   *55*
Is rather dear!—I'm sure I mean no harm.

VIII

Great men have always scorned great recompenses:
  Epaminondas saved his Thebes, and died,
Not leaving even his funeral expenses:
  George Washington had thanks and naught beside,   *60*
Except the all-cloudless glory (which few men's is)
  To free his country: Pitt too had his pride,
And as a high-souled minister of state is
Renowned for ruining Great Britain gratis.

IX

Never had mortal man such opportunity,   *65*
  Except Napoleon, or abused it more:
You might have freed fallen Europe from the unity
  Of tyrants, and been blest from shore to shore:
And *now*—what *is* your fame? Shall the Muse tune
    it ye?
  Now—that the rabble's first vain shouts are o'er?   *70*
Go! hear it in your famished country's cries!
Behold the world! and curse your victories!

Pomps and Vanities

(from Canto Eleven, Stanzas 73–85)

LXXIII

Our hero, as a hero, young and handsome,
   Noble, rich, celebrated, and a stranger,
Like other slaves of course must pay his ransom,
   Before he can escape from so much danger
5   As will environ a conspicuous man. Some
     Talk about poetry, and "rack and manger,"
And ugliness, disease, as toil and trouble;—
I wish they knew the life of a young noble.

LXXIV

They are young, but know not youth—it is antici-
     pated;
10   Handsome but wasted, rich without a sou;
Their vigor in a thousand arms is dissipated;
   Their cash comes *from,* their wealth goes *to* a Jew;
Both senates see their nightly votes participated
   Between the tyrant's and the tribunes' crew;
15   And having voted, dined, drunk, gamed, and whored,
The family vault receives another lord.

LXXV

"Where is the world?" cries Young,° at *eighty*—
     "Where
   The world in which a man was born?" Alas!
Where is the world of *eight* years past? *'Twas there*—
20   I look for it—'tis gone, a globe of glass!
Cracked, shivered, vanished, scarcely gazed on, ere
   A silent change dissolves the glittering mass.
Statesmen, chiefs, orators, queens, patriots, kings,
And dandies, all are gone on the wind's wings.

---

17 Young Edward Young, author of "Night Thoughts."

LXXVI

Where is Napoleon the Grand? God knows: 25
   Where little Castlereagh? The devil can tell:
Where Grattan, Curran, Sheridan, all those
   Who bound the bar or senate in their spell?
Where is the unhappy Queen, with all her woes?
   And where the Daughter, whom the Isles loved
      well?°   30
Where are those martyred saints the Five per Cents?
And where—oh, where the devil are the rents?

LXXVII

Where's Brummel? Dished. Where's Long Pole
   Wellesley? Diddled.°
   Where's Whitbread? Romilly? Where's George the
   Third?
Where is his will? (That's not so soon unriddled.)   35
   And where is "Fum" the Fourth, our "royal bird"?
Gone down, it seems, to Scotland to be fiddled
   Unto by Sawney's violin, we have heard:
"Caw me, caw thee"—for six months hath been
   hatching
This scene of royal itch and loyal scratching.   40

LXXVIII

Where is Lord This? And where my Lady That?
   The Honorable Mistresses and Misses?
Some laid aside like an old Opera hat,
   Married, unmarried, and remarried (this is
An evolution oft performed of late).   45
   Where are the Dublin shouts—and London hisses?
Where are the Grenvilles? Turned as usual. Where
My friends the Whigs?° Exactly where they were.

27–30 **Where . . . well?** Grattan, Curran, and Sheridan (the famous dramatist) were wits. Queen Caroline had died in 1821, and her daughter, Charlotte, in 1817.   33–34 **Dished . . . Diddled** Beau Brummel had by this time fallen out of favor and into poverty. The Duke of Wellington's nephew Wellesley was bankrupt.   48 **Whigs** They had been turned out of power.

LXXIX

Where are the Lady Carolines and Franceses?°
50   Divorced or doing thereanent. Ye annals
So brilliant, where the list of routs and dances is—
   Thou Morning Post, sole record of the panels
Broken in carriages, and all the fantasies
   Of fashion—say what streams now fill those
     channels?
55 Some die, some fly, some languish on the Continent,
Because the times have hardly left them *one* tenant.

LXXX

Some who once set their caps at cautious dukes,
   Have taken up at length with younger brothers:
Some heiresses have bit at sharpers' hooks:
   Some maids have been made wives, some merely
60   mothers;
Others have lost their fresh and fairy looks:
   In short, the list of alterations bothers.
There's little strange in this, but something strange is
The unusual quickness of these common changes.

LXXXI

65 Talk not of seventy years as age; in seven
   I have seen more changes, down from monarchs to
The humblest individual under heaven,
   Than might suffice a moderate century through.
I knew that naught was lasting, but now even
70   Change grows too changeable, without being new:
Naught's permanent among the human race,
Except the Whigs *not* getting into place.

LXXXII

I have seen Napoleon, who seemed quite a Jupiter,
   Shrink to a Saturn. I have seen a Duke°
75 (No matter which) turn politician stupider,
   If that can well be, than his wooden look.
But it is time that I should hoist my "blue Peter,"

49 **Carolines and Franceses** lady Caroline Lamb and Lady Frances
Webster, two of Byron's women earlier in his life.   74 **Duke** Wel-
lington.

And sail for a new theme:—I have seen—and
    shook
To see it—the king hissed, and then caressed;
But don't pretend to settle which was best.   *80*

LXXXIII

I have seen the Landholders without a rap—
    I have seen Joanna Southcote°—I have seen—
The House of Commons turned to a tax-trap—
    I have seen that sad affair of the late Queen—
I have seen crowns worn instead of a fool's cap—   *85*
    I have seen a Congress doing all that's mean—
I have seen some nations like o'erloaded asses
Kick off their burthens, meaning the high classes.

LXXXIV

I have seen small poets, and great prosers, and
    Interminable—*not eternal*—speakers—   *90*
I have seen the funds at war with house and land—
    I have seen the country gentlemen turn squeakers—
I have seen the people ridden o'er like sand
    By slaves on horseback—I have seen malt liquors
Exchanged for "thin potations" by John Bull—   *95*
I have seen John half detect himself a fool.—

LXXXV

But "carpe diem," Juan, "carpe, carpe!"
    Tomorrow sees another race as gay
And transient, and devoured by the same harpy.
    "Life's a poor player" then "play out the play,   *100*
Ye villains!" and above all keep a sharp eye
    Much less on what you do than what you say:
Be hypocritical, be cautious, be
Not what you *seem,* but always what you *see.*

82 **Joanna Southcote** See note to *The Vision of Judgment,* l. 224,
p. 147.

A Country-House Weekend

(from Canto Thirteen, Stanzas 50–111)

L

Lord Henry and the Lady Adeline
    Departed like the rest of their compeers,
The peerage, to a mansion very fine;
    The Gothic Babel of a thousand years.
5 None than themselves could boast a longer line,
    Where time through heroes and through beauties
        steers;
And oaks as olden as their pedigree
Told of their sires, a tomb in every tree.

LI

A paragraph in every paper told
10   Of their departure: such is modern fame:
'Tis pity that it takes no farther hold
    Than an advertisement, or much the same;
When, ere the ink be dry, the sound grows cold.
    The *Morning Post* was foremost to proclaim—
15 "Departure, for his country seat, today,
Lord H. Amundeville and Lady A.

LII

"We understand the splendid host intends
    To entertain, this autumn, a select
And numerous party of his noble friends;
    Midst whom we have heard, from sources quite
20   correct,
The Duke of D—— the shooting season spends,
    With many more by rank and fashion decked;
Also a foreigner of high condition,
The envoy of the secret Russian mission."

LIII

And thus we see—who doubts the *Morning Post?*   25
  (Whose articles are like the "Thirty-nine,"
Which those most swear to who believe them most)—
  Our gay Russ Spaniard was ordained to shine,
Decked by the rays reflected from his host,
  With those who, Pope says, "greatly daring dine."   30
'Tis odd, but true—last war the News abounded
More with these dinners than the killed or wounded;—

LIV

As thus: "On Thursday there was a grand dinner;
  Present, Lords A. B. C."—Earls, dukes, by name
Announced with no less pomp than victory's winner: 35
  Then underneath, and in the very same
Column; date, "Falmouth. There has lately been here
  The Slap-dash regiment, so well known to fame,
Whose loss in the late action we regret:
The vacancies are filled up—see Gazette."   40

LV

To Norman Abbey whirled the noble pair—
  An old, old monastery once, and now
Still older mansion; of a rich and rare
  Mixed Gothic, such as artists all allow
Few specimens yet left us can compare   45
  Withal: it lies perhaps a little low,
Because the monks preferred a hill behind,
To shelter their devotion from the wind.

LVI

It stood embosomed in a happy valley,
  Crowned by high woodlands, where the Druid oak   50
Stood like Caractacus° in act to rally
  His host, with broad arms 'gainst the thunder-
      stroke;
And from beneath his boughs were seen to sally
  The dappled foresters—as day awoke,

51 **Caractacus** British chieftain who resisted Roman invasion, 43–47 A.D.

55 The branching stag swept down with all his herd,
    To quaff a brook which murmured like a bird.

    LVII
    Before the mansion lay a lucid lake,
        Broad as transparent, deep, and freshly fed
    By a river, which its softened way did take
60   In currents through the calmer water spread
    Around: the wildfowl nestled in the brake
        And sedges, brooding in their liquid bed:
    The woods sloped downwards to its brink, and stood
    With their green faces fixed upon the flood.

    LVIII
65 Its outlet dashed into a deep cascade,
        Sparkling with foam, until again subsiding,
    Its shriller echoes—like an infant made
        Quiet—sank into softer ripples, gliding
    Into a rivulet; and thus allayed,
70   Pursued its course, now gleaming, and now hiding
    Its windings through the woods; now clear, now blue,
    According as the skies their shadows threw.

    LIX
    A glorious remnant of the Gothic pile
        (While yet the church was Rome's) stood half
            apart
75 In a grand arch, which once screened many an aisle.
        These last had disappeared—a loss to art:
    The first yet frowned superbly o'er the soil,
        And kindled feelings in the roughest heart,
    Which mourned the power of time's or tempest's
            march,
80 In gazing on that venerable arch.

    LX
    Within a niche, nigh to its pinnacle,
        Twelve saints had once stood sanctified in stone;
    But these had fallen, not when the friars fell,
        But in the war which struck Charles from his
            throne,

When each house was a fortalice,° as tell   85
    The annals of full many a line undone—
The gallant cavaliers, who fought in vain
For those who knew not to resign or reign.

LXI

But in a higher niche, alone, but crowned,
    The Virgin Mother of the God-born Child,   90
With her Son in her blessèd arms, looked round,
    Spared by some chance when all beside was
        spoiled;
She made the earth below seem holy ground.
    This may be superstition, weak or wild,
But even the faintest relics of a shrine   95
Of any worship wake some thoughts divine.

LXII

A mighty window, hollow in the center,
    Shorn of its glass of thousand colorings,
Through which the deepened glories once could enter,
    Streaming from off the sun like seraph's wings,   100
Now yawns all desolate: now loud, now fainter,
    The gale sweeps through its fretwork, and oft sings
The owl his anthem, where the silenced quire
Lie with their hallelujahs quenched like fire.

LXIII

But in the noontide of the moon, and when   105
    The wind is wingèd from one point of heaven,
There moans a strange unearthly sound, which then
    Is musical—a dying accent driven
Through the huge arch, which soars and sinks again.
    Some deem it but the distant echo given   110
Back to the night wind by the waterfall,
And harmonized by the old choral wall:

LXIV

Others, that some original shape, or form
    Shaped by decay perchance, hath given the power

85 **fortalice** fortress.

115 (Though less than that of Memnon's statue, warm
       In Egypt's rays, to harp at a fixed hour)
     To this gray ruin, with a voice to charm.
       Sad, but serene, it sweeps o'er tree or tower;
     The cause I know not, nor can solve; but such
120 The fact:—I've heard it—once perhaps too much.

LXV
     Amidst the court a Gothic fountain played,
       Symmetrical, but decked with carvings quaint—
     Strange faces, like to men in masquerade,
       And here perhaps a monster, there a saint:
     The spring gushed through grim mouths of granite
125   made,
       And sparkled into basins, where it spent
     Its little torrent in a thousand bubbles,
     Like man's vain glory, and his vainer troubles.

LXVI
     The mansion's self was vast and venerable,
130   With more of the monastic than has been
     Elsewhere preserved: the cloisters still were stable,
       The cells, too, and refectory, I ween:
     An exquisite small chapel had been able,
       Still unimpaired, to decorate the scene;
135 The rest had been reformed, replaced, or sunk,
     And spoke more of the baron than the monk.

LXVII
     Huge halls, long galleries, spacious chambers, joined
       By no quite lawful marriage of the arts,
     Might shock a connoisseur; but when combined,
140   Formed a whole which, irregular in parts,
     Yet left a grand impression on the mind,
       At least of those whose eyes are in their hearts:
     We gaze upon a giant for his stature,
     Nor judge at first if all be true to nature.

LXVIII
145 Steel barons, molten the next generation
       To silken rows of gay and gartered earls,

Glanced from the walls in goodly preservation:
   And Lady Marys blooming into girls,
With fair long locks, had also kept their station:
   And countesses mature in robes and pearls: 150
Also some beauties of Sir Peter Lely,
Whose drapery hints we may admire them freely.

LXIX

Judges in very formidable ermine
   Were there, with brows that did not much invite
The accused to think their lordships would determine 155
   His cause by leaning much from might to right:
Bishops, who had not left a single sermon:
   Attorneys-general, awful to the sight,
As hinting more (unless our judgments warp us)
Of the "Star Chamber" than of "Habeas Corpus."   160

LXX

Generals, some all in armor, of the old
   And iron time, ere lead had ta'en the lead;
Others in wigs of Marlborough's martial fold,
   Huger than twelve of our degenerate breed:
Lordlings, with staves of white or keys of gold: 165
   Nimrods, whose canvas scarce contained the steed;
And here and there some stern high patriot stood,
Who could not get the place for which he sued.

LXXI

But ever and anon, to soothe your vision,
   Fatigued with these hereditary glories,   170
There rose a Carlo Dolce or a Titian,
   Or wilder group of savage Salvatore's;
Here danced Albano's boys, and here the sea shone
   In Vernet's ocean lights; and there the stories
Of martyrs awed, as Spagnoletto tainted   175
His brush with all the blood of all the sainted.

LXXII

Here sweetly spread a landscape of Lorraine;
   There Rembrandt made his darkness equal light,
Or gloomy Caravaggio's gloomier stain

180   Bronzed o'er some lean and stoic anchorite:—
But, lo! a Teniers woos, and not in vain,
    Your eyes to revel in a livelier sight:
His bell-mouthed goblet makes me feel quite Danish
Or Dutch with thirst—What, ho! a flask of Rhenish.

LXXIII
185   O reader! if that thou canst read—and know,
    'Tis not enough to spell, or even to read,
To constitute a reader; there must go
    Virtues of which both you and I have need;—
Firstly, begin with the beginning (though
190   That clause is hard); and secondly, proceed;
Thirdly, commence not with the end—or, sinning
In this sort, end at least with the beginning.

LXXIV
But, reader, thou hast patient been of late,
    While I, without remorse of rhyme, or fear,
195   Have built and laid out ground at such a rate,
    Dan Phoebus takes me for an auctioneer.
That poets were so from their earliest date,
    By Homer's "Catalogue of ships" is clear;
But a mere modern must be moderate—
200   I spare you then the furniture and plate.

LXXV
The mellow autumn came, and with it came
    The promised party, to enjoy its sweets.
The corn is cut, the manor full of game;
    The pointer ranges, and the sportsman beats
205   In russet jacket:—lynxlike is his aim;
    Full grows his bag, and wonder*ful* his feats.
Ah, nut-brown partridges! Ah, brilliant pheasants!
And ah, ye poachers!—'Tis no sport for peasants.

LXXVI
An English autumn, though it hath no vines,
210   Blushing with Bacchant coronals along
The paths, o'er which the far festoon entwines
    The red grape in the sunny lands of song,

Hath yet a purchased choice of choicest wines;
   The claret light, and the Madeira strong.
If Britain mourn her bleakness, we can tell her,   *215*
The very best of vineyards is the cellar.

LXXVII

Then, if she hath not that serene decline
   Which makes the southern autumn's day appear
As if 'twould to a second spring resign
   The season, rather than to winter drear—   *220*
Of indoor comforts still she hath a mine—
   The sea-coal fires the "earliest of the year";
Without doors, too, she may compete in mellow,
As what is lost in green is gained in yellow.

LXXVIII

And for the effeminate *villeggiatura*°—   *225*
   Rife with more horns than hounds—she hath the
      chase,
So animated that it might allure a
   Saint from his beads to join the jocund race;
Even Nimrod's self might leave the plains of Dura,°
   And wear the Melton jacket for a space: *230*
If she hath no wild boars, she hath a tame
Preserve of bores, who ought to be made game.

LXXIX

The noble guests, assembled at the Abbey,
   Consisted of—we give the sex the pas—
The Duchess of Fitz-Fulke; the Countess Crabby;   *235*
   The Ladies Scilly, Buscy;—Miss Eclat,
Miss Bombazeen, Miss Mackstay, Miss O'Tabby,
   And Mrs. Rabbi, the rich banker's squaw;
Also the honorable Mrs. Sleep,
Who looked a white lamb, yet was a black sheep: *240*

LXXX

With other Countesses of Blank—but rank;
   At once the "lie" and the "élite" of crowds;

225 **villeggiatura** the country season.   229 **Dura** in Assyria.

Who pass like water filtered in a tank,
    All purged and pious from their native clouds;
245 Or paper turned to money by the Bank:
    No matter how or why, the passport shrouds
The "passée" and the past; for good society
Is no less famed for tolerance than piety—

LXXXI

That is, up to a certain point; which point
250   Forms the most difficult in punctuation.
Appearances appear to form the joint
    On which it hinges in a higher station;
And so that no explosion cry "Aroint
    Thee, witch!" or each Medea has her Jason;
255 Or (to the point with Horace and with Pulci)
"Omne tulit punctum, quae miscuit utile dulci."°

LXXXII

I can't exactly trace their rule of right,
    Which hath a little leaning to a lottery.
I've seen a virtuous woman put down quite
260   By the mere combination of a coterie;
Also a so-so matron boldly fight
    Her way back to the world by dint of plottery,
And shine the very *Siria*° of the spheres,
Escaping with a few slight, scarless sneers.

LXXXIII

265 I have seen more than I'll say:—but we will see
    How our *villeggiatura* will get on.
The party might consist of thirty-three
    Of highest caste—the Brahmins of the *ton*.
I have named a few, not foremost in degree,
270   But ta'en at hazard as the rhyme may run.
By way of sprinkling, scattered amongst these,
There also were some Irish absentees.

---

256 **"Omne . . . dulci"** He who blends the useful with the pleasant
wins all votes (Horace, *Ars Poetica*, 343). 263 **Siria** Sirius is the
Dog Star, she, the bitch.

LXXXIV

There was Parolles, too, the legal bully,
   Who limits all his battles to the bar
And senate: when invited elsewhere, truly,   275
   He shows more appetite for words than war.
There was the young bard Rackrhyme, who had newly
   Come out and glimmered as a six weeks' star.
There was Lord Pyrrho, too, the great free-thinker;
And Sir John Pottledeep, the mighty drinker.   280

LXXXV

There was the Duke of Dash, who was a—duke,
   "Ay, every inch a" duke; there were twelve peers
Like Charlemagne's—and all such peers in look
   And intellect, that neither eyes nor ears
For commoners had ever them mistook.   285
   There were the six Miss Rawbolds—pretty dears!
All song and sentiment; whose hearts were set
Less on a convent than a coronet.

LXXXVI

There were four Honorable Misters, whose
   Honor was more before their names than after;   290
There was the preux Chevalier de la Ruse,
   Whom France and Fortune lately deigned to waft
     here,
Whose chiefly harmless talent was to amuse;
   But the clubs found it rather serious laughter,
Because—such was his magic power to please—   295
The dice seemed charmed, too, with his repartees.

LXXXVII

There was Dick Dubious, the metaphysician,
   Who loved philosophy and a good dinner;
Angle, the *soi-disant* mathematician;
   Sir Henry Silvercup, the great race-winner.   300
There was the Reverend Rodomont Precisian,
   Who did not hate so much the sin as sinner;
And Lord Augustus Fitz-Plantagenet,
Good at all things, but better at a bet.

LXXXVIII

305 There was Jack Jargon, the gigantic guardsman;
      And General Fireface, famous in the field,
   A great tactician, and no less a swordsman,
      Who ate, last war, more Yankees than he killed.
   There was the waggish Welsh Judge, Jefferies Hards-
         man,
310   In his grave office so completely skilled,
   That when a culprit came for condemnation,
   He had his judge's joke for consolation.

LXXXIX

   Good company's a chessboard—there are kings,
      Queens, bishops, knights, rooks, pawns; the world's
         a game;
315 Save that the puppets pull at their own strings,
      Methinks gay Punch hath something of the same.
   My Muse, the butterfly, hath but her wings,
      Not stings, and flits through ether without aim.
   Alighting rarely:—were she but a hornet,
320 Perhaps there might be vices which would mourn it.

XC

   I had forgotten—but must not forget—
      An orator, the latest of the session,
   Who had delivered well a very set
      Smooth speech, his first and maidenly transgression
325 Upon debate: the papers echoed yet
      With his debut, which made a strong impression,
   And ranked with what is every day displayed—
   "The best first speech that ever yet was made."

XCI

   Proud of his "Hear hims!" proud, too, of his vote
330   And lost virginity of oratory,
   Proud of his learning (just enough to quote),
      He reveled in his Ciceronian glory:
   With memory excellent to get by rote,
      With wit to hatch a pun or tell a story,

Graced with some merit, and with more effrontery,   335
"His country's pride," he came down to the country.

XCII

There also were two wits by acclamation,
   Longbow from Ireland, Strongbow from the Tweed,
Both lawyers and both men of education;
   But Strongbow's wit was of more polished breed: 340
Longbow was rich in an imagination
   As beautiful and bounding as a steed,
But sometimes stumbling over a potato—
While Strongbow's best things might have come from
    Cato.

XCIII

Strongbow was like a new-tuned harpsichord;   345
   But Longbow wild as an Aeolian harp,
With which the winds of heaven can claim accord,
   And make a music, whether flat or sharp.
Of Strongbow's talk you would not change a word:
   At Longbow's phrases you might sometimes carp: 350
Both wits—one born so, and the other bred—
This by his heart, his rival by his head.

XCIV

If all these seem a heterogeneous mass
   To be assembled at a country seat,
Yet think, a specimen of every class   355
   Is better than a humdrum tête-à-tête.
The days of Comedy are gone, alas!
   When Congreve's fool could vie with Molière's
    bête:
Society is smoothed to that excess,
That manners hardly differ more than dress.   360

XCV

Our ridicules are kept in the background—
   Ridiculous enough, but also dull;
Professions, too, are no more to be found
   Professional; and there is naught to cull
Of folly's fruit; for though your fools abound,   365

They're barren, and not worth the pains to pull.
Society is now one polished horde,
    Formed of two mighty tribes, the *Bores* and *Bored.*

XCVI

But from being farmers, we turn gleaners, gleaning
370   The scanty but right-well threshed ears of truth;
And, gentle reader! when you gather meaning,
    You may be Boaz, and I—modest Ruth.
Farther I'd quote, but Scripture intervening
    Forbids. A great impression in my youth
375 Was made by Mrs. Adams, where she cries,°
"That Scriptures out of church are blasphemies."

XCVII

But what we can we glean in this vile age
    Of chaff, although our gleanings be not grist.
I must not quite omit the talking sage,
380   Kit-Cat, the famous Conversationist,
Who, in his commonplace book, had a page
    Prepared each morn for evenings. "List, oh, list!"—
"Alas, poor ghost!"—What unexpected woes
Await those who have studied their bon mots!

XCVIII

385 Firstly, they must allure the conversation
    By many windings to their clever clinch;
And secondly, must let slip no occasion,
    Nor *bate* (abate) their hearers of an *inch,*
But take an ell—and make a great sensation,
390   If possible; and thirdly, never flinch
When some smart talker puts them to the test,
But seize the last word, which no doubt's the best.

XCIX

Lord Henry and his lady were the hosts;
    The party we have touched on were the guests:
395 Their table was a board to tempt even ghosts
    To pass the Styx for more substantial feasts.

375 **cries** in Fielding's *Joseph Andrews*, IV, xi.

I will not dwell upon ragouts or roasts,
   Albeit all human history attests
That happiness for man—the hungry sinner!—
Since Eve ate apples, much depends on dinner.   *400*

C

Witness the lands which "flowed with milk and
      honey,"
   Held out unto the hungry Israelites;
To this we have added since, the love of money,
   The only sort of pleasure which requites.
Youth fades, and leaves our days no longer sunny;   *405*
   We tire of mistresses and parasites;
But oh, ambrosial cash! Ah! who would lose thee?
When we no more can use, or even abuse thee!

CI

The gentlemen got up betimes to shoot,
   Or hunt: the young, because they liked the sport—   *410*
The first thing boys like after play and fruit;
   The middle-aged to make the day more short;
For *ennui* is a growth of English root,
   Though nameless in our language:—we retort
The fact for words, and let the French translate   *415*
That awful yawn which sleep can not abate.

CII

The elderly walked through the library,
   And tumbled books, or criticized the pictures,
Or sauntered through the gardens piteously,
   And made upon the hothouse several strictures,   *420*
Or rode a nag which trotted not too high,
   Or on the morning papers read their lectures,
Or on the watch their longing eyes would fix,
Longing at sixty for the hour of six.

CIII

But none were *gêné:* the great hour of union   *425*
   Was rung by dinner's knell; till then all were
Masters of their own time—or in communion,

Or solitary, as they chose to bear
The hours, which how to pass is but to few known.
430 Each rose up at his own, and had to spare
What time he chose for dress, and broke his fast
When, where, and how he chose for that repast.

CIV

The ladies—some rouged, some a little pale—
Met the morn as they might. If fine, they rode,
435 Or walked; if foul, they read, or told a tale,
Sung, or rehearsed the last dance from abroad;
Discussed the fashion which might next prevail,
And settled bonnets by the newest code,
Or crammed twelve sheets into one little letter,
440 To make each correspondent a new debtor.

CV

For some had absent lovers, all had friends.
The earth has nothing like a she epistle,
And hardly heaven—because it never ends.
I love the mystery of a female missal,
445 Which, like a creed, ne'er says all it intends,
But full of cunning as Ulysses' whistle,
When he allured poor Dolon:°—you had better
Take care what you reply to such a letter.

CVI

Then there were billiards; cards, too, but *no* dice;—
450 Save in the clubs no man of honor plays;—
Boats when 'twas water, skating when 'twas ice,
And the hard frost destroyed the scenting days:
And angling, too, that solitary vice,
Whatever Izaak Walton sings or says;
455 The quaint, old, cruel coxcomb, in his gullet
Should have a hook, and a small trout to pull it.

447 **poor Dolon** Trojan spy, captured and killed by Ulysses and
Diomedes in the *Iliad*, X.

CVII

With evening came the banquet and the wine;
   The *conversazione;* the duet,
Attuned by voices more or less divine
   (My heart or head aches with the memory yet).   *460*
The four Miss Rawbolds in a glee would shine;
   But the two youngest loved more to be set
Down to the harp—because to music's charms
They added graceful necks, white hands and arms.

CVIII

Sometimes a dance (though rarely on field days,   *465*
   For then the gentlemen were rather tired)
Displayed some sylphlike figures in its maze;
   Then there was small talk ready when required;
Flirtation—but decorous; the mere praise
   Of charms that should or should not be admired.   *470*
The hunters fought their fox-hunt o'er again,
And then retreated soberly—at ten.

CIX

The politicians, in a nook apart,
   Discussed the world, and settled all the spheres;
The wits watched every loophole for their art,   *475*
   To introduce a bon mot head and ears;
Small is the rest of those who would be smart,
   A moment's good thing may have cost them years
Before they find an hour to introduce it;
And then, even *then,* some bore may make them
   lose it.   *480*

CX

But all was gentle and aristocratic
   In this our party; polished, smooth, and cold,
As Phidian forms cut out of marble Attic.
   There now are no Squire Westerns as of old;
And our Sophias are not so emphatic,   *485*
   But fair as then, or fairer to behold.
We have no accomplished blackguards, like Tom
   Jones,
But gentlemen in stays, as stiff as stones.

CXI

They separated at an early hour;
490   That is, ere midnight—which is London's noon:
But in the country ladies seek their bower
    A little earlier than the waning moon.
Peace to the slumbers of each folded flower—
    May the rose call back its true color soon!
495 Good hours of fair cheeks are the fairest tinters,
And lower the price of rouge—at least some winters.